# The Long Journey To You

Vincent Traughber Meis

ISBN: 978-1-915905-33-8



First Edition, Spectrum Books, 2024

Cover design: Vincent Traughber Meis/Andrew May

# Contents

*To all the souls we have lost due to AIDS.*

# Chapter 1

Hope, powerful and enticing, came to me as a man in scrubs. He was sent, it seemed, to care for me. His name was Mateo. Mateo was hope. In my disheveled state, lost in a sad memory and on the verge of tears, I looked up to see this young man walking toward me, his eyes swimming with concern. My first impulse was to be suspicious, hope having entrapped me many times, held me in his arms, and promptly left me in the dust. But my defenses were a poor match for Mateo's quirky smile, freckles that made no sense, and mischievous eyes that set off tiny explosions in my head. Laugh, cry, or jump in the water's fine? I wasn't sure I had a choice.

This astonishing and quite unexpected encounter happened on a day that had progressed like any other, read: uneventful. Over the threshold of my humble abode, I went like I had been telling myself to do since breakfast. Ah, the thrill of the great outdoors, fresh air and sunshine, birds tweeting on the power lines. A couple of steps on the porch, and the great outdoors attacked me. The sharp afternoon angle of the sun stabbed me in the chest and with the next step it targeted my eyes, causing them to retreat behind squinting lids. I wore no sunglasses nor sunscreen nor protective hat, making me feel as naked as a newborn. Reboot. I turned around to retrieve the suggested items for my excursion only to realize the door had locked behind me. When I reached into my pocket, I was hit with another sinking revelation: no keys. I glanced across the street in hopes that the neighbors, who had a spare set for just such occasions, were home. Neither of their cars was in the driveway.

I sighed and turned my attention to a cracked Talavera pot spilling soil onto the terracotta tiles of the porch while the globe of blooming calibrachoa appeared undeterred by the breach. I walked around it for the umpteenth time, and for the umpteenth time promised myself to do something about it. Transplant the flowers to a new pot? Mend the crack? Sit back and admire the resilience of nature? By the time I had reached the sidewalk, the pot had once again slipped from my consciousness, replaced by a new dilemma. Right or left?

Decisions had become particularly hard as of late.

A neighbor turned the corner and came in my direction from the right, not one of the ones I found annoying, but one with whom previous chats had made it obvious we had nothing to say to each other. I doubted she'd be interested in the mid-Pacific cargo spill of rubber ducks that floated to various corners around the world I had been researching all morning for a poem about drifting, another poem that would probably go unfinished. She was still far enough away I could escape with a slight wave and head to the left, pushing my legs, still sore from the exercise routine I had just completed. I picked up speed and put a distance between us.

The streets were relatively free of pedestrians on this unusually warm day, still early for the hordes of dog walkers to do their late afternoon strolls and a little too hot for many of the retirees in the area who waited until the sun was lower in the sky to perform their constitutionals. When I did encounter another walker, there was only about a fifty-fifty chance I would get a nod, a hello, or a smile. San Leandro suffered from being a small city adjacent to two larger ones, Oakland and San Francisco, making people unsure if strangers on the street should be treated with small-town friendliness or big city suspicion.

A half hour into my walk, an apricot tree, bulging with fruit, leaned over a fence and caught my eye, as if it had something to tell me. I stopped and tilted my head just as a gust of wind loosened an overripe cot from its branch and sent it cascading down to splatter on the cement.

I was ripped back in time to another apricot tree in the yard where I had lived in Spain. I stared at the fallen fruit on the sidewalk and remembered a memorial held under the tree for a dear friend, the smell of the ripe fruit bringing back the soft murmuring of inadequate words. On that day, too, during a lull in the conversation, a plump apricot hit the ground with a soft thud, causing us all to turn and look at the orange splat on the ground. My friend, Charlie, quite spontaneously, not meaning to be profound, said, "Another one bites the dust." The partner of the man who had died, and who had maintained a stoic façade up to that point, fell into a chair and buried his face in his hands, weeping uncontrollably. The rest of us looked from face to face, wondering who would be the next to bite the dust.

Some thirty years later I stared at the fruit on the ground with the pits exposed and imagined that each one represented a loved one who had been struck down in a land far away. I stood mesmerized by the palette of squashed orange-yellow fruit and brown pits against the gray concrete canvas, feeling a profound sadness. An inner voice urged me to carry on, to shake myself from the paralyzing sentiment by putting one foot in front of the other, taking myself away from the trigger.

But I couldn't move. Tragedies occupied too much space in my head, tragedies of old and the one more recent.

Who knows how long I might have been stuck there if I hadn't noticed out of the corner of my eye someone approaching along the same sidewalk at a good pace? No time to shuffle over to the other side of the street to hide the tears in my eyes. I turned my head toward a dark-skinned man and suffered a momentary knee-jerk racist panic that immediately sickened me. In the few seconds it took to get over myself, I felt the hopelessness of humans to get better.

He stopped and frowned, joining his thick brows into one dark slash above concerned brown eyes.

"Are you okay?" he asked in a slight Spanish accent. His questioning eyes moved directly to the stain on my T-shirt where the juicy tomato from my lunch had squirted. Looking like blood?

I became acutely aware of my attire: baggy sweats that may have had other stains, a baseball cap with a tattered rim, and faded crocs. He wore neat magenta scrubs that matched the color of his full shiny lips. His nametag said Mateo.

The scenario must have been embarrassingly clear to him. I had wandered off from one of the many senior facilities that dotted the landscape of the neighborhood. If I exaggerated the confusion that I, in fact, frequently felt, he might take my arm, walk me back to the facility, put me in a bath, gently wash my back, and tuck me into bed. The more I looked into his onyx eyes, the more I wanted him to do just that.

"I mean, you looked a little lost...and sad."

"Don't worry, Mateo." His eyebrows separated and bounced at the sound of his name. Then he smiled and touched his nametag, realizing how I knew it. "I'm lost in a memory is all." I chuckled. "I suppose I do fit a profile."

"You're okay, then?"

"Yep."

"My bad. I didn't mean to profile you. I have experience with that, and it's no fun."

I imagined that he was doubly profiled, first for the color of his skin and then a second time when people caught a hint of his accent.

"No harm done. I appreciate your concern."

"It's kind of my job. Sometimes it is difficult to switch out of that mode when I leave work." He lowered his eyes, making me realize I must have been staring intently. How could I have not? He was an amalgam of all the men I had been attracted to my entire life: Mediterranean, Black, Latino, shorter than me, rectangular solid frame, soulful eyes, thick hair. But with an added twist. A dusting of freckles graced his cheekbones and the bridge of his nose.

In a thoughtful gesture, he stared at the sidewalk and raised his hand to his chin, rubbing his index finger over his left cheek, revealing another physical trait that rang my buzzer: little tufts of black hair between his major and minor knuckles, a tiny forest to let my tongue wander through.

Thank God, he couldn't read my thoughts. Or could he?

"I should let you get on your way," he mumbled, still not looking at me. He stared at the smashed apricots on the ground with, I imagined, quite a different take than mine.

I wasn't ready to let him go just yet.

"Do you work in one of these facilities I might have escaped from?"

"Now, look, I didn't mean..." He took a step back in what appeared to be a desire to flee.

"I'm teasing. I haven't seen you around the neighborhood."

He tapped his nametag and twisted his neck to look at it. "Kaiser. It says right here. Kaiser Permanente."

"I have trouble reading fine print." I let out a small laugh, but he didn't join me.

He took another step back. "Just moved here less than a year ago."

I guessed he was mid-thirties, and with his Spanish accent and African features, maybe Puerto Rican? Cuban? I imagined he lived with a wife and multiple *niños.* They spent Saturdays having barbecues in the park and Sundays from dawn to dusk at church events. He looked far too sweet to be anything but a family man. Now I was profiling.

"From?" I asked.

He let out a protracted sigh, as if the conversation had gotten way more involved than he had intended. His forehead crinkled again, hesitating to give me an answer.

"The city. Getting too crazy over there."

Then he raised his head and his eyes met mine with the twinkle of a forest elf. Perhaps he wasn't annoyed with me after all. Perhaps I had been wrong about sizing him up, though my conclusion that he was a family man was much easier to handle. Yet, he wore no ring.

Now it was my turn to say, "I should let you get on *your* way," the implication being he had more important places to go than I did.

"Yes, well...uh...enjoy your walk." He started to go, and then turned back around. "You got my name, but I didn't get yours."

"Nathan. I should probably wear a lanyard with my address on it in case I get lost."

"Stop." He chuckled. "Geez!"

I was anxious to shake his hand for the contact it would afford me, but he had moved too far away. My arm hung at my side like a useless appendage. "*Mucho gusto,*" I said.

"You speak Spanish?"

"Yeah. Sorry. I detected an accent."

"Oh my God. First I'm a nosy bastard and then I can't speak proper English." He delivered his remark in a *Masterpiece Theater* British accent.

In our five-minute conversation, he had gone from concerned to shy to enigmatic to testy to playful.

"Now, I really better go before you punch me."

"Not today, Nathan. I'm too tired after a long shift."

"Goodbye, Mateo." I gave him a little wave and started on my way.

"Bye." And then, as an afterthought. "*Hasta luego.*"

Did he really think he would see me later? Nah. Just an expression.

He walked away...like they all had—walked away, fell away, or were carried away. That ray of light in my day disappeared into a shadow under the trees of the avenue, and the ennui I'd felt when I left the house was back on my shoulder like a gargoyle whispering unpleasant things in my ear.

At the next corner I turned right to avoid the possibility of looking back to see if he was looking back.

"*Hasta luego,*" he'd said, as if we were joining up later for dinner.

*It's an expression, Nathan. You know that.*

In the next block, my brother phoned. He always acted like he had a question for me or news to share, but I knew he was checking on me. I sometimes wondered if he, my friends in the city, Anthony's friends, the neighbors, the guy at the convenience store, and the checker at Trader Joe's had all conspired to coddle me until it seemed I could stand on my own.

"How're you doing, bro?" David asked in that annoyingly chipper voice he'd developed since going on a two-week meditation retreat in Hawaii a couple of years before.

"I'm out on a walk and have managed 5,000 steps so far. I hear birds singing, and I can smell dogshit on the sidewalk right near me, so I guess that means I'm still alive."

He hesitated a few seconds and then laughed. "Still got all your senses. That's good. I wanted to let you know that your niece, Kimmie, just had her baby this morning."

"What is that now? Number sixteen?"

"Don't be mean. It's only her fourth."

People were still having multiple children. I couldn't imagine why. "Congrats, Grandpa. I'll send her a message."

"She'd like that. They named her Jaqueline."

"Jaqueline," I repeated with a catch in my throat. "Mom would have loved that."

"Kimmie always said that as soon as she had a girl, they'd name her after mom. Every time they had another boy, Mom used to say, 'Oh, darn.' Too bad she couldn't have been around to meet little Jackie."

The entrance of Mom into the conversation brought on the usual pang of sadness. It had been three years since she passed. She had never seen the house Anthony and I bought in San Leandro, her health not allowing her to make the trip from Florida where she lived not far from David in St. Petersburg.

After Anthony and I had been together about a year, we traveled to Florida for the official presentation of the new boyfriend. By that time, Mom had stopped resisting her attraction to nice gay men and openly began fussing over him like a third son.

As I watched her warm to Anthony, I had the duh-level epiphany that she'd always had an affinity for the homosexual men of our town. She was friendly not only with her hairdresser but also his "roommate", and she would occasionally go out to lunch with them, always coming home in a slightly better mood. She loved going to the theater productions at the local university, and when my father found an excuse not to go, she would go with a bachelor professor in the music department. Then there was the handsome and multi-talented Dr. B from down the street who would come to our house to play the piano. In later years I wondered if she had an inkling of his proclivities before the scandal that drove him from the town made it obvious to everyone.

# Chapter 2

The San Leandro house still had a grip on me that was both comforting and debilitating, the house where Anthony and I had lived together, the house that had so much of him, but not him. We had spent two years renovating the fixer-upper, so every wall color, window shade, floor tile, appliance, and plant in the yard held an essence of him. Nearly every day I was close to putting it on the market and being reborn somewhere else, possibly far away, another country. I lived on a small pension and had been dipping into savings to make the payments each month. I didn't know how long I would be able to do that.

I wandered the house with Mateo's face on my mind, a new face to take me places I had never been. In the living room, the Turkish carpet under my feet beckoned me, and in a quick moment I was stretched out on its lush ruby, orange, and beige pile. It was one of the few things in the house that took me back to a different time, a different love.

I had purchased the Anatolian rug on a trip to Turkey. It had traveled with me from Van in eastern Turkey to Barcelona to California and held in its fibers the complex essence of my first love in all its joy and pain, Nick Baronian—or Dr. B, as we used to call him—the man my mother had befriended and allowed to play piano in our house.

Sometimes I needed to feel that joy without remembering the pain that both of us knew I would cause him from the beginning, and still we let ourselves open the door to it. From the age of twelve, I lusted after the young doctor down the street without an understanding of what I was feeling. That we ended up together years later was a minor miracle since I never imagined, when he was driven from our hometown, that I would ever see him again.

In the fall of 1969 I headed to college, after what had been a chaotic and historically significant summer: the first man to walk on the moon, the murders of Sharon Tate and four others by the Manson family, the Woodstock Music Festival, and the Stonewall rebellion, often called the beginning of the modern gay rights movement. But most of the space in my mind was occupied by my escape from my Midwestern hometown by going to Tulane University in a city that seemed about as culturally distant as I could go without leaving the country. Unbeknownst to me, Dr. B had also taken refuge in New Orleans.

The Fates had determined at our births that we would find each other again, or so we sometimes joked. Clotho, the Spinner Fate, had spun the thread of our lives, putting us together once again in The Big Easy, but for us to be together as a couple was a trickier weave. It took the Up Stairs Lounge fire in the French Quarter where thirty-two people lost their lives in a gay bar to bring us together emotionally.

Lying on the rug, I could still conjure up the feeling of walking out of the memorial into the light of day, holding Nick's hand for all the world to see, in 1973 when men did not hold hands in public, and it never failed to give me a rush, making the hairs on my legs stand up. Nick and I felt guilty for the bliss we found in each other's arms, the guilt of survivors, and the bewildering acknowledgement that the deadly fire was indirectly responsible for bringing us together.

Anthony would sometimes catch me stretched out on the rug and ask me what I was doing. I couldn't say, "Oh, I'm just wallowing in the memory of my first one true love on the carpet on which we had made passionate love many times in front of a roaring fire in a candlelit room, and where the pile might still hold traces of our bodily fluids." No, I would groan a little and say, my back hurt. Lying on the floor was the only thing that helped.

After the tragedy of the fire, the gay community of New Orleans trudged through the summer heat back to normal life, or I should say, what had been the norm before the fire. The brief radicalization and push for gay rights soon dwindled, replaced by the debauchery of drinking and quick hookups for some and campy parties and bitch-banter dinners for others.

The day after the memorial, Nick returned to work where the administrators at the hospital were suspicious why he had taken two days off, and he wasn't at liberty to tell them the truth that he was comforting friends who had lost loved ones in the fire. I went back to my shift at the restaurant, where my fellow workers, Shelly, Ivette, and I expected all the customers to be in the same funk we were and got pissed when they laughed and enjoyed their meals when they should have been in somber remembrance of the people who had met a horrific death in the arson fire down the street.

A month later, fewer and fewer conversations centered around the disaster, though having come upon the aftermath of the fire while it was still smoldering and bodies were being carried away was something I could never forget. I swore there were nights when leaving the restaurant, I could smell lingering smoke tinged with the odor of burning flesh months after the fire.

Around the beginning of September, I arrived at the front door of the restaurant and saw a notice saying the establishment was temporarily closed by the health department until certain violations were corrected. I hurried over to Sherry's house.

"What the hell is going on?"

"Remember that customer I yelled at and eighty-sixed when he made a joke about the fire?" Sherry said in her Mississippi drawl. "The asshole called the health department and made a complaint, something about finding a rat's toenail or something in his food. Child, if I had known he was gonna do that, I'da slapped him up the side of the head. Probably woulda got charged with assault, but it woulda warmed my soul. They did an inspection yesterday and surprise, surprise, they found stuff not up to code."

"How long are we going to be closed?"

"Probably two or three weeks. I don't know how I'm going to pay rent next month." Shelly and I were both Tulane dropouts whose parents had cut us off. I felt a little guilty that I didn't have to worry about rent since I had moved in with my doctor dreamboat boyfriend, Nick.

That evening, I told Nick about the restaurant closure and was shocked by his reaction. "What I'm hearing is road trip." He danced around the kitchen like a teenager. "Road trip. Road trip." All my badgering for him to relax and enjoy life was paying off. It was endearing and a little frightening because I had created this monster. Before he met me, spontaneous was not a word in his vocabulary.

"You're serious! Can you take time off?"

"Do you know how much time I've taken off since I started working at the hospital five years ago? Two days around the fire and memorial. That's it. They owe me."

"My classes start in two weeks." I had signed up for a couple of business classes at the junior college. I wanted to finish my degree, but there was no way I could afford to go back to Tulane.

"We'll be back by then."

"Where do you want to go?"

His eyes flashed with further evidence of spontaneity. "Montreal."

"Uh...that's where my brother lives."

"I know. I've always wanted to go there, and you said it was a great city. You could visit David."

"Not a good idea."

My moving in with Nick hadn't been divulged to anyone in the family, not even David, who I was close to. My family all knew Nick from when he was our neighbor down the street before he left town in disgrace. On a visit home at the tender age of nineteen, I had hit my parents with the big three: I was gay, had gone to rehab for drug abuse, and had dropped out of college. It ruined the pork chop dinner my mother had prepared especially for me and caused a rift with my dad that never fully healed, but it wasn't quite the gnashing of teeth I had imagined. Telling them I was living with Dr. B would certainly be the revelation that cast me into the outer darkness with great weeping and gnashing of said teeth.

I had barely spoken to my father since I'd divulged all my failures, but I talked to my mother every few weeks, both of us working hard to maintain our relationship. I didn't want to jeopardize that. Whenever the topic of where I was living came up, I made it sound like I was sharing an apartment with Sherry, which was where I got my mail. I rationalized that not telling her the truth was saving her pain and worry.

Nick obviously read the doubt on my face. "You've got to face it some time." Another thing that had changed in Nick. Suddenly he was Mr. Let's-Come-Out-to-the-World.

"Easy for you to say. I think David would be okay with it, but would he be able to keep it from Mom? I'm not ready for that." With Nick by my side like that day we first held hands in public leaving the memorial, I felt like I could face David, and face David we did.

We embarked on our road trip to Montreal, stopping to see my old roommate, Kevin, in Maryland. He would soon start a grad program in ethnomusicology at UCLA. And then we visited Ricky in Boston who had just started med school. Both had been instrumental in the rehab program my friends designed to get me off drugs. Most of my Tulane friends had graduated and left New Orleans, getting on with their lives, doing adult things. I was a college dropout and worked in a health food restaurant, living off tips.

I called David from Boston, announcing my visit and that I was bringing Dr. B, but he should call him Nick now. His initial freak-out that both Nick and I ended up in New Orleans and had found each other gradually morphed into a conclusion that me being with Nick made sense. David and Lola welcomed us with open arms, and a few minutes later, they announced that Lola was pregnant. My parents would finally get the grandchild they were hoping for.

Our time in Montreal was filled with laughter around the dinner table and exploring the city. One evening, I went with David to score some pot in Ville-Marie. He told me to wait outside the building while he went inside to make the deal. On Saint Laurent Boulevard I leaned up against a building, people-watching and delighting in how Montrealers dressed in style and looked at each other with a curiosity in a way I didn't see in the States.

A balloon-shaped older man approached me and spoke in French. My French was passable, but his question took me by surprise. I asked him to repeat it. He switched to a heavily accented English. "What is it that you charge?"

I had hair down to my shoulders, wore faded jeans and a Hawaiian shirt. I figured he was looking to buy drugs. "No, I don't have anything."

"Don't worry. I have a place nearby. I give you twenty."

"What?"

"Okay. Twenty-five. I suck good."

A feeling came over me like I had fallen in a stagnant pond teeming with snakes. I'd had the same feeling several months before when I had gone to the hotel room with a nameless character in a business suit when I was in the worst of my drugged-up/hookup period. He wanted to pay me after we had sex because he only enjoyed sex if he paid for it. I had thrown the money back in his face and stormed out of the hotel room.

"No. I'm not...go away," I mumbled to the round little man.

I didn't care that people saw me as gay, though being taken for an escort gave me that writhing snake feeling, something that a few months later would seem absurd. But at the time, at least some of the elements of my Protestant-Puritan background still held sway.

He shouted some choice phrases in French, basically saying that I wasn't worth even a dollar. David and I laughed about it later, but I asked him not to tell Nick.

"Why not? It's hilarious."

"Please. He wouldn't find it funny."

He looked at me strangely but promised not to tell.

As I lay on the carpet forty-some years later, I still remembered how I felt and how that incident stuck with me for months afterward, planting the seed of an invasive herb inside me.

*I never meant to hurt you, Nick.*

Why did memories of the good times with Nick always slide into the times I was a shit to him, the things I did and the things I hid? But as my mother always used to say, "Truth will out." He saw me at my lowest and somehow managed to keep loving me.

I got up off the carpet, went to the door, and opened it onto the front yard, a door to the present and a clear reminder of how much my life had changed. I needed air. I sat on the redwood bench and grabbed one of the sun-faded pillows, hugging it tightly. I stared at the broken pot and wept silently. I cried it all out and took a deep breath. One of my traits, for better or worse, was my ability to pick myself up and move on. Life had forced me to. That or die.

My thoughts turned to Mateo's kissable lips, saying, "*Hasta luego.*" I should have said something clever. I should have invited him for coffee. I should have faked a fainting spell, so he'd have been obliged to take me home. Lock the door and thrown away the key. Never let him leave.

I had to chuckle at myself. In the last several minutes, I had, from the library of my mind, checked out a cozy read, let it slip into a maudlin memoir of betrayal, and ended with a fantasy rom-com. The golden years could be vastly entertaining, that is, if you looked at your life like it was someone else's.

# Chapter 3

Forty years after those early days with Nick, I knew it was not a good idea to dwell on the failings of my past, but as a survivor with a considerable stash of memories, time on my hands, and living alone, it was inevitable that some of the old stories would escape the shelves in my head and run through my brain like ticker tape. I was in denial about how greedy the past was, devouring me without giving anything back, flooding in when I least expected it. My therapist kept telling me I needed to build a dam where I would have control, releasing the waters gradually so that they didn't overwhelm me with the recurring feeling that there was a connection between my failings and the hurt I caused people, that I was punishing myself for the bad things I did. Going to a therapist helped me staunch those notions, and the fact that I hadn't touched drugs for twenty years, aside from an occasional drink and pot, was something. I survived. I kept going. And something told me I wasn't done yet.

I dressed in some nicer sweats, making sure they were free of food stains. I wore my favorite baseball cap, a pair of Camper sneakers I had bought in Spain, and a sky-blue T-shirt that people often told me brought out my eyes. And marching out my door past the broken pot without a glance, I retraced my steps to where I had met Mateo. I was the walking, breathing poster boy for hope springs eternal. But unless Mateo turned out to be a vampire and gave me the gift of eternal life, assuming, of course, I managed to find him, the greater part of my life had passed. This might be my last chance for a connection. But I was jumping ahead of myself.

Both excited and terrified by my quest, I kept telling myself to keep it simple. Seeing him again would be enough. This was not a stalking adventure, which in my past, admittedly, I had been guilty of, occasionally with the desired result.

I strolled along the street where we had met, taking my time, noting details of houses and yards I had never noticed before. I focused on gates left open and back doors ajar, thinking of my youth where the yards and homes in my neighborhood were my domain. This was a different time and place, land of security cameras and gates, alarm systems and neighborhood watch groups. The innocence of the 1960s in the Midwest might still exist in some form somewhere, but not here in the Bay Area where even the suburbs had big-city crime. I didn't worry that I was going to start finding ways into the houses of my current neighborhood, because, in addition to the security issue, I wasn't interested in their lives. A neighbor a few streets over had a sign in his window that said, "I shoot first. Ask questions later." I was sure that was the attitude of more than a few residents.

I reached the apricot tree, where that day, in a few minutes, I had gone from a person who didn't care if I looked like a schlumpy old man to someone determined to make the most of what attributes I still had left. I had cleaned myself up and I observed, as I lingered under the tree, that the sidewalk had also been cleaned of fallen fruit. But Mateo was nowhere to be seen, despite my careful calculation of the time the meeting had taken place.

I considered making a trip to Kaiser and sitting outside the hospital around the time I imagined he finished his shift. 3 p.m.? Then I would have to come up with an excuse why I was there, which for an older person, claiming a doctor's appointment wouldn't be difficult.

I continued in the direction he had gone, turning my head so often to look up and down streets I must have looked like I was casing the area. No doubt I was caught on several cameras as a suspicious character. I went up one street and down the other until the foolishness of my pursuit hit me, and I headed to Peet's for a coffee and a pastry to smooth over my frustration.

A homeless woman sat on a low wall not far from my outside table, rearranging her belongings and carrying on such a mundane conversation I thought she might have been talking to her daughter through earbuds. "Honey, you know that won't work. It's too late for that," she said. "But one thing at a time. You'll get there." She pulled a pair of sunglasses missing a temple from one bag and transferred it to another. "Have you had your dinner? No, don't wait for me. I'm delayed." And then, she began to laugh with such shrillness it made me shiver. Her voice changed from concerned mother to damaged soul. "Motherfuckers got me permanently delayed." She glanced at me, and I couldn't look away fast enough to avoid eye contact. She abandoned her bags, though glanced over her shoulder at them a couple of times as she approached my table.

"Sir, could you give me five dollars to get something to eat?"

Her voice was pleasant, almost girlish. Her hair was tied up in a colorful scarf, and she was clearly well fed, an observation that made me feel guilty to point out if only to myself. Had inflation gotten that bad? I remembered when panhandlers asked for one thin dime. I was inclined to give her something, but would a dollar be insulting since it was the only bill I had besides a couple of twenties in my wallet?

I made the offering, and she took it, turned around without saying thank you, and returned to her bags. She reminded me of someone, and it took me a moment.

The second man on my relationship dance card was a Cuban named Vladimir. We lived together in Spain for a couple of years and then in San Francisco. In Spain he was my savior; in the U.S my crown of thorns. After we had been together a few months, he convinced me to make the trip from Spain to Cuba because his mother was dying to meet me. Exaggeration, if not a downright lie. When we arrived at her humble home surrounded by a chain-link fence in Matanzas, she stared at me with cold suspicion in the same way the homeless woman had. And like her, she had a pie-shaped chestnut face with dark eyes, her head wrapped in a scarf.

"Mami, look what Nathan and I brought you."

He opened his backpack and drew from it wonders from the east: French perfume, products to conk her hair, scented soap, makeup, a sewing kit with twelve colors of thread, and a small fake Gucci purse he had bought on the Ramblas in Barcelona from Africans who spread out their wares on the blanket so that they could bundle them up in a couple of seconds when outlooks whistled that the police were coming.

With the gifts she warmed up considerably, or maybe my own trepidation about meeting her had made me misinterpret her chilly greeting. She grabbed her son and smothered him with kisses and then hugged me warmly as well. Within seconds, she was in full welcoming mode, offering us tiny cups of thick sugary black java. As soon as she had served the coffee, she fired up the gas stove to heat the tons of food she had prepared. We sat down to a meal of rice and beans mixed together called *moros y cristianos,* fried fish—Vlad had warned her I didn't eat beef or pork—fried plantains, and yucca in garlic and oil. She had probably used up a month's ration of oil to prepare the food. She apologized throughout the meal about the meager offerings and kept talking derisively about the *libreta,* which Vlad explained was a ration system allowing Cuban households to purchase a limited amount of staples each month at a fraction of the regular cost.

Every time I was reminded of my relationship with Vladimir, I felt a little sick to my stomach. I had never been able to echo Edith Piaf and sing "*Non, je ne regrette rien.*" I knew early on the relationship was a mistake. I was weak. I broke all the rules my friends laid out for me. "Don't start something so soon after Nick." "Give yourself time to mourn." "Don't date a bartender." "Don't get involved with a Cuban." I ignored it all. I was hurting.

He wasn't happy in Spain and was fixed on going to the United States, his goal all along, though I didn't fully understand why. In a conversation with his mother at the beach while Vladimir was in the water, she mentioned something about Vlad's wife and two kids who had managed to get to the United States through her father in a family program. She assumed he had told me about his little family, but when my stunned expression told her I was in the dark, she downplayed it and said they were a bad match. He probably only wanted to see his kids, but not get back with her. I waved it off as I did every red flag that was put before me in relation to Vlad.

Being in Cuba was like being in another universe, under a dome of sensory overload, cut off from the rest of the world. Smells of the sea, musty buildings, and fried food fill the air already flavored with dance music and frolic, making people glide and shimmy down the street rather than walk. And out of the portals of crumbling structures, men and women of uncommon beauty emerged in designer clothes supplied by overseas relatives or paramours they'd charmed. The people had become experts at thinking outside the box because the box was empty. They were poor when it came to possessions but rich in laughter, playing the long game with their foreign conquests. It was the movie of life in vibrant color and endless drama, starring everyone I met in Vladimir's town.

I returned from that trip feeling like I knew Vladimir a little better, having seen him in his element, but frankly, the mysteries he still encompassed were of little importance to me when he held me through the night and eased my pain.

Despite all the hurtful things he later did and the awful decisions he made, I looked back with certainty that he was the most affectionate man I had ever met. He had the gift of tenderness, unbridled affection, and sweet gestures in the moment. Did it fit into his plan? Most definitely. Was he aware of his goal every time he shared half of whatever he was eating, absentmindedly ran his hand up and down my arm as we sat side by side, whispered sweet things in my ear like we lived in a universe of two, and held me down when I said I needed a snort to ease my pain? It was hard to know.

In a reality-is-stranger-than-fiction mind boggle, Nick had introduced me to Vladimir. I came home from work one day and a young man stood at the mantle, examining photos of Nick and me and our friends going back to our days in New Orleans. He must have heard me approach, as he spun around with a smile calculated for maximum effect. His eyes latched onto mine, framed by dark wavy hair, longish, covering his ears, and he had a several-day growth of beard.

Over cocktails in the living room, I learned he was a student in the business program of the institute where Nick and I taught and worked as a bartender in one of the gay bars of the town. It was difficult to imagine him as a businessman, but someone in the Spanish resettlement office for Cuban refugees picked up on his abilities and thought it was a good idea to enroll him in the program. He was clearly smart. He was intelligence smart and socially smart and, I later found out, sexually a genius.

Vlad had finagled his way into our home, no doubt flirting with my boyfriend as he and Nick rode the train together back to Sitges at the same time every day. Nick, in his innocence, was oblivious to scammers and plotters.

We moved out onto the terrace for more drinks, and when he left, saying he wanted to go home and get a couple of hours of sleep before his bartending shift, he invited us to come by one night and he would hit us up with free drinks. He hugged us at the door like we were old friends.

Nick and I went back out onto the terrace and watched him strut down the street as if he was smiling inside with secret information. We sat down to finish our drinks, and I asked Nick why he had invited this young man to our house.

"I thought you'd be pleased." Nick grinned, obviously assuming I would appreciate the young man's beauty, which I did. But I was much less naïve than my boyfriend.

"Did he cruise you on the train?"

I loved how he still got embarrassed when I implied he might be in a sexually flirtatious situation.

"No! He was just a friendly guy. We are often on the same train."

At the time, I entertained the possibility I was being overly cynical after having fallen under the spell of at least a few charmers in my life. When I had seen Vladimir, still a stranger, gazing so intently at our pictures that day, I imagined him wanting to crawl into those photos, be part of our life, a scene from one of those horror films where someone maneuvers their way into a family and destroys it. Everything I felt in that instant came to pass, though I couldn't blame him for being a homewrecker. The disease took care of that.

My Peet's coffee had gone cold and threatened to form a milk skin on top as I shook myself out of the memories. I got up from my table and nodded at the homeless woman, who glanced at me like she'd already forgotten me and my piddling donation.

On my walk home I carried with me both sadness that my mission to find Mateo had failed and relief that my mission had failed. What would I have done if I had run into him again? In waiting for the light to cross the street at Bancroft, I considered giving one last sweep of the area where I had seen Mateo, but I had forgotten to use the bathroom as I usually did at Peet's, distracted by the homeless woman and my journey into the past. It was time to go home.

I crossed the street and was a quarter of the way up the block when I heard someone shouting, "Faggot," that automatic stun gun of a word, no matter how many times in my life I had felt its electricity. But it was daylight in a relatively progressive suburban town where front yard rainbow flags were not uncommon. I felt confident enough to turn around and satisfy my curiosity.

A young man on a beat-up one-speed crossed the intersection against the light and shouted at the cars that were reluctant to stop for him. “Faggots! You’re all faggots.” He rode in my direction, and I surveyed the landscape in case I had to run.

As he came up beside me, he continued his rant. “And you, too, you little bitch!” He was close enough that I detected the look of wild, uncontrolled anger in his eyes. He pedaled on; his new obscenities whisked away by the breeze as he approached the next corner at a good clip. It had been quite a while since I’d been called a little bitch, and the last time had probably been in jest.

I arrived home without further incident and closed the door on the outside world, disappointed at my failed search but safe inside my sanctuary.

# Chapter 4

When Nick and I got back from our trip to Montreal the fall of 1973, I was full of hope and relieved that my brother now knew of my relationship with our former neighbor, Dr. B. I was about to start my classes and eventually get a degree, which would lead to the fantasized career of an international businessman, possibly in France like Nick and I had talked about it. Doctors could work anywhere, right? As I would soon come to learn, the universe had other plans, and I wasn't quite the master of my fate that I had thought when I came out of rehab with all the notions my caregivers/friends had put in my head of how powerful I was, in control of my destiny, and surrounded by love and support.

My classes were in the morning and I returned to the newly reopened restaurant for evening and weekend shifts. The owner had hired a new waiter at Sherry and Ivette's request, a young man they had befriended who everyone called Sniffy due to his frequent sniffling, which he attributed to his allergies. Despite the annoying habit, he was "a total babe" as Sherry said. He was Cajun with black hair, blue eyes, and a naturally athletic body, reminding me of Marc, who held the distinction of being the first man I'd had sex with. Though I felt the pull of his charms in the way everyone did, Nick and I were still in our honeymoon phase and a little voice told me Sniffy was a danger zone. We did, however, become friends almost instantly. With Nick back to working long shifts at the hospital, Sniffy and I started hanging out after our evening stints at the restaurant while Nick was still working.

We would go to one of the French Quarter bars, where the two of us walking in would generate a buzz. Men would buy us drinks, which might have been a disaster for a person with an addictive personality like mine, but I had never developed an interest in alcohol, and rarely drank more than a cocktail or two. Sniffy was happy to take care of the drinks that sweated on the coasters in front of me. Though alcohol didn't do it for me, I still had dreams about the diet pills I had started taking in high school and later became addicted to, those and the downers I would take to soften the crash. The sense memory of the rush was always with me, those times drugs brought me out of myself and made me a more social, likable person.

Sniffy went to the bathroom a lot, and when I commented on it, he'd mumbled with a downcast look that he had a bladder problem. One night he wandered off and split without saying goodbye. The next time I saw him, he apologized and said he had hooked up with a guy, which sounded completely normal since men were constantly all over him. It started happening a lot. I admired him in a way but had no desire to go back to my druggy hook-up days. I had my dream man, albeit one who worked way more than I would have liked.

I started taking notice of the men Sniffy would flirt with. They were older and generally unattractive, and then he would disappear without a word. I imagined that he loved being adored and was attracted to men who gave him the attention he felt like he deserved. Silly me. Of course, he was hustling.

One evening after Sniffy left, I sat alone at the bar nursing a drink. An older man, thin but with a big gut that made him look like he was with child, sat down beside me and kept glancing at me as if waiting for me to start the conversation. I remember thinking that if I had a little bump, I would start chattering away with absolutely no goal except to voice my witty thoughts. But in my mental state at the time, I preferred to simply sit and observe people, silently amused by their strange behavior. He was not to be deterred and clearly *did* have a goal. He moved one seat closer.

"Say, there," he said in a low voice. "I bet your friend is feeling pretty good right now."

I assumed he meant that he was probably screwing his brains out. "I suppose." I stared at the almost full drink in front of me.

"I hooked him up with the...ya know...blow. I've got some more. We could go back to my place and see what happens. The stuff's expensive, but you could do all you want if you let me..." he looked at my crotch and giggled nervously. "You know, a blow for some blow."

I was angry with myself for being such an idiot. Of course, Sniffy was not only an escort, but a cokehead. He frequently had on nice new clothes and shoes. On a waiter's salary in one of the city's not-so-fine dining establishments? It had been right in front of me for weeks and I didn't see it. The whole thing pissed me off so much I felt like taking it out on the man beside me.

"You think I'd let you touch me for a little toot? Maybe a toot and fifty bucks." Nick used to say I didn't have a mean bone in my body. I beg to differ. It may not be a major bone like a fibula, but perhaps one of those little metatarsal bones in my foot that had gone over to the dark side and, at times, made me cruel.

The guy shook his head and walked away, apparently deciding I wasn't worth it. What if he had agreed? God knows I could have used the money, but to my upbringing, prostitution was horribly wrong. I remembered the guy in the hotel room chiding me for thinking I was so superior when I wouldn't accept money for sex and the man on the street in Montreal who cursed me.

The next time I went out with Sniffy after work and he headed to the men's room for one of his "pee" breaks, I grabbed his arm. "You're so full of shit. You're going for a little blow before you wander off for a big blow." I felt ridiculous paraphrasing the weasel from the week before. "And getting paid for it to boot."

At first his blue eyes popped. And then he laughed cruelly. "A little slow on the uptake, aren't you, Sherlock? Wanna join me?"

"No way. I'm in recovery."

"But you drink all the time."

"Alcohol, I can take it or leave it. Never been a problem for me. It's the other stuff."

"Like?"

"Speed mostly, and then the downers to crash."

"Cocaine's different. Easier to control."

"I have to be good. For Nick, if nothing else."

"Suit yourself. And by the way, one of my guys has been pestering me to get you into a three-way. He thinks you're so hot."

"Go do what you have to do. That's not me."

"As you like, cher." It was the first time he's used that Cajun endearment and it nearly knocked me off my chair. I had worked so hard to get Marc out of my head, but it all came rushing back with that single word he used to call me, his half smile, his charming way of speaking, and the way he shouted out during sex. Marc and

I had sex during that confusing period when I was trying to figure things out. It turned out that he was more confused than I was.

"I've got to go. See you at work tomorrow."

I ran to the streetcar, and when I sat down in the nearly empty car, I was shaking. I shook while the car rattled and swayed, and I thought of my wonderful boyfriend and what I was going to do as soon as he got home.

He walked in the door tired, but I felt no shame in begging him for sex. I wanted him to pound the craziness out of me, making me forget what I had found out about Sniffy, and how I was a millimeter away from going to the john with him and snorting cocaine, ending up in a three-way.

Nick got a second wind and indulged me because he knew how much I needed him. After I came, I cried, and he held me, and I loved him so much I wanted to die.

In the morning, I made him breakfast and, since it was his day off, we went for a walk in Audubon Park and reminisced about a walk we'd taken there before we got together. In a secluded spot under a live oak tree, I kissed him, and he chuckled nervously. There was still an innocence about him. Before I went off to the restaurant for my dinner shift, we made love again and I got there ten minutes late with Sniffy giving me the evil eye because he had to do all the setup. I didn't care because I had resolved to keep my distance from him. Instead of going out, I would stay home and study since I was already falling behind in my courses.

One night as I sat at the kitchen table, bored out of my mind, with an accounting textbook and notes spread out in front of me, Sniffy rang.

"Come over," he said.

"Nope. I'm studying."

"I really need you to come over." His voice sounded troubled.

"Are you okay? Is something wrong?"

"Just come over. Please!"

I surveyed my mess of papers on the table. I glanced at the clock. "Alright. I could use a break. For an hour, and then I have to come back and study."

"Cool."

He answered the door and walked me down the hall into the living room. Sitting in a ratty armchair was one of his gentlemen from the bar, presumably the one who wanted a three-way. I did a military about-face and headed back down the hall. Sniffy followed after me. "Wait. Wait. Wait," he hissed. "You don't have to do anything. You can just watch."

"Are you out of your mind? You're such an asshole."

He pulled me into the bathroom off the hall and closed the door.

"I didn't have a choice," Sniffy said in an agonizing voice. "He threatened me. He's from Slidell and knows my parents. Please. You can just sit there. Maybe take off your shirt or something."

"No."

"He's got a shitload of money. It's just a one-time thing. I'll never ask you again. I promise. He'll give us fifty each."

I had about two dollars in my wallet after a bad couple of weeks for tips at the restaurant. I had to buy books for my courses. Whenever Nick would ask me if I needed money, I always said no. It was a pride thing. He was already supporting me enough.

I sighed. "Half hour max and I'm leaving." A part of me knew that if I didn't leave the bathroom at that very moment and walk out of his house, I would be doomed. Nick would discover the real me I had been trying so hard to repress. He would kick me out. I had nowhere to go.

"This will help," said Sniffy. He took a little vial out of his pocket and formed some lines on the edge of the sink. He rolled up a bill and handed it to me.

A surreal voice in my head said, "You're an addict. You can't fight it. It's a one-time thing. No one will know."

I took off more than my shirt. I went home with money in my pocket. I got in the shower and scrubbed every inch of my body. When Nick got home, he crawled into bed and wrapped his arms around me. I pretended to be asleep, though I was buzzed from the coke. I felt cold and empty. My head hurt.

The next few months were a blur. Sniffy arranged sessions like we'd had with the guy from Slidell. I could now afford cocaine, and if there was cocaine, I was down for whatever. I had always been an expert at hiding what was going on with me. I hid my new activities from Sherry and Ivette. I hid it from the members of Nick's MCC church who sometimes came to dinner. And I hid it from Nick, even blamed him. If he hadn't worked so much and left me alone so often, I wouldn't have strayed. It was his fault. I was right back to that horrible time before Nick and I got together, the nights of debauchery that led to my overdose and near death. Except this time, it didn't make sense. I had my perfect boyfriend who loved me and sexed me, and I lived in a nice house, and, though many of my close friends had left New Orleans, I still had the people at the restaurant and others. I hated myself. I was clearly sick.

One night I ran into Marc on the street, and in his searching eyes I saw he was still floundering around in his sexuality and had drunk enough that he was open. We went to his house and snuck up the back stairs. I didn't want his housemate, Betsy, who was a friend of mine, to know I was there. I stayed a couple of hours, snuck down the back stairs, went home, and took a shower.

I scrubbed my body again and got into bed before Nick came home. He crawled into bed and pulled me into his arms. I lay awake, plotting ways to kill myself.

I wanted Nick to catch me. I wanted him to show how much he loved me by saving me (again) and I would show how much I loved him by letting him. Years later, my therapist had a field day with that notion, but at the time, it made perfect sense.

My therapist and I talked about the movie *Goodbye Columbus* where the Ali MacGraw character sabotages her relationship by deliberately leaving her diaphragm in her drawer for her mother to find, thereby realizing she was having sex. She knew it would lead to her parents forcing her to end her relationship.

From a young age, I had been an expert at hiding things I didn't want people to know about. I snuck in and out of the houses of my neighborhood without being discovered. I had even hidden in the closet and watched Nick, then the young married doctor down the street, have sex with a guy he played tennis with while his wife was out of town. I had hidden my use of diet pills, starting from the time I was a sophomore in high school, until it got out of control and I overdosed on Seconal in New Orleans. And for a long time, I hid from my parents that I was using drugs, had dropped out of college, and was gay until there was no other choice but to tell them as part of my recovery process.

So, that scene in the movie shook me enough that I remembered it many years later when normally I had difficulty remembering a movie I watched the night before. It confounded me that someone would deliberately sabotage what looked like a satisfying sexual relationship for no other reason than she felt ambivalent about it.

# Chapter 5

With the new day came a new resolve and a practical realization. What did I have to lose? If I found Mateo and it was awkward, so what? I had a burning desire to see that face again, if only to fill a poem with his broad nose, those searching eyes, the splash of freckles, and the hard eyebrows.

Based on my knowledge of the town's geography and transportation offerings, triangulation using the point where our encounter had occurred, and a smidgen of guesswork, I speculated that he took a shuttle from the hospital to the BART station, and then walked the rest of the way home.

I drove to Kaiser around the likely time he got off and parked in the lot, luckily finding a space with a good view of the shuttle stop. I had picked up a cappuccino with an extra shot for my stakeout, though I'd opted out of the donuts, a decision I was beginning to regret.

From three to three-thirty, a sea of employees in scrubs of all colors exited the building, heading for the parking lot and the bus stop where the shuttle as well as regular buses passed. I looked for his magenta scrubs, but then realized he might not always wear the same color.

The coffee had made me so jittery I jumped out of the car without a plan and walked toward the multi-colored wave of Kaiser employees, a fish swimming upstream. Not only did the double shot of caffeine make me nervous, but also delusional, hints of the old days of diet pills causing me to do things and say things I never would have done normally. I imagined singling him out of the crowd, chattering at him incessantly about the weather and the state of the world before grabbing his arm and steering him toward my car for a ride home.

A couple of minutes later, I was standing alone. The crowd had scattered as if a bomb had gone off. I sat down on a bench and leaned forward with one arm on my knee and my chin in my hand, contemplating what frozen meal I might heat up in the microwave, my standard dinner fare of late. Would it be the veggie lasagna or the Kung Pao chicken?

"You look like you're posing for that statue. What's it called? Yeah, *The Thinker*."

He so startled me my boney elbow slid off my boney knee in a movement that must have looked like I was having a fit. From my awkward position, all I could see was his black sneakers and the trousers of his scrubs, but the voice was unmistakable. I supposed that burying my head in my arms like I was preparing for a nuclear attack would have looked even more ridiculous, so I lifted my head to meet his eyes. And suddenly, I didn't give a fuck what he thought. He was right in front of me with those beautiful white teeth shining through absurdly kissable lips, smiling, fine lines at the corners of his chocolate eyes. Day made. I could have died right there. "I missed being Rodin's model by a couple of years."

He let out a chuckle. "What are you doing here?"

"I had an appointment."

Oops. I wasn't going to do that because then he would ask in what department and I would have to make up something that wasn't scary, certainly not oncology. I hoped he was too discreet to ask, which he was. Thank God because I'm a terrible liar and with my luck would have blurted out some department they didn't have at this Kaiser.

"What a coincidence. I'm just getting off work."

I produced a sick smile. "My lucky day, I guess."

"Are you being sarcastic?"

"No, really. No. It's nice to see you again."

His unibrow snapped shut above squinting eyes. "Well, it is a surprise."

Okay. I said it was nice to see him and he said it was a surprise. He didn't say nice surprise. The best course would have been to tell him to have a lovely day and scurry back into the hole from which I had emerged. But no.

"How was your day at work?"

"It was fine." His smile faded. "Actually, it wasn't fine. It was kind of shitty. One of my patients got some bad news."

"I'm sorry."

"I shouldn't be telling you this. Let's go back to it was fine."

My mind took off into a crazy fantasy that I would be the one he talked to when he had a bad day and then I would massage his shoulders and then...and then...I snapped out of it and became aware that he was staring at me like he had asked me a question and I had taken off on an exploration of space.

"I'm sure it must be tough sometimes, doing what you do."

"But I'm off now and I just want to get home and out of these clothes."

His arms hung at his sides like all the weight of the day had caught up with him. Damn, those were some nice forearms. I gauged a deliciously toned body just from those meaty flexors of the forearm. But he wanted to go home, and I was keeping him. It didn't seem a good time to ask him if he wanted to go for a coffee, which was the last thing I needed at the moment. My brief high took a nosedive.

And yet, that little guy inside my head told me not to give up yet. "I have my car here."

He tilted his head. "Are you offering me a ride?"

"Unless you don't want me to know where you live."

He huffed. "Why wouldn't I want you to know where I live?"

"It was a joke. Ax murderer and all that."

"You and your jokes."

If I could read auras, I would have seen his like a string of Christmas lights blinking blue and then white and then red, his moods changing by the minute like the first time I met him.

"I would be happy to give you a ride home."

"I do not know sometimes if you are being serious or not." He said it like we had been dating for months.

"My car's over there." I pointed at my BMW across the street in the parking lot. "*Vámonos*, Mateo."

We got to my car, and he looked it over.

"*Que chévere*. Fancy."

It was really Anthony's car. He had been driving my car that night because he was in a rush to get to work and his was almost out of gas. BMW was not my style and I planned to sell it. But Mateo didn't need to know all that.

Mateo went silent and pensive in the passenger seat, staring at the hands in his lap like a kid I had enticed into the car with candy. I kept thinking of conversation starters, but bit my tongue because they sounded stupid or sarcastic or something that might make him question if I was being serious or not.

"Uh, directions?" I said.

"Oh, yeah."

He indicated the way to an apartment complex on Haas Street where there must have been over twenty units in the building, so I knew generally where he lived, but I wouldn't be able to go banging on his door in the middle of the night in a desperate move to see him. He didn't jump out of the car as I thought he might.

"This is nice," I said. "You have the creek running along the back."

"I live with my mom."

"I live alone."

"She needs care."

"I'm widowed."

"I work a lot."

"I'm retired."

"I'm from Colombia."

"I'm from Illinois."

"I stay home most of the time."

"I'm a member of AARP."

"I'm older than you think."

It was a bizarre rapid-fire conversation like we were on a game show and had fifteen seconds to learn about each other. We both took a breath. "That was weird," I said.

"Did you really have an appointment at Kaiser today?"

"Of course. With my dermatologist."

He turned to look at me with a half-smile. "There's no dermatology department at Kaiser San Leandro."

"Shit."

He turned to stare at the tall trees along the creek. His aura became soft and gentle pale blue. He spoke almost in a whisper. "It's okay."

"What?"

"If you wanted to see me again."

*What the hell?*

"I'm not a stalker."

"Uh...you came to my work."

"I need to get a hobby. Look, I'm sorry. That was not cool."

"It wasn't unpleasant. A little weird maybe."

"I won't do it again."

We sat almost a full minute in silence. He still hadn't fled the car. "I have a vehicle," he said, turning his head to look at me.

"That's nice."

"It's in the Kaiser parking lot."

"You're shitting me."

He laughed. "I usually walk to the BART station and take the shuttle. I like the exercise. Today I was running a little late."

Things were getting curiouser and curiouser. If I was a stalker, he was an enabler.

"Do you want me to take you back to get it?"

"I'll get it tomorrow. My mom's expecting me. I should go." He opened the door.

"Wait. Can I get your number or something?"

I opened the console between the seats and rummaged around for a pen and a scrap of paper.

"What are you doing?"

"I'm looking for something to write with."

He shook his head and pulled his cell phone out of his pocket. "We have these new gadgets called cell phones. You can store numbers in them. It's like magic."

"Hahaha."

He opened his contacts and then looked at me sheepishly. "I forgot your name."

"Nathan. N-A-T-H-A-N."

"Last?"

"Landis. L-A-N-D-I-S."

He typed in the letters and handed me the phone. "Put in your number. Then I call you, so you'll have mine. You *do* have one of these, don't you?"

"I left it at home."

He called my number and listened to my message with a grin. I had been meaning to change it. It sounded like a person who couldn't care less if someone called.

"Falla," he said into the phone.

My Spanish was far from perfect, but I was pretty sure "falla" meant failure or flaw. Why would he say that? I panicked that he was saying this whole thing was a failure from the beginning.

He must have noticed the anxiety on my face.

"That's my last name. Falla. F-A-L-L-A. Falla Alvarez. A-L-V-..."

"I can spell Alvarez. Thank you very much."

"When you get home, send me a text that you got home safely."

"It's like six blocks."

"Okay, don't."

He was now out of the car, and I had missed my chance to touch him, put a hand on his shoulder, throw myself on top of him and stick my tongue down his throat, some small gesture to show I cared.

"I will."

"*Hasta luego.*"

"*Ciao, bello.*" He leaned down and looked at me strangely.

*Had I gone too far?*

"Bye," he said and closed the door.

When I got home, I rushed to find my phone. I was desperate for physical evidence that what had happened had really happened. I hit the voicemail button. In his beautiful tenor voice, I heard "Falla."

I fell onto the sofa and composed a text. **I managed the six blocks without incident**. After I hit the send button, I realized it sounded snarky and cold. I sent another. **Thank you for accepting the ride when you didn't need to. And for sharing your phone number. And for telling me a little about you.** That went too far in the sappy direction. I almost erased it, but I wanted him to see something quickly to counter the first message. I sat waiting for a reply. And waiting.

We had barely met, and I was already a mess. A chill passed through me. Mateo had just sat in Anthony's car in the passenger seat in an unsettling re-creation of a scenario, though a rare one, of me driving and Anthony occupying the passenger seat. Anthony preferred to drive on our many trips into the city for a show and dinner or to wine country or down the coast to Half Moon Bay. But occasionally, he would have a little too much to drink and I would take the wheel. Now I was the sole driver of the BMW since my slightly less glamorous Prius—a car I felt comfortable driving—was totaled.

The horror of that night, always lingering in the back of my mind, rushed to the front, or in my therapist's words, overwhelmed the dam. If he hadn't taken my car, he might have come home safely. It was a useless what if, but it kept weaseling into my brain. Then the worst part. The reason he was late and didn't have time to stop for gas was because I had forced him into a conversation he didn't want. I had whined about his spending so much time at the restaurant and getting home late, sometimes early morning, working six days a week and on his day off, all he wanted to do was sleep. We barely saw each other. At the same time, I knew it meant everything to him to make the restaurant a success, his lifelong dream. It was selfish of me to provoke an argument. Life was good. The restaurant was doing well and getting good reviews. I had taken an early retirement and had published my first book of poetry. We had made the rather plain house we purchased in a boring suburban neighborhood into something we jokingly called our oasis in a desert. We had parties with friends in the yard we had designed and landscaped ourselves. We had flowers for the bees, tall shrubs to block out the neighbors around us, and fruit trees and a vegetable garden, producing things we ate. Suburban living was new and surprisingly gratifying after spending most of the last forty years living in city apartments.

In the middle of our argument, he got a call from the restaurant, a crisis of some sort. We hadn't resolved anything, and the air still held the petrichor of a brewing storm when he left. It haunted me that I couldn't remember if I had said "I love you" when he went out the door, as was my habit.

As everyone kept telling me, the car, the argument, whether I said, "I love you," none of it had anything to do with the accident. There had been several incidents in the news of freak shootings on I-580, a sniper. It wasn't the bullet that entered the car that killed him. The shock of the cracked windshield must have made him lose control of the car—probably driving faster than he should have—and it turned over several times. Was he rushing home so we could patch things up? I normally didn't wait up, but I was wide awake that night, my apologies all lined up, my arms ready to hold him. Instead, I got the nightmare call.

# Chapter 6

For years I awoke without fail to find Anthony by my side followed by months of waking up, sometimes from a sweetly sexy but unconsummated dream, only to find that life sucked and I had been robbed a second time of a person who, all joking aside, was my better half and loved me unconditionally. The morning after giving Mateo a ride home, my emerging consciousness was met with another irritating and confusing sensation. It took a minute to fully pinpoint the source of my annoyance. Before falling asleep I had checked my messages one last time only to find that there had been no response from Mateo.

I sat up on the side of my bed and stared at the black screen of my phone, afraid to awaken it for fear of what I wouldn't find. All those mornings of opening my eyes to the new reality of being alone were gut wrenching, but I was sustained by the feeling that day by day, things would get better. I might even feel so bold that one day I would be able to capture my pain in a poem. But this juvenile panic that, "Oh, God. He didn't answer my text. He must not like me," was like being shot from a cannon back to my teenage years, when, of course, there were no cell phones or text messages, but sentiments of rejection were equally devastating.

To be rejected, I realized as I raised my eyebrows trying to force my eyes open and rolled my head around on my shoulders to get rid of the cricks in my neck, you had to have offered something. What I had given him was one snarky text followed by a second one that hinted at human emotion to try and soften the flippant tone of the first.

If I had learned one thing in my relationship with Vladimir, it should have been to handle people you have recently met and are interested in as if you are playing a game of chess. If you want something from them, you have to play the game rather than expect that magically the stars were going to align in the heavens to produce the outcome you hoped for. The first step in that game was that you had to admit you wanted something. Did I really want something or was I just bored? And if I wanted something, was it reasonably attainable in this universe? I didn't even know if Mateo was gay. I knew that he lived with his mother and wore no ring, worked as a nurse, and at times made the tiniest gestures or facial expressions that could be interpreted as an interest in me. As a friend?

Though Vladimir had been frustrating, there was a mystery in his personality, a way of interacting with people that I had the desire to unlock, though I doubted I ever would. Had he planned his incursion into our lives, hoping for a throuple, or had it developed over time? Whatever plans he had, he couldn't have known, of course, that a few months after our initial meeting that Nick would start coming down with a series of opportunistic infections and a few months after that he would be gone. But it became certain that he knew how to get what he wanted. He knew how to cajole. He never forced anything or was cruel or obviously manipulative. He put out the bait and let us take it.

In the mid-eighties, all relationships breathed under the shadow of AIDS, and the disease was taking its toll in Spain. Nick and I naively thought that we had dodged a bullet when we moved from San Francisco to Barcelona in the early eighties. The reports from New York and San Francisco were devastating. Two friends from New Orleans who had inspired us to move to San Francisco passed away early on.

Vladimir brought a new energy into our lives. Nick and I had known each other for over twenty years, though we had only been living together as a couple for about twelve. When Nick got sick and the fun times ended, Vlad could easily have drifted away. But he stayed and helped take care of him. And he took care of me. I had been off cocaine and speed for ten years, but the deep, dark hole of depression after Nick's death seemed impossible to crawl out of without help. I had to go back to work, and drugs seemed the only way to make that happen. Vlad was smart enough to realize that if I went off the deep end, he might never reach his goal of getting to the United States. Every time he caught me doing drugs—he had moved in at that point—he took them away and replaced them with sex, the kind of sex a grieving person needs, hardcore sex that took away the pain. And then he would hold me through the night like he truly cared. A part of me was aware of what he was doing, but I was too weak to stop it.

When my HIV test came back positive and his negative, he had another opportunity to make his escape. He didn't. His reasoning was that the devil you know is better than the one you don't. We were using protection, so he felt safe, certainly safer than hooking up with others who lied about their status or didn't know.

Things were bad in Sitges. Two of the bartenders where Vlad worked got sick. Every week we heard about another person dying. We started talking seriously about going to the United States. I needed a plan if I got sick. As long as we were outside of the U.S.,

I was confident that Vlad would stick around. But I had a feeling that once we got stateside, he would be gone with the wind. I never expected a long-term relationship, but I felt like I needed him until I was stronger.

When I angrily accused him of deliberately hiding the fact that he had two kids and a wife in the States, he acted like it was of little consequence.

“Were you going to wait to tell me until they showed up at the front door of our house, bags in hand?”

“What? You’re buying us a house?” He scooped me in his arms and kissed me.

I pushed him away. “Who are you?” I screamed. “I thought people like you only existed in movies.”

“You think I’m a movie star?”

Wallowing in memories of Vladimir and Nick was exhausting, and I let my head fall back on my pillow and considered crawling back in bed. But my phone made a funny little chirp and the screen lit up, sending my pulse into a sprint. Oh, shit! It was Cindy, my BFF extraordinaire. I had forgotten it was our regular check-in day.

After Anthony’s accident, she stayed with me a few days until she was sure I wasn’t going to do anything harmful to myself or the world but continued to insist we get together for a meal, a walk, a drive, or a movie once a week. A month ago, we had switched to every two weeks, which was less pressure but more difficult to remember. Like Mateo, she had reminded me we had devices called cell phones with calendars where you could put dates and be notified of them.

“These lumps of precious metals and lithium ions are taking over our lives,” I moaned in a recent conversation.

"We have to control them, and not let them control us," Cindy said.

"You mean like Dave in *2001:A Space Odyssey,* who was forced to put the computer HAL in its place?"

I remembered calling Cindy the day after seeing the movie for the first time high on mushrooms. We must have talked for over an hour about the movie and my experience with mushrooms and what happened afterwards. It was before I knew Nick was in New Orleans.

"I met someone," I told her, and I was certain I could hear her smiling over the phone. "I spent the night in his bed after watching the movie. We were intimate in that hazy, druggy kind of way but no real sex."

"Perfect," she said.

"It's probably not real. Just the drugs doing their thing."

"I've been telling you for years you need to move on." Of course, she meant from my teenage infatuation with Nick. "What's his name?"

"Marc. He's Cajun."

It felt strange to be talking to her about meeting a man. If it wasn't for that little twist of nature that made me special, Cindy and I would have ridden off into the sunset after we met that beautiful summer day by the pool at our swim club and realized we were in the same French class at Westwood High. We made a brilliant but brief attempt to defy nature.

Soon after Nick and I moved to San Francisco in 1976, she went through a nasty divorce and moved from Los Angeles to the Bay Area with her boyfriend and later husband. She had a difficult time with me being with Nick after having held my hand through the whole scandal of Nick's wife shooting Nick's tennis partner. Nick's daughter, Judy, had been one of her best friends until Judy made her choose between her and me. She chose me.

Her devotion to me didn't stop things from being awkward when Nick, Cindy, and I first started getting together in those early days in San Francisco. The pall of the hometown scandal continued to hang over us. With time and frequent awkward get-togethers, she came to accept Nick and his undeniably basic goodness. Forty-five years after our first meeting she remained my best friend, the sister I never had, and now my mother after my real one had passed.

Her text reminded me we were having lunch at Zuni Café in San Francisco, a place not in my budget, but she had insisted on inviting me as she had oodles of money from her divorce settlements and her own successful career as a graphic designer.

"Did you get a haircut?" she asked from across the table by the window facing Market Street. Outside a homeless man's grubby jeans had fallen around his hips and he had stopped just in front of our window to make adjustments with hands that were nearly black with grime. Ah, San Francisco. Where else could you pay top dollar for such a view?

"It's been a couple of weeks. Why?"

"You look different."

I had made more of an attempt than usual to be presentable, putting on a linen shirt with a collar and uncomfortably tight jeans rather than the sweatpants I had grown accustomed to. I had even put product in my hair to keep it from sticking out in all directions.

"I'm two weeks older?"

"Oh, shut up. You look, dare I say, like the worst has passed."

"It's just a façade, so I don't have to listen to another one of your it-gets-better pep talks."

"I don't know why I try. You're just as ornery as you were forty-whatever years ago. God, I can't even say it. It makes me feel old."

"Butcha are, Blanche."

"Say what you will, you'll always be older than me."

"One month!"

"Anyway, Marcelo doesn't think so."

"You're seeing someone?"

She made a sign to wipe my chin. "You have schmutz on your chin. Probably the guacamole." She smiled. "Yeah."

"Italian?"

"Brazilian."

"Child, you have gone over to the dark side."

"I'll ignore that comment, but just for the record, he's from the far south of Brazil and whiter than you."

"Oh, the Nazi area of Brazil." She broke off a crust of bread and threw it at me.

Through the salad course with several kinds of lettuce I had never heard of and the entrée of Mesquite grilled fish with potatoes that had been raised to the level of gourmet by being fried in duck fat, she talked about Marcelo and how they met, admitting that he was a bit younger.

"A bit?"

"Well, what's fifteen years?"

One of the issues she'd had with my relationship with Nick was the age gap. I was dying to tell her about meeting Mateo, but I wasn't sure how she'd take it, not the even wider age gap, but the fact that it was so soon after Anthony. Though she had come to accept Nick, she strongly opposed my involvement with Vladimir despite his using all his charming trickery to win her over. But

Anthony, she absolutely adored and was devastated by his loss. The evening after I got the nightmare call, she came over, and we went through a whole box of tissues. When one of us would start to calm down the other would go off in spasms of choking and gurgling emotion. If I mentioned I had a tiny attraction to another man, would she be pleased or shocked? Would she consider it a turning point or a betrayal?

"At our age I don't suppose it matters much," I said in a moment of wishful thinking.

"And what's going on with you? You're looking at your phone every two minutes."

"No, I'm not."

"You are."

Since nothing had happened except in my addled brain and as each hour went by without a response, it looked like nothing would, it seemed silly to mention Mateo, a mere blip on the screen of my life.

"I sent off a poem to a magazine, and they were supposed to let me know by today if they were going to include it in the next issue."

"That's great. I'm so glad you're writing again."

I wasn't. But I could rattle off who had won every tennis tournament since the beginning of the year and who they played in the semi-finals and finals and what the scores were. My one indulgent expense was paying for the premium cable package that allowed me to watch every professional match on the face of the earth. I had erotic dreams about Rafael Nadal's arms and Jo-Willie Tsonga's chest and would wake up with a smile on my face that was quickly wiped away by images of Nick and our many hours on the tennis court. In Spain we used to play on red clay and the memory of scrubbing our socks to get the red out would leave me teary-eyed and then I would feel guilty I was crying about Nick and not the person I had just lost.

"When do I get to meet this Marcelo? Though I'm warning you, as soon as I hear that accent, I might try to play footsie with him under the table."

I was traipsing on dangerous territory, but I couldn't stop myself. If I had the gene to be gay, she was cursed with the gene to be attracted to gay and bisexual men, leading to several relationships that didn't work out.

"Not this one," she said with a wry smile. "We had that discussion after our first night of glorious sex, and he assured me he had dabbled as a teenager but decided it wasn't for him."

"Dabbled? Is that what we're calling it now?"

"Are we having dessert or not?"

"Maybe we shouldn't." I patted my stomach.

All my lying around and eating crappy food in recent months had given me a belly. My phone buzzed and I hungrily turned it over to see who it was.

"Are you sure you haven't met someone? It's okay, you know, to go on with your life."

"It was my brother," I said, holding up my phone. "In any case, I wouldn't even know how. Do you have any idea what it's like to go on a dating app and tell your true age and reveal your HIV status?"

"No."

"Neither do I, and I'm not doing it."

We parted with the agreement that our next encounter would be a walk around Crystal Springs Reservoir and a picnic. She also made me promise to send her some of my recent poems.

On the drive home, I turned my phone off and listened to the chillout channel on SiriusXM, grateful for a friendship with someone who would never abandon me regardless of how snippy or sarcastic or maudlin I might be. It was nothing less than true love. And yet, I lied to her about my recent writing.

At home I sat in my worn rolling chair, swiveled back and forth a few times, did a couple of complete rotations like a dog trying to settle in, and opened a blank Word document on my desktop. I stared at the screen for several minutes before tapping a few words on the keyboard that magically appeared on the screen. They didn't look right. They refused to go together in any meaningful way. I pleaded with them, rearranged them, and promptly erased them. Tapped in and tapped out. Defeated by a malaise that consumed me.

# Chapter 7

With my mid-morning coffee mug in hand, I waded through fallen leaves and twigs and brushed off piles of dried flowers fallen from the bushes before I could sit down on the woven plastic patio furniture. The backyard was in the process of doing what nature does, breaking out of its manicured self, branches jutting out at weird angles for best sun and water access, neighboring plants competing with each other as vines strangled nearby bushes, weeds bullied weaker plants, and crabgrass wrestled with its cultured cousin. In the last few months, I had done nothing to stop the garden from becoming a wilder, untamed version of itself. The butterflies and bees couldn't have been happier, but a mockingbird screeched with annoyance that a human dared invade the area where it had a nest.

A warm breeze carried a curious aromatic blend of chocolate from the Ghirardelli factory across town and lemon blossoms from the tree over my head as I turned my chair toward the sun, absorbing its warmth on my face. When I leaned back, my phone, which had been dormant since the evening before, slipped out of the pocket of my loose sweatpants and landed with a crack on the ground. The protective cover saved the screen, but the phone was shaken to life. The first thing I saw was that it was Saturday. Oh, that was interesting. Who knew? Next, I noticed a banner notification of a text from Mateo Falla. The name rang a bell.

**Playing fúbal (don't make me call it soccer) today at 3pm at Pacific Rec field off Marina. Annual Kaiser benefit game.**

How was I supposed to respond to an FYI-type message? I imagined for a moment that it had been sent by mistake or sent to everyone in his contact list. It was weird. Nothing for two days and then an impersonal public service announcement. I wasn't sufficiently awake to determine if there was some kind of hidden message there. Was I supposed to go and sit with the Kaiser soccer families and marvel at his skills and drool over his muscular legs and then join them all at the local brewery for craft beers afterwards? Since it was a benefit, maybe his only intention was to gather the most attendees who might donate to the cause. His message was far more annoying than mine.

**Do I know you?** I typed, but then erased. I tried again. **Is this meant to be an invitation?**

His answer was immediate. **If you're busy, no problem.**

"What do you want from me?" I screamed, though it was much too hysterical to write in a text. Tick, tick, tick. I assumed he was waiting for a response. What would Vladimir do? **Let me see how the day goes.** That's the ticket. Keep him hanging. Maybe hanging wasn't exactly the right word as I had no idea if he cared whether I went to his terribly important benefit soccer match or not.

I tried to forget about it, think of errands I needed to run, fish I needed to fry, hairs in my nose that needed trimming, but at three in the afternoon, I found myself pumping up my bicycle tires. I put on sunscreen, grabbed my helmet, filled a water bottle, and began pedaling vaguely in the direction of the Pacific Rec complex where I might ride by and catch a glimpse of Mateo running around chasing a ball.

I entered the parking lot of the rec center next to Marina Square shopping center around 3:30, and the match was underway. In the distance, I saw a large crowd along the sidelines cheering them on. As I was too far away to distinguish who was who, I moved closer where I found a bench to lean my bike against and sat down, still far from the crowd, some of whom were curiously wearing bunny ears, Hawaiian shirts with plastic leis, Mardi Gras beads, floppy hats, large sunglasses, and paisley pants. Mateo had neglected to mention I should wear a costume, though it might have been nice to have a disguise to hide behind.

I discreetly removed a small pair of binoculars from my backpack—I was no fool when there were soccer players' legs to look at—and spotted Mateo. I had been right about one thing. His legs were hairy and nicely muscled. I also saw that it was a coed game and during a break, he moved close to a slightly overweight woman with a long, blond ponytail, and they chatted. The game was casual, with lots of breaks, giving him multiple chances to chat up the woman. It soon became obvious that Mateo was one of the few players on the field who knew what he was doing and scored all the goals for his team.

A couple of times he gazed in my direction, once even shading his eyes to get a better look, though never gave any indication he recognized me. A small wave might have been nice. I settled on the bench, and though I hadn't intended to stay for the whole game, after what must have been a half hour to forty-five minutes, the players came off the field, the crowd cheered, and some of the players began to pack up their belongings. Mateo continued talking to the woman with a ponytail as they left the field. I hopped on my bike and rode away.

I pedaled leisurely up Marina Blvd, trying to stay away from traffic on the wide street. After a few minutes, I felt the presence of a large vehicle behind me, moving slowly but not passing me. I looked over my shoulder and saw a black pickup truck. Why didn't they just pass? I hated when cars were overly cautious. After another couple of minutes of the truck keeping pace, I began to get paranoid. I had heard stories of trucks plowing into cyclists for no other reason than they were pissed off in an extremely uneven battle of road rage.

At one point the right lane ended, and I had to merge to the left. I pulled over to the right as far as could in the merging area, giving the truck plenty of room to pass. The dark monster moved to the curb and stopped behind me. Mateo got out and approached me, still wearing his soccer shorts, his legs glistening with sweat. I stared at the polyester fabric of his orange jersey gripping his pecs, showing his perky nipples.

"Why did you leave?" he said with a bite to his voice and angry-bird eyes.

"I don't know. It felt weird, and you seemed occupied with your friends."

"I was going to come over and say hi, but you disappeared."

"It didn't seem like you cared if I was there or not."

"I invited you, didn't I?"

I shrugged. "You played really well."

"Did you see me score the goals?" Mood switch. Now, he sounded like an ecstatic teenager after a big game.

"You mean when you kicked the ball, and it went into the little net thingy?"

"Yes. That's called a goal, and you're pulling my leg."

I laughed and glanced at his sweaty legs, which I would have been very happy to pull at that moment. I glanced at the traffic speeding by, and people stared at us as if we might be having a confrontation.

"I don't think this is the best place for a conversation."

"We can put your bike in the back, and I'll give you a ride home."

"Aren't your friends waiting for you to go out for beers? Like maybe one in particular."

He ignored me and put the tailgate down. He lifted my bike like it weighed nothing and laid it gently on its side in the truck bed. He turned to me with squinty eyes.

"*No. Nadie me espera,*" he said, slamming the tailgate shut.

"When you said you had a car the other day, you didn't say it was a truck."

Mateo threw up his hands. "Do you not ride in trucks?"

"Not, normally. I guess I'll have to make an exception since my bike is already in."

"But you get to ride in the cab unless you prefer to be with your bike."

I walked to the passenger door and tried to open it. It was still locked.

"Sorry," he said and clicked the doors open.

The outside of the Ford truck was shiny and without scratches while the inside was immaculate and smelled new. "Did you just get this?"

"No. Had it about two years."

Check. He took care of things and kept them like new. He must have been horrified at the state of the BMW, dirty, unvacuumed, and probably smelly.

"You looked pretty good out there."

"You mean my outfit," he said with a campy lilt to his voice. For someone who seemed so ungay most of the time, he occasionally let a feather fly. With everyone talking about toxic masculinity, maybe he was just one of those men who had loosened up.

"Though your outfit is cute, I was referring to your running around the field and..." I gawked at his legs. With his right leg working the pedals, his muscles were deliciously taut. His shorts had ridden up, revealing a thick thigh. "...and the...uh...kicking."

"I wanted to be a professional soccer player when I was growing up."

"What happened?"

"Life."

I waited for further explanation and forced my eyes away from his legs. "Oh, turn left here."

"Now I'm going to know where *you* live."

"Not worried. Should I be?"

"I could be a vampire."

I titled my head, pulled the collar of my shirt down, and exposed my neck to him. He shook his head and let out a low chuckle.

"Back to your life answer. That's it? Life?"

"Too complicated to explain. It is sufficient to say, I moved to the United States and my life turned upside down."

"Take a right here, and that's my house on the left. You can pull into the driveway."

He lowered the tailgate and lifted the bike out, putting it in my hands. For a moment, we were inches apart on either side of the bike, looking into each other's eyes. He backed off and the bike nearly toppled over since, in my distraction, I hadn't firmly grasped hold of it.

•

Mateo moved forward to catch the bike. "Whoa, there."

"I got it," I said.

I held on to my bike, negating any possibility of a hug, not that it seemed an occasion for it, or even a handshake. He stood as if unsure what to say and pulled at his crotch through the shiny shorts in the way men from other parts of the world did, especially athletes. I had learned the hard way, that most of the time it had no meaning beyond a simple adjustment.

"Um...could I use your bathroom? I've had to pee for the last hour."

"Oh, sure." I fished the garage door remote out of my pocket and opened the door. "We can go in through the garage."

I stored my bike on the rack and hurried to open the door. Now knowing his propensity for neatness, I was embarrassed to invite him in. What could I do? He was a man in need.

Once we got inside, I pointed at the evil eye hanging from a ribbon next to the door. "That's my anti-vampire device."

He shielded his eyes as if it was painful to look at.

"Oh, and I had to let the maid go."

"No worries."

"Caught her nipping at the sherry."

"What a shame."

I moved around the kitchen, putting dirty dishes in the sink. The mayonnaise, which I had used for my sandwich, sat on the counter. I whisked it into the fridge, though it was probably too late, and I would have to throw it away. My place at the island counter where I sat for all my meals was littered with magazines, books, and unopened mail. I gathered it all up into a neat pile while Mateo stood patiently in the middle of the kitchen. He picked at his crotch again. "Uh...the bathroom?"

"I'm so sorry."

I was sure the bathroom was a disaster zone far exceeding the kitchen, but I couldn't make him wait while I went in and made it slightly less of a disaster. I hoped I'd remembered to flush. "This way."

I led him into the hall and pointed at the doorway at the end of it. "Pardon the mess, I don't usually..."

"It's fine." He disappeared into the bathroom.

The quiet was unsettling. I dashed into the bedroom—hopefully he hadn't peeked in as he walked by—and threw the covers over the pillows to give the illusion of being made and tossed all the clothes on the chair into the closet. I heard the flush and then the water running at the sink. For a long time. Probably scrubbing his hands like a good nurse to ward off the contamination of the surroundings.

The door opened before I had a chance to get back to the kitchen, so I hid around the corner in my own home from the man I had already spent way too much time fantasizing about being in my house. The creak in the floorboard told me he had paused outside the bedroom. Was that a little snigger I heard? He continued along the hall to the kitchen. I walked in a moment later.

"Could I get you something to drink?"

"Water would be nice."

"Sparkling or still? I could put lemon in it. We have a lemon tree." The "we" slipped out. Force of habit. He blinked and raised one eyebrow.

"Regular water, no lemon, no ice would be fine."

I filled up a tall glass from the water dispenser in the refrigerator door and set it on the island in front of one of the stools.

"Have a seat."

He took the glass but didn't sit down. He put the glass to his lips, and I was mesmerized by his prominent Adam's apple sliding up and down while he finished the glass in one long gulp. There was something decidedly sexy about a thirsty man.

"I'll get you another."

He handed me the glass with a nod. "I can't stay."

Was that a I-can't-stay-and-have-sex-with-you or I-have-to-be-somewhere-else or let-me-out-of-here-as-soon-as-possible kind of I can't stay? He must have noted the confusion on my face.

"My mother."

"I see."

"The woman who usually stays with her was busy today, but the neighbor said she'd check on her every so often."

"That's a good neighbor."

Despite saying he had to leave, he sat on the stool to drink his second glass, this time taking it slowly.

"You said the other day you were widowed."

He had definitely heard the "we."

"I lost my partner a while ago." Partner was a copout. Anthony and I were legally married. I still hesitated to use the word husband, thinking that it made others uncomfortable.

"I'm sorry."

"Did you hear about the 580 sniper and the guy who crashed by the Dutton exit about eight months ago?"

"That was him?" He sank into his stool as much as one can sink into a stool. He blinked and water pooled in the corner of his eyes. "That must have been...must have been..."

"Devastating? Yes, still is."

He unfolded himself and stood up. "I have to go."

"Your mother."

"*Sí,*" he mumbled. He pointed at the door to the garage. "This way?"

I walked him out through the garage, engaged in my usual attempt at analyzing what was going on in another person's head. He stared at the ground and his shoulders slumped. "Sorry," he said.

Again, I had to hypothesize if he was sorry for what happened to Anthony or sorry for leaving so quickly or sorry he couldn't be more comforting.

"Thanks for the ride home," I said.

"Thanks for the...uh...water."

He got in his truck and backed out of the driveway.

Every time we separated, I felt the emptiness of a missed opportunity.

# Chapter 8

Nick stared out the window at the racing gray clouds, offering glimpses of the vast green and brown of Texas down below. I sat next to him with my eyes closed, staring inward, wishing that the much darker clouds in my brain would go away and give me some clarity. We were on a flight from New Orleans to San Francisco. All our clothes and personal items were in our luggage. Nick's house had been sold and the furniture sat in storage, waiting to be shipped to the coast. It was 1976.

The reasons we decided to move to San Francisco were varied and numerous. The pall of the Up Stairs Lounge fire hung over New Orleans and particularly the gay community. The MCC church that Nick had become so dependent upon for his emotional and spiritual health had a hard time recovering after losing the pastor and so many of its members in the fire. Several of the surviving members moved to Atlanta and a few of Nick's closest friends to San Francisco. Nick was unhappy with his job at Charity Hospital, and he complained that the administration was backward and racist. But the X factor was on me, the urges I couldn't control, the trails of my bad behavior that flowed a winding course through the city like the muddy Mississippi.

In the months following our trip to Montreal, I had fallen more and more under the influence of Sniffy, which meant becoming more and more dependent on cocaine and escorting to pay for the cocaine. The night I hooked up with Marc was a crisis point. Something had to give.

On a chilly winter day with a seamless dove-colored sky, I wandered through the house on my day off, trying to shake my depression. I sat in a cold living room, gripped my journal in my jittery hands, and tried to write down my feelings as Sherry had encouraged me to do. But the evening found me sitting on the edge of the bathtub, huddled over a mirror, cutting lines of cocaine with a razor blade. The door was ajar. I heard a noise and turned my head like in a drug flashback nightmare as the door inch by inch swung open. I jumped up like the edge of the tub had suddenly turned ice-cold, knocking the mirror into the sink and scattering the white powder. Nick looked at me with a disappointment that sliced through me. I hung my head and gripped the edge of the sink to keep from crumbling onto the floor.

Did I know he was coming home early that night? Did I deliberately leave the bathroom door ajar? At that point it didn't matter. I had been caught, and despite the flashing hot and cold in my gut and the monumental weight of embarrassment, I felt a tinge of happiness. Whatever happened, things wouldn't continue in the way they were, and that alone was a relief.

As an obstetrician, Nick was good at crisis management and pulled back the devastation on his face in a matter of seconds. "I wish you had come to me, but since you didn't, this is partly my fault."

I gasped-choked, sputtering my words. "You can't...take the blame. Something. Is. Wrong. With. Me. Always has been."

"We can work on that." What? We? He wasn't leaving me? Any sane person would. "But I came home early because I wanted to talk to you. We have something else to deal with. The other day I felt a burning down here." He pointed at his crotch. "I went to the clinic and it's a venereal disease." The implication was obvious. No way in hell had he been with anyone else.

I burst out sobbing. I suppose I hoped he would take me in his arms and make everything better, but he didn't. We were way beyond that. This wasn't a simple cut on my finger. This wasn't a simple incident of having a snort of coke for old times' sake. This wasn't a one-time cheating fuck that I could swear didn't mean anything and would never happen again. This was a pit deeper than the Grand Canyon and I wasn't sure I could climb out of it.

"When you're done feeling sorry for yourself, come out into the living room." He turned his back on me and left. That was the coldest he had ever been with me, and I felt the pain in every cell in my body. I deserved it.

He sat in his favorite chair, staring at the hands folded in his lap. I skulked into the room and fell in a heap on the sofa. "I have utterly and totally failed you, and I honestly don't know how you could ever forgive me." I took a deep breath. It was time to reveal the full depth of my depravity. "It's worse than you think."

"I know."

"What?"

He sat without moving a muscle and spoke in a monotone with his eyes closed, as if that was the only way he could get the words out. "I called one of my friends at the church who still goes out to the bars and asked him if he had seen you and that Sniffy character. He didn't want to tell me, but I made him. I believe I actually threatened him. This is what it's come to. I won't repeat what he told me, but I will give you the opportunity to explain yourself."

"I can't. I'm sure the truth is probably worse than what he told you."

"Things are going to change," he said forcefully, but without rancor. "Number one, you are taking time off from the restaurant so that you won't be in contact with Sniffy."

"What do I tell Sherry?"

"I suppose you can leave out the...uh...late night activities, but you have to tell her you can't be around Sniffy and why. His habit."

"He'll probably get fired."

"From what I gather, he doesn't need the money. Tomorrow, we search for a rehab facility, a real one this time."

"I'll do whatever you say."

I wanted with all my heart to make it up to Nick, to put one foot in front of the other down the long road to regaining his confidence. I felt the tiniest spark of hope that it could work. Before going into rehab, I met with Sherry and told her everything, and I mean everything. I knew I couldn't shock her. I told her how much I wanted to get rid of my drug habit for Nick.

She shook her head of wild curls. "Don't do it for Nick. Do it for yourself."

And I did.

A lot of people who knew my history thought it was a strange decision for us to move to San Francisco with its reputation as a den of iniquity, a place of sex, drugs, and rock and roll. Temptation would be everywhere, bad enough for a person without addiction, but for someone like me disastrous. Nick and I talked about it a lot, and he had long conversations with his friends who had moved to San Francisco. We became convinced that if we lived in a more open place, a place where we were free to be homosexual, it would make our relationship stronger. Nick also felt that a change of jobs to a more enlightened environment would make him happier. When we explained it to some of our friends, they laughed or shook their heads sadly. Everybody had stories of gay couples moving to San Francisco and breaking up within a year like a gay man in a candy store absolutely couldn't control his sweet tooth.

We were determined to make it work. Were we one hundred percent successful? Far from it. But I stayed off drugs and Nick found a job he loved at SF General Hospital. We fell into a community of like-minded people thanks to our friends from New Orleans. It wasn't the free love and drugs in the city that led us to move again a few years later. We had arrived at a turbulent time, though if you look at the history of San Francisco, when wasn't it a turbulent time? Our arrival in the city was right before the Pride Parade of 1976. Two years later, events shook the city to its core and affected us personally.

Nick got a job in San Francisco General Hospital's OB/GYN department and was thrilled to be working with forward-thinking colleagues who were open to the needs and wants of their patients. He fit in easily and made friends in the first week.

It wasn't as easy for me to find work. I searched for waiting jobs because that's what I had on my resume, and I had never finished college. Nick encouraged me to look for something else. One of our friends from New Orleans was working as an English as a Second Language teacher and said they were looking for teachers at his school since large numbers of Southeast Asian refugees were beginning to arrive. The school offered a four-week training course. I could start working as soon as I finished. I was confident I had a good knowledge of my own language, but teaching it ended up being much more difficult than I thought. And the pay was low. I complained to Nick that I was sure I could make more as a waiter.

"But as a teacher, you're building a future. San Francisco State has a master's program in teaching English to speakers of other languages. It would lead to better paying positions."

I was still a half year's worth of credits short of getting my bachelors. Nick suggested I work part time at the school and finish my degree at the same time, cleverly trying to keep me busy and out of the late-night restaurant world with its temptations. Though I felt strong after my last rehab, he was right, and finishing my degree and getting my master's ended up being prescient in terms of where we would end up next.

Exciting things were happening politically in the city and in the gay community, a far cry from what was going on back in New Orleans. A progressive mayor, George Moscone, had been elected and a new group of politicians was determined to challenge the old guard. Our New Orleans friends got us to work on the campaign of Harvey Milk, running for a seat on the Board of Supervisors. If successful, he would become the first openly gay man elected in California. We spent a lot of weekends canvassing neighborhoods and addressing envelopes at Milk's camera shop on Castro Street. It was an exciting time, and yes, I was much too busy to party down.

After a few months of working at General, Nick came home with a story about one of his patients. It wasn't ethical for him to talk about the woman personally, only that she was a member of Peoples Temple. The church and its founder were frequently in the news, and we started paying more attention now that Nick had a personal connection. The patient was so fond of my Dr. B—people at the hospital logically fell into using the name we had called him when I was a teenager—that she told all her pregnant friends at the Temple about him. He ended up with several patients from the church, both Black and white, women enthusiastically endorsing the church's commitment to integration, expounding on how they were trying to create a new world free of racial injustice where Martin Luther King's dream could be realized.

The next time we were at a campaign meeting with Harvey, we asked him about the Temple. He was a passionate supporter of the church and lauded Reverend Jim Jones for his fight against racism and anti-gay ballot measures, many of which were against gay teachers around the country. Peoples Temple was also a political force that could turn out votes—they helped get Moscone elected—and showed up at rallies for social justice causes. The more we learned about Jim Jones, the more we realized what political power he wielded in the city with many rising politicians begging for his support.

One day Nick showed me a letter he had received through one of his Temple patients from Jim Jones himself. The letter spoke of how highly his patients regarded him and expressed in flowing language his vision for the future. At the end of the letter, he gave a number for Nick to call to set up a meeting because he had a great desire to meet him in person. Nick was flattered and arranged the meeting for the following week. We thought it would be a good idea to go to Sunday service at the Temple to get a preview of the man he was going to meet.

Security to get into the service was daunting, something one might expect going to a concert of a major rock star. The security guards scanned the entering crowd with intimidating eyes, searched some and separated others, taking them aside for questioning. Nick and I were relieved that we were able to enter what used to be a Scottish Rite Temple without incident, but several times during the service I felt the gaze of the guards who were positioned along the walls. The church's reputation as a haven for the disenfranchised was evident in the congregation made up of a mix of older church ladies in their Sunday finery, young hippie types, and African Americans who had adopted afro hairstyles and colorful garb in African patterns. Though we had heard the church welcomed sexual diversity, we didn't spot other obvious gay couples around us.

Despite the security presence, the energy was electric in anticipation of the Reverend Jim Jones's appearance, and when he came out, the joy on the faces of the crowd, basic good people from all walks of life, was contagious. He stepped into the spotlights in his burgundy leisure suit, his jet-black hair glistened, and his signature dark aviator shades reflected light as if from heaven. Many stood and put their hands in the air, while others clapped and shouted out greetings to their pastor. The older Black woman next to me closed her eyes behind her large-frame glasses, and with a beatific smile smoothing her face, produced a low contented hum.

While Jones basked in the adoration, a pair of attendants brought a young Black woman in a wheelchair from the wings onto the stage, her leg in a cast from foot to knee. He directed the light people to focus on her and began berating the city leaders for abandoning the Fillmore neighborhood, making it difficult for good people to walk down the street without danger of injury due to the horrible condition of streets and sidewalks, implying that governmental neglect had been the cause of her broken leg. Until everyone was treated equally in every corner of the city there could be no peace. Broken promises from civic leaders and broken streets shouldn't lead to broken bones. This sister didn't deserve her injury, and he would right the wrong by healing her on the spot. He prayed over her and had the attendants remove her cast. Stepping back, he bid her to get up out of the chair, and when she made her way to him, cautiously at first, before putting full weight on her leg, he embraced her. Cries of amazement were followed by a wave of ecstasy flowing through the congregation.

I glanced at Nick who was transfixed by the scene, and then at a nearby guard who I felt watching me from behind dark glasses as if detecting my skepticism.

Nick and I had very different approaches to the question of organized religion. I had grown up in a secular home. Both my parents had come from strict religious households and vowed that my brother and I wouldn't be subjected to the same. Nick had found solace in the Metropolitan Community Church in New Orleans that held the belief that all people, gay and straight, were part of God's family. The church's approach to a higher power was steeped in the atmosphere of true Christianity. It was something he needed after the tragedy of his marriage and his flight from our hometown. I respected his involvement with MCC, though rarely participated in the church functions.

Later, I was relieved when Nick admitted that he didn't believe the healing any more than I did, but defended the theatrical nature of it, which brought the crowd together to focus on the message we both agreed was seductively positive. Jones had railed against a nebulous "skygod" that needed to be replaced by bringing heaven down to earth, to the streets with action, building a utopia of social justice, no rich or poor, no racial inequality. Though he was clearly white, he referred to himself as a "nigger" and that we were all "niggers in the eyes of corporate America." I couldn't argue with the message, but I also witnessed how the congregants were not only swayed by the words but also by the deliverance, his gift of the oratory power of a southern preacher. His words affected the people physically, their bodies swaying to the rhythms and cadences of his voice as if he had the ability to sync it to the beating of their hearts.

The following week, Nick came home from his meeting with Jones in a daze, making me think for a second the man had worked a spell on him, and he'd agree to give all his worldly possessions to the church and devote his life to Peoples Temple. The reality was far more frightening. Jones had told him about the land they had bought in Guyana, the socialist utopia they were building in the jungle. They needed doctors, and most importantly, doctors to deliver babies into the new world they were creating. Since Nick had already delivered a few babies of church members, Jones wanted him to go to Guyana as the chief obstetrician.

I stared at him in shock. "What did you say?"

"I said I'd think about it."

"No fucking way!"

"What else could I say? The pressure in the room was intense. A few members of the church hierarchy, mostly white women, one who kept staring at me in a creepily seductive way, and a couple of bodyguards I wouldn't want to mess with were all breathing down my neck. But the weirdest thing was that he knew all about me. He said I could bring you as all relationships were valued. They would need teachers as well in the new community. He even knew about my ex-wife and my flight from our hometown. It was eerie. He also offered me a lot of money."

"This guy is dangerous. I don't like it." Now, I shudder every time I think of what could have been, if somehow, he had convinced us to join the crusade in the jungle.

# Chapter 9

When Mateo had left the day of the soccer game and my big reveal about Anthony's demise, I had an unsettling feeling that I wouldn't see him again. After an entire day of interior whining about being old and undesirable, I picked myself off the floor and came to a place of being okay with it. Things had slid into uncomfortable territory too fast. Aside from being unusually attracted to him, I wasn't sure I liked him with his rapidly changing moods, his enigmatic responses, and his actions that left me confused. There was also the big question: I didn't know if he was gay or one of those confused men who liked to flirt with other men and drive them crazy. Because of Marc in my early coming out days in New Orleans, I swore I would never get involved with another man uncertain about his sexuality. It's too much work, and you get burned in the end. Yes, there was Vladimir. What can I say about that? He wasn't confused. He knew exactly what he was doing. He knew how to use sex to get what he wanted.

I went back to my routine of sitting in front of a blank computer screen, trying to put one word after another in some way that meant something before slinking off to the couch and watching hours of tennis on TV. When I reached a level of potatoness that even I found disgusting, I got up and made an attempt to clean the house, and by clean, I mean making sure I could walk from one room to another without tripping over shoes, laundry baskets of washed but unfolded clothes, pizza boxes, and cushions that had slid off the furniture.

I cautiously entered the kitchen afraid that little creatures might have taken over due to my lack of attention to cleanliness, making the room a far, far cry from godliness. There was absolutely no excuse for the clutter of filthy dishes since I had a dishwasher. I gathered everything from countertops, sink, stove, and various stations around the house, filling the dishwasher only to panic I had run out of the cute little pods that eliminated the drudgery of measuring and possibly overfilling the soap tray.

For the next few minutes, I rummaged through the forest of cleaning supplies under the sink to no avail, followed by a trip to the garage where in the back of one closet I came upon an unopened package of multicolored all-inclusive pods among the backup supplies that my dear husband had been so diligent about keeping well stocked. I reached for the box with a shaky hand. It was the minor events such as this that hit me the hardest and made his loss unbearable. I had a moment with choking sounds trying to escape my throat. At the same time, I knew he would want me to carry on, break the seal of the packaging with the zeal of discovering something new, and let the suds do their job. He was inordinately fond of running the dishwasher, doing the laundry, washing his car, and stocking vast quantities of detergents and products to complete those functions.

I entered the bathroom and my spirits that had been so lifted by my accomplishments in the rest of the house immediately fell to the tiles. Okay, triage. Dump some Soft Scrub into the toilet and swish it around to take care of the smell. That done, I was exhausted. Enough cleaning for the day. I found the latest New

Yorker and curled up in Anthony's mechanized lazy chair that held the occupant prisoner. I conked out after reading two paragraphs of the short fiction selection.

At an undetermined point of darkness, I woke up with severe hunger pangs and extricated myself from the chair after several unsuccessful attempts at finding the right button to return the chair to a position one could get out of. I shuffled into the kitchen and made a peanut butter and jelly sandwich.

While I sat at the island and munched, I thought of my mother and how she used to leave a PB&J wrapped in wax paper on the kitchen table for my brother and me when we got home from school. She would have been pleased by the house, the beautiful kitchen Anthony had designed, and the few pieces of family furniture I had claimed and had shipped out west when she moved from the Midwest to Florida. Like everyone, she was charmed by him, especially after he insisted on cooking her favorite foods. She kept telling me how happy she was for me, and then a few minutes later she would tell me again because she couldn't remember if she had told me. On her coffee table she had copies of the magazines that had printed some of my poems. She pointed at them and said how proud my father would have been because he always dreamed of having something published other than his academic papers. A couple of minutes later she said, "You know your father would have been so proud of you."

"I know, Mom," I said in a dreamy way like my father and I hadn't had a falling out that was never repaired. I was living in Spain when he died and couldn't make the funeral because Nick had just died, throwing me into an emotional morass. I couldn't bear the thought of conversations at my father's funeral about how Nick died and what the implications were for me.

Mom had also implied that Dad would have liked and accepted Anthony, but I had my doubts he would have been won over so easily. He'd shared with my brother and me on several occasions that he had a recurring nightmare about a Black man chasing him with a knife. And Mom would confirm that he often woke up thrashing and shouting like he had PTSD. As far as I knew, there had been no real incident in his life that provoked the bad dream.

The emotions triggered by the peanut butter sandwich zapped my appetite and I threw the last half in the overly full trash bin, the smell reminding me it needed to be taken out.

A week went by without hearing from Mateo, and though I knew it was best to leave well enough alone, I composed several texts, which lingered in the draft stage. Even these attempts at communication ended up being erased, and with time I began to breathe easier, letting the Mateo loop in my brain fade like an old film that wasn't properly stored in its canister.

I had started making my bed for a reason that was obscure to my own thinking. One morning as I pulled the covers up, I thought about how silly it was. The chance of anyone seeing if my bed was made or not was even less than when I used to complain to my mom when I was a teenager. What was the point? An unmade bed was easier to crawl into at night.

In the middle of this terribly important internal dialogue about bed making, my phone chirped, causing me to jump as it happened rarely, especially so early.

***Discúlpame.*** That was it. It had taken him a week of thinking before he brought himself to apologize, and per his typically cryptic texts, I wasn't sure what he was sorry for. I had been having a perfectly pleasant morning debating with myself about the pros and cons of making my bed and now I was thrown into a dilemma of whether I should bother answering a text from out of the blue from someone I had nearly deleted from my files. But as it would have been rude to ignore someone who had just apologized, in a language that wasn't mine, I might add, I responded.

**For what?**

**You must have wondered why I bailed.**

**Not really.**

I had no intention of making this easy for him. I could give short cryptic answers as well.

Time passed lazily. I finished with the bed, picked up some clothes from the floor, put them on a chair, and wandered into the kitchen to start the coffee. The coffee gurgled into the pot. I poured some granola into a bowl and smothered it with yogurt, determined to start eating healthier. I filled my cup with blackness (no cream or sugar for me in my new regimen), sat down at the counter, and tried to pick up where I had left off in the fiction piece from the New Yorker. Was this the kind of material the esteemed magazine was looking for? A whiny piece about how mean the writer's ex-wife had been. I punctuated the end of each paragraph with a comment from the virtual peanut gallery. "You got what you deserved, you blithering idiot!" And then in the next paragraph he would say he got what he deserved because he was a blithering idiot. I had sent the magazine fifty of my best poems and they had never printed one because, I surmised, they had to leave space for this drivel.

My phone chirped.

**Please meet me at Peet's at 4 p.m. *Puedes*?**

Maybe he did have a little of the Vladimir cheek. Propose a mysterious rendezvous and see what happens. Who can resist a mysterious rendezvous?

***Puedo.***

Despite the huge "why" flashing in neon lights in my brain, I arrived at Peet's shortly after four, a little sweaty on the brow from hurrying and damp palms from nervousness. He stood in line ordering a coffee, and I had the great fortune of being able to stand behind him for a couple of minutes without him being aware. He wore a salmon polo shirt and tight jeans in which his delightfully amazing ass was nestled. Jesus, his mother let him leave the house like that? He made his order and gave his name as Matt.

"Hello, Matt," I said.

He whirled around and then shrugged. "Mateo can be hard to spell."

The girl at the register with a nose ring and green hair tsked, her hand on her waist, elbow jutting out. "I *know* how to spell Mateo."

Mateo smiled and turned back to her. "Mateo then. But wait. Nathan, what can I get you?"

I was buzzing from the pot of coffee I had drunk throughout the day. "I'll take a peppermint tea. Thanks."

While waiting for our drinks, we grinned awkwardly and glanced around the room. I touched his arm, letting him know we needed to move out of the way to let other customers get to the cash register.

"I'd been hoping to see you out of your scrubs," I said to fill the space.

His mouth twisted. "Out of my scrubs? Like in...?"

"I mean, in something other than scrubs." I felt my face go hot because I totally wanted to see him out of his scrubs.

"I wore athletic clothes the other day."

"You certainly did," I said with an enthusiasm to show how much I had appreciated the outfit.

He shot me a taken-aback look that I had already witnessed several times and it made me smile.

"Matt Mateo," the barista shouted.

We sat outside at the same table where the homeless woman had approached me, which seemed to complete some kind of circle, though I was hard pressed to say what kind. He took a sip, and I took a sip.

"Yee-ow! That's hot," I said.

"Mine, too. Very hot."

The light changed and the traffic roared down 14th Street like they all had some important meeting they were late for. We looked at the traffic, stared at our drinks, glanced at other people at their tables, letting our eyes land on anything that wasn't each other.

Mateo cleared his throat. "I'm afraid you might have the wrong impression of me."

I took a sip of tea. Here we go, I mused. He was going to give me a little speech about how he wasn't like that and he was sorry if I was misled.

"I understand."

"Do you?"

"I think so."

"I *don't* think so. I haven't, you know, met anyone in a long time. I work a lot and take care of my mom. And San Leandro doesn't exactly have a lot of options." It was like he was cranking out the words from an old Victrola that needed repair.

I felt sorry for the guy. He had been trying to make a friend, and I took it the wrong way. He was letting me down easy. "It's okay. You don't owe me an explanation. It's always nice to meet a new friend."

He gave me a look of total exasperation. "You say friend, but you don't seem to like me much." He let out a big puff of air, like he had been holding it for the last three weeks. "*Por Dios!* I find you are a handsome man."

A leaf falling from the tree above us could have knocked me over. I surely must have misheard him. "But you acted like you didn't think much of *me*."

"Do you really think I invite random people to come and watch me play fútbol?"

"That's just it. You didn't invite me." I raised my voice slightly. "You informed me of an event."

He countered with a more agitated tone. "With the time and location, and you were late! Then you ran away."

I took it up one more notch. "Of course, I did. You barely let that blond ponytail out of your sight."

He rumble-laughed, deep and victorious. "She's a lesbian. I told her I had invited someone to come and watch me play. I tried to get her to look discreetly in your direction."

"Weirdest invitation I've ever gotten."

"I doubt it," he said with jumping eyebrows. Now that he had gotten things off his chest, he was loose and ready to spar. His shoulders twitched and his eyes sparkled as if the bell had rung, and it was fight time. He cracked his knuckles and his biceps bulged like he was turning into the incredible hulk in front of my eyes.

"Don't do that."

"Crack my knuckles?"

"No. Look so damn sexy."

His body was literally taken aback this time, his head moving away from me, and shoulders leaning back. He glanced around in case someone might have heard. "You think so?" he whispered.

"Don't be so naïve. I haven't exactly been discreet with my wandering eyes."

"The ones that wanted to see me out of my scrubs?"

"The very same." In my wildest dreams, this was not the way I'd expected the day's conversation to go. Where was all this leading?

"I need to explain something." He turned serious again. "The other day when you told me about your ex. I felt bad to be in the house, imagining he was present, watching us. I wanted to comfort you, maybe give you a hug, because no one deserved to have so much pain, a death so sudden like that, so tragic. But it wasn't right for me to be there and make an excuse to come into your house and hope maybe I could get to know you a little. That was before I knew."

We had painstakingly gotten to a joyful point. It was thrilling to realize that someone I found agonizingly attractive believed there was something in me he could work with. He was sweet to say I was handsome, but it had been a long time since I felt the least bit attractive.

With the mention of Anthony, I felt myself sliding back into the sadness that had been my constant companion the last few months. "He wasn't like that. I mean, if he was watching us, it wasn't in a scary way."

"Sorry to make you sad again. It was nice to see your smile a few minutes ago."

"How could I not smile when I've got a view like this?" I stared straight into his eyes.

"*Oye, sinvergüenza.* Be careful now."

"I know. *Despacito.*"

"You never told me where you learned Spanish."

"I lived in Spain for a while."

"Ah, I bet you learned from a nice Spaniard, whispering things in your ear."

"Not exactly."

Most of my time in Spain I lived with Nick. That was a story for another day. I didn't want him to think I was like the spider woman whose kiss put her lovers in the ground. The last couple of years in Spain living with Vladimir helped perfect my Spanish, but I wasn't keen on Mateo ever learning of Vladimir. He didn't need to know.

"Sometimes I hear something like a little Cuban accent."

Shit! Cuban Spanish has an addictive cadence that anyone who has lived with a Cuban will inevitably pick up. "Uh...my teacher was Cuban."

"Strange to have a Cuban Spanish teacher in Spain."

"I know, right?"

We finished our drinks, and the conversation reached a pause. Mateo pouted his lips and looked at his phone.

"Do you have to get back to your mom?"

"I have a little time."

"How much?"

He did the knitted unibrow thing, like he knew what I was thinking. "Are you having bad thoughts?" he asked.

"No, Father, I swear." I made a sign of the cross and hoped he wasn't a good Catholic who might take offense. "I meant, maybe we could go for a walk."

"That would be nice. I walked here, so you can walk me home."

With the confirmation of a mutual attraction, I thought about suggesting he walk me home, an empty place where we would be free to explore whatever we wanted. But once we got there, it would be weird if I didn't invite him in since he had already been in my house, and if he came in, I might be tempted to make a move, putting him in an awkward position since he had already expressed discomfort at being in the house I shared with Anthony, causing him to push me (most likely gently) away, and then we would both feel like something was wrong and we probably wouldn't talk about it because we hadn't really gotten to the point where we could honestly discuss our feelings, and he would leave and not text me for a week or maybe ever. I had the whole film scripted and played out in half a second.

"I would be happy to walk you home," I said.

It was both odd and extremely gratifying to be walking the streets of my town next to Mateo, adjusting my normally long strides to match his, our hands occasionally brushing, and I was freed of any nervous anticipation that he would invite me in because I knew he couldn't with his mother at home.

Mateo's complex was larger than I thought, consisting of two large buildings. He led us in the direction of the second building that bordered the creek and as we moved down the sloping driveway, his jovial step since leaving Peet's noticeably stiffened and slowed.

"We were able to get an apartment that faces the creek, which was lucky because they don't come available very often. We have a balcony with a little table and two chairs where you can sit and look at the creek through the trees, big trees, though there's not much creek to see this time of year because it's dry. I guess we're in a drought. Sometimes in the winter when it rains a lot you can hear the water flow and it's comforting, especially for my mom, who says it reminds her of where she grew up in a rural area near Santa Marta in Colombia." He paused, but only a second. "Sometimes the neighbors are a little noisy, so it's not ideal. Thin walls, you know. Eventually I'd like a house, but I don't know. Things are so expensive." He stopped outside the entrance to his building. "Sorry, I'm babbling."

I wasn't paying a lot of attention to the words but rather the sound of his soft, slightly scratchy voice that I could have listened to all day. A shaft of light shot through the branches and gave his dark hair a reddish tinge and a bead of sweat made its way down from his temple. He must have felt my stare on his cheek and swiped a hand across it.

"You should probably take a breath at some point in the near future."

"Oh, yes. Thank you." He took an exaggerated gulp of air. "I have to go inside."

"Of course."

He continued standing in front of me, shifting his weight from foot to foot, looking at the ground and then up at me in the most adorable way. "Thanks for meeting with me."

"Anytime you want."

"Tomorrow?"

"Seriously?"

"I may be slow to react sometimes, but I don't throw things out that I don't mean."

"Do you have a bicycle?"

"In storage. I could dust it off and fill the tires."

"How about a ride to Alameda?" I leaped on the moment without considering the distance. "Come to think of it, that might be a little ambitious. I haven't been riding mine either."

"I have to take my mom to church if she feels up to it. Most of the time she gets dressed and decides not. We'll see. But we might do a short ride over to the bay."

"Call me in the morning. Or if you want later tonight."

Neither of us seemed to know exactly how to end the conversation.

"Can we hug?" I said. "Or would that be too...?"

Before I could finish, he had pulled me in. It was strong but brief, a socially acceptable length of time.

"You smell nice," I said.

"Hair stuff."

I started backing away. "I'm going."

"Be careful on the walk home."

"The only danger in this town is right in front of me." I laughed to make sure he knew it was a joke, but he still shook his head and twisted his lips.

"Goodbye, Nathan."

"*Hasta luego*."

# Chapter 10

I woke up the following day in good spirits despite not hearing from Mateo the night before. I had craved one of those conversations, curled up snug in bed like Cindy and I used to have in high school when we would talk for hours about our hopes and dreams. Since he had been so adamant about not suggesting activities that he had no intention of following through on, I was fully confident we would get together later in the day for a bike ride.

After coffee, I went into the garage, pulled my bike down from the rack, and filled the tires. I hadn't been riding much lately, even though San Leandro was in some ways an ideal place due to its flat terrain. In most of the city the biggest hills were the overpasses over the freeway.

I opened the garage door with the idea of taking a little spin around the neighborhood. Before heading off, I straddled my bike at the end of the driveway and watched the crows sitting on the power lines, cawing like something was amiss. A squirrel scurried down a tree trunk with something in its mouth and ran across the neighbor's yard while one of the crows swooped down, nearly grazing its back in hopes of getting it to drop what it carried. The squirrel dashed under a parked car and hid.

A Porsche pulled into the driveway across the street, someone visiting my neighbor, and the crow took flight, allowing the squirrel to dart across the yard and up a tree. I flashed on the day I, barely a teenager, was out riding my bike and stopped to watch the new family move in down the street. One of the new owners, Mrs. Baronian, directed the movers, and a girl about my age was plopped in an armchair on the front lawn as if supervising. I straddled my bike and watched from a distance, but the girl saw me and sneered, making me feel like it was time to continue my ride. Just as I put my feet on the pedals, a black Porsche pulled into the driveway, and a man with movie star good looks got out wearing Bermuda shorts and a Lacoste polo shirt. It was the woman's husband, the young Dr. B. That was the day Nick Baronian came into my life and changed everything.

When Nick and I got to San Francisco years later, one of the first things we did was acquire bicycles, something I could never in a million years have imagined that day I watched his family move in. We lived in the Cole Street neighborhood with its own commercial street, including a lesbian bar, a hardware store, and an alternative bakery that made a dynamite potato bread I have never found the likes of since. It was just a few blocks up from the decadence of Haight Street with drug addicts and boarded-up storefronts, but a few blocks from Golden Gate Park where we could ride the three miles all the way to the ocean through one of the most beautiful parks in the world.

In those early days in the city, we were high on the thrill of being in a place where we could live openly as gay men, where city politics had taken a turn toward the progressive, and where groups like Peoples Temple were preaching racial equality and social justice. Though we had missed the Summer of Love by about ten years, we thought we had arrived at a reasonable facsimile of paradise, at least compared to those latter years in New Orleans. Our bikes became symbols of happiness and freedom as we rode around, discovering new places in this magical city. Two and a half years later, the city had become a living hell rocked by assassinations and a mass suicide, both incidents to which we had personal connections. Our bikes then turned into vehicles for maintaining our sanity as we rode through the park as often as we could, surrounding ourselves with plants and trees to block out the horrendous events.

The man who emerged from the Porsche across the street, a bald, paunchy gentleman caller for the woman across the street, glanced at me with a look that made me feel like a nosy neighbor. He was a far cry from Nick Baronian. I pushed off to ride around the block, remembering all the other cities I had lived in and all the bicycle rides I'd taken in those places. I was anxious to add a bike ride with Mateo to the long list of fifty-odd years of feeling the wind in my face while on two wheels.

When I returned home, there was a message from Mateo. **Sorry. Please don't think I'm a liar. I had every intention of going on a bike ride today. I was looking forward to it. I told my mom I was going out and the lady next door would stay with her for a couple of hours. She became very agitated. I will call you later.**

Yes, I was pissed, but mostly disappointed. I put my bike back on the rack and called Cindy.

"What's up, sweetie?" she said.

The mere sound of her voice perked me up. "Am I interrupting anything?"

"Perfect timing. Marcelo just left." She had that bubbly sound in her voice that still held the previous night's pleasure.

"Don't you need to go get cleaned up or something? Wash that man off your body?"

"You are rude and crude and socially unacceptable."

"That's why you love me. So, things going well?"

She hesitated a moment as if she didn't want to rub it in that she had someone, and I didn't. "So far, so good."

"Remember the other day when you suspected I might have met someone, and I denied it?"

"You can't hide from me, Nathan Landis."

"I've spent forty-five years trying."

"So, you did meet someone? What's going on?"

"I didn't want to tell you because the word was still out and still is."

She must have picked up on the despair in my voice. "Please tell me this is not another Vladimir situation. I swear I'll come right over and slap you silly."

"He does live with a woman."

"God, Nathan! I'm getting my car keys right now. Why in the world can't you find a man who's one hundred percent gay?"

"Anthony was one hundred percent."

"Now you're making me sad."

"Before you go jump in your car, the woman he lives with is his mother."

"Thank God! But I suppose that could be worse."

"He's a nurse at Kaiser, and then he comes home and has to take care of her."

"Definitely gay."

"I was kind of shocked when he admitted as much. He's butch and plays soccer. And the body! I haven't gotten the full reveal, but I suspect he could pose for a *Men's Health* magazine cover."

"I want a picture right now."

"It's moving very slowly. We haven't arrived at the can-I-take-your-picture-for-my-later-enjoyment stage."

"Okay. I get it. It's lust. You deserve that. But is there anything there?"

"Now you're making me feel like a typical body-centric superficial faggot, which I suppose I am."

"You're not. Maybe you want to be, but you're not."

"Okay. He's sweet and reserved, overly serious at times, and frustrating as hell."

"Except for the last part, he sounds the exact opposite of Vladimir."

"Can we never mention Vladimir again?"

"Gladly. It's just that I was so mad at you during that period I almost lost my best lifelong friend. I wanted to kill him."

"Me too."

"Good thing you didn't. What's his name?"

"Mateo."

"Back to the Latino thing, huh?"

"I believe we're supposed to say Latinx, now."

"Pardon my politically incorrect ass."

"He's more Blatino, or do we say Blatinx? From Colombia. If you take all my previous boyfriends, even the one whose name we shall no longer mention, and roll them into one, he's it."

"Sounds delightfully dangerous. How did you meet?"

"I was out on a walk. He was on his way home from work in his scrubs, and we started talking. I'm sure he thought I had wandered off from one of the nursing homes around here."

"Shut up."

"I wasn't having a good day. It was one of those days like why bother putting on clean clothes or combing my hair, and not a spec of makeup. *Quelle horreur!* I live in San Leandro, for God's sake. Who cares?"

"Just when you least expect it..."

"It was a simple, casual encounter, but I couldn't stop thinking about him even though I was almost sure he wasn't gay. Either my gaydar was on the fritz or he had a blocker."

"Did you exchange numbers or something?"

"No. I tell you it was a totally random brief street conversation, but he was wearing a nametag that said Kaiser."

"You went into stalker mood, shameless one that you are."

"I hate you knowing me so well."

"And it worked?"

"You can only stalk the willing."

"That is total bullshit, but I'll ignore it. Did you go to his work?"

"Outside his work. Does that count?"

"It's still pretty low."

"You know what the mofo did? He accepted a ride home from me when his own car was sitting right there in the parking lot. He is com-pli-ca-ted."

"That was the sign, right?"

"I was still confused, thinking he was lonely and had no friends. Then he told me I was handsome."

"That was sweet."

"Then I was sure he was desperately lonely and had absolutely no friends, so he would say anything just so I would stay around and talk to him for five minutes."

"Honey, he's into you."

"We were supposed to go on a bike ride today. Nice healthy date, right? Mama got wind of it and said no dice."

"She wouldn't let him go on a bike ride?"

"He said she got agitated, which is probably a nice way of saying she threw a fit. Apparently, she's unwell. Sometimes has panic attacks when he leaves."

"Patience, my boy. Give it time. Hey, I've got to go. I have an appointment with a client."

"Sure. Leave me alone in my agony."

"We're still on for the walk around the reservoir next week, right?"

"Absolutely. Unless I have to take a raincheck because I'm on my honeymoon in Bali."

"Bitch! Love you."

"Ditto."

I sometimes think that I wouldn't have survived as long without Cindy who had been there in person or by phone for countless important moments in my life. When Nick died, she flew to Spain even though I didn't ask her to. That was when she first met Vladimir. She had his number from the get-go.

"Honey, I know you're hurting. I can't even imagine. Just be careful. Don't do anything you'll regret later."

At first, I thought she was talking about falling back into drugs. Then she nodded at Vladimir across the room. "He's trouble."

She had seen him holding me up. She had seen him find a seat for me and run to get me something to drink. She had seen him tuck me in, kiss my forehead goodnight and leave. What she didn't know was how he kept me alive, how I most certainly would have gone on a drug binge without him around.

She stayed as long as she could, but after a week, she had to go back home. I had other friends I normally could have depended on, but a lot of them were dealing with their own illnesses or that of their partners. My best girlfriend in Spain and a colleague at the institute had an African boyfriend who tried to go back to Togo to see his sick mother and was stuck in immigration limbo somewhere. She spent all her time trying to locate him and help him get back to Spain. He never did. He died of AIDS at an immigration detention center in Morocco. She couldn't be there for me. I was left with Vladimir, who was present and very caring in his own way. Aren't all relationships transactional, I reasoned?

After my conversation with Cindy, I zoned out watching tennis on TV. I had leftover pizza for dinner. No call from Mateo. I went back to the TV and watched an old movie, *Gentlemen Prefer Blondes,* which I had seen about twenty times and it always cheered me up. The Jane Russell number, "Ain't There Anyone Here for Love?" had lifted me out of many a depression and brought a smile to my face as the campiest, gayest, most homoerotic song in musical history. I did fall asleep before the tiara issue was solved.

I woke up to someone knocking on the front door. I looked at the clock. It was 11:30. No one ever knocked on my door at night. I was terrified it was someone who was going to say their car broke down and then ask to use the phone. I would let them in, and they'd murder me and ransack the house, stealing all the precious jewels and priceless art. I peeked out the window and saw a black pickup truck parked out front. I opened the door.

He stood there breathing like he had just run a marathon, his eyes dancing, unsure, his hands hanging at his sides but poised like a swimmer about to dive in the pool. It was the sexiest thing I had seen in my life.

"Why didn't you answer my message?" he said.

"I didn't...I haven't..."

A second later he was inside the house, and I was up against the wall with his mouth on mine, his hands on either side of my face as if he was afraid I would pull away. This was a dream, right? This didn't happen in real life. His tongue rolled over mine and he kept starting to release me but would change his mind and dive back in as if he had no control. It wasn't fair because his breath was all minty and mine pepperoni-y. I pulled him closer, knowing that if this was a dream, it would end before anything serious happened.

Then he let go for real and stared at me. "I'm sorry. I didn't know what to do."

"This is what you do when you don't know what to do? You can not-know-what-to-do to me anytime."

"Stop. This is serious. I'm serious. I've wanted to do this since..."

"That first day under the apricot tree?"

"Well, maybe not..."

"Oh, come on. Just say yes."

"Yes. Yes. Yes. Kissing you is awesome."

Before that night I had declared that adjective to be thrown on the trash heap of overused words. When people said it, I cringed. But his lips breathed new life into it, his pronunciation made it a new word. Awesome. Awesome. Awesome. He could whisper it in my ear the whole night if he wanted.

"I think I better close the door. If the neighbors want to see more, they'll have to pay."

I walked around him, pushed the door closed, and flipped the lock. The click was like a gear shifting into place just before a race car taking off...or maybe not. Whatever had overtaken him appeared to have subsided. He stood with a silly, contented grin on his face. I grabbed his hand and led him into the living room.

We sat on the sofa and with our hands still interlaced he rubbed the back of mine along his cheek which was, in my estimation after many years of observing men's beards, a three-day growth where it had just reached the scruffy-sexy stage before venturing into wild unkempt territory. It sent tiny rivulets of pleasure up my arm.

I glanced around the room, wondering where my phone was. "What did your message say?"

"That I had just gotten mom to sleep, and I wanted to see you. It's been a rough day. She had a panic attack. I gave her something to sleep."

"You drugged your mom so you could come over to see me?"

"That's not funny." He tried to extricate his hand, but I held on.

"Sorry." I kissed the back of his hand, letting the hair on his knuckles tickle my lips.

"She often takes something to sleep. I don't feel comfortable leaving her for a long time, though."

"That's why you put on the brakes?"

"No. I didn't want it to be like that."

"Like what?"

"Like animals. Boom, boom, bye."

"Are you saying you want to have growling sex, *and then* we hold each other until our rapidly beating hearts calm down and maybe through the night?"

He tilted his head, grinned, and gave a little shrug. "*Sí, señor.*"

"Is that ever going to happen?"

"*Sí, señor.*"

I rubbed my eyes. "I was asleep when you knocked on the door."

He pulled my head to his chest. "Rest, *cariño.*" He ran his hand through my hair, which was almost as good as sex, maybe better. It was safe sex, and I didn't have to take care of that pesky little business item before we got down to business if he still wanted to after I revealed my status.

# Chapter 11

I often wondered why I was spared to go on living and so many were not and why Nick's life was so full of tragedy and mine more tragedy adjacent. By the summer of 1977, things were beginning to unravel for Peoples Temple, but Nick had an inkling before the bad press hit the newsstands. Not long after he had gotten the offer to go to Guyana, one of his Temple patients opened up to him. He had learned to be very cautious with them and they trusted him. In the more progressive San Francisco General OB/GYN department, fathers were encouraged to be involved in the pregnancy and birthing process. Whenever he casually asked the Temple mothers about the fathers, simple questions like if the father was excited about the new little one, they would clam up or begin talking about how successful the latest food and clothing donation campaign had been. But one of his patients, a young woman eight months pregnant, had a minor breakdown in their consultation. She said that people were making plans for a large contingent of church members to move to the jungle in Guyana, something she didn't want to do.

Nick naively said that she should simply tell the church authorities that she didn't want to go. Tears rolled down her face as she said, "I can't, especially as a woman carrying the future in my belly."

"You mean you're being forced to go?"

She suddenly pulled back her tears and her face turned hard, realizing what she had done, spoken against the church. "I'm just being emotional. Forget what I said."

"It's okay," he said. "Everything you tell me in this room is confidential."

She nodded but examined the ceiling and upper part of the walls as if looking for cameras.

When Nick told me the story as we lay in bed engaged in our habit of talking to each other about our days, we turned to each other with fear in our eyes. He still hadn't given Jones an answer about Jonestown. I had visions of the Temple guards breaking down our door and kidnapping us, putting us on a plane to the middle of the Guyanese jungle. Since they seemed to know everything about us, they certainly knew where we lived.

A few weeks later an exposé of alleged Peoples Temple atrocities and the Jim Jones personality cult was published in *New West* magazine, sending shock waves through the political, journalistic, and DA's offices in the city. But before the article hit the streets, Jones had already fled to Guyana. Nick and I breathed a sigh of relief.

Into the fall, more reports came out about abusive treatment of members who wanted to leave the Jonestown community. Since Nick's pregnant patient never came back, he assumed she had been forced to move to Jonestown and would have had her baby there. Several other of his Temple patients had missed appointments.

Many of the politicians, newsmen, and local officials who had once praised Jones, including the renowned columnist Herb Caen, began distancing themselves from him. One who remained steadfast in his support was our friend Harvey Milk. We continued to work on his campaign for the board of supervisor seat, but our enthusiasm had waned. At a press conference we attended, a reporter asked him how he could continue to support Jim Jones. He didn't hesitate a moment in answering and challenged the reporter to name another prominent church leader who was outspoken about gay rights, who denounced violence against gays and lesbians, and who worked tirelessly to give homosexuals a seat at the table.

During those joyous first months in San Francisco, we had attended a rally where Harvey spoke. He began with his catchphrase, "I'm Harvey Milk and I'm here to recruit you." Nick winced, but I was thrilled that he was throwing the conservative accusation back in their faces. He ended his speech with the message, "Hope for a better world, hope for a better tomorrow, hope for a better place to come to if the pressures at home are too great." To that, Nick nodded enthusiastically. It was the message that had drawn us to San Francisco and the message we were living every day.

Though we didn't understand why Harvey continued to support Peoples Temple and Jones specifically, we joyfully celebrated when he won his election in the fall. Dancing with other gays and lesbians at the victory party was one of the highlights of my life.

In the next year, the news was constantly filled with stories of Jonestown custody battles and congressional investigations led by Congressman Leo Ryan. Nick contacted an organization called The Concerned Relatives to see if they had any information about his former patients. I convinced him to let it go as he was obsessing over something he had no power to change.

And then in November, Nick and I sat in front of the television in horror as the images and stories of the mass, and in many cases forced, suicides emerged from Jonestown. Nick was inconsolable as he lamented the deaths of the former patients he had grown to know and love. But what drove him to despair was the three hundred children that perished that day, a few of them babies he had delivered and others he would have delivered if they hadn't gone to Guyana. The footage of bodies sprawled all over the jungle floor in colorful outfits stuck with us for a long time. Nick had nightmares, something that had never happened in the time we had been together. We soon found that the Furies were not finished with us yet.

Not even two weeks after the Jonestown massacre, George Moscone and Harvey were assassinated in City Hall. The joyful bubble of our new life in San Francisco, on life support for the last nine days, burst with more wailing and tears. Our dream shattered.

Nick spent the rest of the year in depression, and I tried to think of ways to pull him out of it though I was also wary about the future. One night in early 1979, Nick said, "I'm done." He said it with a finality that rocked me.

"You mean with San Francisco?"

"San Francisco, my job, everything." I rose on my elbow and stared at him in panic. What was he saying? "Except you."

"Thank God for that. I feel like we came to the end of the rainbow and instead of a pot of gold, we found a pile of shit. Where is there left to go?"

By everything he meant a change of profession as well as a change in location. He had been practicing medicine for close to twenty years. Doctors in their mid-forties didn't normally dump their careers and start over. I had finished my bachelors but was still working on my masters. When Nick and I first got together, I had mused about going to France, thinking that Europe had more enlightened attitudes about homosexuality. I fantasized about being an international businessman and speaking fluent French. The business part had long been discarded but living in Europe and speaking a foreign language was still something that excited me. "What about Europe?"

"When you mentioned that years ago, I thought you were going to run off without me. I've always wanted to live in Europe, but I didn't know how I would practice over there. Once you finish your masters, you can teach anywhere. Maybe I can find a different sort of work in another country."

We spent the next year perusing foreign job ads, thinking we shouldn't limit it to Europe though that was our goal. I still hoped for a French-speaking country. While I completed my masters, Nick plodded to his job at the hospital, his heart not in it. Each day there reminded him of the patients and babies he'd lost.

In the fall, I signed up to go to an ESL teacher's conference in San Diego. Nick accompanied me. It was good for both of us to get away. I had heard that foreign schools sometimes recruited at conferences and we took copies of our resumes just in case. An English language school in Barcelona was looking for teachers, not a place where I could use my French, but it was in Europe. The real stroke of luck was that the school had recently begun a new program of English for medical professionals. We both applied for jobs with a why-not attitude. A couple of months later, we got letters of our acceptance for the fall 1980 school year.

Our spirits picked up, knowing we had an escape plan. The night we got our letters, Nick got into bed and turned to me. "*Hola,*" he said. "*Como esta usted?*"

"*Muy bien,* but I think you can use *tu* with me since we've been sleeping in the same bed for six years." That was about the extent of our Spanish. The dark cloud over our lives was lifting and we made love for the first time in months. As we lay in bed, our bodies warm and satisfied, and my head on his chest, I said, "I thought of another one. *Te quiero.*"

"Me too. *Quiero* you."

"Tomorrow we begin with Spanish lessons every day. Not a bad language to know, since there are about three hundred million Spanish speakers in twenty different countries."

"You'll have to help me. I failed French in high school."

"You'll be fine."

# Chapter 12

The decision to go to Spain and learn Spanish changed my life in ways I couldn't have imagined at the time. After studying with audiotapes and lesson books for a year, I felt comfortable in simple conversations when we arrived in Barcelona in the fall of 1980. Nick struggled. The immigration official asked him how long he would be in Spain.

"*Cuarenta y seis,*" he answered. He had learned the numbers very well. He thought they had asked his age.

"*Dias?*" the agent said.

"What?" He turned to me.

"He's asking how long we'll stay in Spain."

The man looked at me curiously and asked if we were together. Instead of giving a direct answer, I pulled our work contracts out of my bag and said we would be teaching at the same school on one-year contracts. I gave him the name of the hotel where we would be staying until we found an apartment. I managed the whole conversation in Spanish, and Nick looked at me in awe. I was high both from negotiating my first complicated conversation in Spanish and the relief of being far away from the problems of San Francisco and the United States, where it was almost certain that Ronald Reagan would be elected in November.

Nick and I were starting a new chapter in our lives. I had read that same-sex sexual intercourse was decriminalized in 1979 in Spain and that in the post-Franco era, particularly in Barcelona, ideas about homosexuality were changing rapidly.

In my first week of teaching, still high on my ability to speak Spanish in the country where it was spoken, I had a rude awakening regarding another post-Franco development. Though we were encouraged to always speak English in the classroom, there were times that being able to provide a simple translation in Spanish saved time and appeased frustrated students.

One day a student said, "Teacher, why aren't you speaking Catalan? You are in Catalonia."

Under Franco, the Catalan culture and language were repressed, but the language—I learned it was a separate language with its own set of rules and vocabulary—was now spoken openly, taught in schools, and some even pushed for an independent state with its own government.

I didn't want to insult the student, but I reminded her I had just arrived in the country and I needed time to perfect one language before starting another. And though I did become proficient in Spanish during the years I lived in Spain and the couple of years I lived with Vladimir in San Francisco, I didn't manage any more than a passable understanding of Catalan.

As time went on, I realized that learning a language was not just memorizing vocabulary and applying grammar rules. It's absorbing a culture as well. Granted, the culture of Spain was quite different from the culture of Cuba, the culture of Mexico, and the culture of Argentina, but as I learned bits and pieces of how Spanish was spoken in each of the geographic locations, I got hints about the culture and its people. In the relationship hiatus years between

Vladimir and Anthony, I traveled to as many of those twenty Spanish-speaking countries as I could and felt privileged to be able to speak to the people in their language.

In the short time I had known Mateo, I felt my knowledge of Spanish gave me a little window into his soul, even knowing that we probably wouldn't be speaking very much Spanish together. When he called me *cariño* without hesitation that night on the sofa after our first kiss, it was so much more impactful than if he had said sweetheart, which might have sounded peculiar. That one word carried inside it a whole culture, a culture I felt completely comfortable with even though it wasn't mine.

When he left that night, he said he had a busy week ahead with his regular work and several doctor's appointments for his mother, and not to get upset if I didn't hear from him.

"You can send me texts from time to time to let me know you're alive, can't you?"

"You are so dramatic. Of course, I'm going to be alive...*y pensando en ti.*"

When he switched languages, it was part of that phenomenon of culture embedded in the words. It might have sounded strange for him to say "and thinking of you" or he wanted to use words that were more meaningful to him. Having two languages to work with allowed us a richer communication, at least, that was my theory, and I was sticking to it.

I had a whole week to think about his kiss. In other news, he did text, actually quite a lot, and I wrote a poem. About a kiss. I called it Spider Woman, and that was not in any way suggesting that either of us was a woman or that there was death in the kiss. But it was about how you die a little bit that first time you have a passionate kiss with someone you've been pining for. Then you're reborn.

He said one last thing that night as he left my house after another long kiss at the door. "Your house is two-bedroom, no?"

"Uh...yes. Why?"

"Well, I just wondered."

He took the stepping-stone walkway through the out-of-control, drought-tolerant hot lips salvia and Mexican sage brushing his trousers on the way to his truck. He opened the car door and waved. "Waiting is good," I said softly. "Waiting is good." If I said it enough times, I might believe it.

I closed the door, remembering his question about two bedrooms. What the hell was that about? And then it hit me. He was thinking ahead. He seemed to have gotten over being in the house I shared with Anthony, but sleeping or other activities in the bed we had shared might be a hurdle too high to clear at this early stage. I felt myself getting hard. Five days until I might see him again? Of course, that didn't necessarily mean five days until D-day. And what were we going to do about Mama Falla?

With Mateo's mother in my thoughts, I called my brother.

"What's up, bro?"

He always answered my calls the same way. I marveled at how different we were, and yet we grew up a few years apart with the same parents, in the same house, in the same town. We couldn't have been that dissimilar deep down. He had always been supportive of me being gay, and he was the only important person in my life who didn't have an adverse reaction to me being with Vladimir. In an unexpected way, they got along very well in the limited time they were together.

"I was thinking about mom. Do you think she really liked Anthony, or did she just want to keep the peace as she tried to do when we were growing up but wasn't that successful?"

"She really liked him. She told me so a bunch of times."

"If I had been her only son and lived with her because she needed care, do you think she still would have liked him?"

"Where's this coming from? Weird question, bro. I hate hypothetical questions."

To continue the topic would have meant giving him the details of meeting Mateo, which I wasn't ready to do yet. "I'm glad she and dad got back together before he passed."

"Yeah. It was good for both of them."

"It felt sucky when they separated, and I believed it was because of me. He could never handle me being gay and Mom wouldn't put up with his shit. And the whole Dr. B thing put him over the edge."

"Hey, you don't get all the cred. He wasn't that crazy about how I turned out either, the whole draft dodger thing. He blamed Mom for everything and didn't like her more enlightened parenting ideas. Having kids myself, I've often thought about the parenting arguments they had. I didn't want to be like Dad. I'm so glad Lola and I were on the same page about that. Now being a grandparent is a whole other ballgame. None of that shit matters. You love them with all your heart and then say, 'Bye, bye. See you soon. Love you, mean it.'"

I laughed.

"I wonder if Dad had seen Anthony and I together, he would have come around."

"Definitely. You guys were awesome together. You were like a power couple. Sorry. Hope that doesn't make you sad."

Power couple we were not. Anthony was part owner of a restaurant, and I was a community college teacher. David imagined my life as much more glamorous than it really was. "The sadness is always there, though a little less every day."

"I'm sorry you didn't get to be around Dad in the last couple of years of his life. When he and Mom got back together, he changed. He let go of a lot of that anger. I never told you this, but about a year before he died, I caught him looking at a travel brochure for Spain. I asked him if he was thinking about traveling and he said he regretted never going to Europe. I told him he should go to Barcelona and see you. He said he was too old. You guys talked on the phone a couple times, right?"

Odd that he thought he was too old to take his first trip to Europe. He was my age when the heart attack took him. The two times we talked on the phone, certainly instigated by Mom, were short and free of controversial topics—we didn't talk about anything meaningful in my life—and ultimately unsatisfying. But he had made the effort. The second time was after Nick died. I was in the depths of depression with an intense hunger for drugs, having black thoughts of leaving this wretched life. I was anxious to speak to Mom. I wanted to hear her voice, possibly for the last time. She didn't say anything specific, but in her tone, there was a softness telling me she knew my pain.

"I hope you're eating well and taking care of yourself," she said. She was still connected to friends from the hometown where the gossip mill had undoubtedly kicked into high gear. She put Dad on the phone. In his long pauses, I sensed his struggle to find words when an estranged son's lover had just died of AIDS and who was the center of the most scandalous tragedy the town had ever known. I knew it was way beyond his capabilities to address it, but he did end the conversation saying that he hoped I would think about coming to their place for Christmas because it would make Mom so happy.

Two weeks later, Dad was dead, and when Christmas came around, my emotional state had improved greatly, but not enough to go to Florida. I had to admit that the improvement in my well-being was largely due to Vladimir. He kept me away from drugs and gave me reasons to go on living, stayed loyal to me, and took care of me. We began planning the move to the States, an idea I wasn't thrilled about, but it was something I could do for him in return for what he had done for me. San Francisco was the logical destination. Despite the bad memories and the AIDS epidemic ravaging the city, I couldn't think of anywhere else I wanted to live. I had friends there. If the disease was going to take me, I didn't want it to be in a foreign country. It took another year of complicated arrangements, some of them illegal, to get Vladimir to the States. We knew that once he got there, he would be free and clear thanks to the government's preferential policies for Cubans. He would get benefits and an automatic pathway to citizenship.

# Chapter 13

On Friday night, I lay in bed reading, trying to pry my eyes open to get through another page, when a text came from Mateo. **Are you up?**

**For you, yes.**

**Can I call you?**

**I can't think of anything more delightful.**

"What are you wearing?" he said with a silly sexy voice when I answered. It was hard to believe this was the same person from a couple of weeks before.

"Whatever suits your fancy?"

"I have a plan."

"Shoot."

He laughed. "Yeah. That's part of it."

"*Sinvergüenza tu!*"

He let out a shameless cackle. "I've arranged for the caretaker to spend the night with my mom tomorrow. After she goes to sleep, I'll be over."

"I'll put clean sheets on the bed in the second bedroom."

"Oh."

"Say no more. I get it."

I spent the following day pretending that we were good to go; that I was a thirty-something hot guy in horny anticipation of the man of my dreams coming over for a night of passionate banging; that HIV didn't exist; and that my first time having sex with him would be an earth-shattering, lust-driven experience without any pauses for negotiation of any kind.

As I dutifully changed the sheets in the guest bedroom, to distract myself from what was coming, I had a porn-worthy creeper fantasy about someone's cousin coming to stay, and I snuck into the bedroom in the middle of the night, arousing him from sleep. Must have been my morning coffee that sent my brain into hyperdrive.

And then the caffeine wore off. The left brain jumped up and slapped me with a reality check. I tumbled. For the first time in a long time, I had a sharp craving for speed or coke or anything that would bring me back up. I had been good for so long.

The craving subsided as the mechanics of scoring drugs seemed way more complicated than I had the capability for. It was partly the age thing, not having the energy to find a source, put myself in a scary situation in an uncomfortable neighborhood, not to mention the guilt I would feel afterward. I turned on the espresso machine and had a double.

After cleaning the house—it was beginning to be a habit—I went outside and sat under the shade of the umbrella. The peacefulness of the yard helped me think. There I rehearsed my little speech for Mateo in my head. I reminded myself that the status reveal had been relieved of most of the trauma that it had in the 1980s and 90s. We had maintenance drugs now. Science had rescued many of us from the grips of death, but had hit a wall in finding a cure. I drew my mind back from speculating on the political, moral, and financial reasons a cure was still unfound and forced my brain back to what I was going to say to Mateo.

I went off on a tangent, wishing we had just done it the night he came over unannounced, full of the heat that had mysteriously overtaken him. We could have done it like animals like he had said as if there was something wrong with that. Then I could have told him my status and lamented what a horrible person I was for not telling him before, and he would agree and would leave, and I could go back to my simple, miserable (but not terribly so) life with occasional bouts of feeling sorry for myself. I could spend the rest of my days sitting in the yard, watching the cycles of life of the local bird population, feeling proud of how the many flowering shrubs were helping the bee crisis, and thrilled by the occasional monarch butterfly that got separated from the pack and took a detour into our yard.

The night owl ringtone, the one I had specifically chosen for Cindy, startled me. It wasn't the first time I had the eerie sensation that our many years of connection allowed her to pick up on the wavelengths of my brain from a distance and call me when I was in crisis.

When my hello wasn't up to her perkiness standards, she said, "Are you okay? You sound down. Has something happened with Mateo?"

"You got all that from hello? You know I don't like answering the phone."

"All right then, tell me how wonderful your day is going."

"I'm writing my withdrawal speech."

"What are you withdrawing from this time?"

"From the candidacy of being Mateo's boyfriend."

"Wait. The last time we talked, you still had doubts about him being gay and now you're breaking up with him? What the hell has happened in the last week?"

"He's coming over tonight for a canoodling session. We almost got into it the other night, but he put on the brakes, wanting something more romantic than a wham-bam-thank-you-ma'am."

"And this is the guy you're dumping? Are you out of your mind?"

"Let me remind you way back when I told you I had the gay plague, and we might as well say goodbye because I didn't know how long I was going to be around."

"And may I remind *you* that was like thirty years ago and your sorry ass is still roaming the planet."

"Roaming the planet with said plague roaming my bloodstream plotting to leap to another carrier given the slightest opportunity."

"Honey, I don't mean to be insensitive, but you're being a fucking drama queen. You have a manageable condition that is not dangerous to anyone, including your canoodling, whatever the fuck that means, partners. Tell him you're undetectable. He understands that. He's a nurse for God's sake. If he bolts, he's a coward who's just using it as an excuse."

Cindy, as usual, gave me the tough love I needed. That didn't mean I would have an easy time telling Mateo, and in the best-case scenario, it was still a mood killer. But I was looking forward to putting the question behind me in a few hours.

Mateo sent me a text around ten. ***Prepárate.***

I wanted to tell him the same, that he should be prepared for something he might not expect. ***Listo,*** I answered, but was I truly ready?

When I opened the door and saw him, I was a millimeter away from abandoning my plan of having the talk first. He wore a collar shirt unbuttoned enough to reveal a patch of curly hair that blasted the message: all resistance was futile. He had shaved but left a soul patch, which was almost immediately pressed up against my chin as his mouth landed on mine in an enthusiastic kiss. His arms wrapped around me, pulling me so close there was no light between us, and my lower regions came to life before I had a chance to control it. This was going to be hard. I mean, difficult. As leisurely as I could without making it seem like a rejection, I pulled back. "Good to see you." It came out croaky and not sincere, even though my body was clearly happy to see him.

He put his hand over the tuft of hair on his chin. "What? You don't like my thingy?"

"Oh, I'm sure I'm going to like your thingy." Keep it light, I told myself.

"What's wrong?"

"Nothing. Would you like something to drink?" I put a hand on his shoulder, pushing him toward the kitchen.

"You're right. Take it slow. I get so excited when I see you."

Since my experience with Vladimir and other charmers who had the gift of syrupy but extremely effective phrases, I wanted to call out his bullshit. But Mateo had a way of being genuine. I knew his words weren't manufactured for maximum profit and came from the heart, which was almost as scary. When someone was bullshitting me, I knew how to protect myself. Mateo took away all my shields and left me vulnerable.

"I'm going to have a shot of tequila." I had no idea where that came from. I hadn't drunk tequila in years. I wasn't sure if there was any in the house.

"A shot of courage? Are you having second thoughts?"

"No way. When I opened the door and saw you, it took away first thoughts, second thoughts, and basically my ability to think at all."

"Not sure that's a good thing, but I'm flattered...I guess."

I stooped down in front of the liquor cabinet and banged around bottles until I came upon one of Don Julio. "Will you be joining me?" I muttered, grasping the bottle and staring into the dark corner of the liquor cabinet.

He hunched down beside me and put his hand on my back. "Nathan, turn around. Tell me what's going on."

It was an awkward position from which to turn around, and I ended up falling on my butt with the bottle between my legs, my knees raised, staring at him, surprised and a bit overwhelmed. He positioned his legs, one on each side of mine, and rested his hands on my knees. He tilted his head and disarmed me with the power of his brown eyes.

"I'm positive," I blurted out, on the verge of tears.

His eyes went blank for a minute and my emotions slid to the floor. He nodded and seemed to be searching for the right words. The seconds ticked by. I couldn't look at his face and instead examined the patterns in the wood floor. My body twitched as if I was about to stand up.

"Oh, that," he said, squeezing my knees. "You had me *asustado* for a minute there. I thought you were going to tell me you were dying of cancer, or not that into me, or trans, not that there's anything wrong with being trans. It's just that I'm more traditional."

"Traditional as in two men rubbing their private parts together?"

"I was hoping for a little more than just rubbing them together."

All the pent-up emotion of the day came rushing out in laughing-crying tears. I let my head fall onto his hands on my knees. He moved in closer and raised my head with one hand. "*Cariño,* what's all this? Are you undetectable?"

I nodded.

"You're healthy? You look healthy."

I nodded.

"Then, I don't see a problem." With a thumb, he brushed away a tear on my cheek.

"You don't know what it's like. You grew up in a different time."

"Don't play that you're-too-young-to-understand card. That's shitty. I wasn't born yesterday."

"No. Like the day before yesterday."

"I like you so much I don't want to punch you."

"You could spank me instead." His eyebrows lifted his eyes wide open. "I was kidding," I added.

"If you're naughty, it might be necessary." He pulled me even closer and kissed the tears, kissed my mouth, and planted a small one on the bridge of my nose. "Let's have that shot of tequila." He stood up and pulled me up with him.

"I most likely contracted it before we even knew what it was."

"I appreciate you telling me, but it's really not an issue. I don't care if you got it thirty years ago or last year as long as you're healthy and undetectable."

My brain spit out a series of questions: Why was he so quick to dismiss it? Is he really okay with it? Is it going to sink in later? Will he change his mind?

I found some shot glasses in the cabinet, cut up a lemon from the tree in the yard, and poured salt into a tiny condiment dish. We clinked our glasses, said "*Salud,*" gazed into each other's eyes, and downed the shots at the same time. It was so smooth we didn't need the lemon and salt.

"We should sip the next one," he said.

I removed the small information card still attached to the neck of the bottle and read the description out loud. "It enters sweet and leaves spicy but is easy on the throat." I giggled. "Sounds perfect."

"No way. You made that up."

"Swear to God. Read it."

I filled the glasses a second time, and we held them up to the light, examining the color. "This will be it for me. I want to be conscious," I said.

"Are you such a cheap drunk?"

"Yeah. And easy, too."

Mateo ran his hand through his thick hair. "You haven't been easy so far, making me afraid I had done something wrong."

"I'll make it up to you."

"I might need multiple sessions. I'm feeling psychologically damaged."

"I'll put you in my calendar with appropriate notes as soon as I find out the best therapy to fit your needs, which I plan to do momentarily."

"Can we please go to the bedroom now? My clothes are...like...*apretado*."

"Tight?" I put my hand on his crotch and was made certain I would like his thingy, still, I guessed, only at half-mast. "I see you need immediate attention. Your therapy session starts now."

We stumbled to the guest bedroom, kissing and caressing along the way. When we got in the room lit by multiple votive candles, he pushed me away and slapped my butt. "I hate you. You made this big deal like I was going to run away, and yet you took the time to light a million candles and turn the dimmer down low. Where are the flower petals on the sheets?"

"You're really okay with it?"

"I'll tell you a story someday. Not now. I've got other things on my mind."

I began unbuttoning his shirt, watching the candlelight flicker in his eyes and his grin go wider and wider. I lifted the shirt over the back of his shoulders and had a little trouble with the sleeves over his biceps. The shirt fell to the floor and I let out a spontaneous, "Wow!" I wish I had thought of a better word. Fucking wow? Fucking awesome wow?

He had a developed torso, which seemed to have taken his natural squareness and enhanced it enough to be defined without going overboard to someone entering a physique contest. Perfect hair distribution. The previously mentioned patch in the middle of his chest, some around his nipples, and the treasure trail down the middle of his flat stomach to the top of his jeans. And wait. What's that? A lizard's head poked out just above his waistline while the rest of the tattoo was buried in the nether regions I couldn't wait to explore. He was full of surprises. I outlined the lizard's head with my finger.

He shrugged. "I wanted a tattoo that would be mostly hidden. Only for special people."

He grabbed the hem of my T-shirt and, in one swift move, pulled it over my head. "Nice," he said. It wasn't a wow, but I'd take it. He raked his fingertips up and down my torso, leaving in their wake goosebumps like a field of wheat bending to the wind and springing back as his hand moved on to my arms. The tingling brought my nipples to life, and he leaned in and bent his head, the perfect height to flick his tongue over them, which sent me up like a rocket into the sky. My body jerked as if having a fit.

"You don't like?" he asked.

"Love it, but let's save that for later."

He moved his head up and kissed me, which ended up being the longest kiss in my recent history and possibly the longest kiss in my whole history of kissing. "Are we trying to set a record?" I said after another minute of oral exploration.

"Shut up. I like kissing. I love kissing."

"It's just that I'm really fascinated by your tattoo and dying to see the rest of it."

"This is a trick. You can't fool me. I wasn't born yesterday or even the day before yesterday or the day before that."

I already had his belt buckle undone and was in the process of lowering his pants that seemed to have gotten snagged on a rather large lump. "This thing needs to be free."

"Yes, it wants to travel to unknown places."

"And visit all the dark and mysterious territories?" I got on my knees. "This one is not exactly undiscovered, but new to you, at least."

I pushed him back gently, so he was sitting on the edge of the bed and slid his underwear down the thighs that had caught my eye in the car that day. "It must be painful to be so hard like that. Let me give you some relief."

"I hope it's like the tequila." He chuckled.

"What?"

"Easy on the throat."

"So funny," I said.

Though his lips were parted, he had gone speechless. He closed his eyes and nodded his head. I sat back on my haunches, staring at it. I had such an incredible sense of gratitude I felt like I should say grace first. He opened one eye as if to say, "Well?"

I touched my tongue to the tattooed end of the lizard's curled tail and followed it up on the ridge of the detailed green body. Just as I reached the head, staring at the beady eyes in the flickering light, his cell phone rang, muffled from his pant pocket. "Do you have to get that?"

"*Sí.*" It was the saddest *sí* I'd ever heard in my life.

He reached down and fished the phone out of his pocket. By the time he had it in his hand, he was soft. He stared at the screen. "No, no, no, no, no," he moaned.

To no one's surprise, it was the woman taking care of his mother. His mother had woken up and called for him. When the caretaker went into the room, Carmen realized Mateo wasn't there and panicked.

"I'll be right there," Mateo said.

He got off the phone and put a hand over his eyes. "I'm so, so sorry. I don't know what to say."

"You don't have to say anything."

"I have to go."

"I know."

"I swear to God I'll figure this out."

"I know."

"Don't hate me."

He groaned as I lifted him up and put junior back inside his underwear. "To be continued," I said. "And I can't imagine ever, ever hating you,"

# Chapter 14

I blew out all the candles in the bedroom of our thwarted desires, leaving the air heavy with the acrid, nauseating odor of smoke like a smoldering house after the firefighters have left. The suffocating atmosphere made me flee to the kitchen, where the bottle of tequila and two lonely shot glasses on the counter sent me further into the doldrums until I slapped myself out of it. Get a grip, I told myself. Be happy the desire was there. That was a miracle in itself.

I picked up the bottle, took a swig, and shuddered with the burn. I held Don Julio to my chest, remembering that Anthony and I had acquired the bottle on our last big trip together to Mexico City and Oaxaca two years before. One of the things that had drawn us together when we first met was a mutual love of travel. At the time, he was working in someone else's restaurant, allowing him actual days off and holidays. The dream of having his own restaurant with his two partners was still a dream, put on hold by the financial crisis of 2007-8. But once the new restaurant opened in 2010, foreign travel came to a halt, and we were lucky to do a weekend trip to Mendocino or Santa Cruz on the two days a week the restaurant was closed. Even on his days off, there was business to attend to: working on the menu, ordering supplies, going to restaurant supply stores, or looking over applications for hiring new staff when someone left. Before I became a real widow, I often felt like a restaurant widow. I knew he was living his dream, and though I loved and respected him for that, it did take a toll on the relationship. Anthony promised that as soon as things settled down—with three partners they could alternate taking time off—we could travel again. The universe had other plans.

I put the bottle back in the liquor cabinet and the shot glasses in the dishwasher. I turned out the lights, did one more check of the guest room to make sure all the candles were out, and went into my bedroom.

I lay in bed and mused about how my mother had tried to protect me from an older man, albeit a much different scenario where my older man was involved in a scandal involving a gun and a death and it was the 1960s and 70s when attitudes about homosexuality were quite different. Now, so many years later, I was the older man, and though I believed Mateo's mother was still in the dark about our budding relationship, she was trying to protect him from something she might only have suspected through a mother's intuition. I had no idea what her thoughts on homosexuality were, and it was possible that she was only petrified of losing him.

The library books on my nightstand were stacked according to due date. I took the top one, a novel I had been struggling with, and only got through a few more pages before moving it to the return pile. My brain begged for mindless entertainment, and I surfed through the various offerings on my streaming services without coming upon anything that sparked my interest. My grandmother always used to say that idle hands were the devil's workshop, so I took those hands into the guest room and retrieved the joint I had left beside the bed.

I hadn't had the chance to ask Mateo if he wanted to smoke it and didn't know if he was a fan of getting high, which reminded me there were a lot of things I didn't know about him. I didn't know how he got to the United States, if he had been in a relationship before, if he had any siblings, if his father was alive and if he still lived in Colombia. I was working with very little data. He was a nurse, liked to play soccer, was a dope kisser, and took care of his mother, though I didn't know what her condition was. He also got high marks on care of his body and hygiene. That was it. The file was thin but of good quality, and I was thrilled to do the work to fill in the gaps.

I fired up the joint with a bit of trepidation about the potential for paranoia, considering the potency of pot these days. I hadn't gotten high since Anthony's death, not wanting to be led down the path of rehashing the circumstances that led to his accident and if there had been anything I could have done to stop it.

Paranoia did, in fact, creep in, not taking me to the night of the accident, but instead to a place of vulnerability as if I was in a haunted house where the dangers inside the house (and inside my brain) were far worse than the cruel world outside the walls. I resented the fact that I was alone, and I was angry because it wasn't supposed to be that way. Though Mateo had never promised to spend the night, in my fantasy he had, or at least until I went to sleep.

I heard a soft thump. Someone at the window? Someone inside the house? It persisted and took the imagined form of someone buried alive trying to scratch their way out of a coffin. I closed the shades and checked all the locks. The scratching ceased until I lay back down on the bed. It started again. Louder this time. A memory refresh reminded me that Anthony was not buried but cremated. In fact, everyone I could think of who died in recent history wouldn't be scratching their way out of a coffin, real or imagined, because they had chosen to be cremated. Fear of being alone, not normally high on my list of fears, consumed me, and I was convinced that my mind was playing tricks, something gnawing away at my vulnerability. My heart pounded in my chest and my breathing was ragged. For one bizarre moment, I considered calling Mateo and telling him I was having a panic attack and needed him. No, it would have been a cruel joke and he would probably never speak to me again.

After a time, a calmer self took charge and identified the sound as an animal on the roof or possibly in the attic. After a few minutes, it was quiet. But as soon as I began to breathe easier, the noise started up again. I got little sleep as the pattern continued for the rest of the night, and I resolved to call a pest control service on Monday.

In the morning I was able to write, taking the frustration of interrupted sex, the paranoia of my high, the image of the two shot glasses sitting on the counter, the smell of smoke and wax, mixing in weird noises from the attic, and voila, a horror poem of sorts. I spent the rest of the morning and early afternoon working on the verses.

In the late afternoon, I received a text. ***Prepárate. Segunda ronda.*** Round two? Were we boxing now?

**Meaning?**

**Have to run to the market. Can stop by for a minute.**

**A minute?**

**Or ten.**

**I'm here.**

I jumped in the shower and was still drying off when the doorbell rang. I wrapped the towel around me and answered the door.

"I didn't expect you to be that prepared."

"Just got out of the shower. I can put some clothes on if you like."

"I'd only have to take them off you again." His mouth was on mine, and he gently pushed me toward the bedroom like we were doing a frantic two-step and I had the trickier part of dancing backwards.

The bedroom was dim with the shades pulled down. He flipped on the light as we passed through the door.

"I want to see," he said, discarding his baggy shorts and T-shirt faster than I could drop my towel. He wore no underwear.

"I didn't expect *you* to be that prepared," I said.

We had seen each other naked during our first thwarted attempt at this, but I still wasn't used to the vast difference in level of fitness between his body and mine. I felt especially naked in the bright ceiling light, unlike the candlelight of last time. V-cut or six-pack or ripped, even when I was in my best shape years before, had never been used to describe me. Like many gay men, I believed that muscly guys only looked for other hunks, and large gatherings of gay men seemed to confirm that belief as likes grouped together. Gym bunnies with gym bunnies. Nerds with nerds.

I was at the point of ruining this perfect moment we had waited for, obsessing over my inadequacies, when Mateo pushed me back onto the bed, caught my wrists in his strong hands and pinned my arms to the pillow on either side of my head. The force of his urgency shocked me for a moment, that fear of being physically hurt, of it turning into something violent, though nothing Mateo had shown me thus far warranted my reaction.

"Too much?" he said.

I shook my head. "You're full of surprises."

His eyes bore down on me. "You can trust me, you know."

"I do." And I did.

A few minutes later, we fell in a sweaty heap, and he pulled my head to his chest. I listened to the thump of his heart, giving me joy that it was beating for me. A man who would hold you after sex and allow you to put your head on his chest, knowing you might fall asleep and drool all over him, was my personal test of a man.

"Did I hurt you?" he said. One hand lazily massaged my head while the other raked along my arm. Instead of creating goose flesh this time, his fingers now left a trail of warmth.

"It's been a while."

"For me, too." He sighed. "I'm sorry. I didn't want it to be like this."

"Sometimes you have to be animals," I said to reassure him.

He must have picked up something in my voice. With a finger he lifted my chin to face him. "Are you okay?"

I grimace-smiled.

"You're angry. Fuck, I knew this was a bad idea."

"I'm not angry."

"It won't happen again."

"If this is what we've got, this is what we've got. By the way, we both kind of exploded. There's that."

"I know, but it's not right."

"But it's okay," I sang. "I'm gonna make it anyway." I stopped when I remembered the next line about packing your bags and leaving.

"Uh-huh. Whitney." Despite the age gap, there were cultural things we shared. We both knew our gay history and its host of tragic heroes.

He began to fidget and looked at his watch.

"I know you have to go. Don't feel bad."

A minute later, he was gone. And for my next song, "My Life as a Senior Booty Call." I started thinking of kitschy lyrics like: *If only I could find my glasses, I could see what you're doing to me. And you rock my world, but the chair's making me dizzy. I fell for you and now I can't get up.* I imagined Bette Midler singing them.

***

First thing Monday morning, I called Rodent Rooters. They'd had a cancellation and were able to send someone out right away.

I opened the door to a technician in goggles, a helmet, gloves, and a mask, wearing coveralls with Alejandro embroidered over his heart. He was prepared for a natural disaster, and I felt vulnerable in my sweats and T-shirt. I expected an evacuation order to be the first thing out of his mouth.

"Hi, I'm here to..."

"Yeah, I think I know why you're here." I waved him into the hall and pointed at the hole in the ceiling. He extended his telescoping ladder to the height that allowed him to reach the attic entrance, lifted the cover, and tilted it sideways.

Rat droppings rained down on him and landed on the floor at my feet. "Oh!" He shook his head and squinted at the oblong black pellets on the floor. "I guess you know what that is."

I stood in the narrow hallway, my eyes at the level of Alejandro's crotch. "I've been hearing noises up there at night."

Alejandro went higher on the ladder and took his phone out of his pocket. "I'll make a video so you can see what the active situation is. I take it you haven't ventured up here."

"Uh, no. I only started hearing the noise recently." In truth I had never been in the attic. Even pre-rat noises it hadn't seemed like a fun thing to do. With Anthony's fear of spiders, I doubted he had been up there, either.

Having rats in the house was creepy enough, but I thought of the story a childhood friend told me about rats being an incarnation of the devil. Tom went to Catholic school and one day a priest came to their classroom to talk about exorcisms. The priest said agents of the devil often took the form of rodents to enter your house. When I said it was a bunch of malarkey, Tom swore he had personal experience and explained how you had to use a crucifix to tame the beasts. It made me glad I didn't go to Catholic school.

"Hey there," said Alejandro, half his body in the attic. "You've got an infestation."

"What?" I was lost in the story of the rat-devil. "Let me go get a broom and dustpan to sweep up the mess."

When Alejandro descended the ladder, I was bent over sweeping. He bumped into me and I looked up, again his crotch at eye level. "Sorry," he said. "I've got something to show you." I pointed toward the kitchen to get out of the close quarters.

He pushed his mask down around his throat, took off his gloves, and lifted his goggles to snap into place above the rim of his helmet, revealing the good looks I had suspected based on a bit of beard peeking out of his mask, curly black hair edging the helmet, and the way his prominent Adam's apple bobbed under his brown skin. He was the perfect bearded, bright eyed fantasy workman of porno films. This was a test. I had a petty notion that to make a move on this guy would somehow be getting back at Mateo for the predicament in which we found ourselves—two adults not being allowed to properly explore their desires.

"What is it?" said Alejandro with a slight grin.

He had caught me staring and an excuse came to me quickly. "For a moment, I thought you might be one of my former students."

"What do you teach?"

"English."

Alejandro raised his bushy eyebrows. "Nope. I'm sure I would remember you. I remember all my teachers, especially the nice ones."

"That's...uh...good to hear."

"Cool. Anyway, I want to show you the video." He moved closer so we were hovering over the phone, heads nearly touching as the video started. From the first scenes of pink insulation peppered with black feces, it was like a horror show. He narrated as if he were the host of an Animal Kingdom episode, almost in a whisper, like the rats might hear him. "You have to get rid of all the insulation where they nest. It's full of rat feces, as you can see. A typical rat excretes anywhere from eighty to a hundred droppings a day." His voice got increasingly more excited as he spoke. "And look at those stains on the wood. That's urine that has seeped into the beams. Once you've gotten rid of the insulation, you have to sanitize everything so outside rats won't be drawn to the space. The peppermint essential oil we use kills bacteria, fungi, and viruses like hantavirus, leptospirosis, salmonella, and others." He paused for dramatic effect with a wild look in his eyes. "The final step is to seal all the entry points and the rodents are left with the only food being in the traps we set...or they resort to cannibalism. Gets pretty gory up there. We come back in a couple of weeks and check the traps."

"Okay," I said, both sickened by the images and excited by Alejandro's delivery.

"Rats have a strong sex drive and are motivated by the smell of urine and feces, looking for new mates to start the frenzy of breeding all over again." Alejandro rolled his tongue over his lips to wet them. Most likely it was involuntary, but I wondered.

"I see," I said with heat running up and down my arms and legs.

"What do you want to do?"

"Have you ever thought of using a crucifix? I hear rats can't handle it."

At first, he was stunned, as if he had encountered a weirdo Jesus freak. "You're pulling my leg, right?" he said with a hopeful chuckle.

I laughed. "Sorry. A friend I grew up with told me a priest had recommended using a crucifix to ward off rats, which are really just manifestations of the devil. But I guess we have to resort to your professional methods to stop the frenzy of breeding."

Alejandro laughed. I stared at his hands with trimmed fingernails and hair on his knuckles. I took a step back. "Can you give me an estimate?"

He rattled off some figures and possible outcomes, procedures, follow-up, but I couldn't concentrate on the words, only his red lips in a nest of dark beard and his golden-brown eyes with a rim of darker brown.

"You look worried." He laid his hand on my arm. "We'll be the least intrusive as possible and be out of your hair in no time."

It was undoubtedly the same routine he used with countless housewives, horrifying them to the point they would be willing to spend any sum to get rid of the beasts. And if that didn't work, having the crisis explained in such an enchanting manner by a fetching young man was certainly part of the business plan. I was torn between asking tons of questions to keep Alejandro there and shooing him out of the house before I said or did something stupid.

"I can put you on the schedule for next Monday. Would that work?"

"Monday is good for me."

"We start early. Is that okay? 8 a.m.? Don't want to catch you in your pajamas."

"I look forward to it. I mean, getting rid of the rats."

"Gotcha. Later, man."

# Chapter 15

On our first day in Barcelona, Nick and I walked from the Christopher Columbus statue at the foot of Las Ramblas to Casa Vicens in Gracia, and with each step we were, for the second time in our recent history, infused with the optimism that we had found a better place. We were going to be Europeans, but since it was the first time in Europe for both of us, we didn't know what that meant. Our lives in the U.S. had been fraught with ostracism, tragedy, disappointment, heartbreak, and family strife, especially for Nick.

His parents had disowned him. They had survived the hometown scandal and were relieved he found a job at a hospital in New Orleans and managed to avoid further scandal. Nick speculated that they may have been pleased he was just far enough away that they didn't have to see each other. The heated phone arguments began after he told them we were living together, got more contentious when he announced our move to San Francisco, and the final break came when he told them we were moving to Barcelona and he planned to give up practicing medicine. As his father was also a physician, Nick giving up medicine was the blow that essentially ended his relationship with his parents.

My connection with my family was less contentious, at least, with my mother and David who both lived in Florida, and though we didn't speak often, I felt we were okay. Mom worried about my wanderlust, as she called it. But we had already proven her prediction wrong that Nick and I wouldn't last. We had been together for almost seven years. I had no contact at all with my father, who stayed in the hometown after my parents separated.

Barcelona in the 1980s was not the trendy destination it later became, but somewhat of a backwater emerging from the repression of the Franco years. The phenomenal modernist buildings along Paseo de Gracia were blackened by years of pollution, the beaches were littered with trash and junkies' needles, and thieves roamed parts of the old town looking for marks. But we were thrilled to be there and could see the beauty beneath the grime and cacophony. The architecture in some ways reminded us of New Orleans, though on a much grander scale. We rented an apartment in the Gracia neighborhood for the equivalent of a hundred and fifty dollars. We both had jobs that didn't pay a lot, but we had benefits, and living was cheap. Public transportation was easy.

At the school, we were discreet at first about our relationship. Our public story was that we knew each other from San Francisco and were now sharing an apartment. It didn't take long to figure out there were several other gay men and a few lesbians on the staff. No one cared. We soon had a ready-made social group of fascinating people, many of whom had been on the expat circuit for years, teaching in Iran, Saudi Arabia, Afghanistan, Portugal, and South America, and they were full of stories about those experiences. We were invited to parties, went out to dinner in groups, and took weekend excursions around Catalonia and south to Valencia, using the trains, which were frequent and inexpensive.

Just down the coast was a beach town called Sitges that was becoming a gay playground for people from all over Europe. With a couple of the gay men who worked at the institute, we took the train to Sitges for the weekend. We went to a beach that was mostly gay, a restaurant with other tables occupied by gay men, and we dragged Nick, kicking and screaming, out to one of the town's gay bars. Having lived in San Francisco, it wasn't surprising to see so many gays and lesbians freely having a good time, but there was something about the atmosphere that was more relaxed. Spain in general seemed more relaxed and fun-loving. After our experiences that weekend, we talked about living in Sitges one day.

Not long after our arrival in the city, we were invited to a party near Parque Güell at our new work friends Sylvie and George's apartment, high on a hill overlooking the city. Sylvie and George were not a couple, but childhood friends from Montreal. I had a chance to talk to them about my trips there to visit my brother. They were pleased when I told them I found it a beautiful city with a great cosmopolitan vibe and the people were warmer and kinder than people in U.S. cities.

I also spent a lot of time chatting with Ronnie, a thin woman with short-cropped hair and a dry wit who became one of my dearest friends at the school. In our discussion she would occasionally turn to her boyfriend, Kossi from Togo, trying to draw him into the conversation, and while he crafted a careful response in his limited English, she would look at him adoringly.

Nick was drawn to a woman named Claire with a full afro and dangling earrings who had taught in several countries and was in the Peace Corps in Yemen. Out of the corner of my eye, I noted the intense dialogue between them and overheard the word Jonestown. Later he admitted that she reminded him of one of his People's temple patients back in San Francisco. Another gay couple at the party joined my conversation with Ronnie and Kossi, Charlie from Wisconsin, who also worked at the school and his boyfriend, Gor, a Turkish Armenian whose family owned a chain of clothing stores.

Sylvie, George, Ronnie, Kossi, Claire, Charlie, and Gor quickly became our core group of friends. In addition to them at the party were a few other teachers along with a couple of staff members, Jaume and Marta from SNAE (School of North American English). Charlie liked to add an "L" to the acronym, making a joke of the pace at which our students learned English.

On the way to the kitchen to refresh my drink, I ran into Nick, and with a simple smile we acknowledged that we had found what we had come to Barcelona for: a life amongst a group of friends with international life experiences and who embraced us as a couple without question. We stood a moment in the hall, listening to Charlie talking with someone in the kitchen about being an expat.

"We live in an intriguing middle ground," said Charlie. "As foreigners we're neither bound by the constraints of the local culture nor the overpowering pressure of being an American. Some of us even pretend to be Canadians if we can get away with it. Americans grow up with the notion that we're the freest people in the world, and it wasn't until I traveled that I had the wisdom to challenge that. Within a few months of living abroad, the bubble of our exclusivity burst, and I saw how freedom in the U.S. depended on so many unspoken rules regarding relationships between Blacks and whites and Latinos and Asians, how gays and lesbians as well as anybody different were viewed by the general society, how patriotism and religion kept us all under control, how people didn't talk about politics, and how a whole section of the country, the American South, was allowed to keep its racist and insurrectionist symbols. Our so-called freedom comes at a price."

Nick and I nodded at his words, and I was overcome with the relief of being outside of the United States and being introduced to a whole subculture of Americans who abandoned their country to work abroad, many of whom stayed away, moving from country to country.

The night progressed and the noise reached a level of laughter and banter I hadn't experienced at many American parties, even though most of us were from the States. At one point, Charlie, Sylvie, and George disappeared into Sylvie's room. Several minutes later, Sylvie stuck her head out and handed flashlights to Claire and Ronnie, telling them to turn off the lights the next time the door opened. She also asked Jaume to cue the music they had talked about.

The door cracked open, and the lights went down, making us notice that just beyond sliding glass doors that led to the terrace, the city of Barcelona was lit up like jewels at our feet, a dramatic backdrop to the show we were about to see. The opening bars of Diana Ross's "Upside Down" rang out and Claire and Ronnie moved their flashlights around the room like movie premiere searchlights.

Charlie emerged first in a black curly wig and one of Sylvie's black cocktail dresses with black stockings and pink fluffy slippers. He had a thick mustache, so it was more genderfuck drag than real drag. Everyone cheered and shouted. He sashayed through the center of the room and out the sliding doors to the huge terrace. We all followed him and danced under the stars while Charlie threw his arms up and bent back over the railing, nearly losing his wig over the edge. Being so far from my Midwestern town in a world, as Diana said, turned upside down, made me happier than I could have imagined. I put my arm around Nick's shoulders in hopes he was enjoying the party as much as I was. I worried how he was dealing with the craziness since he was more conservative than me, had grown up in a different time, wasn't big on public displays of affection, and was often uncomfortable at parties. He turned to me and kissed me, giving me my answer. His shoulders relaxed and he wrapped an arm around my waist. We had found a special place.

The music changed to Earth, Wind, and Fire's "Boogie Wonderland" and George burst out of the living room onto the terrace in a silver dress, blonde wig, and a pink feather boa wrapped around his neck. George had a soft, handsome face that translated well to feminine beauty, but several women at the school affirmed that he was straight, or at least enjoyed the intimate company of women. It was easy to tell it wasn't his first time in women's clothes, as he knew how to rock a dress.

The next song was "Another One Bites the Dust" by Queen. Charlie initiated a conga line with him at the beginning and George at the end. Who could have imagined what that song would come to mean later? But for now, it was joyful, and the thumping bass made us want to shake our butts. The conga line dispersed and reformed into a big circle, with everyone holding hands, dancing around the barbecue pit as if it were a bacchanalian celebration that would end in an orgy. The orgy didn't happen, but the party was talked about for a long time, and the bond we formed lasted for years. The memory of that night was special, but the thought of it later filled me with sadness. A few years after that party, five of the attendees were no longer on this earth.

The party wound down at about three in the morning. Our apartment in Gracia wasn't far from the gathering, and Charlie and Gor said they would walk us home before continuing to their place in Eixample. We walked along Calle Verdi and crossed Travesera de Dalt into our neighborhood. Lots of people were on the streets, leaving bars and parties. Groups of teenagers that might have made us wary back home didn't bother us.

I turned to Charlie. "Now tell the truth. Is George really straight?"

"He looks fabulous in drag, right?"

"He seemed quite comfortable in a dress," said Nick.

"Is anyone really one hundred percent straight?" said Charlie. "I know George has dated women, but he's also totally relaxed with his feminine side. I'm glad there are straight, or whatever he is, men like him."

"We could do a test," said Gor. "Lock him in a bedroom after a few drinks with a hot guy."

"Are you volunteering?" said Charlie.

"Oh, no, dear. Not me," he said, putting his arm around Charlie's waist and pulling him close. "I was thinking of that Italian guy who said he was a model."

I laughed. "I think all Italian guys say they're models and a lot of them have the goods."

Nick looked at me. "Hmph! I noticed you were right behind Giovanni in the conga line."

"Were you jealous?"

"Jealous you got to stare at his ass."

I stopped and turned to our friends, grabbing Nick's arm. "I don't know who this person is. I went to the party with my reserved boyfriend, but someone must have switched personalities with him and I'm going home with a whole new person. This could be fun," I joked.

"I just know a nice ass when I see one," said Nick, his speech slurred after a night of alcohol.

"I have never once in the years we've been together heard you comment on a man's ass."

"Boys. Boys," said Charlie. "That guy was hitting up every single woman at the party. I don't think any of us need to worry about him stealing our partners."

Nick laughed. "I don't want to be stolen. I only want to look."

"And look you may," I said.

# Chapter 16

I steered my bicycle into the front parking lot of Mateo's building and sent him a text, praying that the postponed ride would happen on this sunny Saturday afternoon while simultaneously reminding myself I had to be patient. Plans could always be canceled at the last minute. While I waited, I stared up at the four stately redwood trees planted in a row, towering over the front building as if sentinels guarding over the parking lot. They seemed out of place and forced to grow in a line when they might have preferred to be in a more sociable cluster. Another example of humans bending nature to fit our needs or sense of esthetics.

A few minutes later, Mateo dashed into view from around the back, looking very unnatural in a helmet, goggles, and very tight shorts, but exuding confidence in his body as he pedaled faster than was necessary and came to a stop with squeaking brakes. He had an awkward moment as his feet tried to reach the ground and nearly toppled over. "Oops!" he said.

"Nice shorts."

He looked down at his crotch. "Is anything showing? I could be having a spontaneous reaction to seeing you."

"Is that a pistol in your pocket or...?"

"What?" he said, staring at me like he didn't have a clue what I was talking about.

"Never mind." Mae West must not have fit into his historical knowledge of gay icons.

He did a quick scan of the parking lot before leaning over and kissing me. "We're doing this."

"What did you tell your mother?"

"That I was going for a bike ride and would stop at the CVS to pick up her prescription on the way. Luisa is with her."

"The caretaker?"

"I scheduled her for a couple of hours, but she said not to worry if we went over."

"Should be enough time to go to Oyster Bay and then along the Marina."

"Lead on," he said. "I'll follow your ass anywhere."

"Jesus!"

"I didn't mean it like that."

"Aw, shucks. It sounded kind of like you were proposing."

"A proposal, not *the* proposal."

"Let's see how the bike ride goes. If it goes well..." I laughed.

"I'll do my best. So, we're going to the bay?"

"Let's go over to Washington and then to Williams. It's the best way to get to the water."

We took a detour into the downtown shopping center and stopped at the pharmacy. I waited outside with the bikes while he went in. He came out a short time later with a small bag and slipped the meds into the pack he had over his shoulder.

"Does she need them right away?"

"It can wait until I get back."

Of the streets that crossed over the freeway to get to the bay, Williams had the least traffic. It went through a residential area with schools on one side and later an industrial area with lots of warehouses, a boring ride though not dangerous. There was one tricky intersection where traffic entering from Merced Street jagged over to Westgate Parkway, and cyclists had to move across the flow of right-turning motorists into the center lane to go straight.

I glanced over my shoulder, and seeing no right-turners, I crossed to the center. The light was green, and I pedaled through. I was part way into the next block when I heard tires screech, but traffic noise drowned out any resulting thud. The tire sound still made my bones shiver. I slowed to a stop but was afraid to turn around, afraid that I had once again become the kiss of death. I waited for what seemed like eons to look back, though it was only a matter of seconds.

Mateo lay on the ground, a car stopped next to him with the door open. A woman stood over him. I turned my bike around and retook the intersection, riding against traffic, my stomach churning and my head spinning with the agony of disaster. He struggled but managed to get up, and I breathed a sigh of relief until I remembered a story in the news of a cyclist who, after getting hit by a car, stood up and walked around before falling over dead.

"Mateo," I shouted. "Sit down. Don't walk around." He lifted his head toward me but gave no sign he knew who I was.

As I got close, I saw his skinned knee with blood trickling down, scrapes on his arm, and a dazed look in his eyes as he stared at his mangled bicycle as if he was more worried about it than his body.

"Did anyone call 911?" I shouted.

A teenager who I guessed was a passenger in the stopped car said, "Yes. I did."

"Somebody, call again just to make sure."

The driver of the car was crying and saying she was sorry, trying to explain how it happened, and not being particularly helpful. Several other cars had stopped to check on him and people got out in morbid curiosity mixed with true concern.

I laid my bike on the ground and ran to his side. "I think it's better if you sit on the curb over there." I pointed and led him with my hand at his back to sit down.

"I'm not in pain," he mumbled. "I think I'm in shock."

The woman, still with tears on her face, approached us with a dirty rag in her hand.

"What's that?" I asked, giving her a look of guarded disgust.

"For the blood on his leg?" She held out the rag at the end of her limp arm.

I waved her away. My biggest concern was his head. "You know where you are, right?"

He grinned. "Next to my boyfriend?" I wasn't sure it was the time to declare our relationship status, but it did seem appropriate as the paramedics would be there soon and probably ask who I was. At the hospital, we would also need to be on the same page to allow me access. I took his hand and squeezed. He gave me a shy smile. I held up three fingers. "How many do you see?"

"Three nicely shaped fingers on a beautiful hand. I noticed your hands that first day."

"I'm not sure if the fall knocked some sense into you or made you batshit crazy."

The paramedics arrived and took control before I had a chance to clarify what he meant by the boyfriend statement. After a brief examination, they suspected he had a concussion, a broken clavicle, and possibly some cracked ribs. They would take him to the hospital for tests and x-rays. It was heartbreaking to see the medics put him in the back of the van, a prone Mateo sliding away from me, but just before they closed the doors, he gave me a look that said I was the person he most wanted near him.

"I'll follow on my bike," I shouted as the doors closed.

When I walked in the glass doors of Kaiser emergency, a woman in scrubs greeted me. "Are you Nathan? Our dear Mateo is in here." I nodded, and she led me through the doors. First the boyfriend statement, and then the realization he had notified them of my impending arrival. I was both touched and shaken by this new responsibility I had been thrust into. As the doctor was examining him, the nurse told me to wait, indicating a chair outside the curtained area. I played with the straps of my helmet and again wondered if I was some kind of curse on people.

When they let me through the curtains, he beamed at me with tears in his eyes. Pain or joy, I wasn't sure.

"You scared the shit out of me," I said.

"You just had to go on a bike ride."

He was teasing, but it played right into my fears. "I know it's all my fault."

"Shut up. I'm fine, well, except for the broken collarbone and three ribs." He thought a minute. "And the concussion. And the scrapes."

"You're making me feel worse."

"I'll heal. And I'll get some time off work. They want to keep me overnight because of the concussion and to make sure the ribs don't do anything funny like puncture my lungs."

"Maybe they'll let me stay and we can have our first night together."

"How romantic! I'll be drugged up. My clavicle is hurting like hell. But I need you to do something."

"Anything."

"Where's my little pack?"

"Over there with your clothes."

"My mom will need her meds. Can you take them to her?"

"Sure," I said in a voice that was anything but sure. My expression must have looked like I had just been assigned a mission behind enemy lines.

"Don't worry. I'll call Luisa and let her know you're coming. Just knock on the door and hand her the bag."

"Okay. I'll ride home, get my car, drop them off, and come back here to give you an intel report."

"If you get caught, deny everything. You've been trained for this. If you talk, the whole network will be compromised."

I snickered. "I'm here to serve. Wish me luck."

"Go, so you can come back." I turned to leave. "What? No kiss?" he said.

"You're not worried about your reputation?"

"I meant a quick kiss, not a make-out session. No one will even know. And I wouldn't care if they did."

***

Showered and in a change of clothes, I rang the doorbell of Mateo's apartment, the closest I'd gotten to the place he lived, the place where he lay his head, the inner sanctum of what I was gradually beginning to feel was my right to know. I pictured his bedroom with his mother in the next room, his hand over my mouth to keep me from screaming out my pleasure as our bodies moved in sync.

The door opened, cutting my fantasy short, and I stood dumbfounded with a half erection and a stricken look on my face as a fragile but elegantly dressed older woman stared me down. She wore a mahogany-colored turban that blended with her warm brown skin, lighter than Mateo's, a beige silk blouse with a string of pearls and loose-fitting tan slacks. Since so much attention had gone into her outfit, it was curious that she was shoeless, her small feet sheathed in sheer anklets. I held out the bag between us like it was a magic potion to protect me from the arrows of her black eyes. "Your medication," I croaked.

"You don't look like a delivery boy." Her English was accented but fluent.

"I'm just doing a favor for a friend."

My knees felt weak and about to buckle as I was face to face with the woman I had demonized, imagining her an old crone in a wheelchair or bedridden, peeking out over the sheets with a wild look. A notion zipped through my brain that Mateo had fabricated her frailty as a shield against commitment, an excuse to run away when things got intense. I was almost certain it was his mother, Carmen, the eyes in shape and color identical to his, though she scrutinized me in a way Mateo never had.

"And who would that friend be?" She put her hand on the edge of the door for support.

Luisa came scurrying around the corner in a flowery smock with her face wrinkled in worry. "I was in the kitchen cooking and didn't hear the doorbell. Ah, it's the delivery person." She reached for the bag I still held out in front of me.

"Hmph," said Carmen. "Already we have determined he's not a delivery person."

Luisa looked at me sheepishly as I stood on the rough carpet of the hallway with the ceiling light bearing down on me like I was expected to confess to a crime.

"Where's Mateo?" Carmen said with a surprising urgency.

"He's...um...delayed," I said.

"Yes," said Luisa. "He called."

Carmen gazed at her as if communicating a message that she wasn't a doddering old fool or possibly doddering but not a fool. She turned to me. "Come in." It sounded like a command.

Luisa grabbed the hem of her smock and twisted it in her fingers. "I'm sure the young man is busy."

Carmen let out a high-pitched, garbled laugh. "Young man?" She continued to chuckle, and it was the first crack in her polished veneer. She stopped her cackling with a cough and bowed her head slightly. Then she made a welcoming gesture with her arm, pointing down the dimly lit hall. Luisa shrugged and whispered, "It'll be okay."

"Please, Luisa," said Carmen. "You know I can't tolerate whispering." Her hearing seemed intact. I thought back to my fantasy of being in Mateo's bed with her in the next room, able to hear everything.

We passed a bedroom on the right with the door half open. There were weights on the floor and a framed poster of Prince on the wall. My nerves tingled with excitement. Once we got to the living room, I thought of asking to use the bathroom, and like I'd seen a hundred times in movies and detective shows, sneak instead into Mateo's room on a reconnaissance mission.

"Sit," said Carmen, pointing to a worn sofa. The décor was that of an older woman with heavy drapes, shelves topped with old photos and chachkas, and mismatched furniture that had been collected over the years. On the coffee table were oversized art books, one featuring the work of the Colombian painter Botero. She lowered herself slowly but gracefully into an armchair while Luisa hovered.

"Young man," Carmen said with a sardonic grin. "You haven't introduced yourself."

"Pardon me. My name is Nathan. Nathan Landis."

Carmen turned to Luisa and spoke in Spanish, telling her she smelled something burning in the kitchen. Luisa rushed from the room.

We sat quietly for a minute, both of us with stiff backs.

"How do you know my son?"

"From the hospital," I blurted out. It was the only answer that made sense since I knew very little of the activities of his life, somewhere we could have met.

"You also work at the hospital?"

Luisa hurried back into the room with a glass of water and a couple of pills, which she handed to Carmen. Anti-anxiety medicine, I hoped.

She downed the pills quickly and drank some water. "Could someone please tell me where my son is?" Her voice was increasingly more anxious, and she stared at me with intense eyes, giving me the urge to jump up and run out of the room.

I wondered if I should try the bathroom trick and escape out the front door. Mateo had always given me the impression she was unstable, and I had already noticed hints of that. If I told her the truth, it might set her off, and I would be responsible. But I didn't want my first encounter with Mateo's mother to be one of lies.

I was saved by the ringing of Luisa's phone. She answered and nodded her head as she listened. Then she handed the phone to Carmen. "*Su hijo.*"

"*Que?*" She stared at the phone and then at me like she had no idea who I was or how I had gotten there.

We could hear Mateo's voice. "*Mamá*?"

She took the phone. "*Mijo?*"

While in the kitchen, Luisa must have contacted Mateo, and I mouthed a thank you to her.

As Carmen held the phone slightly away from her ear, Mateo's soothing voice in the even cadence of Colombian Spanish reassured her that everything was okay. I caught sight of Carmen's unstylish but comfortable shoes under the coffee table that she must have kicked off earlier, and then forgotten when the doorbell rang. Out of the corner of my eye I detected her upright posture withering, her face drooping.

"*Mijo*," was all she said. "*Mijo*."

Carmen was in a daze when the call ended.

"Let's get you to your room for a rest," said Luisa. While helping Carmen up, she motioned for me to go.

As I passed by Mateo's room, I stuck my head in, and standing on the threshold, I was twelve again, sneaking into people's houses, wandering around, touching their things, my feet itching to take the next step. Like an alcoholic or an addict, the urge was with me, even after many years of controlling it. I could hear Luisa in the next room, her voice low and comforting as she readied Carmen for a nap. However things turned out with Mateo, I didn't want to screw it up by snooping through his things. I needed to get out of the apartment and back to the hospital. I backed away and felt a rush of having overcome temptation.

# Chapter 17

With those guardian redwood trees looking over my shoulder I stood outside Mateo's building and texted him.

**Now that was an experience.**

**I had no idea she would answer the door. Sorry.**

**I'm not. I got to meet your mother.**

Hesitation. **If you're tired, you don't have to come back over here.**

*Was he feeling uncomfortable about me meeting his mother?* **Are you tired?**

Hesitation. **Yeah.**

**I'm coming anyway. Even if I just watch you sleep. See you in fifteen.**

**Okay.**

It was the first time I got to watch Mateo sleep, see him in his innocence, the mind at rest from the plotting and planning we all engage in every waking moment. His vulnerability brought a tear to my eye as I sat by his bedside. I wanted so badly to crawl into the bed and wrap my arms around him, but I was also content to simply sit there. I had nowhere to be, no one waiting for me. I was thrilled with each flicker of his eyelid, each twitch of his hand, each guttural breath.

And like sometimes happened when watching someone sleep, he opened his eyes as if the intensity of my staring caused him to stir.

"Hi," he said with a smile working its way out of slumber. He extended his hand, and I covered his with mine, inserting my thumb into the cup of his palm. "Been here long?"

"A little bit."

"That must have been boring."

With my free hand I wiped away the tear that was threatening to escape the corner of my eye. "Actually, it was kind of fantastic, though I'm a tiny bit upset I'm having this first time observing you asleep in a hospital room."

"How was my mother?"

"She was suspicious, understandably so, this strange man coming to her house delivering medicine that her son was supposed to bring her. After talking to you on the phone, she was sad, confused."

"You probably think it's weird."

"What?"

"My relationship with my mother."

"I had a mother."

He gave me a skeptical look, both of us knowing my situation had never been the same. "It's just been the two of us since she brought me to the States when I was twelve, and we've never been back to Colombia. I didn't know at the time how complicated it was, how she must have planned that move for years behind my father's back."

"Is your father still there?"

"I assume so. I haven't had any contact. At first, we went to Miami and stayed with a cousin, but then started moving around a lot. I later realized we were hiding from my father."

"Afraid he'd come after you?"

"My parents were high school sweethearts. They grew up in Santa Marta in poor families. My grandparents didn't want my mom to marry him because of his lack of resources. He went off to Medellin supposedly to go to university, but he got involved in what Medellin became famous for. He came back to the hometown with nice clothes and a car, not a big fancy car, just a regular one, enough to impress my grandparents. They got married, I was born, and he bought a house in Cartagena, though he still spent most of his time in Medellin. I grew up in luxury. When I was five, my dad bought a bigger house with a pool. I started private school and had a security guard drive me around. He never talked to mom about his work, but she knew. Once, when I was ten, some men tried to kidnap me."

"Oh, my God. This is like *The Sopranos*. Were you hurt?"

"I didn't realize what was going on. It seems they were idiots and bungled the whole thing, but Mom freaked out and Dad ordered extra security. That's when she decided we were leaving. I think she still loved my father, but protecting me was more important to her. She had to keep her plans secret from my dad, of course, but also from the security guards loyal to my father. One weekend my father didn't come home, and she badgered the security until one of them told her he had been arrested but it was no big deal, and he would be out soon. The next day we went to visit relatives. While the security waited out front, we slipped out the back, a cousin drove us to the airport, and we got on a flight. All we had when we arrived in Miami were the clothes on our backs and my mother's purse full of jewelry and the house money she had saved. It was the end to our life of luxury."

"She gave up everything for you."

"After a couple of months, our money was almost gone, and she realized there were too many Colombian connections in Miami for us to ever remain anonymous. In the last apartment we stayed in belonging to a friend of hers from grammar school, there was a postcard of San Francisco's Golden Gate Bridge on the refrigerator. She took it as a sign and made a spontaneous decision. We got on a Greyhound bus and traveled across the country."

Again, I felt bad for any negative thoughts I'd had about his mother, the annoyance with her for keeping us apart. Like millions and millions of mothers before her, she sacrificed for her son. They had a mother-only-son bond that was fierce but could also be damaging in its intensity.

He continued the story of how they slept in a horrible transient hotel near the bus station in San Francisco, the horror of going from a luxury home with a pool and private security to a rat-infested smelly room with the toilet down the hall. His mother had to struggle to survive, first as a maid, and then as a bilingual secretary when her English was sufficient. She clawed her way from nothing, so that Mateo could have a better life.

"You should sleep," I told him.

"I just wanted you to know. I owe everything to her. Now she's suffering and I need to take care of her. She has the early stages of dementia."

"I get it."

"But I will find a way forward for us, that is if you want it."

"I wouldn't be here if I didn't."

"I'm feeling groggy again. You should go home and get some sleep."

"I can come back tomorrow and take you home if they release you." I leaned over to kiss him just as a nurse walked into the room.

"Excuse me," she said.

I whispered in his ear. "I think I just outed you."

"Everybody knows," he said loud enough for her to hear.

"Uh-huh. You don't know how many hearts got broken when we found out, I mean, among the female staff. Looks like hearts are gonna be broken among the guys too."

"Don't listen to her," Mateo said. "I didn't get a single Valentine this year."

"That don't mean there weren't a whole passel of 'em wanting to be sent. All I'm saying, Mr. Nathan, you better treat him right."

"I will if he lets me."

"He playing hard to get, huh?"

"I'm not," Mateo said. "You two go gossip somewhere else. I'm tired."

I kissed him again. "*Hasta mañana.*"

As I left the room, the nurse gave me a look like she couldn't fathom what a hot young man like Mateo was doing with someone like me. My sentiments exactly.

In the ride home my head bounced between anxiety—afraid I would do something to screw this up or he would change his mind or his mom would make it impossible—and ecstasy that he found something in me that made him want to be with me, to kiss me, to get naked with me, and now to be open about it with other people...except one.

Still vivid in my brain was the image of standing in the doorway of his room, the timeworn impulse, a carryover from what seemed another lifetime, to enter his space and be part of it, pick up a shirt and smell it, see what was in his bedside drawer. I had resisted the urge, but it surprised me how strong it was, leading me to question how much I needed to reveal about my past. Would he reject me for a pre-teen and early high school habit of snooping? Would he reject me for the problems I'd had with drugs? What about the year Sniffy and I had acted as escorts? I strongly believed I had left the worst of my bad behavior behind, and the notion of dumping all my baggage on a potential mate out of guilt seemed misguided.

Though I had been clean for many years before I met Anthony, moving to San Leandro with him felt like the final rejection of the surroundings, circumstances, and unstable people that led me to drugs. There was something symbolic about buying a house in suburbia and settling down with a person who was so even keeled and loving, a commitment to, dare I say, a boring life. The antidote to that boredom was supposed to be our regular trips out of the country, to recharge our batteries with doses of new cultural, gastronomical, and adventurous experiences. First, the trips had been put on hold, and then our life had been shattered. There was absolutely no reason for me to stay in a house too big for one person and a considerable distance from anyone I cared about. I had been edging toward one more move in my life. And then, along came Mateo.

I pulled into the driveway of our bastion of middle-class mediocrity, knowing full well I had made the concession willingly, and as long as Anthony was alive, didn't regret the venture into the suburbs for a minute, or at least, I could say I didn't dwell on it more than a minute. I had bought a lawnmower for the backyard as well as an edger, taking me back to the years of my youth when I cut the grass of the neighborhood to earn extra money. And like my grandmother, who had lived two doors down from us on Oak Street, we grew vegetables and delicious red tomatoes in the garden. I had, in some ways, moved back to a version of my hometown, the same averageness. San Leandro had about the same population, a large working class, lots of chain stores and fast-food restaurants but few fine-dining options or trendy shops so common in other towns of the Bay Area.

We had made the yard a little paradise with bird baths that attracted a variety of feathered friends, flowering shrubs that drew bees and butterflies, and patio furniture that lured our friends from the city for a day of sunnier weather. The inside of the house we had renovated to our liking and filled with furniture from our past lives and new pieces that complimented the mid-century style of the house.

As I sat in the car, staring at the front porch that we rarely used, the paint job seemed to have faded in equal measure to the novelty of our suburban lifestyle. I had a sudden craving to be in Barcelona despite the jarring remembrances of losing friends, or bouncing on a bus through the Tunisian desert despite the sickness we all had that led to Nick's diagnosis. I craved the otherworldly atmosphere of being in Cuba, visiting Vladimir's mother despite the memories it conjured up of a person I had lost all contact with. I recalled the delight on Anthony's face when we traveled through Brazil surrounded by Black and brown people and the awe-inspiring sight of the Iguazu Falls. Had I jumped into this thing with Mateo too fast to comfort my lonely heart?

Excited by the mental journals of my travels, I spent the evening planning a trip. Since I wasn't flush with cash, my destination had to be somewhere economical. It had to be culturally rich and hopefully not involve a long flight. Mexico was the logical choice.

I could spend a couple of weeks away and test my feelings. I could have the perspective of distance to figure out what I wanted to do with the rest of my life. But I wasn't so callous that I would go before Mateo healed. I could help him and nurse him back to health.

With Anthony, there had been no hard decisions. Everything flowed. My feelings for Mateo had tossed me right back into the ring of difficult choices. In my dilemma, I chose to use my call-a-friend option, wondering if Cindy got tired of my dependence on her in times of crisis, going on forty-five years now.

About a year into my relationship with Anthony and everything going so well, she joked about hanging up her crisis counselor hat. "Not so fast," I told her. "I might need to call you if I'm traumatized by the tomatoes getting a nasty bug infestation."

I lay in bed, my favorite phone conversation position, and called her. It was rare she needed more than the sound of my hello to pick up on my mood. "Let me guess, you are canceling our walk tomorrow because you *will* be off on that honeymoon to Bali."

"No, but I do have travel on my mind...uh...a solo trip."

"Hold on. Let me dust off my crisis line hat. What's going on?"

"Yesterday was quite a day." I told her about our bike ride, the accident, the boyfriend affirmation, meeting his mother, and the history of Mateo's arrival in the United States.

"That all sounds positive, progress being made. Yes, the mother thing is a bit of a snag, but understandable, right? I'm not getting the crisis that makes you want to go walkabout."

"Meeting Mateo was a kick in the butt, what I needed to feel alive again. But the problem with having real feelings is that you wake up and look around. Is this the life I want, going from my blank computer screen to vegging out watching TV in a house I don't need, full of memories and a yard threatening to return to jungle mode? I can travel. Why am I not traveling? There is the sticky point that my finances are shit, but if I sell the house, I can become a perpetual nomad and post videos on YouTube."

"You seem to be forgetting the part about having real feelings for a real person. And what? Are you going to dump him while he's down and out with broken bones, poor baby?"

"No. I'll stay around until he's recovered. Which reminds me, I *do* have to cancel tomorrow. I'm picking him up at the hospital and he's not sure what time they'll release him."

"Well, good on you for not being a heartless bitch. You're going to wait until he's more attached after you lovingly nurse him back to health, and then dump him!"

"Wait. I thought as a crisis counselor you're supposed to bring me back from the edge and talk me down gently."

"You forgot who you're talking to. Honey child, I've earned the right to call it as I see it. Am I wrong?"

"I can think of a shitload of times when I should have listened to you. But this, it's all been so unexpected. I never thought anyone could love me again, and I'm not saying he loves me. He's curious for some reason."

"What is love but an immense curiosity about another person?"

"Never thought of it that way. Brilliant!"

"Get some sleep so you can be fresh in the morning when you pick him up. And smile. No one can resist your smile."

"Maybe I want him to resist my smile. I'm not sure I can be in a relationship right now. It might be a rebound. Not real."

"You're not making sense. Go to sleep. See how you feel in the morning."

# Chapter 18

I stayed up late looking at destinations I could get to in Mexico from the Oakland airport on nonstop flights. I was surprised how many there were. I could go to Mexico City, Guadalajara, Puerto Vallarta, Cabo, Morelia, and Guanajuato via the Leon airport. On a legal pad, I dutifully made my pro and con columns for each city, an exercise I had been using since my brother told me about it in high school when I was trying to decide what colleges to apply to. I had been to Mexico City, Puerto Vallarta, and Guadalajara, but the other three would be new to me. I was bogged down in the old dilemma of traveling: return to a familiar place I had enjoyed or go for the more adventurous option of trying a new place. I researched each possibility online and wrote down the positives and negatives. It was a little like being back in college, doing the initial research for writing a paper, though back then I probably would have been high on diet pills and unsurprised when I heard the early morning birds calling outside the window.

In this case, the surprise was glancing at the clock and seeing that it was three in the morning, the latest I had stayed up in a long time. Without finalizing my decision, I turned out the light and tucked myself into the large bed I had shared with Anthony. "I wish you could go with me," I whispered.

I overslept and missed Mateo's text and call and the second text and the second call where a woman in the background said, "You better be on your way."

I called him back, and he answered right away. "I'm so sorry. I'll be there as soon as I can."

When I walked past the nurses' station, the woman from the night before gave me the evil eye. I hurried into his room and felt a gut-punch as I saw him in a wheelchair with an abandoned look on his face, his left arm in a sling to protect his shoulder and wearing his cycling clothes minus the blood from the day before. I cringed at the raw skin on his leg. He saw my reaction.

"I'm going to have scars."

"We all have scars of some sort."

"You won't mind?"

"Are you sure your head is all right 'cause you're sounding a little batty. Mind? I'll even kiss them for you."

"I told her you'd come," he said. "She wanted to call a taxi."

"I was up until 3 a.m. It was stupid. Forgive me?"

"Your friend, Claudine, took my clothes home last night, washed the blood and grit out of them, and brought them back this morning."

"My friend?"

"The one who was here yesterday."

"Oh, the one I just passed in the hall who was about to tear my head off for being late."

"I heard that." Claudine stood sentry-like in the doorway. "Punctuality is a sign of respect. I told you you better treat him right."

Mateo winked at her. "Oh, Claudine, you know how hard it is to remember things when you get to a certain age."

"He can have all the senior moments he want just not when he made a solemn promise to pick you up."

"You're ganging up on me. I swear I'll make it up to him."

"Hmph. He's not supposed to have any rambunctious activity."

I got behind the wheelchair and put my hands lightly on his shoulders. "Can you believe it, Mateo? She thinks we might do something rambunctious. Tell her I'm a gentleman."

"That's not what I heard," said Claudine with a laugh.

"I do hope you haven't been blabbing to the whole hospital what we do in private." In truth, there hadn't been a lot to blab about.

Claudine raised her heavily filled in and extended eyebrows. "I was referring to the stalking. I don't want to hear about the other stuff."

"Goodbye, Claudine." I pushed the chair, but it wouldn't budge.

Claudine threw up her hands. "Oh, Lordy. Don't you know these things got brakes?" She bent down and released the levers.

We headed out the door with Claudine hot on our tail, still behind us when we got to the elevator. I peered at her over my shoulder.

"I'm going with y'all to make sure you don't run off with my chair."

In the elevator, Claudine rested one hand on the back of the chair. "You gonna be okay with your mom and all?"

"Sure," said Mateo.

Claudine glanced at me with raised eyebrows, obviously trying to cue a response from me.

"I can always help," I said.

"You got to do better than this morning," said Claudine.

"I will. I promise."

I got Mateo in the car and wheeled the chair back to Claudine waiting at the door. "No messing around," she said.

I laughed. "I'll pass the word on."

In the car, I patted Mateo's leg. "Claudine said no messing around."

He shook his head. "I'll need a minute before I'm up to anything. Can we stop at Safeway? Luisa said food is running low."

"And who's going to cook? You?"

"I can cook."

"I'm sure you can, but your arm."

"I'll get prepared things, maybe a roasted chicken, potato salad. Mom won't like it, but..."

"I can always go shopping for you or pick up food to go. Anytime."

"You'd do that for me?"

"Of course, not that I have much choice with Claudine breathing down my neck."

"She's a sweetheart under that gruff exterior."

"I'm not taking any chances."

We drove on Marina Blvd, and I pointed to the lane in front of the Ford dealership. "That's where you ran me off the road. I could have been the one in the hospital after a bike accident."

"What an exaggeration! You left in a fit of jealousy because I was talking to a girl, so I had to come find you. I was afraid you might do something to hurt yourself." He laughed and immediately grabbed his ribs. "Ouch! It hurts."

"Serves you right for talking nonsense."

"Come on, admit it. You were jealous."

"No way." I felt giddy inside.

We got to Safeway, and I offered to go in.

"I can walk, you know. I'm not a cripple."

"I could get you one of those motorized carts for seniors."

"You probably have experience with those."

"Watch it. That's two senior jokes in one day."

"Okay, *papi.*"

"No, no, no. None of this papi shit. I'm nobody's daddy."

"I'm not saying you are. It's a term of affection. We use it for friends, relatives, lovers."

I wanted to ask which one I was, but let it go.

As we got out of the car, I noticed his grimace of pain. It sent a squeamish chill through me, but if he insisted on playing the macho guy, I had to let him. We grabbed a shopping cart and as we entered the store, he leaned heavily on it though I refrained from commenting that he was using it as a walker.

"Just tell me what you want, and I'll pull it off the shelves or run and get it."

We quickly ended up knee-deep in a discussion or argument about each item.

"You know, Costco has better roasted chickens," I said.

"Do you want to drive me to Costco right now?"

"No."

"Fine. Next time we'll go to Costco."

We? Next time? Oh, yeah. I promised Claudine. I chose the biggest lemon-herb chicken from the heated compartment.

"You know, biggest isn't always the best."

"I'm not touching that one with a..."

"Stop. Not in the mood," he said, making me feel like an incorrigible potty-mouth homo.

In the deli aisle I picked up the tub of potato salad he pointed at and read the label. "This has a high fat content and is loaded with salt. Look at this. One serving has fifty percent of a day's maximum cholesterol. Sodium, thirty-five percent."

"That's the brand my mom likes."

"I imagine at her age, she needs to cut down on fat and salt."

He huffed and a thick vein popped up on his neck. "Which one of us is in the medical profession here? I can take care of my mother, thank you."

"I'm just saying."

In the frozen food section, he braced himself with one hand on the cart, opened the frosty door, and took out a pizza. He turned it over and read the label before putting it back and shaking his head.

I had a big grin on my face.

"Shut up. I guess I can order a gluten-free vegetarian pizza from delivery with low fat cheese that tastes like plastic."

There were no vegetables in the cart, not even frozen ones. "Do you eat vegetables?" I asked.

"I eat a lot of vegetables. If I had known you were going to be the food police, I would have come here on my own."

Nearby, an older woman doing her own label reading over the top of her glasses turned and smiled at us. Her knowing look seemed to say, "Love is love, and couple shit is couple shit."

Mateo smiled back at her and then glared at me. "*Insoportable,*" he grumbled.

"Me?"

He leaned over and surveyed the items in the cart. "You didn't get the milk."

"I forgot to ask if you wanted whole, two percent, fat free, lactose free, fortified, or soy."

"I only drink orangutang milk. *Por Dios!* Get the two percent so I don't fall over with a heart attack in the next week."

"This is fun." I started off to get the milk.

"You think you know everything about food because..." He stopped himself, his annoyed face cringing into horror at what he had almost said.

I turned around and gave him a baffled look. I was sure where his angry words were going, a reference to my chef husband until he remembered he was dead of a freak accident, and I might still be feeling just a little bit sensitive about it. "Because?" I asked.

"Nothing."

He looked traumatized, and I knew it wasn't his nature to be mean though everyone can be pushed to the edge. I didn't want to make it worse.

"You mean because I used to work in a health food restaurant? Did I tell you about that? It was right after college. And yes, I learned a lot about food."

He looked at me with grateful eyes that I had let him off the hook and hunched over the shopping cart as if he was exhausted. "I'm being a bitch. Sorry."

He was undoubtedly feeling the effects of the accident, the pain, and having to take time off work, but I questioned if there was another source of tension. Throughout our merry shopping adventure, we avoided the topic of what would happen when we got back to his apartment. He wouldn't be able to carry all the groceries himself, so I would have to accompany him back into the den of the lioness.

I had been thinking of ways to decrease the anxiety Carmen might be feeling about me stealing her son away, though it was conjecture on my part, not knowing if she had any idea what was going on with Mateo. But something about the way she scrutinized me the day before told me she knew. If I showed up a second time, it would likely confirm her suspicion. I would soon be removing myself from the situation by going on a trip, thus making things easier for her. But another part of me was pissed that she was trying to impede her son from living his wonderful gay life.

We got to the car, and he groaned as he struggled to get in.

"Are you okay?"

"I didn't take any pain meds this morning because I didn't want to be groggy."

"You should have. Maybe you wouldn't be so grouchy."

He clammed up, not saying another word until we got to his building. "You can park where it says guest."

I reached over and touched his arm, causing him to flinch. "You'll need help with the bags."

"Obviously."

"I don't want to upset your mom."

"This is her nap time."

By the time we got to the third floor, Mateo was breathing heavily and wincing. His hand shook as he put the key in the lock.

"Should I come in?"

"It'll be okay. Don't worry."

Somebody on the other side of the door certainly wasn't napping, and it seemed she had been sitting on a chair in the hall, waiting for the sound of the lock.

"*Gracias a Dios!*" said Carmen. Mateo hugged and kissed his mom, telling her she should be resting. Then she looked at me like I seemed familiar, but she wasn't sure. "Who's he?"

"That's my friend, Nathan. You met him yesterday."

She gave me a hard stare. "Delivery boy," she said in a way that sounded like a put down.

"No. He's my friend and he's helping me."

She pointed at his arm in the sling. "What's that?"

"Remember I told you I had an accident. But I'm okay." He was extremely patient with her, a lot more patient with her than he had been with me in the supermarket.

Luisa came into the hall and picked up the bags off the floor. "I'll put these away before I go."

"I can help," I said to escape Carmen's harsh stare.

"No. No. You all go in the living room, and I'll make some tea," said Luisa.

"Mateo, I think I should go," I said.

He put his good arm around Carmen's shoulders and ushered her toward the living room. He glanced back at me and nodded for me to follow.

This time Carmen sat on the sofa and patted the seat next to her for her son. I was left to sit on one of the armchairs. She leaned close to Mateo and spoke in Spanish in a low voice, either thinking I wouldn't understand or forgetting I was there. She claimed "*esa mujer*," pointing toward the kitchen, snuck out last night and left her alone. Mateo said he didn't think so and that Luisa always took good care of her. Then she said she'd seen her go in his room and take some money. Again, he calmly explained that Luisa doesn't need to take money because he paid her very well. She countered that he paid her too much.

I fidgeted in the chair across the room, and Mateo gave me an apologetic look. "Mami, Nathan was an English teacher. Now he's retired and writing poetry. He just published a book."

Carmen smiled politely and turned to Mateo, asking if he got the potato salad she liked.

"Yes, mami." He twisted his mouth, smiling weakly at me.

"Nathan was nice enough to pick me up at the hospital and took me shopping."

Instead of being pleased, she appeared perplexed by the information. Mateo's attempt at presenting me in a good light wasn't working.

Luisa brought in a tray with a pot of tea, milk, sugar, and some everyday cups.

"Where are my lovely Meissen cups?" asked Carmen.

Mateo's brow wrinkled. "The blue ones?"

*"Sí, mijo."*

"We haven't had those since we left Colombia."

"I just saw them the other day."

"No, we left everything in Colombia."

"*Dios mío*," she said, and tears came to her eyes.

Luisa served the tea and passed around a plate of butter cookies we had bought at Safeway. Though my churning stomach didn't want a cookie, I took one to be polite and sipped the tea while Carmen continued to talk dreamily about the house in Cartagena and all the beautiful things they had there.

Luisa announced she was going to leave, and I stood up. "I should go too."

Mateo looked disappointed. "You haven't finished your tea."

Not that I didn't enjoy a tea party, but this one was a little too much like the mad tea party in Alice in Wonderland. I stuck out my hand to Carmen and thanked her for the tea. She took my hand and said the pleasure was all hers. For a moment, she was warm and gracious, her eyes softening.

"I'll walk you both to the door," said Mateo.

Luisa said goodbye, and I lingered a moment. "Well?"

"Baby steps. She's more confused than normal today. I don't think she slept last night."

"Let me know if there's anything I can do."

He leaned in and sneaked a kiss. "I'll call you later."

# Chapter 19

For the rest of the afternoon and evening a series of images bounced around my brain: Mateo in a wheelchair with his arm in a sling, Claudine giving me the evil eye, the amused woman in Safeway overhearing our conversation, an elegantly dressed Carmen either ignoring me or shooting me dagger eyes. But one image that sucked the humor out of me was Mateo sitting in the passenger seat of Anthony's BMW 330i. The car was both classy and sporty—he had gotten the sports package with leather seats. It was an impressive vehicle, a status car that zoomed on the freeway, but since I felt neither classy nor sporty, I wasn't comfortable driving it. I was a retired teacher and poet who didn't need showy things and who had spent the last few years, particularly the last few months, trying to simplify my life.

I had always been suspicious of the never-ending car advertisements that led people to associate a make of car with the ambitions, social class, and personality of the driver. I would never forget the day Mom and I stood at the back door when Dad pulled up in the new car he had gone off to purchase. He wouldn't tell us what it was beforehand because he didn't want to ruin the surprise. It was a white 1959 Cadillac with huge fins capped with bullet taillights, looking like a rocket tipped on its side. I let out a cry of excitement, but Mom was quiet. I gazed up at her and saw a crestfallen face lined with disappointment. I knew that look because I had been the recipient of it many times, like the time I said I didn't want to do piano recitals anymore because they made me nervous or the time I got a B- in math class.

Mom's reaction puzzled me, and after badgering her for a couple of weeks, she finally explained. In her Midwestern 1960s farmgirl mentality, there were two kinds of people who drove Cadillacs: Jewish businessmen who were trying to show how much money they made and Black people who pooled their resources in a neighborhood and bought one Caddy for the block, which they took turns driving. "It just doesn't look right for a university professor to be driving that car," she said. Every time we rode in it, or she drove it herself, she had a sour look on her face. Her silent, pouty campaign against the car was successful, and Dad got rid of it three months later.

Unlike my mother, I didn't associate a sporty BMW with any particular group though if hard pressed, I suppose I could have come up with a profile, though not one including racial or socio-economic elements. What I was sure about was that I didn't come close to that profile.

In addition to the image problem, I had a ridiculous sensation that with Mateo in the car, I was cheating on Anthony many months after he had been gone. That nagging twinge of misplaced guilt served to make me act on what I had been thinking about for months: putting the car in the hands of someone who would appreciate it.

I had heard of a new online car buying operation that made it easy for people selling cars. The beamer was less than two years old, and before it came to me, Anthony had kept it in pristine condition. I went on the website and put in the stats. A short time later, I got a quote for the car that was far more than I imagined. At the time he bought it, I never asked how much he'd paid as it was his last big splurge before devoting himself, and a lot of his savings, to the restaurant. Besides, he told me, he had to look the part of a restaurant owner who strived to one day have a Michelin star.

When I told my brother I was thinking of getting rid of the beamer, he said I was crazy, that I should enjoy it because it was something I would never buy for myself.

"Do you want it?" I asked.

"No, man. What am I going to do with a car like that? I've got four grandkids I have to haul around."

"That's what I'm saying."

"What? You don't have grandkids."

"It's the image thing. It was Anthony, but it's not me."

The more I thought about it, the more it made sense to get a new car, at least new to me as I would likely get something secondhand. The insurance money from my totaled Prius was still in the bank. I could use it to buy something simple and practical. The money from the BMW would come in handy in my current financial straits as well as pay for my trip still in the planning stage.

Having made that decision, I was in good spirits when Mateo called in the evening.

"How's your mom?"

"She seemed a little better when I got her to bed, though at dinner she was convinced Luisa had stolen the jewelry she brought from Colombia. I had to remind her that she'd sold it so we could put food on the table and pay for our move to San Francisco."

I could tell immediately he was in a better mood, making me guess he had taken something for the pain. Good thing, because I felt a tease coming on.

"This is probably not the time to ask, but you're legal, right?" I wasn't serious and quickly added a comment with the distracting b-word. "I'm not sure I signed up for a boyfriend who's illegal."

"I think you mean undocumented, asshole...boyfriend...asshole boyfriend."

"You know I'm kidding, but the thrill of being with someone outside the law is somewhat enticing."

"Such a rebel. Sorry to disappoint. I'm an anchor baby, which to right-wingers is probably worse. It was the best thing my father ever did for me. He realized the precariousness of his career choice, so when my mom got pregnant, he devised a plan to send her to the States and stay with a cousin before she was obviously showing. I was born in a Miami hospital and got a U.S. passport with my one-week-old baby picture in it. My father arranged everything. We returned to Colombia and Mom renewed my passport whenever it was necessary. Twelve years later I came here on my American passport thank you very much. Unfortunately, when Mom's visa expired, she was undocumented and had to take what jobs she could, you know, cleaning, sewing, robbing banks."

"Did she take you into the banks in a stroller and then pull a gun out of your diapers?"

I pictured his eyes sparkling with wildness. "Just until I was old enough to see over the counter, then I went in alone."

"Uh, warning. My line might be bugged by the FBI."

His laugh made me happy. I loved talking to him, lying in bed. Our inane little conversations soothed my soul.

"Oh, I forgot to tell you. Mom has a doctor's appointment tomorrow. We can take a taxi unless..."

"Of course, I'll take you. I need to accumulate all the points I can with her."

"She'll come around...like I did." There was his laugh again, hearty and sweet, and then, "Ouch! It hurts. I have to remember not to laugh. Wouldn't that be something if laughing made my ribs puncture a lung and I literally died of laughter? Help! My boyfriend is killing me."

"If you come over, I can think of some ways to take the pain away that don't involve laughing."

"Hah! Remember what Claudine said." His sigh was like a gust of wind over the line. "You know, the day of the bike ride, I thought we'd go back to your house after."

"For ten minutes?"

"Maybe fifteen. I really wanted that."

"I hope that isn't what distracted you, fantasizing about my naked body."

"Hell, no. That bitch wasn't watching where she was going. I shouldn't say that. Poor thing was devastated."

"Do you think the universe is trying to tell us something? Every time we..."

"Stop. The universe also put us together under an apricot tree."

"And that would have been the end of it if it hadn't been for me."

"It's not my fault if you recognize a good thing when you see it."

Zing!

Good thing it was, but short on practicality.

***

The next morning, I woke up to three different alarms two hours before I had to pick them up because the image of Mateo's face when I was late to the hospital still haunted me.

Carmen and Mateo were waiting outside the building when I pulled up. I jumped out and ran around the car to open the passenger door for Carmen. "Am I late?"

"Not at all," said Mateo. Carmen remained stoic, and Mateo opened the rear door. "Mom prefers the back seat."

"Oh, okay." I moved to take her arm to help her in, but she spryly was inside the car before I touched her, staring at me again like I was a homeless person at her window asking for a handout.

Mateo folded his body into the front seat, biting back a moan. I got in and let out a big puff of air that sounded heavier than I had intended. Mateo gave me a startled look. Here we were. Not only did I have Mateo again in Anthony's car, but also his mother in the back seat in one of those how-the-hell-did-I-get-here moments. It was like a bizarre dream. In the rearview mirror, my eyes met hers. "Everybody buckled in?" I asked.

Mateo turned to look over his shoulder but grimaced as if sharp teeth were clamping down on his broken bones. "*Todo bien*?"

"*Sí, mijo.*" She continued to glare at me in the mirror as I backed up and headed out to the street. Her perfume filled the car with old lady essence, and I cracked my window enough that I could breathe, but not so much there would be a draft on her.

"My son tells me you're a teacher." The amiable voice came from the back seat but seemed disembodied from the person who, a moment before, had been staring me down in the mirror.

"Yes. For many years. English."

"Teachers don't get respect in this country."

I glanced at her again just before turning onto the street. She smiled pleasantly. We were having a normal conversation, everything suddenly normal, a normal day taking a friend's normal mother to the normal doctor.

"I still remember my first English teacher when we got to San Francisco," said Mateo.

"You were an excellent student and learned quickly," said Carmen in a strong voice full of pride.

"Apparently I still have an accent." He turned to me with a crooked smile, sticking out his tongue.

"Oh, nonsense," said Carmen. "Your English is perfect."

"I agree," I said. Though an image jumped into my head of us lying in bed, and Mateo whispering spicy nothings in my ear with an exaggerated accent in hopes of driving me wild, which it did. Lost in my thoughts, I didn't turn where I should have.

"You know where we're going, right?" said Mateo.

"I'm taking a shortcut." I started to reach over and squeeze his leg but caught myself.

He gave me one of his endearing sidelong glances I had become used to. "Uh-huh."

When we got to Kaiser, I said I'd come back later and pick them up. "Do you need help getting in?"

"No, we're fine," said Mateo, half out of the car, his voice a little shaky.

I hopped out of the car and ran around to the passenger side. "Here, let me help you."

"I said I'm fine."

I opened the rear door. "*Señora.*" I gave her my hand, and this time she took it.

"*Gracias, joven.*"

What I imagined to be the real Carmen, gracious and warm, had made an appearance. Holding her hand briefly while she got out of the car felt like progress.

Mateo took a ragged series of breaths from the simple effort of getting out of the car. "Did you take anything today?" I asked.

"I forgot." He adjusted his arm in the sling and grimaced again.

"I'll run to the pharmacy and get pain medicine right now."

"No, I'll be fine. I'll take something when I get home."

"Don't be ridiculous. I'll get some Tylenol and bring it to you. What's the room number of the doctor?"

"I said no." He sounded unusually stubborn, almost angry. I supposed he didn't want to look weak in front of his mother or didn't want her to know the extent of his pain.

We stared at each other for a moment and then both turned at the same time to look at Carmen, standing patiently but with a confused expression like she was witnessing something she had never seen before. Mateo offered her his good arm, and the two of them hobbled to the entrance.

An hour later I pulled up to the glass doors where Mateo and his mother were waiting. I got out and helped them into the car, immediately seeing that Carmen's evil twin was back as she stared at me with vacant eyes. "I thought we were getting a taxi," she said to Mateo. "This isn't a taxi."

Mateo spoke to her in Spanish, explaining again who I was and reminding her I was the teacher who had dropped them off. She responded that it wasn't good to take rides from strangers.

I went back to the driver's side and let him negotiate with his mother, feeling that the progress we had made a short time earlier had been lost but realizing how much more difficult it must have been for her, unable to process the things happening around her, new and changing situations. I promised myself to be more understanding and to stop thinking of her as my adversary.

After a few minutes, he had Carmen in the car, and he got in next to me. I dropped a box of Tylenol and a bottle of water in his lap. "Take it," I said. "No arguments." He started to protest but let it go as if he didn't have the energy. He got the box open and made an attempt at the tamper-proof bottle. I took it out of his hands, opened it, shook out two pills, and offered them in the palm of my hand. He managed the twist-off cap of the water bottle on his own and downed the medicine.

"How about some lunch?" I suggested.

Mateo shook his head. "I think we should go home."

"But you have to eat something." I sounded like Anthony when I used to be ambivalent about eating. I didn't believe in strict mealtimes or eating at all if I didn't feel like it, but I was desperate to hold on to the progress I'd made with Carmen, hoping sweet Carmen would come back. "I could get some Chinese takeout and bring it over." I looked in the mirror. "*Señora,* do you like Chinese food?"

"No."

Mateo shrugged in a defeated way. "We have food at home. Thanks, though."

I dropped them off. This time I let them manage their own exit from the car. Mateo gave me a cool, "Thanks," and closed the door.

On the way home I agonized over his icy word of thanks and the troubled look in his eyes. Hadn't I just done everything I could to get in good graces with his mother, showing how much I cared? He couldn't have been upset that I forced him to down some pain pills. I had taken time out of my day—okay, it wasn't like I had to reschedule anything—to help him and what do I get but a cold goodbye.

In pulling into my driveway, I realized I was making the day all about me, something I had been called out for by just about every guy I had been with. Instead of being sympathetic about the impossible position Mateo was in, I was being selfish. He had to deal with the heartbreaking predicament of watching his mother going in and out of sanity without the means to do anything about it, and that very day might have received some bad news about her worsening condition in the doctor's office. And now, on top of that, he had to care for her while in pain from the injuries of the bicycle accident. And he had to worry about how to tell his mother he had met someone he cared about, though I was making a couple of major assumptions that, one, he wanted to tell her, and two, he truly cared about me. If all that wasn't enough, he might have sensed my frustration—I had done my best to hide it—and feared I might do something like run away on a trip out of the country, leaving him behind in his loneliness and frustration, which was exactly what I was planning to do. Shit. Asshole boyfriend was right.

But were we really boyfriends? It hadn't been a true declaration of relationship status but rather a ploy to make sure the medics and hospital would allow me to be by his side after the accident. Since then, it had been sort of a joke we'd never had the chance to have a proper conversation about. We had barely gone beyond the good feels stage, knowing there was an attraction, the nature of which I still doubted, but not having enough opportunity to fully explore it. I knew that deep inside me and for as long as I could remember there was a skepticism about anyone showing an interest in me.

When I first met Cindy in high school, she was my dream girlfriend. She was pretty and popular and had the exotic quality of having dabbled in the alternative. She had associated with real-life hippies the year she spent in California, adding elements of that contact to her style of dress, but most importantly she said things in conversation that no one else was saying in my high school, new ideas about our society, speaking out against the Vietnam war and for racial equality. The diet pills a friend turned me on to allowed me to come out of myself and feel like I might be worthy of her friendship and possibly something more. The speedy sensation of the drugs made me engage in conversation, tell jokes, and show confidence despite the fact I was not a jock, a class clown, a school politician, or member of multiple clubs. I was a nobody that a somebody noticed. It was hard to believe that the same doubts of my youth were still with me today. Mateo had youth, beauty, a good job, and a sweetness that captivated me. What could he possibly see in me?

I sat in Anthony's car in the driveway, staring at the house we had bought together, but my thoughts were dominated by this new person in my life. I became suddenly aware of the stuffiness inside the car, the powerful smell of the leather interior, and the last remnants of Carmen's perfume. I threw the door open with force, a symbolic gesture heralding my escape not only from the car but the current dilemma. I would go ahead with my plan to travel.

# Chapter 20

In the relationship drought between Vladimir and Anthony, travel became my new drug. I had gotten a taste of the high while living in Barcelona, a gateway to Europe, North Africa, and the Middle East. Visiting different countries provided, like drugs, an escape from the mundane and whatever miseries, real or imagined, that I was going through. In the first few years back in the United States, I stayed put, partially out of obligation to Vladimir and partly for fear that if I ventured too far from work or home I would keel over dead in the street. The life expectancy of someone with HIV was not good. After Vladimir made his exit, I no longer had to feel responsible for him, confident the U.S. government, in its preferential treatment of Cubans, would keep him from falling through the cracks as he cruised along the highway toward permanent residency and citizenship. And, since I lived alone, I didn't have to inform anyone about my trips except the U.S. Post Office to hold my mail and Cindy so she wouldn't freak out if I didn't respond to one of her check-ins.

With my teaching experience in Spain, I snagged a full-time contract at City College, giving me a salary to indulge my whims. Saving for a future that was still very much in doubt seemed pointless, though I was able to buy a humble condo in Potrero Hill through a series of circumstances, including a surprise bequeathment of some money Nick had tucked away (half to me and half to his daughter) and a city-funded program for first-time home buyers,

Not only was I a proud owner of a tiny spot of real estate in San Francisco, I had the means to jet off to South America, the Caribbean, Southeast Asian, Australia, interspersed with trips back to Europe. I was unattached, had disposable income, and a wealth of vacation time. But the most important stroke of luck—and I say luck because it seemed the only way to explain why I had been able to avoid opportunistic infections—was that I had remained healthy. An old friend from my first period in San Francisco with Nick now worked for a foundation and kept my hopes up by informing me about new HIV drugs that were coming out regularly and vaccines that were in clinical trials, a vaccine we still didn't have thirty years later.

After Vladimir moved out, I embarked with a ton of apprehension on my first trip out of the country since coming back from Spain, a long weekend in Puerto Vallarta. But from the first moment of stepping into the balmy air of seaside Mexico and taking a taxi through the old part of town, I felt alive. I remained healthy throughout the trip and didn't suffer from even a small bout of intestinal trouble Mexico was famous for. After a night of dancing in a club, I had my first in a long series of no-strings-attached safe sex encounters as if I had set out to have sex in every country in every continent. Subsequent trips were farther afield and of longer duration. The travel years rapidly became similar in many ways to my years of debauchery in college, but without the destructive results. I had replaced drugs with the buzz from travel, and the one-night stands didn't leave me feeling empty as it was part of the territory. I rarely stayed more than a few days in one place as I was anxious to see as much as possible, not knowing how much time I had left on the planet. And it wasn't all party time and meeting local talent. I visited museums, monuments, and wonders of nature, occasionally with a local who would spend the night, and the next day show me his favorite places in the city. I would come home to San Francisco and my cozy apartment, feeling rejuvenated, ready to go back to work, and grateful for what I had, mostly the fact that I was still alive.

Occasionally I would meet someone at home who would stick around for a week or a month before one of us decided it wasn't working. It wasn't an unhappy time. I imagined that this respite from the trauma of my earlier years would gradually fade into the end of my days, without a partner but surrounded by a few close friends and family members. I wrote a poem depicting my grand finale, replete with drama, tears, parting speeches, and costumes. My mother was the Queen and Cindy, the high priestess, my brother, the court jester, wiping away the sadness with humor. I sent a copy to Cindy. "Nice poem," she said. "A little drama queen-ish. I'll show you this in twenty years when you're still gallivanting around the globe breaking hearts."

This new life began the day I got my freedom from Vladimir, which is an odd way to put it since it had never been a true relationship and we hadn't lived together for a couple of years. But I continued to do what I thought was my duty in leading him down the true and righteous path, or better said, not fuck up the opportunity I had given him. He was only a couple of years younger than me but had the discipline and sense of responsibility of a twelve-year-old.

In those first couple of years in San Francisco, we were more like roommates than lovers, living in the same space but with our separate lives. From the government, he got food stamps, Medicaid, and refugee cash assistance each month. The cash was usually gone within a few days of receiving it. He lived rent free. Not a bad gig if you can get it. Sometimes he would sneak out after I had gone to bed and take my car. I wasn't aware until one night I got a middle-of-the-night call, saying he had been in an accident. Fortunately, it was a parked car he hit, and no one was injured, but he got a DUI, causing our insurance to skyrocket.

It was a warm fall day the last time I saw him leaving me forever, and I wondered if any of my time and effort trying to steer him toward a goal ever paid off. I dropped him off at the place he was staying since he moved out, and he got out of the car with a cool thanks and a stern look that was hauntingly similar to Mateo's recent exit from my car. He had been periodically showing up on my doorstep after a spat with his current squeeze. The first year after moving out, it was an older woman, and recently it had been a guy he worked with that he claimed was just a friend, but I knew they were having sex. He would ring my doorbell and stand with his brown muscled arm extended along the door frame and eyes like a sorry puppy. I would let him into my house and into my bed. Sometimes he would stay around for a few days. I shouldn't have put up with it, but I did because it was easy and sex with him was always good.

After that last time, I expected to hear from him in a couple months, as was his pattern. I never did and never learned what happened to him. I hoped that he finally took the responsibility to be with his two kids who were living in North Carolina, though I doubted it. It was an anticlimactic ending to a seven-year affair that, I had to keep reminding myself, had served a purpose and very possibly had kept me alive after Nick's death. Despite all the things the long affair was lacking, I always believed we had true affection for each other that resembled in many ways love. When I realized a few years later he was never coming back or even contacting me, it hurt. It was some consolation that I felt I had done everything I could for him.

With every man that I'd been attracted to, there had been an element beyond the obvious appreciation of the soulful eyes, the enticing smile, a nicely shaped body, a strong but gentle hand that was a perfect fit in mine. That extra something was a force pulling at me like a fishing line once the hook had taken hold. At times, it was a slow, gradual pull, as if ruled by destiny. At others, it was a reel-in-let-out back and forth to counteract resistance. But beware the times it was a sudden jerk sending me flying through the air, flopping out of control. Was the power and the quality of the pull an actual chemical reaction, the chemistry that people offered as an explanation? Did the pheromones documented in the animal kingdom function in humans, as so many wanted to believe? Researchers said no, but people were desperate to put a name on that inexplicable feeling.

My attraction to both Mateo and Vladimir was of the more volatile variety, leaving me with the sensation of being out of control. But because the two attractions happened at very different points in my life and because Mateo and Vladimir were very different people, my ability to handle the sense of ungroundedness was distinct. Vlad caught me at a vulnerable time and at an age where hormones continued to have an advantageous seat at the table, reaching out and laying a hand on my leg under the table just as I was about to make a presentation. Meeting Mateo many years later still threw me into the air, but I had learned from my past, or thought I had, and my sexual appetites had waned, or I thought they had. But one thing was certain. Mateo was a much better person who didn't wield his charisma like a weapon, and was earnest in his approach. The risk factor, so thrilling in youth, no longer held sway, though the fact remained that one can be hurt at any age, and having seen my share of it, I very much preferred to avoid it.

I felt extremely mature and clever to have analyzed my way out of the Mateo quandary. I would gladly offer him whatever help I could while he recovered from his accident, but I would move forward with my plans to sell the car, plan my travel, perhaps with an extended trip, and seriously consider putting the house on the market. I spent the rest of the day reading, going for a walk, fixing a light dinner, and searching for a movie I could snuggle up with.

I was stretched out on the sofa, remote in hand, and my brain in a haze from the hit I'd taken off a joint—all I needed for my evening's entertainment—when my phone buzzed with a text from Mateo. I considered waiting until later to read it, but the voice in my head kept saying, "What if it's an emergency?"

**I'm going to take the trash down.**

Mateo's texts had a way of jumping into the middle of a conversation, no doubt one he'd been having in his own head.

**Okay. Do you need help?**

**No. I can manage. But can you meet me by the trash bins?**

**That's the most romantic offer I've ever had.**

**I want to give you something.**

Since he was incapacitated and probably still hurting, I doubted we were going to have a hot bang behind the bins.

**I have sunk into the sofa and I'm afraid I would need a crane to get me up.**

**Please.**

I swear I could hear the reel spinning and feel the line tightening. It wasn't fair. I was in a state of complete comfort, and it was chilly outside. A simple no would suffice. Whatever he had to give me could wait. I imagined him patiently holding the phone in his hand pressed against the dark creases of his palm I had traced with my finger one evening (or was it in a dream?), the hand he had run along my cheek and the fingers that had moved through the strands of my hair in gentle strokes. Damn him.

**Give me a few minutes. I'll text you when I'm on my way.**

When I pulled into the guest parking place, he was sitting on the steps by the entrance with a bag of trash by his side. In my headlights, he looked like a bear that had been caught raiding a campsite and he threw his good arm up to shield his eyes.

I cut the lights and got out. I pointed at the bag. "Is that what you wanted to give me? A bag of trash?"

"It might be a bag of cash." He grabbed the railing with his right hand and pulled himself up, smiling grimly.

"Are you okay?" I lifted the plastic bag and some bottles and cans rattled. "Doesn't sound like money."

"Precious metals. Follow me."

As we walked around to the side of the building where there was a fenced area for the garbage bins for landfill and recycling, he tried hard not to show pain in his walk. With his one good hand and the other limited due to the sling, he struggled with the gate, but I let him do it.

"Which one do I throw it in?" I asked.

"Normally, I separate things, but I..."

"It's okay." I lifted the top of the landfill bin and tossed the bag in.

He pointed to a bench on a patch of grass that sat inexplicably close to the garbage area. I supposed it was for those kinky folks who wanted to meditate on the smell of garbage or for residents who invited their boyfriends for clandestine chats with the excuse of taking out the garbage.

He grabbed his lower lip with his front teeth. "I felt bad how I left you earlier. I was upset."

We sat down on the cold metal bench. "Bad news about your mom?"

"It doesn't look good. I had a private chat with the doc. She said her condition is deteriorating rapidly."

"For a while earlier, she seemed fine."

"I'm glad you got a glimpse of the true Carmen. The times when she is distant and even rude, that's not her."

"I had a feeling that was the case. I'm truly sorry."

"I know you're probably getting disgusted with the whole situation."

"No. Not at all. I told you I would be there for you. Whatever you need."

"That's very kind. But you don't have to."

"I feel responsible in a way for the bike accident."

"That's why you're being nice? Because you feel guilty? You feel sorry for me?"

"No. That's not what I meant." I put my hand on his. My heart was racing in the exact opposite direction from the exit plan I had determined only a few hours before.

He raised his chin and gave me a beguiling smile, making me think I might have underestimated him, again having that feeling he was capable of weaponizing his charms and using them on me in the way Vladimir had. In the soft yellow light from the street his skin shined golden, and I leaned in, really to touch a freckle that appeared out of constellation, but our lips had other ideas. I wiggled closer and put a hand at the back of his head, pulling his face closer to mine, our lips snapping together like pieces of a puzzle. He had reeled me all the way in, and now I was in his net.

As much as I was lost in the kiss, the smell of fish coming from the garbage bin made my body shake with a cosmic giggle. "What is it?" he said.

I couldn't possibly explain the whole fish thing. "It's just funny that we're having this passionate kiss with fumes of garbage all around us."

"If I wasn't messed up like this and it was the only place available, I'd throw you in the dumpster, jump on top of you, and fuck you silly."

"I repeat. You say the most romantic things."

"Must be the drugs. Forget what I said. I want to make love to you in a bed with clean sheets and stay wrapped up in your arms all night until the birds sing in the morning."

"That sounds a little boring compared to the previous proposition."

He chuckled, and then his face turned sad in the pale light. "You're not thinking of going anywhere, are you?"

"What do you mean?" I tried to sound light, but I trembled inside, wondering if I had unwittingly given him the password to access my brain and read my thoughts.

"You don't seem to have much reason to stay here. I know you love to travel."

"I think I have a pretty good reason." I leaned in to kiss him again. Why was I doing this? He had basically opened the door and told me I could go.

He pulled back. "My wounds are burning. It hurts to breathe. My collarbone is painful. But you know what's really throbbing?" He took my hand and put it on his dick. He moaned. "I've got to go back upstairs, though."

"Life is so unfair. I'll walk you to the door. Wait. What did you want to give me?"

"My apology for earlier...and...uh...a kiss. God, I sound like I'm ten years old."

"More like sixteen. At least, I hope you weren't kissing men when you were ten."

"Not at ten. Not at sixteen. It took me a while to figure it out."

"And lucky me to be the recipient of that realization."

His eyebrows snapped to attention. "Are you being sarcastic?"

"No. I'm serious. You are..."

"What?"

"More than I could ever have imagined."

The two versions of me, one flirtatious and the other plotting to run away, battled it out right in front of innocent Mateo without him being any the wiser. We said goodnight, and flirtatious me kissed him one more time while the transient me dragged me away with a snarly laugh.

# Chapter 21

I met Anthony at a party in a house above the Castro. The owners of the house, Emilio and Wilson were famous for throwing big gay parties with drag shows, dancing until the wee hours of the morning with plenty of alcohol and substances to abuse. I went with a group of Spanish-speaking friends that I often spent time with, and one of them was the first to join in when they brought out the wigs, dresses, and makeup. I had seen Anthony once before at their annual New Year's bash, but I hadn't spoken to him. I thought he was cute, and our eyes met, but there was no feeling of being jerked out of the water from across the room. Anyway, I was a committed bachelor, and he didn't look like the type, in his designer glasses and pork pie hat, that went home with the first guy who smiled at him.

The second time I saw him at Emilio and Wilson's was a President's Day weekend party. He sat alone on the sofa in the part of the vast living room where they had bunched up all the furniture to create a dance floor and stage for the drag show. He had arrived with the same guy I had seen him with at the last party, who I assumed was his boyfriend. The friend had wandered off. A group of my friends had lit on the furniture around him like a flock of birds and begun prattling away. He didn't laugh when they made jokes and in general looked lost. I squeezed in next to him on the sofa. "Do you speak Spanish?" I asked. He shook his head.

"*Oye, chicos,*" I said. "Our friend here doesn't speak Spanish."

"Sorry," said Pedro, who still wore makeup from his performance but had changed out of his wig and dress into a sparkly T-shirt and shiny tight pants. "What's your name, honey?" Pedro asked.

"Anthony."

"What happened to your boyfriend?"

"He's not my boyfriend."

"That's good news," Pedro screamed.

"Why's that?" said Anthony. He looked serious and uncomfortable, and, I had to admit, endearing in a vulnerable kind of way.

"That means you're available."

"Not necessarily."

I jumped up. "Anthony, could I get you something to drink? I'm going into the kitchen."

"I'll go with you."

"*Escúchame,* Nathan," said Pedro, "you bring him right back because we have a lot more questions."

"Thanks for rescuing me," said Anthony as we entered the kitchen. "I really should learn Spanish. I know they were talking about me."

"It was nothing mean. They just thought you were adorable, which you kind of are."

"I'm not sure adorable was the look I was going for, but thank you."

In the kitchen we perched on stools on either side of a small island surrounded by the clutter of bottles of alcohol, mixers, remnants of food trays, and overflowing trash cans. We nursed beers neither of us seemed to want. Despite the mess around us and the constant traffic in and out of the kitchen, we fell into an easy bubble of conversation. We talked about travel, the favorite places we'd been. I told him about living in Barcelona and Sitges, and his eyes lit up like we had just found the holy grail of relationships that would bind us together forever and ever. Barcelona was his favorite city in the world, and he was jealous I had lived there. I talked about my time in New Orleans, and he said his grandmother's family was from there.

He had grown up with his grandparents and had worked in his grandmother's restaurant starting as a teenager. After working in several other restaurants and hotels in his twenties and thirties, he entered the cooking program at City College. Again, his body lifted off the seat with excitement when I told him I taught at the same college. He felt it necessary to point out how many connections we had, ticking them off like it was some kind of interview while I smiled but didn't see it as a path down the aisle or even a spare bedroom in the upstairs of the house. It was admittedly peculiar that I had avoided using "we" pronouns when talking about all my life experiences and moves and travels, not wanting to bring in the boyfriends who had been a major part of my life during those times. He casually revealed, without my asking, that he was single after having recently ended a long-term relationship, which again was information that edged too close to the interview-for-a-new-partner setup.

Despite the slightly uncomfortable emphasis on his single status and the things we had in common, I felt at ease with him. He had a warmth and innocence that was refreshing, and a kind, handsome face that could make one think boyfriend material. His skin was perfect, and I imagined getting lost in it for a night or two, though it was now clear he wasn't that kind of guy. At one point he covered my hand with his, which made me have a tingly moment of the kind of connection I didn't know I had been missing. It wasn't the sloppy, inebriated kissing and grabbing that I was used to in hookups. I was relatively certain that his index finger tracing mine was not an invitation to hop in bed, but to move in and buy furniture.

We were shaken from the trance of our prolonged conversation when my friends flowed into the kitchen to see where I had disappeared to. They were going out to a bar, and I said I'd find my own way home.

"I bet you will," said Pedro with a wink. And under his breath he mumbled, "Bitch."

Anthony and I went back into the living room, now looking like a disaster zone, and the crowd had significantly dwindled. Anthony did a quick sweep of the house and decided his friend had already left. "Do you need a ride home?" he asked.

That would be the easy option, but I wasn't looking forward to an awkward goodnight. Invite in or not? Kiss or not? "I live in Potrero Hill. I'm sure it's out of your way."

"Not really. I live in the East Bay, so I can get on the freeway from there."

Public transportation at that hour was depressing and a cab would be expensive. "Okay. Thanks."

We sat in his car in front of my building. "It was kind of you to drive me home." It sounded like a very nonsexual gentlemanly thing to say. I had one hand on the door latch, hoping for a graceful exit.

"I'd really like to see you again," said Anthony.

"Yeah. Maybe. I don't know."

"But we have so much in common."

"It was great talking to you. But I'm not looking for anything. I can tell you're a relationship person, and when you say you want to see me again, what I'm hearing is you want this to go somewhere."

His downcast eyes gave me a power I didn't want. "I get it. You're not into me."

"I like you a lot. But I'm not looking. I haven't been involved with anyone for a long time and that's fine with me."

"You're such a nice guy. I can't believe you wouldn't want someone in your life. I don't necessarily mean me, but someone."

"I don't, okay? That doesn't make me a freak or less of a person." I couldn't believe we were having the relationship conversation a couple of hours after we met.

"Sorry. I'm not saying that."

It was the goodnight I had wanted to avoid. I couldn't wait to get out of the car. He didn't try to kiss me. Why would he when I had my arms crossed in front of me like a coat of armor? I felt like such a jerk that when he asked for my number I agreed.

He called and texted me over the next couple of weeks. Sometimes I took his calls, and he made me laugh with his stories about the restaurant where he worked, the crazy things that customers did and how the servers found subtle ways to get back at rude diners. Yes, we did have things in common, and as we talked, I remembered the party and the sleeves of his polo shirt gripping his biceps, the feel of his hand on mine, and the shape of his body as I walked behind him into the living room. I let myself fantasize about how it would be in bed with him. I imagined traveling together, spending the day exploring the back alleys and hidden places of a city, and then share a hotel bed wrapped in each other's arms all night. I guessed he was a cuddler and kisser, leading me to visualize exploring his body, running my tongue up and down his silky brown skin. Stop! All those delicacies came at a price. I enjoyed my freedom. Traveling alone and living alone had its advantages. Relationships were complicated.

Anthony wore down my defenses, not with a battering ram, but brick by brick. I agreed to go out to dinner with him and let him order us a meal. I still remember it because he took the time to explain the ingredients and how they were prepared and why the combinations worked. He was charming and funny, and this time when he put his hand on mine, we interlaced fingers, and I didn't fight the rush it sent up and down my body.

In the next few months, everything I had imagined—the hidden places in strange cities and cuddles in hotel beds—came to pass. He taught me to trust again. I revealed my status, and he handled it without the slightest bit of drama. I tried to tell him about my checkered past, but he wouldn't have it. He said he had all the information he needed, and the past was the past. Having someone who accepts you just the way you are is nothing to take lightly. When we got to the moment of revealing our ages on that first real date, we were both surprised. I had guessed he was a good ten years younger, but it was only five. And when he said I looked a lot younger than my years, I knew it wasn't one hundred percent flattery because I had been hearing it my whole life. My good genes had managed to counterbalance the years of drugs, HIV, and the emotional ups and downs. I had reached my mid-fifties, already living years beyond my expectations and it looked like I was going to be around for a while longer. I was being given a chance at love, maybe my last chance. Why not take it?

In learning about Anthony's past, I realized he had done quite a lot of living himself and wasn't the innocent babe in the woods

I had imagined at first. In his work life of restaurants and hotels, he often joined his co-workers at bars and discos, knocking back drinks and paying the price the day after. Some of those party nights must have led to liaisons of the sexual variety. But maybe it was what I wanted to believe, so my past didn't look so depraved in comparison. When we met, he worked in a high-end restaurant in Berkeley, and he assured me his wild nights had for the most part been put to rest. Turning fifty had hit him hard. It was time to realize his dream, and with a couple of friends, the plans for having their own restaurant began to materialize.

Anthony and I got married in June of 2008 during the brief window when marriage licenses were issued in California before the haters took away the right in the same November election where Obama made history. Though our marriage remained valid, it did put a small stain on the celebration of sending a Black man to the White House. Soon after we moved into our house, we sat on our new imitation mid-century modern L-shaped sofa and bawled our eyes out as we watched the Obama family take the stage on election night. I had gone from a cynical confirmed player when I met Anthony to a married homeowner with a mortgage in the suburbs. What was next? Kids?

I took in the expression on Anthony's face as he watched someone who looked like him ascend to the presidency and couldn't check the "audacity of hope" I felt. It was the same sensation I'd had when Nick and I moved to San Francisco and got involved in the campaign to elect Harvey Milk as part of a citywide movement toward progressive politics and racial equality. And then I'd felt it a second time when we moved to Spain, work contracts in hand, to pursue our dream of living in Europe and leave the pain of the United States behind. Remembering what had happened in both circumstances sent a jolt of disquiet through me. I got up off the sofa and went into the dark kitchen where I stood at the window and downed a glass of water. Anthony came in and flipped on the light. "You okay, babe?"

"Yeah, sure. The moment just got to me. Maybe we can relax a little bit about the way of the world." He wrapped his arms around me, and our bodies heaved with a new round of weeping. I loved the feel of him, the smell of him, and his fierce way of loving.

Our relationship lasted a presidential term. Anthony and I had met about a month after Obama announced his candidacy in 2007 and were together until disaster struck almost at the end of Obama's first term. The night of the 2012 election I sat on the same sofa alone, this time with two reasons to weep. I was grateful that despite the rise of white supremacist and right-wing forces, the country decided to stick with the Black man. But it was painful that I couldn't share with my husband the re-election of the first president who came out in support of gay marriage.

It was cruel losing someone in the prime of a relationship, and in such a freakish manner. I could easily have fallen into an even worse depression than I did, paranoid that opening my heart to someone always ended in disaster. But the legacy of Anthony was that two middle-aged men could take vows, buy a house together, and live in relative harmony, side by side caring for and supporting each other, laughing and doing fun things as a couple, jetting off to see the world. I came from the generation of gay men, many of whom decried the pursuit of same-sex marriage, warning against trying to emulate heteronormativity. It was Anthony that first proposed the idea that same-sex marriage was a rebellious act. We weren't trying to copy heterosexuals; we were demanding the same rights they had. And the way right-wingers got all frothy at the mouth about it proved that Anthony was right.

Anthony had paved the road for me to even consider that Mateo was worth the effort. Admittedly, that day I stalked Mateo at the hospital had a lot to do with the disconcerting sexual pull he had over me, that desire to rip his clothes off every time I saw him. But among the many things my experience with Anthony taught me, was the need for patience, that staying with something could lead to unexpected treasures. And Mateo, for his part, seemed adept at playing the impetuous sex card and the romantic card at the same time.

Putting things in perspective with Mateo didn't give me an answer as to what my next move should be or if any move should be made at all. I focused on a simpler task. I went into the kitchen and took some ground turkey out of the freezer. I found a couple of jars of marinara sauce and a box of lasagna noodles in the cupboard, very likely bought by Anthony months ago. I put them all out on the counter. A few things were missing. I hopped in the car to the local gourmet market a few blocks away and came home with mozzarella cheese, ricotta cheese, parmesan cheese, fresh spinach, salad ingredients, and a baguette to make garlic bread. I set to work making two large lasagna dishes, one for me to eat over the next week and one for Mateo and Carmen. I divided the baguette and made two garlic breads. While the lasagna was in the oven, I threw together a salad. I tried not to think if there was any particular significance to what I was doing. It was simple. Mateo was banged up physically and his mother banged up mentally. I was being a good neighbor. I sent Mateo a text.

**I'm coming over. I want to give you something.**

**Does it involve a large plastic bag?**

**No. It's something to put in your mouth and hopefully will make you feel better.**

**Do I need to lock my mom in her room?**

**I'm glad you said that and not me.**

**I'm a bad son. Forget I said that.**

**It's something to eat. I'm afraid you aren't getting enough nourishment.**

**The nourishment I need is to see your face.**

**You must be really, really bored.**

***Sí, cariño.* And it would be great to see you. One thing is not related to the other.**

***Hasta pronto.***

In the bedroom, I went through several changes of outfits until I got on my own nerves. "You're going over to drop off some food, for Christ's sake," I shouted at the mirror.

I arrived at his apartment with the salad in one paper grocery bag and the lasagna and garlic bread in the other. He opened the door with a big smile. "Come in," he said. "I suppose you'll be wanting a tip."

I gave him my best dumb, innocent delivery boy look. "No. I want the whole thing."

He burst into laughter and looked over his shoulder down the hall.

I clapped a hand over my mouth. "Shit!" I whispered. "Sorry. Your mom?"

"She's watching TV in her room. She usually has the volume up high. You are a nasty boy."

"I'm afraid it's the effect you have on me." I cleared my throat. "Okay, then. Let me carry these into the kitchen."

"What is it?" he asked.

I put the bags on the counter and turned around. He was so close behind me we ended up nearly bumping noses. "It's lasagna. You probably should heat it up for ten minutes." He stared at me so sweetly I wanted to slap him. "And there's a salad and garlic bread."

"I'm wondering about the salt and fat content of this meal."

"All right, smarty pants. I put very little salt in it. The meat is lean ground turkey, and the ricotta is low fat."

"You do know that lasagna is one of my favorite things. And I can eat the garlic bread because you won't be around after. I would ask you to stay, but Mom isn't having a good day."

"That's fine. I'm looking forward to a relaxing evening at home."

"Lucky you."

He was still standing close. "I guess I'm ready for my tip now," I said in a low voice.

"It will have to be the tip of my tongue 'cause..." He leaned in and kissed me. The kiss turned into a little more than expected, and, as if in a scene from a Hitchcock film, we separated, and with a screeching violin soundtrack in my head, we turned to see his mother in the doorway.

"*Mijo,*" she said in a heartbreaking voice. She did an about-face and went back toward her room.

Mateo threw his head back and looked toward the ceiling. "*Madre de Dios!*"

"Sorry," I said. "I feel terrible."

"Not your fault."

"What are you going to do?"

"Eat dinner, I guess. Thanks for the food."

"I'll talk to you later." I went one way toward the door, and he went the other toward his mom.

"*Mami, donde estas?*"

# Chapter 22

The gods smiled on Anthony and me again a couple of years after we moved into our house. Or better said, the gods smiled on Anthony because it wasn't the best thing for our relationship. The owner of the restaurant where Anthony was the chef decided to sell. Anthony and his two partners pooled their resources and jumped at the chance, making an offer to buy the business.

I had taken an early retirement to pursue my dream of producing a collection of my poems and to be available for the trips Anthony and I constantly talked about and researched. We had a giant map on the wall dotted with green pins on places only I had been, red pins for places only Anthony had been, and blue ones for places we had been together. One night, before the opportunity to buy the restaurant came up, Anthony arrived home disgusted. The owner had nixed some of the changes he wanted to make to the menu, a customer had sent back a plate of perfectly cooked food, and he'd had to reprimand one of the line cooks because of a screw-up. "I've had it," he said. "Let's move to Portugal."

Portugal was one of the places we had visited together and loved. He had been impressed by the food scene there. "Would that you were serious, my love," I said.

"I am."

The idea excited me, but I knew his moods. His frustration would pass, and he would backpedal, but for the moment we could dream. We spent the next hour discussing how much we could get for our house, what we would do, and where we would live in Portugal. I went to sleep with visions of our new life back in Europe, walking the hilly streets of Porto and stopping in a bodega for a glass of port, coming across an outdoor restaurant in a little plaza in the Alfama neighborhood of Lisbon like we once did, finding a hidden beach along the craggy coast of the Algarve. The following week the owner of the restaurant called him in to say he was selling in case Anthony and his partners were interested. Our Portuguese castle on a rocky mountain against a blue sky fell to ruin overnight.

Travel plans no longer came up in conversation, and every waking hour he wasn't working, Anthony met with his partners. Though our love was strong enough to weather the inevitable changes not only to our daily routine but our future, I had to constantly make an effort not to feel disappointed. At the same time, I knew if he didn't pursue his dream, the resentment on his part and the guilt on mine might grind us down. I took a part-time teaching job, more to fill time than to supplement my retirement, and used the nights home alone to write.

I resented those solitary nights, though a good bout of writing tended to mitigate the loneliness, and I chastised myself for being petty. But many nights when the writing wasn't going well, and boredom set in, I fell into the disappointment of the great distance we were from how I thought our life would be. Enter some motherfucker who thought his beef with society or an ex-employer or ex-girlfriend (or maybe it was the ex-girlfriend with the beef—we always assumed it was a man) combined his anger with a gun, causing Anthony's death. The months following the accident, I would have gladly traded a thousand nights of being home alone for one when I knew he would be returning, and I didn't care what time. True loneliness was not just feeling lonely, but not knowing if there was ever an end to it. Still, humans are good at adapting to horrific realities. In the weeks before meeting Mateo, I had stopped waking up in the middle of the night sure I had heard Anthony's key in the lock. The adaptation had become complete.

When I realized there was a mutual attraction between Mateo and me, the part of me that had been coddled and allowed to develop by the certainty Anthony would always come home to me started to live again. I had been spoiled by the assumption that a relationship meant you spent the night together. I didn't expect that Mateo and I would be having nightly snuggle fests, but the craving for an occasional all-nighter had been awakened and promised, a craving that was not being fed and didn't look like it was going to be anytime in the near future. Aren't two people having sex but never spending the night together just fuck buddies? And that was the trouble with habits and cravings and expectations and assumptions. They took on a life of their own and often led you down the road to disappointment.

About halfway through Mateo's recuperation period, I got a call from Cindy saying Marcelo had a business meeting in Oakland and they could swing by San Leandro for lunch. If Mateo was available, she'd love to meet him. I made a reservation at Paradiso and asked Mateo if he would be able to join us. He got Luisa to stay with his mom, and I picked him up.

"Don't you look handsome," he said. "This person must be very important to you."

I had no words to explain the significance of Cindy in my life. This would be the fourth man I was involved with that she had met, and it was a bit like taking him home to meet my mother, especially since I no longer had a mother to take him home to. But the focus wouldn't be all on me and my new squeeze as she was also introducing me to her new beau.

When Cindy and I kissed, she whispered in my ear. "How do you do it?"

"What?"

"Another wow boyfriend."

"You're not doing so bad yourself, cradle robber."

"Well, that's the pot calling the kettle beige." It was one of our favorite lines from *The Boys in the Band.*

We eased into the conversation with Marcelo saying he was from Brazil and Mateo from Colombia, and I said something stupid in a rapper accent like, "South America in da house."

"This may sound weird," said Mateo, "but you don't look Brazilian." Marcelo was tall and blond and had blue eyes. He was striking. I gave Mateo a little kick in the ankle.

"That's because my grandparents were Nazis," he deadpanned. Mateo and I let out twitchy chuckles. "It wasn't a joke. It's a fact I must live with. Lots of Germans went to southern Brazil after the war. My mother was just a little girl. My grandparents tried to hide their past, but she found out. Not surprisingly she married my father, a rebellious young union activist from an old Portuguese family. My grandparents had a fit."

"Sorry. I didn't mean to bring up bad memories," said Mateo.

"Not at all, Mateo," Marcelo said with a sweet smile and his very Brazilian accent, despite his Germanic looks. "I don't mind talking about it because we must face our pasts in order not to repeat it, right?"

"What was your meeting in Oakland?" I asked Marcelo.

"I work for a foundation that funds the creation of urban gardens and organizes intercity kids to work in them. We want to partner with a group in Oakland."

"They have a fundraiser at Chez Panisse coming up," said Cindy. "We should all go."

"That's brilliant work," I said. "It's great to hear that not everyone on the peninsula is into making money hand over fist." I glanced at Mateo, struggling to cut the chicken breast he ordered. "Here, let me help you."

"I'm fine." He got irritated every time I tried to help him, a stubborn streak that occasionally showed itself. I smiled awkwardly at Cindy.

"And about your work, Mateo?" said Marcelo. "It must be terribly difficult in the emergency room."

I knew the off-work Mateo, the sweet, fun, and sometimes overly sensitive man sitting beside me. The working Mateo, I had a feeling, was intense, strong, no-nonsense, not fazed by large quantities of blood, broken bones, and grotesque injuries I could only imagine. I wouldn't have lasted five minutes in the ER.

"It is, but right now I'm missing it a lot." He lifted his arm still in a sling. "This is so boring."

"I try to help. When he lets me," I said.

"Nathan has been very sweet. He helps me take out the garbage." He looked at me and smiled. I dropped my hand into his lap and squeezed.

"I hear you play soccer," said Marcelo.

Mateo turned to me. "So, you tell Cindy everything?"

"You're the one who brought up taking out the garbage."

Cindy and Marcelo looked confused. "Sorry," I said. "Inside joke. Or outside joke, really...never mind."

"Ignore him," said Mateo. "Did you play in Brazil?"

"I played in school. I admire you for keeping up with it. That must be what keeps you in such fine shape." Cindy and I shared a raised eyebrow look. "What?" said Marcelo. "I can't comment on another man looking good?"

"Of course you can, sweetheart," said Cindy. "And I love that you feel comfortable doing it."

"Hey, Mateo, can I get your number?" Marcelo winked at him and laughed.

"I'm kind of seeing someone right now," said Mateo. "But if it doesn't work out..."

"Well, this is awkward," said Cindy.

Marcelo turned and kissed her. "I'm happy with this woman."

"Anyway," said Cindy. "We should all exchange our information, so we can coordinate on the Chez Panisse fundraiser."

On the drive back, Mateo said he loved Cindy, and I was lucky to have someone like that during the many, many, many years of my life.

"Watch it, buster. I'm surprised you noticed as you were staring at Marcelo so much."

Mateo giggled with delight. "You're jealous. But, of course, I was not staring. Well, maybe a little, since he is so charming and handsome."

"It's funny, well, not funny for her, but Cindy has a tendency to fall for men that are gay or bisexual."

"Do you think he is?"

"She swears he's not."

"I think it's a good sign that straight men can joke with gay men. It shows they are comfortable with who they are."

I couldn't help but think of Vladimir and how he went beyond joking, beyond flirting, to the point of abusing...in a psychological way.

***

With time, a nodule formed on Mateo's clavicle where the bones fused together, his ribs no longer hurt, and scar tissue formed pink medallions on the brown skin of his leg and arm. Until that happened, we had shared several stolen kisses, making sure we couldn't be seen by Carmen, had a few mutual jackoff sessions in my car in the far corner of his building's parking lot, and engaged in the occasional sexting to climax.

"My doctor said I can drive now," Mateo told me by phone one evening.

"That's nice," I said, determined not to get my hopes up.

"I can dr...ive!" He dragged out the word, obviously trying to communicate a message I was too dense to understand.

It was like we were sixteen and had to speak in code to plan the long anticipated first fuck. Even though it wasn't the first, it had been so long, it felt like it. "Would you be dr...iving over here?"

"Saturday night. I'm starting back to work on Monday. This is it, *querido.*"

I didn't ask if it would be a bump and run or what the arrangements were with his mother or if he wanted me to greet him at the door in a towel wrapped around my waist. I was determined to be very Zen and accept whatever happened, even the possibility that it might not happen at all. "If you're ready, I'm ready."

"You don't sound very excited."

"If you could see me, you'd know that I am."

"Hey, save it for me. Don't touch yourself until you see me."

"I'm all yours, baby."

Of course, I was excited, but why did I feel like I was playing a game? And then my next thought was that it's all a game à la Shakespeare's "All the world's a stage, and all the men and women merely players." The speech from *As You Like It* also came to mind, "and one man in his time plays many parts." I often felt Mateo was a master at playing many parts, combining the humility of a mature man with the raw emotion of youth, the loyalty of middle age with the playfulness of the child. That first day I met him, I saw his mood change several times with matching facial expressions, but I wouldn't call him moody in the negative sense. It seemed that a bundle of emotions inside him were vying for position. I had told Cindy that he was complicated, but that wasn't quite right because through it all, the ups and downs, the back and forths, one thing remained constant and simple: his inexplicable attraction to me. Every time I saw him, he acted genuinely happy to see me, and if he was acting, it was the truest performance I had ever seen.

And that was how he arrived at my door on Saturday evening, simple and complicated and bright-eyed and playful and humble and ready to give me all. He took my breath away, not just because of his beauty, but I was also in awe of how he kept all those disparate parts together. He quickly shut down my chattering brain by pushing me inside up against a wall and kissing me with tenderness and uncontrolled desire at the same time.

I tried not to think about how much time we had. He didn't seem to be in a rush. I thought about asking him if I could count his freckles, which might have kept him there into the next week. He let me kiss his body from toe to head, running my lips over his scars, his healing bones, and then the parts of him that were most calling for attention. We rubbed our bodies together and made animal noises and gripped each other's hands so tight our knuckles hurt, and we squeezed sweat from each other's flesh and licked the sweat and spread saliva everywhere and thrust and met the thrust and grasped and edged time after time until we couldn't stand it anymore. For moments we entered the cliché zone of two bodies becoming one, where I ran my hand on skin I didn't know if it was his or mine, but of course it was his because it felt like silk and I opened my eyes to see him staring at me, wanting to devour me like he was a boa, and I was the alligator I had seen in a nature video.

We lay in the flickering candlelight, and with my eyes closed, I pictured a pine forest since one of the candles was balsam scented. The violent nature scene had dissipated, and we were now two boys lost in the woods, comforting each other, and bound together for warmth on a bed of pine needles. Neither of us said anything because any words trying to qualify what we had just experienced would have been absurdly inadequate.

I felt a tear escape my eye and begin a long roll down my cheek and somehow he knew without looking and reached up and coated the tip of his index finger with it. "Mateo," I whispered.

"Nathan."

I wanted to say, "I love you" but couldn't. It wouldn't have been untrue. But I was suspicious that it would have been triggered by post-sex bliss. Could I be trusted to say something so profound at that moment? Especially when I was going to start hating him in about five minutes when he began fidgeting and saying he had to go.

He sighed, and I sensed the first twitch. "Don't do it," I said.

"What?"

"Look at the time."

"I'm sorry." He reached for the phone he had left on the night-stand. "It's...I..."

"I know." I felt the bitch coming out.

"I don't want to leave. You must know that."

"Next week I'll be leaving myself for a while." Words were escaping from my mouth and I couldn't seem to stop them.

He untangled himself from me and sat up. "Where are you going?"

"Mexico."

"What? For a few days? A week?"

"Longer."

He jabbed his feet into his underwear. "How long?"

"I don't know."

He stood up, and even though he wasn't tall, he seemed to tower over the bed, casting a giant shadow on the wall. "You're just saying that because you're upset with me."

"No. I've been planning it for a while."

"You mean like before you met me?"

"Yeah." I lied.

"And nothing that's happened makes you want to change your mind?"

"It's not about you."

He had his jeans and T-shirt on now, and I could look at him. His nakedness might have made me lose my resolve.

"But it affects me, Nathan. It affects me a lot."

"You could be a little more sympathetic to my needs after going through a traumatic loss and having to make a lot of decisions that I've been avoiding. Then I met you, and things spiraled out of control. I don't know what I want."

"You seemed pretty certain about an hour ago."

"That was sex. Sex confuses things."

"You just want a fuck buddy, then?" There was anger in his voice, and I had provoked it. It didn't feel good to see him hurt, but I had to take care of myself.

"That's kind of all we're allowed since..."

"Just shut up. I can't listen to any more of your bullshit."

The Mateo emerging in the dim light and rattled atmosphere was one I had never seen before. What did I expect? You poke the tiger, he's going to react. "I didn't mean..."

He stood in the doorway, half out of the room, his body trembling with anger. "I have to take care of my mother. Don't you see that?"

"Yes," I said weakly.

"Have a nice trip!" His shoes pounded the wood of the hall on the way to the front door. I got out of bed.

"Mateo!"

The door slammed.

Asshole boyfriend me. Or more likely, asshole ex-boyfriend. I didn't expect him to be thrilled about my trip, but I was stunned by his violent reaction. I never imagined him to be the door slamming type. All right, my timing was shit. And maybe I did want to get back at him for leaving after one of the best sexual experiences of my life, definitely in the top five. And maybe I did just want a fuck buddy (hahaha, a fuck buddy at my age) because anything else got too convoluted. And yes, I thought he should have cut me some slack since my life had recently gone through yet another catastrophic episode, and I was still trying to figure it out. But what really set him off was my implication of the obvious. His mother's condition stood in the way of us having anything resembling a natural progress toward being boyfriends for real. My reservations for Mexico were made. I hated leaving with anger hanging in the air, but a break was probably a good idea.

# Chapter 23

From the balcony of my hotel room, I had a bird's-eye view of a monumental 17th century basilica painted saffron yellow and trimmed in rust red that matched the massive dome. Below me in the Plaza de la Paz, a group of troubadours with guitars, mandolins, and tambourines, sporting medieval outfits of black velvet jackets with puffy sleeves and white leggings, serenaded a group of people. They belted out a traditional song that a minute later was drowned out by the three layers of bells of the church tower ringing the hour. Beyond the church, the hills had turned golden, and the houses tumbled down the hill in every color imaginable, as if a backdrop colored by a group of schoolchildren told to use every color in a box of crayons. I took an emotional breath and tasted the magic of travel.

I had chosen Guanajuato, a city in Mexico unknown to me, but particularly important was that it wasn't somewhere I had been with a partner, not wanting memories to distract me from a total disconnect from my life. Guanajuato was perhaps a strange choice, a city where one of its biggest tourist attractions was a museum of mummified corpses in glass cases, the poor souls having been kicked out of their tombs when the families couldn't pay the grave tax. My grandmother always used to say there were only two things certain in life: death and taxes. In the Guanajuato graveyard, it seemed, taxes were a certainty even after death.

I hadn't seen or spoken to Mateo since the night he stormed out. The evening before I left, I sent him an apologetic text and told him I would be flying out the next day to central Mexico and would be posting photos on social media if he cared to follow my trip. He didn't respond.

I also sent a text to Cindy saying that I would be away. I didn't call because I knew she would detect something in my voice, and I would probably blurt out the story of what happened with Mateo. I didn't want her to know. She texted back.

**Won't Mateo miss you?**

**Idk. But he's cool with me going.**

I wondered if she could discern my lies even in a text.

**Don't stay away too long. He's a keeper. Don't screw it up.**

Too late. I had already screwed it up. I planned to indulge in my healthy drug of travel and try not to think about home.

Coming in from the airport, the taxi dipped into what I thought was a tunnel, but it soon felt like we had descended into Dante's first circle of hell. When we came to a stoplight and the underground passage branched off in various directions, it was obviously not a modern version of the torturous afterlife but unsettling, nonetheless. Upon seeing my stunned reaction in the rearview mirror, the driver grinned and explained Guanajuato was known for its series of nine underground tunnels with intersections and footpaths that diverted traffic under the historic city center. It reminded me of the ant farm I had as a kid where I watched troops of ants scurrying about from one end to the other.

From my hotel room I saw another city hotspot, the mammoth statue of El Pipila high on the opposite hill, offering the best views of the city. I headed out in the golden light of late afternoon and walked to the foot of the hill, where I ascended the small mountain via funicular. At the top, I learned the story of this Mexican revolutionary hero. No wonder the figure was so huge. El Pipila, as the story from 1810 goes, strapped a flat stone on his back to ward off bullets while approaching the Spanish garrison and lit the main entrance on fire, allowing the rebels to enter, thus starting the war of independence from the Spanish. In Spain I had grown to love the Spanish people and their culture. Back in the New World, they were the bad guys, and their acts of cruelty throughout Latin America were legendary.

I wanted to visit the site of El Pipila's heroic act, but it was too late in the day. Instead, I tagged along behind one of the many *callejoneadas* where groups of troubadours led gangs of tourists through the narrow streets and alleys, entertaining them with songs, stories, and legends. We ended up at the Alley of the Kiss, so narrow that while standing on a balcony on one side, you could kiss your loved one on the balcony opposite, guaranteeing seven years of happiness together.

"Why seven?" asked one of the tourists.

The leader of the troubadour band with a twinkle in his eye brought up *la picazón de los siete años* or seven-year itch. Nothing was guaranteed after seven years. I thought sadly how Mateo and I hadn't even made seven months.

Then the group leader put on an exaggerated sad face and told us the "true" story of El Callejon del Beso, involving a tragic Romeo and Juliet type legend where the girl was stabbed by her own father for disobedience. How dare she fall in love with a young man from the lower classes!

"How could a visit to the location of that tragedy end up leading to seven years of happiness?" someone asked.

"What tourists would come to this alley and kiss their loved ones if they knew the real story beforehand?" the young man said with a laugh. "Okay. Who's going to be the first to give it a go? Pucker up."

That night I went to sleep, thinking about this city of color, mystery, music, secret alleys of legend, revolutionary heroes, and a bizarre fascination with death. What was not to love?

The following day I paid homage to El Pipila by visiting the site of the first battle between the insurgents and the Spanish at the Alhondiga de Granaditas. It was now a museum, and I got lost in the emotional murals of Jose Chavez Morado. The Spanish, in dark clothes with somber expressions, did not come out well at all in those murals.

I saved the mummies for my last day in Guanajuato and almost became one of them. The taxi I hailed in the plaza below my hotel took me off the main road on a winding street into the hills outside the center of town. I paid my entrance fee for the pleasure of seeing emaciated corpses of desiccated skin, hollow cheeks, wisps of hair still clinging to scalps, a few yellowed teeth protruding from prominent jaws, and dusty burial clothes like a fashion show from *Night of the Living Dead.* These were the poor devils not only thrown out of their graves, but their remains were never claimed by relatives.

One was a French doctor who had spent years taking care of the medical needs of the townspeople, but because he had no family to pay the grave tax, he was disinterred, stored in a warehouse, and eventually put on display in a glass case where people were charged to see him. The doctor's story was sad enough, but there were also several children on display, one still in a silk dress possibly used for a christening and another in a powder blue sweater. A sad poem ambled through my head, and I couldn't wait to get back to the hotel to jot down my thoughts.

I left the museum, exhausted after days of walking from morning until night, wandering up and down hills through alleys and squares and parks. I stepped into the burning sun, unusually hot for October, shaken after my bizarre museum visit and with a sick feeling in my stomach. Not only had I missed breakfast and set out on an empty stomach, but I had also forgotten my water bottle and none of the souvenir stands sold anything useful, like a cold drink.

The museum had been almost empty, so it was not surprising there were no taxis. My head was spinning, and I sat on the curb at the edge of the parking lot without shade, hoping for a taxi to pass. After twenty minutes, I gave up and started walking, thinking it would be better than waiting in the sun and it wouldn't be strenuous as it was all downhill. Undoubtedly, I would come across a corner store where I could buy water or Gatorade.

I plodded through poor neighborhoods with mangy dogs and children in tattered clothes staring at me, but no one bothered me. After a mile of the winding road with no shade, no taxis, no stores, I sat on a low wall to rest. I felt tinges of panic and wondered if I should ask someone for help. I could see that I was still a good distance above the town, but not knowing what else to do, I stood up and continued walking. A couple of times I stumbled on rocks and nearly lost my balance. In my stupor I had the sensation of walking in place, making no progress, and with no sidewalk to guide me, I didn't know if I was going in the right direction. Sweat coated my forehead and rolled down my torso under my clothes.

I weaved on the edge of drop-offs where a misstep could send me tumbling down a precipice, and the view of surrounding hillsides blurred in front of me. A dog across the street transformed into a wolf before my eyes, and I imagined being attacked and dragged into the woods. After several more minutes of walking—I had lost all sense of time or distance—I saw an Oxxo sign, the ubiquitous corner store in Mexico, and tears of joy rolled down my cheeks. But when I reached the store, it was empty, abandoned, and my tears of joy turned to tears of utter frustration. I had shortness of breath and a massive headache. I thought of calling Mateo and saying goodbye, telling him I was sorry for running off to Mexico. Maybe the sound of his voice could revive me. I leaned against the wall of the empty store and struggled to take my phone out of my pocket, wondering if 911 worked in Mexico.

I woke up alone in a sparse room with green walls and an IV in my arm. I had a faint memory of being lifted up by some men and putting up a fight. One of them kept saying, "*Tranquilo, hombre.*" I thought they were going to put me in a grave like one of the mummies I had read about in the museum literature. They believed the woman had been buried alive because of the position of her body when they dug her up. Why hadn't I stayed with Mateo and made up with him? I had let my disappointment over him not spending the night, my ambivalence toward the relationship, and my doubts lead me to nearly dying alone in a foreign land, a very lovely country, mind you, with colorful houses and a rich culture.

A nurse told me some men had found me on the ground, put me in a truck, and driven me to the Cruz Roja (Red Cross) on Benito Juarez. Angels again had come to my rescue like the ones who found me many years before, passed out in the mud at the West Palm Beach Pop Festival, and the one who found me when

I overdosed on Seconal after a several-day speed binge in New Orleans. Those two incidents were drug related, but this one was just negligence. I was severely dehydrated, she said, and they wanted to run at least one more bag of fluid into me before letting me go. I was dizzy and sore, most likely from the fall. She asked me a few questions and determined that I probably hadn't hit my head, giving me a concussion.

A couple hours later I was in a taxi back to the hotel where I explained to the receptionist what had happened and asked if someone could pick up some food and a couple of bottles of water for me. I only ate about half the takeout before I stretched out on my bed and entered dreamland. Twelve hours later I awoke to the sound of bells, the chimes at the end telling me it was six in the morning. I had booked a seat on a bus to San Miguel de Allende, a trip of a little more than an hour, but it was too early to go to the bus station. I sent Cindy what I thought was a hilarious email about my pilgrimage to Las Momias de Guanajuato, and how it had been such a frightening experience I had a psychedelic flashback, running through the labyrinth of the museum trying to find my way out while the mummies broke out of their glass coffins and chased after me. It had been so traumatic I passed out and was taken to the Red Cross where I was attended by a strapping young male nurse who sat next to my bed holding my hand and kept asking my name to make sure I was okay. Okay, I embellished the story a bit. She texted me right away.

**I hope this is a joke.**

**Well, most of it. I did go see the mummies and passed out from dehydration. They took me to the Red Cross. The nurse unfortunately was a woman about eighty and reminded me of my second-grade teacher who I was petrified of.**

**I want you to come home right now.**

**I'm fine. Going to San Miguel de Allende today.**

**Why did you lie about Mateo being cool with your trip?**

**OMFG! You contacted him?**

**I had to communicate some updated info about the Chez Panisse fundraiser and just happened to mention something about how he was probably missing you.**

**You are such a liar. You didn't believe me when I said he was on board.**

**He didn't say what happened. Don't want to know. Come home and fix it.**

**He won't answer my texts. I'm better off here. The weather is great, the men are beautiful, and the history is badass.**

**So, when?**

**Idk. Will let you know.**

My humorous email was a mistake. Funny story backfires. I was dying to know what Mateo said to her, but no. I was supposed to be unplugging from home, and since I had a couple of hours before I had to be at the bus station, I went to a travel blog on the Internet. People had a lot to say about San Miguel de Allende, and I couldn't wait to see if it lived up to all the hype.

***

If San Miguel and Guanajuato were sisters, San Miguel was the older, more sophisticated, educated, and impeccably dressed in designer clothes in the red-yellow-orange part of the spectrum. The younger sister wore whatever she wanted in whatever color she felt like, drank a little too much and got sloppy, but everyone loved her because she was so much fun. After having spent a lot of time in the Mission District of San Francisco, I knew something about gentrification. San Miguel was gentrification on steroids, infused with outside money, a lot of it from the States but also rich Mexicans, transforming the colonial buildings into galleries, boutiques, restaurants, and homes for the wealthy. Everything was done with taste and design, attention to detail and art, combining traditional with modern in a dizzying display of beauty.

My hotel was a restored colonial home just outside the center, with one of the rooms being in the former chapel. Since the place was nearly empty, they had given me the chapel room with appropriately lofty ceilings, religious artifacts for décor, a fireplace, a bathroom tiled from floor to ceiling, and a giant canopied bed fit for a king. I appreciated their offering me the primo room, but I asked to change to a humbler one, much to the surprise of the young woman who checked me in. I felt I would have to pray on my knees each night at the side of my bed and confess my sins, which would take a lot longer than I wanted to spend on my knees, and once I got into bed, I was sure bats and the ghosts of saints would be flying around the rafters. The simpler room I took had a balcony facing spectacular sunsets every evening.

In the last minute of packing my bags for the trip, I had thrown in a few copies of my poetry book, *Faces Take Me Places.* Sales had been rather dismal, not that I expected a best-seller book of poems, but there was always the possibility of getting the book into the right hands, a person who might make it fly, and it could happen anywhere. What if fate had me sitting next to Maya Angelou on the plane and I gave her a copy of my book? What if I ran into Ocean Vuong coming out of a restaurant in Guanajuato and I slipped him a copy?

I had read about the Biblioteca Pública or Public Library in San Miguel. It was not just a library with a huge collection of books in English and Spanish, but a cultural center with a courtyard café, theater, and bookstore, making it a place that seemed a bit like heaven on earth with people sitting in patios surrounded by books and murals and fountains. On my first day in town, I rushed over to this cultural oasis.

The director agreed to see me and examined my book, commenting on the striking cover of multiple faces representing various ages, ethnicities, and expressions. She told me that book events had to be organized months in advance, but they had a bilingual poetry group that met on Wednesdays, and she gave me the name of the facilitator who might let me join the group. I was honored he agreed to allow me to sit in as a guest poet.

The gathering was a mix of foreigners and Mexicans, mostly people my age, but a few younger ones. I introduced myself in Spanish and English. Each person in the group read a couple of poems and the others commented. First, I read a humorous poem I had written in Spanglish, which came from listening to a couple of Puerto Ricans I overheard on a subway in New York City. Then I read a more serious one about watching the twenty-one emotions a Black person's face (Anthony's) went through on election night in 2008. When I finished and looked up, I noticed a young man with a head of jet-black hair, very thick and very straight, staring at me with doe eyes as if I was generating a light that he couldn't escape from.

After we finished the serious part of the gathering, they served tea and cookies, and I spoke with several of the group members, none of whom seemed like a poet laureate who might review my book for the New York Times, but lovely people, nonetheless. The young man approached me with soft brown eyes framed by extra-long lashes and told me how much he had enjoyed my poems. His name was Carlos. He wanted to buy my book if I had any to sell. Taken by his earnest approach and Donatello model face, I offered to give him one, but I didn't want to do it in front of the others as I only had a couple of copies.

"Then I should come to your hotel to retrieve it?" Carlos said a slow deliberate English, finishing with a bit of tongue sliding over his thick lower lip.

"How about we meet in a café? Perhaps you can recommend one."

"Yes, of course. And then I can take you to some of my favorite places." We made a plan to meet the following day, and when the group started to break up, Carlos and I took a selfie where he slipped his arm around my waist. Then we took photos of the group, and of me with various members individually. I left the library and floated back toward the center of town after experience #5385 of why I loved traveling. What could be better than sharing poems with like-minded people in an architectural jewel of a city in an enchanting country and making a new fan in the process?

In El Jardin park, I sat on a bench amongst Mexican families and ex-pats, admiring the carefully manicured laurel trees, which in their thick sharp lines reminded me of Carlos's haircut. The square was the beating heart of the town with foreigners basking like iguanas in the sun on the south side and Mexican papis buying balloons for their kids and gossiping grandmas dressed for winter though it was quite warm, leaning into each other with the latest health problems of Conchita's cousin's brother. Looming over the square was the iconic church of thousands of photos, the Parroquia de San Miguel de Arcángel—named for the head honcho of the archangels, who cast out Satan—guarding over this little slice of paradise on earth. In contrast to the warrior image of Michael, the church with its pink spires and towers had the appearance of being a fairy castle made of peppermint ice cream. Sitting in the town square amongst the people was #5386 of why I loved traveling.

# Chapter 24

Carlos gave me a nervous wave as I entered the cafe. I ordered a coffee and joined him at the table, where he stood up and hugged me. Nice gesture, but we barely knew each other. I presented him with the signed copy of the book, and he held it to his chest as if he was Moses receiving The Ten Commandments from God. I was both flattered and creeped out, wondering if he was going to start stalking me around the town. With promotion of my book always in the back of my mind, I asked him to pose for a photo as if he was reading the book in the little café at a rustic table with a spot right above him and art on the walls. The staged photo turned out much better than I could have imagined. His angelic face glowed as if the words themselves were heavenly.

When we got to the topic of our personal lives, he told me he had moved to San Miguel to be with his Dutch boyfriend, but the guy had dumped him for someone younger. Younger? Was the man a pedophile into twelve-year-olds? Carlos's family wanted him to come back to Mexico City, but he had fallen in love with San Miguel. I told him I was happily married and flashed my ring, causing scant reaction on his face as if he wouldn't be deterred by a tiny detail like someone being married, happily or not.

A couple of months after Anthony died, I had decided it was time to remove the ring he had put on my finger and keep it in a safe place. It didn't mean I was over mourning or wanted to forget about our brief but happy marriage. I never particularly liked wearing a traditional wedding band and all it represented. The whole idea of marriage, moving to the suburbs, being a responsible gay man in the new order of things was novel for me, but I did it for Anthony and had no regrets.

Before I left on the trip, I took the ring out of the box and slipped it on my finger. It wasn't that I was trying to ward off hordes of young men following me about like the ones that made short work of Sebastian Venable in *Suddenly, Last Summer*. I liked the image of being a married man while traveling, which was ironic since my husband had died and Mateo was no longer in the picture. There was nothing to keep me from having a mad affair except my image of myself as a person too mature to return to the habits of my youth. I honestly hadn't anticipated someone like Carlos where it would seem wearing the ring would come in handy after all. Or not. He didn't seem to care about my age or the ring. He had a whole list of activities he had planned for me and only some of them involved tourism.

The first stop on my personal tour was a giant art shopping mall situated in an old textile factory, La Aurora. The sprawling complex held artist studios, galleries, furniture shops, design studios, and a couple of restaurants. Carlos knew several of the gallery owners, shopkeepers, and furniture salespeople—he admitted the Dutch ex had allowed him to shop and decorate their home—and I cringed when they eyed me as the new sugar daddy. Aside from the awkward feeling, I appreciated the quality of the art and saw lots of pieces I wouldn't mind having if I owned a mansion in Malibu. The prices, too, were more what I would expect in Los Angeles than Mexico.

After lunch at a restaurant in La Aurora, he told me we were going to see the Sistine Chapel of Mexico. It sounded intriguing, but I was already tiring of being constantly in the focus of his adoring eyes, especially since I was suspicious of his intentions. He convinced me it was something I couldn't miss, but after the long taxi ride to the dusty little town of Atotonilco and seeing the stark white walls of the church complex that had the look of a fortress, I questioned his judgment. Once we had passed through the simple arched entrance and I feasted my eyes on the astonishing interior where of every square inch of the walls and ceiling was covered with murals, sculptures, and paintings, I turned to him with a big smile expressing my thanks. In all my travels, I had never seen anything like it. Never a big fan of religious art—these murals elaborately depicted the story of Jesus's life—I did appreciate the sheer ambition and passion of the project, almost inspiring me to be a believer. Okay, I didn't rush to the baptismal font and grab a priest to pour holy water over me, making me part of a worldwide organization that had seriously misinterpreted a good deal of the words of the rebel from Galilee, but I had to admire the church's ability to motivate/cajole/force artists to create great works.

And then Carlos told me we were only viewing a chapel, and the best was yet to come. We passed through a small arch into the nave of the church with three times the amount of wall and ceiling space filled with color, making me feel like I had fallen into a Flemish painting with bearded men wearing long flowing robes who pointed at me, tried to instruct me, invited me to sit at a banquet table to make me one of them. The experience fell short of an epiphany, but I was thankful that Carlos had shown me this marvel, though not so thankful that I reciprocated when he tried to take my hand while we were sitting in one of the pews with our necks back gazing at the ceiling.

"Uh, I'm married, remember?" I whispered.

"So?" He giggled. "Is your husband here?

When we returned to San Miguel, I told Carlos I was going back to the hotel and thanked him for the day. It was almost time for the sunset, and I had made it a ritual to watch the sun go down every evening from my balcony. I reminded Carlos once again that nothing was going to happen between us.

"At least I have your book," he said with downcast eyes. "And I'll follow you on social media."

I sat on the balcony and watched the clouds and sun create a palette as spectacular as the murals I had seen earlier, and for brief moments clouds became bearded men in long robes with mouths open, pointing at me as if they had something to tell me. I imagined Mateo sitting in the empty chair next to me, sharing the moment.

I had spent the day with an attractive young man and felt nothing beyond friendship. But the mere thought of Mateo filled me with longing to feel his touch. I sent him a picture of the sunset with a message that I was thinking of him. He didn't respond. I didn't cry myself to sleep, but I did suffer a fairly serious bout of melancholy, missing his playfulness and even the spats. I fantasized an extravagant makeup sex scenario, knowing it probably wasn't going to happen. Missing someone who was likely lost to me made me reiterate my desire to sell the house and leave San Leandro behind.

I returned to Guanajuato for a couple more days, and then headed back to the Leon airport. I had been gone for two and a half weeks, which was about the limit my budget could sustain until I made some of the financial decisions I had been thinking about.

My flight home was delayed, and an annoying person sat next to me in the center seat. He couldn't sit still and kept making me get up so he could go to the restroom without once apologizing. I did not arrive in Oakland in a good mood.

I passed through customs, gathered my luggage, and exited the doors to the lobby of the airport with my head down. The feeling of someone watching me made me look up. A man that looked very much like Mateo stood at the waiting gate. It was surely a mirage created by my tired eyes. I blinked and forced my eyes open. Damn! Mateo was awaiting me. There is no feeling quite as wonderful as coming home from a trip and seeing the person you have missed there to pick you up. I wanted to get down on my knees and make a scene in the airport, begging his forgiveness for abandoning him. In my joy, I was oblivious to the decidedly stern look in his eyes. I approached him and pulled him into a hug. He was stiff. I stepped back.

"How did you...? Ah, Cindy." He neither smiled nor said a word. Something was wrong. Was he here to assassinate me rather than take me home? "You came to pick me up but won't hug me? What's going on?"

His blank face worked its way into a searing glare. He pulled out his cell phone and with trembling fingers, opened Facebook and jab-scrolled through photos. Arriving at the one he wanted, he thrust it in my face. It was the pic of Carlos with his arm around me at the poetry gathering. Taking the phone back, he scrolled to the picture of Carlos sitting in the café reading my book. "Who is that?" he growled.

I had about fifteen emotions doing battle inside me. He had come to pick me up and was being emotional, which were pretty good indications that he loved me or at least had strong feelings.

He was confronting me as if he were my boyfriend, which made me angry, and he was doing it with a lot of people around, which was embarrassing. In a matter of seconds, he had thrown a wrench into my all-night pondering and laid-out plans to leave San Leandro. I was confused and happy and furious and touched.

"Mateo," I said with a big sigh that did a poor job of communicating everything I was feeling. "You didn't answer my texts for three weeks."

"So, you went to Mexico to screw around?"

"Nothing happened. He was some wide-eyed kid who thought he had met a famous poet. He showed me around a bit." I realized that he probably showed up in more social media photos than Mateo had pushed in my face.

"Did you offer me a copy of your book? Did you think I wasn't interested? Did you think I couldn't read English?"

He was shouting and people were watching. I grabbed my bags and put one hand on Mateo's back. "Let's start walking out."

He looked around, also becoming aware that we were putting on a show. "Sorry."

"Maybe you should have punched me, so we would have properly entertained them. They're hungry for it." I was able to draw a tiny smile.

"You know I would never do that."

"Just to clarify, you are here to pick me up, right? Or pick a fight?"

"You are so annoying."

"I guess you missed me being annoying so much you rushed to the airport to get a dose of it." I got another grin out of him.

We got outside and he took a deep breath. His eyes trailed back toward the glass doors we had passed through. "Watch this, gawkers!" He took me in his arms and kissed me passionately. As we separated, I swore I heard muffled cheering from inside the terminal.

"Was that for the crowd or for me?"

"This one is for you, my asshole boyfriend...if you want to be my asshole boyfriend." He kissed me again, harder this time.

"I'll try to be less of an asshole if you promise me regular make out sessions, preferably with less of an audience."

"I'm thinking about a lot more than making out. Maybe second base?"

"Not sure what that is, but I'll try it."

***

Mateo pulled his truck into my driveway and sat a minute without saying anything. I wanted him to come in. There was never any doubt about my attraction to him, but I didn't trust my emotions to not fall into our usual pattern of sex, wind down, and then the sense of abandonment when he left. It was a cycle I wanted to avoid. But how?

"Are you coming in?" I asked.

"If you want me to."

"It's not about wanting, but about controlling my feelings when you leave."

He lowered his eyes. "I know. So, I shouldn't come in?"

I reached over and took his hand. "Come in. I got you something." I had bought him a winged heart *milagro* carved out of wood he could hang on the wall for good luck. "Even though I didn't know if I'd see you again."

"Seriously?"

"I had never seen you so angry when you left that night. It frightened me."

"I wasn't so much angry at you but everything. I calmed down and thought about how I should respond to your texts. Then I saw those fucking pictures. You obviously weren't even thinking about me."

"I thought about you a lot. I told that kid I was married, though, to be honest, he didn't seem to care."

He looked at my hand with concern. "I see you're wearing a ring. I never saw this before."

"I thought it might be a good idea while traveling."

"Because you have so many boys trying to get in your pants?"

"Honestly, it's usually the hot grandmas who think I'm the stud they're looking for."

Mateo laughed. "Can we go inside now?"

There was a bundle of accumulated mail on the front porch, and the plant in the cracked pot looked like it had finally gone to meet its maker. Mateo stared at it sadly. "I could have come by and watered it."

"I sent you a text about that, but since you didn't read any of them, look at the results."

"I read every single one, and I'm absolutely sure there was no text about watering your plant."

"My bad." I pushed the door and was hit by the bottled-up smell of loneliness wafting from the house. "I hate that smell when you come back to a house that's been closed up."

"Did you send me a text asking me to stop by and air out the house, too?"

"If you think I'm giving you a key the next time I go away, think again. You'd probably go through all my things and discover my secrets."

His face pinched like I'd just slapped him. "You're going away again?"

I dropped my bags and pulled him toward me. "I was joking. But if I have to go away for a few days like to visit my brother, I will give you a key to water and stuff."

"Stuff like what?"

"Like be waiting for me naked in bed when I return."

"You know better than to say something like that when we're standing this close, and you have your hands on my waist." He put his hands on either side of my face and planted a kiss on my lips. "I almost forgot what it was like to kiss you."

I knew where this could very easily go. I broke away. "Would you like something to drink? There should be some beer in the fridge." That was a subtle way of asking if he was going to stay long enough to drink a beer.

He hesitated and looked at his watch, the simple gesture that provoked an automatic rise in my blood temp. "Sure. And I know what you're thinking. I have a plan."

"A plan? Pray tell. Let me get the beers."

We sat at the island in the kitchen and clinked our bottles. "*Salud!*" we said at the same time.

"I talked to my mom's doctor and told her about our situation."

"You talked to the doctor about us? I wish I could have been there because I'd like to know about us, too."

His face fell. He started to speak a couple of times, but only puffs of air came out. "Would you just listen for once? This is not easy for me."

"Sorry."

"I asked the doctor if in Mom's current state she could grasp that I had needs. She said that Mom's reactions were pure emotion: fear and confusion. The only thing that makes sense to her and makes her feel comfort is having me around, and when I absolutely can't be there, Luisa, who she's known for a long time, is acceptable. The doctor asked if you would be willing to spend more time at my place so that Mom could get more familiar with you. And...this is a big one, we could try having you spend the night. It seemed like such a simple solution. I don't know why I didn't think of it. I would be there if she woke in the night and was frightened. And you would be with me rather than the other side of town, angry with me because I left you alone after sex."

I questioned the word simple. It had been years since I spent the night in someone else's bed, the last time being at Anthony's before we moved in together. I had a frightening image of getting up in the middle of the night to pee and running into Carmen in the hall. It would not go well. "It seems like you've got this all figured out. Do I get a say in it?"

"Of course, you do. But I really think it could work. It's not ideal, but it would give us the chance to spend the whole night together."

"Would they be whole nights of platonic love or could we do things?"

"Personally, I can't imagine spending the night in bed with you and not doing things. I might have to slap my hand over your mouth because you can be kind of noisy."

"Me? What about you?"

"I have self-control, or haven't you noticed?" I thought of the times he was on the verge of orgasm and had pulled back.

"I don't know. It's so like teenagers having a sleepover."

"Please, just say you'll consider it."

I nodded and leaned toward him, putting my head on his chest. "Did she ever say anything about our kiss?"

"Not a word."

# Chapter 25

We set a date for our first sleepover the following Saturday night, and I looked forward to it with both eagerness and dread. I had entered the set-in-my-ways phase of life and kept thinking of all the little things that would be uncomfortable. But since I had made such a big deal about being disgusted with our bump and run encounters, leading to our biggest fight, I couldn't back out of Mateo's plan. I had selfishly always imagined that a whole night together would be at my house and certainly not lying on the other side of the wall from a woman who would most likely rather see me fall off the face of the earth.

That first night of the experiment I entered his room cautiously, careful not to trip over his weights and fall flat on my face or spend too much time critiquing the décor, which had some cool things like the Prince poster and some rather awful things like the striped comforter that looked like it came from Walmart and a dream catcher hanging from a lamp. Yes, a dream catcher!

"That's your side," he said, pointing to the queen-size bed. It was the same side of the bed I always slept on with Anthony. "There's a robe hanging on the closet door in case you have to get up in the middle of the night."

"About that," I said. "You can count on me having to get up, and I'm going to wake you to hold my hand. I am not chancing an encounter in the hallway with your mother and scaring the bejesus out of her."

"*Entendido.* I'll hold anything you want."

"This is serious."

"Okay. I can stand outside the bathroom door while you hold your own thing." He stood on the other side of the bed and took off his shirt. He folded it and put it on a chair in the corner. He did the same with his jeans, but left his underwear on. I followed suit and stood with my clothes in my arms, looking around for where to put them. "Oh. You can put them on the desk chair."

Assuming we survived this trial sleepover, I imagined things would get easier on subsequent occasions, which we agreed would be limited to weekends. What was especially not easy was looking at his almost naked body for the first time in a while and trying to remain calm. "Have you gone back to working out?" I asked.

He rubbed his abs. "You like?"

I quickly got under the covers. "Maybe just cuddling would be best this first time. I'm feeling a little awkward."

He crawled into bed and moved close to me, taking my hand in his. "Yes, it is strange and wonderful at the same time. I will try to behave." We lay in silence for a few minutes, and then he made a move. He leaned over and kissed me, a warm but quick kiss like he was saying goodnight and we had been together for years. Belying the chaste kiss was a significant protrusion in his underwear against my thigh as he half covered me with his body.

"What's this?" I said.

"And you?" He reached down and expertly negotiated the waistband of my underwear. "Yep." His mouth went from nuzzling my neck to whispering in my ear. "Nathan."

In the time we had been preparing for bed, we had heard Carmen lightly snoring on the other side of the wall, giving a good indication how thin the walls were. I removed his hand from my underwear. "I thought we just agreed..."

"*Por favor.*" He said it in a teasing way, but the whisper caressed my ear and telegraphed all the way down to my toes, giving a surge to my dick on the way. He moved one leg in between mine.

We noticed at the same time that the background sound to our heavy breathing had stopped. Carmen was no longer snoring. We froze. Faintly from her room we heard, "Sergio? Sergio?"

Mateo groaned and returned to lying on his back. He threw off the covers and dragged his feet over the side of the bed. "It's okay. I'll be right back."

Carmen may have had a tenuous connection to reality, but she seemed to have a telepathic link with her son. Ten minutes into our experimental sleepover and there was a crisis, hopefully minor. I had never heard of a Sergio but imagined it was her ex-husband.

Mateo's low, soothing voice came from the other room along with what sounded like gentle weeping. I couldn't hear what they were saying except the name Sergio came up again and again. I rolled over and got into my usual fetal sleeping position.

I had drifted off but woke up when Mateo got back into bed. "Everything okay?" I asked.

"For now, but in general not good. Lately she keeps thinking Sergio is in the apartment."

"And Sergio is...?"

"Right. I guess I haven't told you. He was my little brother."

"Was?"

"He only lived until he was five. He was born with a heart defect. Unlike me he wasn't born in the States because it was a difficult pregnancy and Mom couldn't make the trip. She has always been convinced that if he had been born here, he would have had a better chance. She took it very hard. But the disturbing thing is that for years she rarely mentioned him. Lately she wakes up and thinks she hears him crying."

"So, it has nothing to do with me being here?"

"No. I'm not sure she's aware. I explained to her last week that I have someone I care about and I want her to get to know you. I reminded her once again that you were a teacher and brought food and helped me when I was injured. She acts like she understands, but then a couple days later she asks me why I'm not married."

"I assume she means to a woman."

"I dated this girl all through high school and she was very excited about it."

"The girl? I bet she was."

"My mother, tonto."

"You've never told your mother you're gay."

In the dim light coming in the window, I saw him put his hand over his face. "No." His voice was laced with embarrassment. "I mean, she hasn't brought up the marriage thing in a long time, and I don't think it's real. It's just part of her confusion."

"This is absolutely not a proposal, but have you ever thought about getting married...to a man?"

He made a grunt of disgust. "If you could see some of the guys I dated in San Francisco, you'd understand why the answer is a definite no."

"That's the first time you've mentioned dating guys."

"Believe me, I'd rather forget about it. There was one guy while I was in nursing school in Hayward that was worth the effort."

"And?"

"That was when Mom first started having health problems, so I moved back to the city and got a job at Kaiser. My friend didn't want to live in San Francisco. He ended up in Portland."

"I've learned more about you in the last half hour than I have in the couple months we've known each other."

"Now, it's your turn. I don't know much about you except that you've had a super interesting life."

"Oh, man. There's stuff you wouldn't believe."

"It's like that Chinese curse, huh? May you live in interesting times."

"Not to be teachery, and I know that's a widely held belief, but they've never found an equivalent Chinese expression that it derived from. That aside, I've lived some really fucking interesting times and it was hell. But I think we should save that for another night."

"You're right. Mom likes to get up early and sometimes she thinks she can fix her own breakfast. One time she almost caught the kitchen on fire."

"I can see the headlines. Nurse and Former Teacher Set Apartment Ablaze on First Night Spent Together."

"Not funny."

"If we can't rub two sticks together, can we at least snuggle?"

"As long as you keep your moans of pleasure to a minimum."

I turned on my side and he pulled me back against his chest. One arm was thrown over my torso and his breath tickled the back of my neck. I let out a low, pleasurable rumble. "This is better than sex."

"Apples and oranges." He took a soft bite of the back of my neck. "*Buenas noches, amor.*"

Hmm, amor? It wasn't exactly like saying I love you, but confusing, nonetheless. Or just sweet. Or something that rolled off his tongue without thinking. He drifted right into sleep-breathing, abandoning me in the contemplation of those four little letters. Where were we? Where were we going? Was this really what I wanted? The last person who called me amor was Vladimir and look how that ended. It came soft and easy to his lips, too. Should I wake him up and ask what he meant by it? In the quiet, I heard Mateo's breathing, his mother's snoring, and my brain chugging into the long night like a locomotive.

I woke up to the smell of coffee and cool sheets on the other side of the bed when I extended my hand. I had gotten what I wanted, a night of entwined limbs with Mateo, albeit skipping the main event that would have made the after party more delicious, but now I wanted more. Was it too much to ask to begin the day sharing yawns, a joke about a morning woodie, a grin? Right on cue, the left hemisphere of my brain played the devil by introducing logic to the argument. The night had been one small step for man, but hardly a giant leap for mankind, or in this case, Mateo-Nathankind. We were in the same bog of impeded steps toward true amor if that's where we were supposedly going. There was the issue of my personal/financial life that remained as boggy as ever, and my plans to get out of that mess would seem to be counterproductive to a future with Mateo.

Before exiting the bedroom, I got fully dressed. No running around the apartment half-naked on the morning after, teasing each other around the dangers of hot coffee and kitchen counters to be lifted up on or a sink to be bent over.

In the kitchen, Mateo, also fully dressed in sweats, stared at a waffle iron next to a large bowl of batter. "I'm making waffles," he said over his shoulder.

"I see."

My lackluster response made him turn around. "What's the matter?"

"Nothing. Is your mom up?"

"The neighbor took her for a little walk around the neighborhood. She didn't want to go, but it's something they do several times a week. She needs the exercise."

He turned around as if he suddenly realized we were alone in his kitchen after we had spent our first night together. He smiled.

My shoulders relaxed and he gave me a hug, nestled his nose into my neck, and inhaled. "That's nice. Did you sleep okay?" He continued to hold me, and I rested my chin on his head.

"That was nice, too." I was making an effort to pump up my enthusiasm. It didn't seem to be working though I couldn't deny that being in his arms went a long way in soothing my anxiety.

He took a step back. "Are you sure you're okay? I know it wasn't all that it could be, but sleeping next to you and holding you was definitely a plus."

"Definitely."

He searched my eyes with a frown, but seemed determined to keep things light. He backed away and opened a cupboard to take out a mug.

"How do you like your coffee?"

"Black and strong."

"I should have known."

When Carmen came in, we were at the table eating waffles piled high with fresh fruit and drizzled with real maple syrup. Mateo got up to greet her. "*Hola, mami. Todo bien?*"

"*Sí, hijo.*" She glanced at me, and her smile withered.

"You remember Nathan, no? He's been helping us a lot."

I stood up. "*Buenos días, señora.*"

She nodded and, as if it was our first meeting, said, "*Encantada.*" It's polite meaning is charmed, but the way she said it and the expression on her face made it sound like another meaning of being bewitched like I had put a spell on her.

"I made waffles," said Mateo. "Please sit and I'll prepare one for you."

She said she was tired and wanted to go to her room. "*Con permiso,*" she said as she took her leave, the polite phrases showing her education, if not her mood.

Mateo slumped into his chair, picked up his fork, stabbed a strawberry, and stuffed it in his mouth.

"The waffles are really good," I said. "I don't think I can finish, though. It's a lot."

He attempted a smile, but his facial muscles wouldn't cooperate. "Me neither."

"I'll help you clean up."

We danced around in the kitchen, avoiding contact as we put things away and loaded the dishwasher. He set the waffle he had made for his mother aside on a plate. "She'll eat it later."

After I was gone, I imagined. "I'm going to take off," I said. "I want to go look at some cars. They're coming to pick up the BMW on Monday."

"Don't buy anything today. It's always good to have someone with you before you make a final decision."

"Are you offering your services?"

"I could go with you after work one day this week."

"I'm sure you know a lot more about cars than I do," I said as he walked me to the door.

"What? You think I'm one of those Latino guys that spends all weekend bent over the engine of his truck, showing his ass crack?"

"No, but I like the image."

"*Sinvergüenza!*"

"You've given me an idea. I think I might go for a drive around the eastern part of town. Maybe one of those ass-crack guys has a car for sale."

"Just so you know, I put one of those jealous husband tracking devices on your car, so I'll know where you are at all times."

Though I knew he was making a funny, the word husband made me wince.

"Oops! Too much?"

"I didn't know you cared." I put my hand lightly on his chest.

He looked down at it. "I care a lot."

Through his fake frown, a grin emerged. It warmed me to see him smile, forgetting for a moment the problems with his mother. He kissed me quickly, and I was out the door.

# Chapter 26

Monday morning the rumble of a large motor vehicle outside my house interrupted my morning coffee accompanied by reading the news on the Internet and shouting at the screen. "What's the matter with people?" I looked out the window at the flat-bed tow truck that would carry Anthony's car away, the first step in easing my financial burden. The day before, I had seen a used, sorry, pre-owned (I was corrected by the salesperson) Prius at the Toyota dealership that would suit my needs, which, in terms of a car, were basic. I wanted something that would get me from one place to another and would have a reasonably small footprint on the environment. Since I didn't drive much, I wouldn't have to spend a lot on gas. I hoped that Mateo would go with me later in the week to look at it.

As the tow truck pulled away, I suffered a deep sadness as another major connection to Anthony, a car I had driven every day since his death, became smaller and smaller with the truck fading into the distance. I held the check in my sweaty palm, thinking of the day Anthony's sister, Leticia, came by the house after the memorial service to pick up some of his things before driving back to Fresno. She had already told me she didn't want any of his clothes, but I set aside personal items, like family photographs and watches that he had collected. Anthony and his born-again sister were not close, and she tolerated me only when she had to. At the memorial service, Anthony's mother took me aside. She had always treated me kindly, though I didn't imagine we would remain in touch. She had come to our wedding; the sister had not. Despite her grief, she took it upon herself to warn me.

"Leticia and them is coming over after the reception. Hold firm." She knew her daughter.

Leticia and her husband rolled out of their Dodge Caravan and waddled over to the BMW parked in the driveway, strolling around it with greedy faces, cupping a hand to their eyes as they put their noses to the windows to look inside, running a finger along the finish with a disgusted look that I wasn't taking better care of it. I came out onto the front porch and the door slammed behind me.

Their heads popped up. "What are you going to do with the car?" said Leticia.

"Drive it. It's the only car I have." I emphasized the "I" as in mine and don't even think about getting your mitts on it. Thank you, marriage equality. Back in the times when a lot of people were dying of AIDS, I saw plenty of families swoop in to claim cars and houses, which were often bought by the couple together but had been put in the deceased person's name. Everything that Anthony owned was now mine, even though he hadn't left a will. Anything I gave his family was a gift from me, and one gift they sure as hell weren't getting was the car.

"Oh," said Leticia. "I thought you might want to get something more practical."

"Would you like to take a look at the things I set aside in the living room?" I tried to sound as pleasant as possible and cranked up a fake smile.

They pawed through the items and snatched up the watches, some of which were probably valuable, but I didn't want to deal with selling them. There were a lot of expensive cookbooks, which they ignored. I left them alone to do their rifling, but when I came back down the hall they were standing by the front door, the husband cradling a single box in his chubby arms. I glanced at the mess they had left in the living room.

"You could probably sell those cookbooks on eBay," I offered.

"We're good," said Leticia.

I escorted them out, and they shoved the box into their car, took one last deflated gaze at the BMW, and drove off. I heaved a sigh of relief, knowing I'd probably never see them again.

After the tow truck left, I walked over to the bank to deposit the check and when I got home, I drew a bath. The day had turned overcast and cool, and I couldn't think of anything better than to treat myself with a good soak among the bubbles. I lay back in the tub that wasn't big enough for my long body and drifted, the hot water soothing my bones. And true to the old riddle: What happens when the human body is submerged in water? The doorbell rang. For real. Probably a salesperson. Another long, anxious trill followed. A few seconds later my phone rang. Shit. Sounded like someone really wanted me to answer the door. I got out of the bath and threw on a robe.

"How did you know I was coming by?" said Mateo, looking me up and down as I dripped on the carpet.

"Wanna take a bath? The water's still hot."

"That wasn't exactly what I had in mind, but it sounds cool...or hot, I guess."

I took his hand and led him down the hall toward one of my all-time favorite things, which very few of my partners had wanted to indulge in. Nick liked his privacy in the bathroom and Anthony had flat-out told me he didn't like soaking in his own juice. Mateo stripped down and it took a little time to adjust our bodies to find a comfortable position. He ended up at the back of the tub and I sat between his legs, my knees bent while I leaned back into the warmth of his chest as he crossed his arms over me, his fingers running up and down my stomach. As lovely as it was, it probably would have been better after sex when we could have stayed there like forever.

A certain part of Mateo's anatomy soon reminded us that we had unfinished business. With my toe I hit the drain lever. While the water receded and bubbles faded away, Mateo nibbled on the back of my neck. "It's soapy," he said.

"I'll turn on the shower."

Next on the agenda was another top-ten activity: shower sex with all the props of steam on the shower doors, water running down brown skin and beading in the hairy bits, a large mirror on the wall, and enough lighting that we could watch ourselves. Add one very horny younger man and one very willing older man. Magic. And clean-up was a snap.

"I hope this wasn't the time you had set aside to go look at a car with me," I said as I toweled his back.

"Would you have rather gone to look at cars?"

"Tough call. It is pretty exciting to buy a new car."

"Yeah, it would have been so much more fun dealing with a smarmy salesman."

"Good point. But engaging in two of my favorite things with the hottest guy in town slightly edges out the smarmy salesman."

"Thank you. I'm honored. Let me dry your back."

He turned me around and vigorously rubbed the towel over my shoulders and down my spine.

And true to form in the world of Mateo and Nathan, a few minutes later I was sitting alone on the edge of my bed wondering what the hell had just happened but reminiscing with a big smile on my face.

***

Mateo wasn't able to go with me to get the car for the rest of the week and I was without transportation, so I faced the smarmy salesman alone, though it turned out to be a saleswoman who was probably a lesbian. She was nice and winked, giving me what she called the friends and family deal.

Mateo and I had a couple more Saturday night cuddle-fests at his house with breakfast in the morning. The second time, Carmen joined us for breakfast. She wore a colorful scarf on her head, but no makeup or jewelry. She first emerged in a bathrobe, but when she saw me, she made an abrupt about-face to her room and changed into a floral print tunic over dark leggings.

Mateo made scrambled eggs and raisin bread toast. Carmen ate slowly and quietly, mostly staring at her plate, while Mateo asked me about my travels, avoiding my most recent trip to Mexico. Carmen looked up and in a clear voice said, "Have you ever been to Colombia?"

"No, but I'd like to go."

"I'll go back there one day," she said with a mysterious grin on her face.

Mateo's fork halted in midair, and silence fell over the room.

Carmen picked up a piece of toast and gawked at it. "What in the world is in this bread?"

"Raisins," said Mateo in a computer-like voice. "It's raisin bread."

She dropped the toast on her plate. "*No temenos pandebono*?"

"No, mami. Sorry."

"I've never heard of that," I said.

"It's a cheese bread made with cassava flour," said Mateo. "Maybe you had *pão de queijo* in Brazil? It's sort of like that."

Carmen shook her head. "No. It is different."

"Okay, mami."

"Very different."

"I don't know where to buy it here. There was one place in San Francisco."

Carmen stared out the window with a wrinkled forehead, as if she wasn't sure where she was.

She turned from the window to me. "Do you live here in San Francisco?"

I didn't know how to answer. I didn't want to correct her.

"He lives just a few blocks from us in a nice house with a garden."

"*Que Bueno.*" She looked at her son. "*Cómo se llama?*"

"Nathan."

"Is he a doctor like you?"

"No, mami. He's a teacher."

Outside the window a blue jay squawked, unsettling Carmen. She shivered.

Mateo had told me that Carmen always wanted him to be a doctor. After finishing two years at City College, he thought of doing something in the medical field, but the long years of medical school and internship weren't in the cards. He needed to start making an income as soon as possible, something more than the part-time job at Safeway to keep them afloat. Carmen had reduced her secretarial work to part-time for health reasons, and the only thing that allowed them to stay in San Francisco was rent control. Still, it wasn't easy. He enrolled in a nursing program at Cal State in Hayward, far enough away where he could justify living on his own—he was desperate to have his own life—but close enough he could come home often if his mother needed him. He found a low-rent apartment in nearby San Leandro near the BART station. Years later, when they needed to leave San Francisco, he was already familiar with San Leandro.

"Your uncle, Hernán, was a teacher. Biology, I think."

Mateo looked at me and shrugged. The human mind was a curious thing. She remembered the profession of someone she hadn't seen in many years, but couldn't remember that her son was a nurse and not a doctor.

Mateo and I were in a holding pattern with weekly sleepovers and the occasional after work romp at my house where we could be as wild as we wanted. Aside from selling Anthony's car, any other decisions about my future were in limbo. Who knows how long that pattern might have gone on if the fickle finger of fate, also known as *el dedo del destino,* didn't stick its boney appendage into the drink of our lives and give it a whirl?

I sat in a sunny spot in the yard reading in the late afternoon. My phone rang and the caller ID told me it was Mateo.

"Are you on your way over?"

"No, sadly. Something's happened."

"Where are you?"

"Emergency. And not for work. Mom had a fall. They think her hip is fractured."

"I'm so sorry. What can I do?"

"Nothing. I just wanted to tell you."

"Is she okay other than the hip?"

"Very confused. I've got to go. I'll keep you updated."

"I'm here for whatever you need."

I tried not to let the thought creep into my head, and when it did anyway, I knew I would rot in hell for it. When they released Carmen from the hospital, she would certainly have to go to rehab. The obstacle would be removed, at least temporarily, separating Mateo and me from having a normal period of discovery to know if we were something that could last. I should have been content enjoying the good times, the afternoon booty calls and the sweet nights of being held instead of selfishly thinking how Carmen's injury could make things better for us.

# Chapter 27

I didn't hear from Mateo for a couple of days while he got Carmen settled into a rehabilitation center on the other side of town. Early one morning I got a text saying he would go after work to visit his mom but wanted to come over and spend the night. The long-anticipated night together in my house was coming to pass, though knowing the way that fickle finger worked, I was reluctant to assume anything. But it did seem like a good time to make some changes in the house to make it more me and less Anthony and me. I struggled with the notion that I was attempting to erase Anthony from my life, but rationalized that my intention was to reduce the number of items I would come across in a day that reminded me of him and what had been taken away. The cookbooks that his sister had rejected had gone back on the bookshelves, but since I never consulted them, I boxed them up. I removed the pinpoints of our travels on the world map but left the map, which I loved to glance at while sitting at my desk and dream of the hundreds of places I still hadn't been. I removed all the photos of us except for the one of our marriage on the mantel in the living room. When we were in Brazil, a street artist had done a sketch of us that we loved, and we had it framed for ten times the cost of the drawing. I took it down from the wall and put it in a drawer.

A couple of days before Anthony's memorial, Cindy had come over and helped me through the arduous task of going through his personal things, separating out things his family might want from what would be donated to Out of the Closet, a second-hand store that gave all the proceeds to HIV organizations. The boxes still sat in the garage, waiting for me to summon the energy to drive across the bay to the store in San Francisco.

In a sweep of the house, adding things to the piles in the garage, I committed myself to purge things from my wardrobe that I hadn't worn in years, something Anthony was always telling me to do. Eliminating the excess would make it easier to prepare the house for putting it on the market. Running parallel to the progress in my relationship with Mateo was the backup plan of liquidating everything and hopping on a plane for parts unknown. I knew Mateo's intentions were good, and that he was good and we were good together, but life had taught me—most recently with Anthony's tragic accident—that you must be prepared for anything and always have a backup plan.

All those shirts I used to wear for work, gone. Those shoes I had forgotten about in the back of the closet, bye. Those jackets that never quite fit right, see ya. By midday, my wardrobe had been reduced by fifty percent, and I was just getting started.

Going through a storage box from under the bed, I came across a kaftan I had bought in Tunisia and only worn a couple of times as part of a Halloween costume. It was a beautiful article of clothing, and as I ran my fingers over the intricate embroidery around the neckline, I was filled with a deep sadness. I pictured Nick and me in front of a stall in the Tunis market as rays of sun passed through the gaps in the awning above, falling on Nick's face, still beautiful but showing signs of age or worry or something else chipping away at him. He saw me eyeing the Kaftan and encouraged me to buy it.

A few years after Nick and I moved to Spain, we went on a tour of Tunisia with Charlie and Gor. Though none of us were big on organized tours, we signed up for one that promised an adventure of a lifetime to the shopping souks and Islamic architecture of the capital, Tunis, the ruins of Carthage, the beaches of Hammamet, and the oasis of Douz, gateway to the Sahara.

We were concerned about being four gay men traveling in an Islamic country and worried who our traveling companions would be since we would be spending the next nine days with them in a minivan. At the airport in Tunis, we gathered with the other tour members and were pleased they were mostly young, travel savvy, and ready to have a good time. Almost immediately we befriended three women in their thirties from Madrid who would not only become our friends but act as our female companions. On the first day we formed a tight group with designated roles. Nick was the father figure who reeled us in when we were too loud and making a scene. Charlie was the entertainer who we managed to limit to only one drag show behind closed drapes prompted by the three women when we were drinking the local beer in their room and they offered clothing and makeup. Maribel, who had instigated the drag show, was a rabble rouser and insisted we could all go skinny dipping in the hotel pool late one night. Her friends managed to talk her down. I was the teacher, filling in information the guide left out about the historical sights we visited.

By the time we got to Douz on the edge of the sand sea, we were exhausted from getting up early every day and spending the whole day touring. It was hot and the air conditioning in the bus barely worked. We arrived at the hotel sweaty, dirty, and tired, but when we saw the glorious turquoise of the egg-shaped pool, we couldn't wait to dive in. After cooling off a few minutes in the pool, Nick went to the room for a nap. He hadn't been sleeping well and was getting dark circles under his eyes.

We started a game of chicken fight, which we had done at several of the other pools on the trip. I was on Gor's shoulders and Maribel was on Charlie's. Maribel was vicious, and soon Gor and I tumbled under the water with our limbs tangled. I felt him grab my crotch. At first, I thought it was accidental, but before we resurfaced, he kissed me. From under the water, I stared at Charlie's legs and Maribel's feet still on his shoulders while Gor pushed his tongue into my mouth. I shoved him playfully away, and we surfaced, laughing.

"Rematch," I said.

"Hey, guys," said Pilar from a chaise lounge by the pool. "We've just been invited to a Tunisian wedding." The tour guide had told us that it was common for locals to ask tourists to attend a wedding, and it was a great opportunity where we would be treated as honored guests.

"I'm in," said Charlie. The three women all expressed their desire to go.

Gor gave me an enigmatic look. "I heard about this bar in town where, as the night goes on, men get up and dance with each other."

"A gay bar in Tunisia?" said Maribel.

"No. Women aren't allowed in bars, so when the men get a little drunk and the spirit moves them, they dance with each other. It's supposed to be pretty homoerotic, but at the end of the night they go home to their wives and mothers."

"Or not," I said with a laugh.

Charlie looked disappointed. "I really want to go to the wedding. We don't know if we'll get the chance again."

"That's cool," said Gor. "You should go. I think Nathan and I are going to check out this bar."

I started to protest, but Gor ran his toes up my shins under the water. Gor and I had flirted in the way that guys in couples do, feeling like it was safe because we were all good friends and wouldn't betray our partners, especially in the new post HIV awareness morality. Stay within your committed relationship and stay healthy.

"Come on if you're going," said Pilar, already on the path to her room. "The guide said he could take us in the tour bus if we hurry."

Charlie and the girls left to go get ready while Gor and I sat on the edge of the pool. He moved his leg over so that our thighs were touching. I dove in and swam toward the center of the pool. He joined me in the water.

"Is there really a bar like you described?" I asked.

"You think I made it up?"

Since Gor had made the first move, he had jumped out of the box of being a friend's boyfriend into a different category, someone mysterious, sexy, and with a hint of danger, a combination that had been disastrous for me in the past. I had always found him attractive. Like Nick, he was Armenian, but Gor's mother was Turkish, and considering the antagonistic history of the two peoples, I wondered what inherited turmoil lurked in his blood. "What if I want to go to the wedding?"

He smirked. "You're free to go, but you better hurry." He splashed me. "Look, they're leaving." Doors closed as the others came out of their rooms and headed for the bus.

"The bar does sound interesting," I said. I had the sensation of falling.

"If we make it there." He had the same expressive thick eyebrows as Nick.

"What's that supposed to mean?"

"I mean, it might be hard to find."

"Maybe Nick would like to go. Anyway, I need a shower."

We got out of the water, and as I dried off, I noticed his furtive glances like he was seeing me in a new way.

He walked me to my room, but when I cracked the door open and we saw Nick snoring loudly, Gor whispered, "Shower in my room. You shouldn't wake him up." I pulled the door closed gently.

"I suppose that makes sense, but I won't have any clean clothes to put on."

"I can lend you some."

I followed him down the hall, thinking I was an adult who could handle it if he tried to lure me into something. I would politely tell him that hooking up was not a good idea, and I didn't want it to hurt our friendship. By the time we got to his room, my speech was written and edited. By the time he closed the door behind us, it was completely forgotten. I blamed it on the fact that Nick and I hadn't had sex in months and that we were traveling. Weird things always happened while in other countries. *But not with the boyfriend of one of your best friends*!

He was cool, at first, and told me to go ahead and shower. I went into the bathroom and closed the door but didn't lock it because, I rationalized, that would be paranoid. I took a deep breath and got under the piddly water pressure, but the cool water felt good after the hot day and put a damper on the steamy thoughts in my head. Pretending to be naïve can be terribly convenient.

I heard steps outside the door. *Oh my God. He's opening the door. He's naked. He's getting in the shower with me.* He wrapped his arms around me and kissed the back of my neck. In freefall now, I reached for the wall.

A short time later, we lay in a tangle of damp sheets. "That was fun," he said.

"We can't do it again."

"Again today?"

"Ever, damnit!"

"I suppose you're right," he said in a completely unconvincing way.

I got up and put on my wet trunks. "I'd better check on Nick."

"You guys want to get together for dinner?"

I looked at him with a baffled expression. Did he seriously imagine the three of us were going out to eat? And what? Play footsie under the table while my boyfriend drank his tea? He seemed to feel no guilt in the slightest. "Yeah, no."

"Oh. Are you angry?"

"No."

"We had a great time. It's no big deal."

I stood at the door. "Right. See you tomorrow, bright and early." We were scheduled to take dune buggies into the desert.

Nick was awake but still lying on the bed in sheets that were wetter than the ones I had just left. "Hi," I said.

"Have you been at the pool all this time?"

"By the pool. Not in the pool. You know, just talking. Some of them went to a Tunisian wedding."

"Why didn't you go?"

"I didn't want to leave you here alone." God, I was shameless. I sat on the edge of the bed and fingered the soaked sheets with an eerie feeling.

Our eyes met. He looked horrible. "I don't feel well. I had a bit of diarrhea."

"I think I have Imodium."

"Already took some. Splitting headache, too."

"Do you feel like eating anything?"

"No. But we're running low on water. I'm so thirsty."

"I'll go to the lobby and ask for a change of sheets. I'll pick up a sandwich or something and a couple bottles of water."

The next morning, Nick was no better. He had night sweats that soaked the clean sheets I had put on the bed. When I went down to tell the others I wouldn't be going on the excursion, I found out that three other people, including Pilar, had the same symptoms as Nick. I breathed a sigh of relief that it was a bug or food poisoning and not the other thing I didn't want to let my mind think about. Charlie marched over to me with twitching eyes and a downturned mouth.

*Fuck, he found out.*

"I'm so sorry to hear about Nick. Pilar's got it pretty bad, too. Is there anything we can do?" *We meaning you and your boyfriend with whom you left me alone last night? No, I think you've done enough. Was I seriously blaming him for my bad behavior?*

"Nothing to do, really. You guys should go and have fun."

"It's sweet of you to stay here and take care of him."

"We have to take care of our partners, right?" *Especially after I betrayed him with your cheating boyfriend.*

On the rest of the tour, several others got the bug, including Charlie. We had to make a lot more pit stops than normal, and at each one, someone stumbled off the bus and ran awkwardly to the bathroom, often just a hole in the ground. Nick felt better after the third day, but I got it the morning we left, making the flight home and going through customs a feverish blur.

For a few months after the trip Nick seemed back to normal and gained the weight he had lost. It was during that time, he brought Vladimir home and he became a regular at our house. Then Nick started going downhill, having one physical complication after another and so many night sweats that we ended up sleeping separately. I kept coming up with excuses not to get together with Charlie and Gor those first months after the trip. When Nick became sick all the time, it was easy to use the excuse that Nick wasn't feeling well.

At Nick's memorial, Gor fell into my arms, sobbing. "Charlie and I loved Nick so much. What we did in no way was ever meant to hurt him. And I ruined our friendship. I am a terrible person. If you can find it in your heart to forgive me, please let me be your friend again. Charlie misses you so much." I needed their friendship. I needed as much love and support as I could get, but, of course, it wasn't enough to ease the pain.

I sat in my bedroom holding the kaftan, the memories bringing me to tears. I cried for Nick, Charlie, Gor, and so many others. Why was I allowed to live? The survivor's question that had no answer. I used the kaftan to wipe my eyes and threw it on a pile of clothes to be discarded.

# Chapter 28

Mateo came over in the late evening for what was supposed to be our double feature of sex and cuddling on the same night in the same bed and maybe morning sex, but I knew none of it was going to happen as soon I saw his exhausted face. He fell into my arms like he needed comfort, his kiss warm but not hot. It was fine with me since I felt drained from my personal *día de los Muertos,* remembering all the friends I'd lost in Spain and the day's effort greatly reducing Anthony's presence in the house.

"Can I get you a drink?" I asked.

"I'd love a shot of that tequila."

We sat at the kitchen counter, sipping tequila, and he gave me the latest reports on his mother. Her bones were so brittle it would take her hip a while to mend. When she came home, she would have to use a walker at all times to avoid falls. Her neurologist said her latest tests showed a steady decline in her cognitive functions. The doctors recommended a care facility, an idea Mateo rejected, though he knew Luisa wasn't qualified to take care of her as her condition worsened.

We held each other in bed, and while he drifted off, my mind became a jumble of new-age spiritualist jargon telling me I had survived so Nick and Charlie and Gor, and others whose lives were cut short could live through me. I had a responsibility to be my best self, enjoy life, and comfort others when given the chance. I squeezed Mateo with such force, he woke up.

"Babe, you're hugging me so tight."

"I want to be with you." I choked on my words.

"You are."

"You make me feel things. Beautiful things. Sometimes I think I survived all the trauma in my life so I could be with you. You are my gift."

He rose up and looked into my eyes. "Are you crying? Come on, amor. It's okay. We're here together. And if you get any crazy ideas about leaving again, I'm going to tie you up."

I laughed through my tears and coughed and generally produced a variety of bodily fluids out of my eyes, nose, and throat. I reached over him and grabbed a handful of tissues. "I've made so many mistakes in my life."

"We all have."

"No, but mine have been worse."

He lay back and pulled my head to his chest. "I hope you're not about to confess to a murder or something."

"Not quite that bad. But I hurt a lot of people. I think I'm a better person now, but what if I'm not? What if there is a sickness in me that can't be healed? I don't ever want to hurt you, but I already have."

"You're being ridiculous. My reaction to you leaving was stupid. I know you weren't doing it to deliberately hurt me."

*I'm glad you're convinced of that because I'm not.*

"It might be way too soon to think about this, but what if maybe someday in the future you and your mom came to live here? There are very few steps to negotiate, and she could sit in the back yard and enjoy the birds."

"I am so, so moved that you suggested that, but it wouldn't be fair to you. Mom's care is only going to get more difficult." He lightly massaged the top of my head. "Wait. Did you just ask me to move in with you?"

I giggled. "Am I crazy? It's how I'm feeling right now. I...I love you."

"*Coño!* You didn't say that. Did you just say you love me? You're killing me. First, you suggest moving in together, and then, I think you said you love me. *Estoy...no sé que decir.* Can you say it again? I'm dreaming, right?"

"I love you. I love you. I love you."

"You make me happy and a little mad." He tugged at a strand of my hair, but not enough to hurt.

"What? I said I loved you, and you're angry with me?"

"I wanted to say it first. I've been thinking about it. And then you just...*hijo de puta!*"

"Maybe you should stop going on about it and kiss me."

"I will, but could you say it one more time?"

"Asshole." I ran the back of my hand over my nose to make sure it wasn't filled with snot that might dribble down as I planted my mouth on his. We had a long post declaration of love kiss, but a part of me was holding back, wondering if I had done the right thing.

"No, no, no, no, no," he said. "That was not an I-love-you kiss. This is an I-love-you kiss." He pushed me onto my back and got on top of me, pressing my head into the pillow with the ardor of his kiss.

"That was acceptable," I said. "I'm just not convinced."

"*Güevon!* If you keep making me kiss you, we're going to end up doing something we said we weren't going to do."

"All right. Okay. I'm convinced. Go to sleep. Turn around. I want to hold you."

"Are we good?"

"We are great."

"We're almost great. I just need to hear it one more time so I can go to sleep."

"I love you," I breathed in his ear.

***

I woke up to Mateo gently nudging me. "Time to get up."

"Why?" I groaned. Long after Mateo had drifted off, my brain had refused to settle down as every single thought, feeling, memory, and heartbreak from the previous day created a traffic jam on the road to sleep.

"We're going to make pandebono."

"Pandewho?"

"Remember the other day my mom wanted pandebono, Colombian cheese bread? I found a recipe. It shouldn't be that difficult. It might cheer her up."

"Don't you have to go to work or something?"

"It's my day off, señor grumpy. *Levántate.*" He proceeded to poke me and not in a fun way.

"This is how you repay me for cooing you to sleep with my sweet words."

"Sweet words? I don't remember. Maybe you need to tell me again."

"I fucking love you! Now, can I go back to sleep?"

He put his mouth near my ear and whispered, "Me too." He inserted his wet tongue halfway to my eardrum, which might have been sexy at another time, but the frisson it gave me felt like a violation. I wanted to kill him. "Now get up!" he said loudly.

After my second cup of coffee, I felt brave enough for us to venture out to the Latino market on East $14^{th}$ to get the cassava flour and other ingredients we would need for the cheese bread. Not only did Mateo choose to rise early on his day off and make something that might make his mother feel a little better instead of spending the morning in bed with someone who had just declared his love for him, but he would also pass the rest of the day after our baking adventure with her instead of said boyfriend. Now that was devotion. Or was it seeping into codependency territory my caffeine-fueled brain wanted to know?

I had to remind myself that though I cut the strings from my mother early on, Mateo's circumstances had been very different from mine. And I had to send grateful thoughts once again to my brother, whose relationship to our mother was similar to Mateo's, as he had both the burden and the special intimacy afforded a caregiver in those final years. When we knew Mom's day was near, I went to spend a week in Florida. Her body was shutting down, but she was relatively lucid until the end, and made every effort to make me feel that despite becoming markedly dependent on David, she loved us the same. She told me again how proud she was of me, even though I knew I had fallen far short of the aspirations she had for me. She gave me that sweet, relaxed smile she had developed in her later years and asked me to read some of my poems to her while she lay back in her morphine-induced dreamy state.

Mateo meticulously separated all the ingredients for the pandebono into little stations on the kitchen counter as if it was a chemistry experiment. The dry things, the cassava flour, corn flour, salt, and sugar were grouped together; the Mexican queso fresco and feta cheese in another group; and the egg and milk in still another. He asked me to get the measuring cups and spoons (luckily, they had been spared in the purge of household items) so he could put the correct measuring device next to each ingredient.

"Are you always so anal when you're cooking?"

He gave me a burning look that if I had been a flower, would have wilted me on the spot. "Are you here to criticize or help?"

*Okay. I get it. This is for your mother.*

"Help, of course."

"Then get me a mixing bowl," he said in a drill sergeant's voice.

When he filled the measuring cup with cassava flour, he squinted and leveled it off with a knife before carefully spilling it into the bowl. I hovered behind him. He glared at me over his shoulder. "Could you give me some space? Here. Take the cheeses over there and start crumbling them into a bowl."

"Crumbling?"

"With your hands. Wash them first."

A minute later he was hovering over me. I didn't enjoy the mushy feeling of the cheese between my fingers. I turned to him with a smile. "Like this?"

He shook his head as if I was hopeless. "I'll do it. You have to squeeze hard. You act like you're afraid of hurting the cheese. Go turn on the oven to 400."

He put the flours and cheeses together, cracked in the egg, and started squishing it all together into a masa. I was glad he was doing it because just watching the raw egg on his fingers gave me the heebie-jeebies. "You forgot the milk," I said.

He gave me that look again. "I did not forget the milk. You add it at the end very slowly to make sure of the wetness level. The masa must be the perfect consistency."

When the masa was ready, he made little balls and put them on a cookie sheet.

"That looks like fun. Do you want me to help?"

"No, thanks. You can make some coffee, though. You must eat them with coffee."

"I thought they were for your mom."

"We must taste them, no? If they aren't right, we must begin again."

Fortunately, the little golden buns met Mateo's approval and we sampled them with strong coffee. "I think Mom will be very happy," he said, smiling for the first time in over an hour. "I must take them to her right away. They're best when fresh."

He packed up the pandebono in a metal cookie tin and got ready to leave. "Sorry if I was a little *exigente* when we were making the bread."

"I understand, really."

"Okay. Tomorrow we get up early and make patacones."

"Oh."

He laughed at the pained expression on my face. "I'm kidding. I'll see you tonight. Thanks for helping."

He didn't exit with the three little words that were now part of our repertoire and I didn't say them because I didn't want him to feel pressure.

As I worried about how Mateo was feeling emotionally and whether he would remember to tell Carmen that I helped with the baking and if she would even remember who I was, I realized that declaring a mutual love for a partner is a monumental milestone in a relationship and wonderfully titillating in the moment, but it doesn't change the people you are or make the deep-seated insecurities and troubling demons magically disappear. Nor did it, in our lives, alter the physical realities of our day to day living situations or the difficult decisions we would have to make soon.

When Mateo came home that night, he said the pandebono put a smile on Carmen's face and perked her up. She sent her thanks to me for helping. I didn't believe that for a second, but it was sweet of him to say.

We fell into a domestic rhythm, spending most nights together, but Mateo dividing his days between working and being with his mom while doctors' reports continued to be grim.

"The rehab center is concerned that she isn't able to perform ADLs," he told me.

"And for the non-medical laymen that would be...?"

"Activities of daily living like being able to bathe and dress herself."

"She was always so put together when I came over to your house."

"That gave me hope. I saw her mind fading into confusion and memory loss, yet she maintained her look, always so important to her. She did it all herself, the hair, picking out the outfits, adding the jewelry. It was the smokescreen she presented to the world, hiding the chaos going on inside her."

Every night Mateo would arrive at my house looking a little more weary and with a few more strands of silver gracing his beautiful dark locks. Though I thought his gray hairs were sexy, the reason he had them was not, and when he had the energy for sex, it lacked the passion of those days when we were trying to figure things out.

"I was so stupid not to consider the steps when we moved into that apartment," Mateo said one night as we lay in bed, his fist pounding the bedcovers.

"I'm guessing she was in a much different state when you moved in."

"It was naïve to think she would stay that way. The signs were already there."

"We live so much of our lives in denial. I suppose it's how we cope."

"Everyone says I should put her in a home. I just can't. She's miserable in that rehab center."

"Should we revisit the idea of bringing her here?" It was partly out of guilt that I made the offer. I couldn't help but wonder if my coming into Mateo's life caused her to panic about losing him. The closer we got, the more she deteriorated. Mateo hadn't said anything about blaming our relationship for his mother's downfall, but I was sure it lurked in the back of his mind.

"She's going to need professional care while I'm at work. It's way beyond Luisa's capabilities. Again, it wouldn't be fair to you for us to take over your home. I have to work something out."

A professional caretaker for a person with Alzheimer's, if he could even find one, would not come cheap. I doubted her Medicare coverage would be very helpful. If he got rid of his apartment and moved in with me, it would relieve his financial burden. But that would be a huge move, possibly causing tension so soon after we had arrived at our new status of being boyfriends that say I love you.

# Chapter 29

The fried plantain tostones and a special Colombian pico de gallo we ended up making the following weekend and more pandebono the weekend after that brought some cheer into Carmen's life but did little to stop the mental and physical downward spiral. Mateo lined up a woman who could take care of her during the hours he was at work and he located a medical supply store where he could get a hospital bed and other equipment he would need to bring her home.

The rehabilitation center said they were making no progress as far as physical therapy for her hip, mostly because she refused to do it, so there wasn't any point in keeping her there once her benefits ran out. Mateo wanted to bring her home as soon as possible, regardless of the benefits, and start having the retired nurse come in. It would take some adjustment on Carmen's part since she was used to Luisa when Mateo wasn't there. Her doctors agreed that since she showed no will to live in the rehab center, maybe if she was home, she would improve.

I was relieved Mateo didn't take me up on my offer to bring her to my house, but I still wanted to help in some way. Cooking had never been my thing and after Anthony and I started living together, I only cooked when I had to. Since most evenings he was at the restaurant, I would throw something simple together or eat leftovers he brought home from work. But now I resolved to make sure Mateo had a good meal when he got home every night, something I could continue to do once his mom was installed at home.

The first few nights Carmen was home, I suggested he stay with her alone and he looked thankful that I had brought it up. One of those nights, the postponed Chez Panisse benefit was finally happening, and I told Cindy I would be attending by myself.

On my way to the event, I arrived at Mateo's door with a serving dish, and his face told me immediately something was wrong.

"When I got home, Mom was crying. She couldn't understand why I would leave her alone for days with this strange woman. I tried to convince her that it had only been since the morning, and the woman was very nice. She couldn't be consoled."

"Sorry," I said, handing him the dish. "It's arroz atollado de pollo y chorizo."

He looked at me in total astonishment. "You made this?"

"It's probably not any good."

"My mom used to make this for me when I was a kid. Are you trying to make me love you even more?"

I shrugged my shoulders with a satisfied smile. "You might not love me so much when you taste it."

"I'm sure it will be good. You look really hot, by the way."

"Not sure about that, but I wanted to dress up a little since I never get the chance."

"Hah! I just remembered Marcelo will be there."

"You think I'm trying to look good for Marcelo? He's your boyfriend, not mine."

"My boyfriend is right here, and I'm so sorry I can't go with you tonight."

He looked down the hall and then leaned in to kiss me. "I don't know why I did that. She can't even get out of bed. Force of habit, I guess." Still holding the casserole dish in his hands, he managed to give me a kiss with enough passion to last through the night and until the next time I would see him. "I'll miss you tonight."

"If I get back early, I'll call you."

***

Cindy and Marcelo were already at the table and stood up to greet me, both looking relaxed and casual chic. They took turns kissing me on the cheek. Cindy had been letting her hair grow long and kept it blond (I'm going to dye my hair until the day I die), reminding me of that night I picked her up for the prom and her hair flashed golden and bouncy as she descended the stairs. From a distance, she could be that high school girl that I hoped could make me a normal boy. After the prom we had gone to a motel, I fumbled about in my cheap champagne drunkenness, failing miserably to lose my virginity and instead painted the bathroom floor with my dinner.

We sat down and the server came by with Deutz champagne as a welcome drink to start the night.

"Here's to Mateo and me officially being not just boyfriends but I-love-you boyfriends," I said, holding up my flute.

"That's wonderful," said Cindy. "I'm so happy for you."

We all clinked glasses.

"I believe then there is no hope for me," said Marcelo with a laugh.

"Absolutely none. Off his feet he has been swept."

"That's a relief," said Cindy with a hoarse laugh that turned into a cough. "Oh! Excuse me."

The first course was tiny grass shrimp cooked with butter and fresh thyme, paired with a Château du Trignon Côtes-du-Rhône Blanc.

I stabbed a tiny shrimp with my fork and popped it into my mouth. "I can't believe Mateo is missing this. He's stuck eating a creamy rice with chicken and chorizo I made."

"That sounds yummy, too," said Cindy. "You're turning into quite a cook."

"Hopefully I learned something after living with a chef for four years." I didn't mean for it to come out so cavalier, and it probably wasn't the best thing to say as Cindy's mouth turned south and she got a tear in her eye.

"So, what is this dish you make?" Marcelo asked me. "It sounds like maybe something Colombian."

"We've been making Colombian specialties for his mother like pandebono, tostones, pico de gallo, ropa vieja a la colombiana."

"Splendid," said Marcelo. "Pandebono must be like our Brazilian pão de queijo."

"Yes, very similar."

"With all this Colombian cooking," said Cindy, "are you making any headway with his mother?"

"Sadly, she's getting worse by the day. Even before she went into rehab, she didn't know, or pretended not to know, who I was after many introductions. Before she broke her hip, I had been sleeping over at their house from time to time on weekends, and when we saw each other at breakfast, she would occasionally speak to me, though never by name. Other times she would only stare at me like she might make me disappear with the sheer force of her will. But since she's been home, we decided it's better for them to have a few days alone. Mateo says he tells her I helped with baking and cooking, but I still don't believe she knows who I am. I'm wondering how long it will be until she doesn't recognize Mateo. Last week he came to my house freaked out because she had confused him with his father. It was only a few minutes, but not a good sign."

"That must be heartbreaking for him," said Cindy.

I turned to Marcelo. "I hope we're not boring you. Not the most pleasant of conversations."

"I also feel the sadness for Mateo. At least you have each other."

It still made me smile to hear his sultry Brazilian accent coming from his pale thin lips and accented by his twinkling blue eyes. "I hope I give him some comfort. It's hard for me to understand exactly what he's going through. My relationship with my mother was intense, but nothing like the mother and son bond Mateo has. It's just been the two of them since they came to the States."

Cindy let out a heavy sigh. "It still makes me shudder when I think about the years after I divorced Ricky's dad. My son wouldn't talk to me. You know what that does to a mother? Loving a son more than anything and not being able to talk to him?"

"But you're all good now, right?"

"For the most part. We still have our ups and downs."

We got a welcome break from the depressing trajectory of the conversation when the server brought our main course: Poached salmon with fresh basil and olive butters paired with a Monte Bello Chardonnay.

"I thought for a benefit, they might tone it down a bit, but they've pulled out all the stops," I said.

"They have a reputation to uphold," said Cindy.

"Marcelo, tell me about your foundation."

He lit up in the way people do when they have the chance to talk about the work they are proud of. "We get funding for urban gardens like the one we support tonight, the Youth Urban Farm Project in East Oakland. It is run mainly by women of color and gives kids access to green, safe spaces and the opportunity to work for something positive that will help their communities. They even get to eat the healthy food they grow."

"Marcelo used to be an investment banker," said Cindy.

"And how did you go from that to this?"

"I must give credit to my first wife, a woman of color who grew up in East Palo Alto. We were like opposites and not just in the skin color, as they say the opposites attract. But also having so many differences can make things too difficult. But the good thing she did was make me realize that life is not only getting money and being this kind of successful. I quit my job and started working for the foundation. I have no longer my wife, but I have a better life." He turned to Cindy. "And a better relationship, thanks to this amazing woman."

I smiled at Cindy. "You hit the jackpot."

"I don't mean to get sappy here, but can I tell you how full my heart is right now?" said Cindy. "I'm with this man I love who's doing wonderful things for the world, and my oldest friend who's found love again after so much heartbreak. I wish Mateo could be here."

The server came by with desert, honey-glazed apple tart with crème fraîche. "Well, we don't have Mateo, but it looks like something almost as delicious. I'm not even going to make a joke about the crème fraîche."

"This is something I like about gay men," said Marcelo. "Sex is never far from the tongue."

"Are we that bad?" I asked.

"No, is good. Part of life."

I took my first bite of the still warm tart and let out a moan of pleasure. "Maybe I should marry this instead of Mateo."

"Wait a minute," said Cindy. "Did I hear the word marry?"

"Girl, that was a joke. I'm not serious. A joke. Not even..." My phone buzzed.

"Somebody's ears were burning," said Cindy.

I had a shy grin on my face until I opened the message, and then I had to stop my face from falling to the floor.

**Mom in emergency again. Infection in leg. I'll be here a while.**

"What is it?" said Cindy.

"Another crisis with his mom. Back in emergency."

I texted him back. **Is there anything I can do?**

**No. I will keep you updated.**

I picked up my fork and tried to return to the scrumptious dessert. I took one bite and frowned. "I should stop by there on the way home."

"Do you need to leave?" said Cindy.

"He said there's nothing I can do, but I feel bad sitting here with this delicious meal in a beautiful setting while he's suffering with his mom in emergency."

"You might miss my wonderful speech," said Marcelo. He was scheduled to give a short talk about his foundation.

"Oh, sorry. I can stay."

"I'm joking. Go be with your love."

I stared at my unfinished tart. "Love you guys."

"Call me tomorrow," said Cindy.

***

In the waiting room, I walked by several people dozing off despite the bright lights, but it seemed like a relatively quiet night in the ER. Claudine was at the counter.

"You two still at it, huh?"

"You didn't think we'd last?"

She chuckled. "Not for me to say. But you being here's a good sign. I'll see if he can come out."

"How is she doing?"

She shook her head. "She's with the doctor now. You might have to wait a minute for Matty to come out."

"You call him Matty?"

"No one else is allowed. Only me."

She disappeared and came back a couple of minutes later. "He'll be out in a little bit."

I loved seeing him even when he was sad, the lovely freckle-stars in the night sky of his face, his mouth I had recently spent so much time with, and his eyes that gazed at me, making me feel like a better person. When the doors swung open and gave me my prince, I couldn't help myself from throwing my arms around him. Claudine raised her eyebrows, scratched the side of her temple, and shook her head all at the same time. He didn't protest at my spontaneous move as I thought he might, but didn't seem to have the strength to hug me back.

"Thanks for stopping by," he said. "You didn't have to."

"We're in this together. Do you need anything? Can I get you some coffee? Something to eat?"

"The coffee in the vending machine is crap, but it might perk me up."

"Do they have the infection under control?"

"They're giving her IV antibiotics. We'll see."

"I'll go get the coffee."

"I'm going back inside. Just give it to Claudine. You should go home."

"I can stay."

"No, really. I'll let you know what's going on."

I nodded. It seemed my presence was a distraction from focusing on his mom. "When she's stable and you need some rest, you can always come to my house."

"I know."

He turned around and walked back through the doors.

# Chapter 30

As far as I knew, I hadn't broken any mirrors in my life, and in any case that bad luck would only have lasted seven years. I wasn't jealous of my brother, David, like Cain was of Abel and certainly didn't murder him and lie to God about it, putting a curse on me and all my descendants. Descendants? And, as a rule, I remembered to spit when a black cat crossed my path.

I did remember a bizarre incident with my grandmother who had some unusual ideas involving the evil eye. She was convinced that the Jamaican exchange student living briefly in our house—I remembered her as a very lovely person—had put the evil eye on me. Gran said witches particularly targeted beautiful children, thank you very much, and she would run and get an egg to rub on my head. Thanks to the egg remedy, I felt safe that none of those supposed curses stuck. There was also that time when Vladimir and I went to visit his mother in Cuba and attended a *santería* ceremony in the back patio of a neighbor's home complete with a bloody chicken sacrifice to the orishas, altars with dolls, tobacco, and rum, and drummers making me feel I had been transported to an African village. Vlad's mother said she wasn't a true believer and leaned more toward Jehovah's Witness, but she liked to cover all her bases. She pointed out the santera who lived in the house and said Vladimir's wife had visited her before she left for the United

States and joked that she hoped she hadn't asked the orishas to put a spell on me. So, the wife knew about me, but I didn't know about her until his mom let it slip? Funny, not funny. But Vladimir's mom assured me the neighbor wouldn't get involved in the shenanigans the wife was known for in the neighborhood. No need to worry.

Why, I wondered, since I had ruled out all the curse possibilities, was death following me around? So many times in my life, I was surrounded by death, some of the time affecting me directly like the loss of Nick and Anthony, and my friend from high school Danny who overdosed, and all our friends in Spain who had died of AIDS. And then there were all the other deaths affecting people I loved like the members of Nick's church who became victims of the Up Stairs Lounge Fire, and Nick's patients and the kids he delivered who died in Jonestown, and Harvey Milk whose campaign we had worked on.

Carmen never returned home after her trip to emergency with the leg infection. She held on for another couple of agonizing weeks. I barely saw Mateo during that time, and I feared he was ruining his health. A couple of times, he came over to my house and crawled into bed, too exhausted to do anything but cuddle. I would force him to eat in the morning before he went to work. He lost weight and had shadows under his eyes.

When she finally passed, he said he needed to be alone, took some time off work, and holed up incommunicado in his apartment. After several days of his ignoring my calls and texts, I began to worry about his welfare. I dropped some food off at his front door, but he didn't answer the doorbell. If the roles were reversed, he would have been able to call Cindy, and maybe she could have gotten through to me. He knew at least one important friend in my life. I hadn't met a single friend of his in the months we had been seeing each other. Did he not have any friends? He was sweet, cute, sexy, fit, and funny. How could he not have any friends? I knew that he had people at work that looked out for him like Claudine, and she'd implied that he had a lot of admirers. There was also the woman with a ponytail I had seen him talking to at the soccer game. He had mentioned the guy he dated at Cal State in Hayward, and I'm sure he must have had dates when he lived in San Francisco, though he claimed none of them were memorable. My original thought when Mateo had shown an interest in me was that he was a lonely guy, and I was available. Before his startling revelation that he found me attractive, I was convinced he was only looking for a friend.

When we met, his life was work and taking care of his mother. It was admirable to give up a social life to devote attention to a mother in need. But the more their relationship bounced around in my brain, the more it seemed just a tiny bit creepy, not Norman Bates creepy, but maybe not the healthiest. Since the time they arrived in the United States when Mateo was twelve, they had always lived together except for the few years he lived in Hayward going to school. And she had a crisis (real or psychosomatic?) that brought him back to San Francisco when he might have wanted to move to Portland with his boyfriend. And as we began to explore a sexual relationship, she managed to have a crisis at the most inopportune times. When I heard of her death, I had to slap myself for feeling the slightest bit relieved, not just because I was selfish and could have Mateo all to myself, but because he could finally be an independent person whose personal decisions didn't always have to consider how it would affect another person, his mother.

I was willing to give him time. He had just lost the most important person in his life. But if his lack of communication continued much longer, I, who admittedly had run off to Mexico a couple of months before to avoid the relationship, was on the verge of going crazy. I was hopelessly in love with him. I made a desperate decision to talk to the only person I could think of who knew Mateo.

"Hi, Claudine," I said, approaching the desk in the emergency waiting room.

She pursed her lips and tilted her head, which looked like she was surprised to see me, but her grin showed she was not. "Do you have an emergency?" she said.

"I kinda do."

"Oh, Lordy. He not talking to ya?"

"Nope."

"Not talking to anybody here neither."

"I don't know what to do."

"All we can do is give him time."

"I thought I had made a breakthrough with him."

"You did. You did."

I wished she looked a little less like she was enjoying my pain. I had written down my number on a note in case I hadn't been able to find her. "Here's my number. If you hear anything, give me a call or text. I just want to know that he's all right."

"I will."

"Promise?"

She bristled a moment at my doubt, but her mouth relaxed, and she grinned. "Cross my heart." She made an X over her large bosom.

"I would hug you if you weren't on the other side of that counter."

She took a step back as if she was afraid I might jump over. "Child...try not to worry. He going through some heavy stuff. Have faith."

A couple of days later, I received a text from an unknown number. **Matty back at work.**

**Thank you, Claudine**.

Good news and bad news. He felt well enough to go back to work, but not well enough to give me a sign that he still cared about us. My desperation turned to panic, but I made a promise to myself that I was not going to stalk him again. *Nathan, you will not sit outside the emergency doors waiting for him to get off work, hoping he will run into your arms. Nathan, you will not stand by his truck in the parking lot like a gay Hallmark card commercial. Nathan, you will not sit on the ground outside his door freezing your ass off, waiting for him to come home.* I tried to turn those and a bunch more desperate situations into a poem, but it came out more like lyrics to a country and western song. *Nathan, if you do any of those things, you're a punk-ass bitch. Damnit, he needs to come to you.*

I felt proud of my self-restraint, but sick about the possibility of losing him. Late one night when I couldn't sleep, I drove over to his building, parked by the tall redwood trees, and walked around the back. The light in his mother's bedroom was on. I saw his silhouette move across the room a couple of times, and it was definitely him, not the ghost of his mother. I wanted so badly to hold him at that moment, I would have sold my pride, my soul, and my left nut to the devil for a chance to comfort him. Another part of me wanted to grab a boulder from the creek and throw it through the window. I said to myself, "Self, I will never talk to you again if you don't get in the car at this moment and leave."

The following day, I received a text from Mateo. **Come over after work. I need to talk to you.**

At least the waiting was over, and he wouldn't be breaking up with me by text but would do it to my face. The irony was too much, but what could I do? We had managed to form what I had believed was a loving bond, walking the tightrope between taking care of our needs and still respecting the needs of his mother. Now that she was gone, there was nothing keeping us apart unless, of course, it was us.

I arrived at his door with my stomach in knots. I imagined that as soon as I got inside, I would have to run to the bathroom and puke. He answered the door in a wrinkled T-shirt and scrub pants in a horrible shade of green. He looked distraught and his eyes were red as if he had been crying. Crying for us? Regretting it didn't work out? He didn't hug or kiss me.

"Sorry," he said.

"Sorry as in you're done with me or sorry you made me have sleepless nights not knowing if you were alive or dead?"

"The former. I mean, the latter. Fuck! I always get those mixed up. I'm not done with you, but I understand if you're done with me."

"Why would I...? Mateo..." I was afraid to blurt out my feelings when my whole body fizzled and popped after he said he wasn't done with me and how I never wanted to be done with him and how I was so afraid he was breaking up with me I wanted to hurl. "Are you going to invite me in?"

"Oh, sorry. I'm such an idiot. Come in. The place is a mess."

"Remember what my place was like the first time you came over?" I teared up thinking of his reticence and his not so reticent request to use the bathroom. I wanted to go back to that day, start all over again.

Halfway down the hall he turned and looked at me, seeming to remember that day as well and maybe having the same thoughts of going back to that innocence. It was the first sign of hope I'd had in a couple of weeks and it tore me apart. "I found something," he said. "It freaked me out. Not that it's an excuse."

"What do you mean?

"Sit," he said when we arrived in the living room.

He sat on the sofa, and I fell into my usual armchair where Carmen used to alternately glare at me or completely ignore me. With his hands on his knees, he stared at a stack of letters on the coffee table, old letters with foreign stamps on them, in those red, white, and blue airmail envelopes that people used to use to make damn sure the letter went by air and not overland by donkey.

"They're from my father. I found them in the back of my mother's drawer."

"Oh." The implication was obvious. He had told me there had been no communication with his father since they left Colombia. Mateo continued to gaze at the letters with an intensity that could make them spontaneously combust. His breathing became irregular.

"Most of them are to my mother, but some of them are addressed to me." His voice cracked like it was over a faulty Internet connection. "They came during the years I was in high school. I was so lost back then and really could have used a father's love."

"What did the letters say?"

"That he would never forget me or my mother, that he had made some bad choices, but he did it for us so we could have a better life. He would always love me even if I didn't write back because I was his first-born son." Mateo's voice had barely crawled to the end of the sentence before struggling to choke back tears, the agony of a loss that might not have been as powerful as the loss of his mother but close.

I sat motionless in my chair, grabbing the armrests, gazing at the person I loved who sat just feet away, utterly destroyed. I wasn't sure he wanted me to, but I forced myself up. He raised his head, sniffling, and in that look, I knew he wanted to be in my arms. I wrapped myself around him, pulled his head to my chest, and let him weep. I could sense how conflicted he was. The woman who he had devoted his life to and sacrificed for had betrayed him, lied to him, kept him from his father. The loss upon loss must have been overwhelming.

After he calmed down and had wiped away some of the tears with his T-shirt, he tried to speak even though his voice was still gurgly. "I'm such a fool. I could have lost you. The best thing to happen to me in, like, forever."

"I told you we were in this together. I wasn't kidding."

"I can't even process why she did it. She was so angry at my father for getting involved with the cartels, she wasn't thinking straight."

My take on it was a little more nefarious, but I needed to stay out of it and let him deal in his own way. She must have known her husband was involved with the cartels for years before doing anything about it. When they came to the States, she made Mateo believe they needed to hide from his father as if he were dangerous. And then, to withhold the letters bordered on cruelty.

Mateo gathered his wits enough to read one of his father's letters out loud. I listened to Mateo's shaky voice and the flow of his father's emotional Spanish. He wrote that one of Carmen's sisters had taken pity on him and given him their address in San Francisco. He missed them terribly after they left but never would have done them any harm or come after them and forced them to return to Colombia. Carmen had made her decision and he had to accept that. He said Mateo's aunt sometimes gave him news, like the fact that he played soccer in high school and got good grades. He remembered how much he loved to watch his son play soccer in Colombia and how it made him so proud.

Mateo broke down again and had to stop reading. "I'm sure he wouldn't be proud of one thing."

"You don't know that."

"You're right. I don't know him at all. That was taken away from me."

"What are you going to do?"

"What do you mean?"

"You have his address."

"The letters stopped almost twenty years ago. How do I know he still lives there?"

"How do you know he doesn't? Is your aunt still alive?"

"Mom cut off contact with her, too. Now I know why. She must have been so angry at her for giving my father our address." He put the letter back in its envelope and placed it neatly on the stack, making sure all the edges were even.

"There is one thing," I said.

"What?"

"She saved the letters rather than burning them."

"God, I can't believe I'm just now learning how complicated my mother was!"

"A little like her son." I took a chance that we were solid enough for a bit of our old banter.

"I'm not complicated. How could you say that?"

"I love all of you, even the complicated parts."

My words hung in the silence of the room. He looked down at his hands, embarrassed, as if he didn't deserve to be loved. "I've missed hearing that. I love you, too. I shouldn't have shut you out."

"You need something to focus on and now you have it."

"What?"

"You're going to locate your father and write to him."

"I can't after all these years. If he's even alive, he probably thinks I hate him."

"You're looking for excuses. It won't be easy, but you need to tell him about your mother anyway. You should contact your aunt, too. Maybe she has information about your father."

"You're being bossy."

"You need a kick in the butt."

"Boyfriend abuse! Boyfriend abuse!"

"Can I tell you how wonderful it is to hear the b-word?" The moment of lightness was like a salve, but Mateo's face became twisted again.

"You know, I was planning to contact my aunt, anyway. I have to take Mom's ashes to Colombia."

"She's being cremated?"

"Remember her cryptic comment a while back about returning to Colombia? She told me a long time ago that she didn't like the idea of cremation, but she wanted to go back to Colombia when she died and that was the easiest way. She didn't want to be a burden after her death."

"That's perfect. Contact your father and tell him you're coming to Colombia."

"I don't know. It's been too long."

"He's your fucking father, Mateo. Did you not read those letters? He deserves an explanation for all these years of silence."

"What if he can't handle what I've become?"

"You mean a wonderful, sweet person who saves lives in the ER and was a devoted son...and a so-so boyfriend?"

"Fuck you. Just for that, you're going with me."

"As your...uh...roommate?"

"If I'm going to do this, I'm going back to Colombia as the person I am and preferably with the man I love."

"That was a quick 180."

"Ignoring the so-so boyfriend comment for a moment, you make me a better person. If my father can't handle it, then I will be back to where I was before, the estranged son."

I looked at the time. "I should go."

"You don't have to. I'm not working tomorrow."

"Why not?"

"Since I started back, I'm doing the rotation others in ER do, twelve-hour shifts. Before, they let me do eight-hour shifts because of my mom. I have the next two days off."

"You want me to spend the night?"

"I have to change the sheets and take a shower. I've kind of let things go."

"You better not say my messiness has rubbed off on you."

"No, *cariño,* I've had a few things on my mind. Help me change the sheets and then you can wash my back."

"In the shower?"

"No, in the kitchen sink."

"I'm just astonished. I get to shower *and* sleep with you. Did I win the lottery?"

“I’m not sure I qualify as a lottery, but I’m yours if you’ll have me.”

We kissed for the first time in what felt like years. “Yeah,” I said. “I’ll have you.”

# Chapter 31

I awoke to the sound of Mateo rummaging around in his mother's room, followed by, "Aha!"

My curiosity drew me out of bed and into a robe. I stood at the door to his mother's bedroom, a room I had never entered. Something gave me the shivers, perhaps the ghost of Carmen, but more likely it was the draft from the open window crawling up my naked legs.

The room was partly cleared out and partly strewn with her remaining belongings where it appeared Mateo had been stymied mid operation, undoubtedly when he came upon the letters. He sat on the edge of the hospital bed that had barely been used, leafing through a small notebook. He looked up. "Did I wake you?"

"I thought we were having an earthquake."

"You always make a mountain out of a mole."

"Molehill."

"What?"

"A molehill is the little hill moles make in the ground. It wouldn't make sense to just say mole."

"But a mole is very small, and a mountain is big."

"Yes, but...it's way too early for this conversation."

"*De todos modos, Gracias, profesor.*"

"What did you find?"

"Mom's address book. There's a number for Tia Julia. I have to call her. That's not going to be easy."

"I guess no one back there knows she's passed."

"How would they? Mom cut off communication with everyone."

"I'll go make some coffee."

The kitchen was clearly not the usual Mateo kitchen. Coffee spill stains and crumbs on the counters and dirty dishes in the sink. I set up the coffee maker and opened the refrigerator, searching for milk. On the middle shelf was the dish I had brought a few days earlier, but only a small portion had been eaten and the foil covering hadn't been put back properly, so the rest had dried out. In addition to the casserole was a container of half-eaten Chinese food, some condiments in the door, a few limp carrots, a carton of expired milk (only a day over, so we could still use it), and browning lettuce in the vegetable bin. I couldn't imagine what he had eaten in the past week. It looked like my kitchen in pre-Mateo days.

A minute later I heard happy screaming coming from the other room. He must have been successful in reaching his aunt. After a few lines of excited conversation, Mateo shifted into a low, serious voice, giving Julia the news. The next few minutes, his voice was shaky, and he told his aunt not to cry. "*No llores, tia.*"

The coffee pot started gurgling so loudly I had to move into the hallway outside Carmen's room to better eavesdrop. After he gave a long description of his mom's decline, he asked about his father. He was silent for a while as Julia gave what must have been a complicated answer, and he followed with a few more questions. When he told her he was going to Colombia to spread his mother's ashes according to her wishes, Julia's cries of excitement were so loud I could hear them from the hall.

Over coffee, sitting on the couch in the living room, Mateo recounted the conversation, and a light came back into his eyes. "All these memories from childhood are flooding back into my head. I have cousins! Cousins I had forgotten all about. Julia had three daughters and they're now married with kids. I have lots of family I don't know. And that's only on my mom's side."

"What about your father?"

"Julia hasn't spoken to him in years, but she's going to ask around. One of his brothers still lives in Santa Marta. Since his mother, my grandmother, died, he doesn't go back to Santa Marta."

The notion of going to Colombia and being surrounded by multiple pairs of Mateo's relatives' curious eyes gave me a reality check. "Don't you think it would be better for you to go alone? I mean, showing up with the grinch who stole Christmas, you would have a lot of 'splaining to do, Lucy," I said in a bad imitation of Ricky Ricardo's accent.

"No. You are not backing out of this. I'm proud of who I am and I'm proud of my *gringo viejito.* And you're much cuter than the grinch, but you *can* be sort of grumpy."

"Me?" I said, punching his arm. "You're the moody one."

"Anyway, I already prepared Julia. Of course, she asked if I was married, and I said, 'Not yet, and it wouldn't be to a woman.' She didn't miss a beat, telling me about her husband's nephew who always liked to wear his sister's clothes."

"I'm not sure performing a drag show for the family would be the best introduction."

"That would involve so much extra packing. I really think we should keep it simple and butch."

"I'll try to keep my wrists from dangling too much. Did you tell her you were bringing someone?"

"One thing at a time."

After having gone to Cuba to meet Vladimir's mother and relatives and all the neighbors and their relatives, and going to meet Anthony's family in Oakland, I figured I could handle Mateo's family. One thing I had observed in my travels was the phenomenon of foreigners being given a certain dispensation. Like when I went to Cuba, I was without a doubt scrutinized as Vladimir's special friend, but at the same time, I was given a pass. Foreigners are, well, foreign and guests, two things that afford them special treatment. I was also willing to suffer a little scrutiny as Colombia was a country I had always wanted to visit. Still, there was one person I was leery about meeting. If Mateo was able to contact his father, I wondered how a man with a connection to the Medellin cartel would react to his son being gay and bringing home his boyfriend. I had never heard anything about cartel members being particularly homophobic, but I couldn't imagine faggotry was looked upon with great warmth. That was not a concern I shared with Mateo.

"What do you remember of your father?"

"I have mostly good memories. He wasn't around a lot because he spent so much time in Medellin. But when he was with us, we used to do a lot of fun things."

"Like what?"

"Hire a boat and go around Cartagena Bay, have lunch at Playa Blanca, and go snorkeling. He taught me to swim and play fútbol. We would go to a field near the house and kick the ball around, take turns kicking goals, and he would yell like a kid when I was able to get a goal past him. Sometimes, we went to Tayrona National Park near Santa Marta and hiked to this amazing beach called

Castilletes with palm trees and giant white boulders, which I used to think were petrified elephants. Mom would pack a picnic and we would spend all day on the white sand with Tia Julia, her husband, and my cousins. Talking to Julia opened the door to all the happy memories of my father that I haven't allowed myself to think about in years."

"Your mom never talked about your dad?"

"Once we arrived in the States, if his name came up at all, it was usually negative. After a couple of weeks in Florida, I asked when we were going home. She squeezed my chin in the palm of her hand and stared deep into my eyes. 'This is home now.' When I asked when Dad was coming to be with us, she said he was involved with some bad people, and we were going to stay in the States because it was safer."

"Safer how?"

"She'd never gotten over my little brother's death, and somehow blamed it on my father, which made no sense. She said we had to work really hard, and I was going to be a doctor so I could save little boys like Sergio. The day they attempted to kidnap me, happening just a couple of years after Sergio's death, was another traumatic event for her, but it also woke up the mother bear in her. Her plan to flee the country must have been brewing for a while. She couldn't lose another son and she was willing to give up everything to bring me to the States. The message was clear. We were never going back to Colombia. We would have no contact with my father."

"How could you accept that?"

"I didn't have a choice. I was cut off from everything I knew. She was my mother. I had to believe she knew what she was doing. She also had a way of putting the pressure on, like the idea that I needed to study hard to become a doctor. I couldn't show my unhappiness because I was supposed to be the man of the family now that it was just the two of us."

It was impossible for me to imagine the war inside Mateo's head between the profound feelings of loss for his mother and the fresh realization that she had cut him out of an important part of his life. It pained me to see him suffer, and yet, there was nothing I could do except support him and give him all the love he needed...and throw in a few jokes to ward off his descending into madness. I put my arm around him and massaged the back of his head.

"We could look on Facebook for your relatives," I suggested, to ease his mind into a realizable task. "What's your father's name?"

"Take a wild guess."

"Mateo?"

"I'm a junior. People used to say I looked a lot like him."

"Hmm. Handsome like you and he would be more my age."

The annoyance on his face told me my joke had fallen flat. "Sorry. Not available. Julia said he has a new family. I guess I have half brothers and sisters," he said as if the words tasted bad in his mouth.

"This gets more complicated by the minute."

"Tell me about it."

A Facebook search for Mateo Falla resulted in the person sitting next to me and a few others, none of whom were in the right geographical area or the approximate age for his father. Since Spanish-speaking countries use a second last name, the maternal last name would have been helpful to narrow the search, but Mateo couldn't remember it.

"Is Julia on Facebook?" I asked.

"She said she didn't have time for that Facebook nonsense, especially after seeing how much time her daughters wasted on it. In my mother's address book, she had conveniently listed the names of Julia's daughters next to her entry. She had cut off ties, but in her head, they were still family, and she didn't want to forget them."

One of them had an unusual name, Daisy, so we started with her and were able to locate a Facebook profile we thought had to be her. Mateo sent a friend request with a message saying who he was.

"Why do you have that funny smile on your face?" I asked.

"Daisy was the cousin I was closest to. We were kissing cousins. My first kiss was with Daisy when I was eleven on Castilletes beach behind a large boulder. I think she was ten. Dad caught us and laughed. He never told anybody about it, but he used to tease me about it all the time."

"And then your budding career as a heterosexual was cut short."

"A year later we were in the States. I wanted to write to her, but Mom wouldn't give me the address. She said there was no point since we were never going back."

"And there was the little issue that she was your first cousin."

"I was attracted to boys, though I hadn't admitted it to myself. There was a boy I liked at school. He was *mono* like you."

"A monkey?"

"No, Colombians use it for blonde people."

"Did he feel the same about you?"

"Who knows? When we left the country suddenly, I thought about him a lot and wondered if he missed me."

"You could look him up when we're down there."

"Not happening." He moved his head away from my hand rubbing his head.

"Should we start booking flights?" I asked.

"I'll let you take care of that, Mr. *vagabundo del mundo.* See if we can fly into Santa Marta. Our return should be out of Cartagena. I want you to see the town I remember best."

After a little research, I found we could go through Panama City on Copa with one stop.

"I thought we would have to go through Miami," said Mateo.

"That's an option, but it's longer and more expensive. Do you want to go through Miami?"

"No way. I haven't been back there since we first moved to the country and that's fine with me."

"Do we need to book a hotel in Santa Marta?"

"Julia is insisting we stay with her. They have lots of room since the girls have all moved out. How do you feel about that?"

"The flights are expensive, so I guess we could save money. But it's also a bit weird."

"Daisy said we'd be better off staying with her, as she doubted her parents had ever had a gay person in the house, let alone a gay couple spend the night."

I didn't know what part of his statement to focus on first. Mateo's referring to us as a couple was still as fresh and thrilling as cracking open a new book, but the fact that there was a competition over who would host us between Mateo's ex-girlfriend/cousin and his aunt who seemed to think gay men wanted to wear dresses was fodder for a sitcom. Sometimes you just had to get as comfortable as possible and enjoy the ride.

# Chapter 32

On the flight from Panama City to Santa Marta, I immersed myself in the ridiculously priced Colombia guidebook I had purchased at a local bookstore, wondering how we were going to cram into eight days—all the time the hospital would give Mateo off—the many things I wanted to see, and the places Mateo wanted to show me. He promised me that the second half of the trip we would spend in Cartagena alone and we booked a romantic hotel in the historic center with views of the sea.

Traveling to a new country with someone I loved was clearly a treat, though circumstances were hardly ideal. We had serious and emotional business to attend to. A couple of days after our arrival, we would go out to Castilletes beach to spread Carmen's ashes, followed by a reception at Julia's house. Poor Carmen was in the overhead bin, neatly packed in TSA approved materials of a plastic bag inside a wooden box. Mateo had done all the complicated paperwork to bring cremains into the country, but the spreading of the ashes we were doing freestyle as we knew getting permission from the park authorities would be a nightmare. We would smuggle Carmen into Tayrona National Park, her final resting place.

As we encountered turbulence over the Caribbean Sea, I had a horrific vision of the bin popping open and Carmen's ashes raining down on us. "You securely closed the backpack, right?"

"Of course."

"I was once on a flight where heavy turbulence forced the overhead bins open, and things got scattered all over the plane. When it stopped, the flight attendants had to hold up items like glasses, cell phones, hats, and jackets, asking people to identify them."

He put his hand on my leg. "Don't worry. Everything's secure." I was sitting in the aisle seat and the man across the way stared at Mateo's hand on my leg. A few seconds later, the plane took a jolly dip, and several people screamed as our hearts landed in our throats. He had just told me not to worry, and now his hand had my knee in a vice grip.

"Just a warning, if the plane goes into a nosedive, I'm going to kiss you hard because I want that to be my last best memory."

"*Te quiero,*" he said, his hand still on my leg but his grip easing.

"Me too," I said with a big smile, hoping the man across the aisle heard his words.

"It's gonna be okay."

The plane leveled and stopped shaking, but as we began our descent, we went through another pocket of bad air, bouncing us around like an amusement park ride.

In the end, it was a smooth landing, though the anticipation of the next phase of arrival in a foreign country brought on the usual tensions: going through passport control and customs and finding our way in a new country. But on top of that, Mateo was arriving in his native country and reuniting with his family after twenty-five years. We had reached the stage in a relationship where a simple look could tell me what he was feeling or a subtle change in the tone of his voice was a sign that things weren't all right or the way his shoulders curved forward I could feel he was internalizing his feelings rather than letting them out. That stage of sharing things without words is significant, wonderful when intuiting the positives, and painful when intuiting the negatives.

After what seemed like a long wait, we were able to get our things out of the overhead bin, including Carmen, and head down the aisle to the jetway.

Once inside the terminal, following the crowd toward customs, I turned to Mateo. “You okay?”

“Why? Do I seem nervous?”

“You have every right to be.”

“Look, I’m very happy you’re with me, but it might be better if you didn’t ask me if I’m okay every five minutes.”

“Gotcha.”

I had on numerous occasions been in the scenario of arriving at a foreign passport control with a partner, boyfriend, or in the case of Anthony, my legal husband, but there was always that awkward moment of whether to approach the agent as a couple or individually with individually winning out. We deserved better. We deserved to enter a country as a couple like straight couples did. And yet, the annoying and sometimes intimidating passport control maybe wasn’t the place to be waving the equal rights flag. We got through it without incident even if we had to enter the country as if we were strangers and didn’t have intimate knowledge of each other’s bodies. On the form I had put Mateo’s aunt’s address as my destination, and I wondered if the agent paid any attention to the fact that the previous person had put the same address and what it meant if he cared to speculate. Once legally inside the country, we were again a couple, gathering our luggage and heading toward the exit.

Mateo’s steps became slow and laborious as we approached the sliding doors to the lobby, making me the first to exit. On the plane we had discussed what we had to do: find an ATM to get cash to pay a taxi and find an authorized taxi so we didn't end up in a ditch somewhere minus all our belongings, or worse. Mateo had expressed his surprise that Julia hadn't said anything about coming to the airport.

I immediately saw that the taxi wouldn't be necessary, and Julia's plan had been to surprise us. A huge sign stuck out from a group of expectant faces, saying, "Bienvenidos, Mateo." I slowed and turned around to smile at Mateo, but he hadn't noticed the crowd as he battled with his rolling bag that had decided to do a Lindy Hop routine.

"Mateo, look!" I said, pointing at the sign.

He got his bag under control and froze, scanning the greeters with something between a scowl and a smile, panic in his eyes. He moved forward and was engulfed by a crowd, inundating him with hugs and kisses from the women and strong handshakes and slaps on the back from the men while I stood aside with the bags. I touched the backpack holding Carmen's ashes and said in not too much of an accusatory voice, "See what he's been missing all these years?"

As if a director held up a cue card, everybody turned to look at me, and Mateo waved me over, presenting me to Julia, her husband, her three daughters, one of the spouses, and several children. Their eyes lit up as I greeted them in Spanish, and no one looked at me with dagger eyes like I was the man who had corrupted their dear Mateo. Daisy was the only one bold enough to let a stare linger, as if she questioned me being there. It seemed that Julia noticed her daughter's scrutiny and stepped in to take my hand, holding it warmly in hers, welcoming me, asking me if it was my first time in Colombia, and wishing me a wonderful stay. Julia had won out in the battle to host us, and we piled into Julia and Oscar's car while everyone else filled the other cars. We went in a caravan to Julia's house in the Gaira area of Santa Marta.

The three-bedroom house had a terracotta roof and was surrounded by palm trees and flowering plants with a small pool in the backyard. We were given a bedroom with two single beds, formerly shared by two of the daughters, but at least they didn't separate us, putting us in opposite ends of the house. In one comical moment, Julia, Oscar, Mateo, and I stood in the doorway of the bedroom and stared at the two beds like travelers opening the door of a motel room that wasn't exactly what was expected. A fresh towel had been placed on each bed.

Oscar drifted silently away, but Julia lingered as we rolled our bags and took in the flowery bedspreads, the thick rose curtains drawn against the heat, and rose-colored throw rugs on the tile floor. A hint of perfume was in the stale, hot air. We weren't used to the heat and humidity, and Mateo stared longingly at the wall-mounted air conditioning unit. Julia grabbed the remote off the dresser and pushed some buttons, explaining how to operate the system. I asked for the bathroom, more to break the awkwardness than a real need, and Julia led me down the hall.

She again assured me I was welcome and if there was anything I needed, to please just ask. By association, I could bask in Mateo's joyful welcome home as if he were the prodigal son though in this case, he wasn't returning destitute after having squandered his inheritance; he had never had the opportunity of an inheritance to waste, which brought to mind the issue of his father. Since our fruitless effort at finding Mateo senior on Facebook, Mateo, as far as I knew, hadn't made more attempts to locate his father, perhaps leaving that up to Julia. I was sure his father was on his mind, but he was overwhelmed by so many new things from the strength-zapping heat to scattering his mother's ashes to reuniting with family in locations he only had vague memories of.

I returned from the bathroom, and Mateo and I sat on the rose-patterned bedspread of one of the beds. His steepled hands were between his legs. "Is this okay?" he asked.

"Nothing a gay interior decorator couldn't fix."

He tsked. "Staying here...with Julia. Is it too much? We could go to a hotel."

"It would break her heart. It's just a few days."

"The whole gang is coming over for dinner. *Prepárate.*"

"You're the one that needs to prepare. I can just sit there, nod, throw in a few words of Spanish and..."

"Look pretty?" he said with a laugh.

"That's not where I was going."

Mateo lifted his head up toward the draft of cool air and swiveled his neck to get the full effect. "I forgot how hot it is here."

"Were they living in this house when you were here?"

"This is an upgrade. Big time. They lived in a simple house in a not great neighborhood. I always felt bad because the house Dad bought us in Cartagena was like a mansion in comparison. I was so naïve. I didn't understand why we lived so well with maids, a swimming pool, tennis court, and I felt sorry for my cousins who had nothing. I could buy all the designer clothes I wanted, the best athletic shoes. And then, we had to leave everything behind. At times in the States, we barely had food on the table. During those times I would have been happy to live in Tia Julia's simple house. At least they had a house and a family."

The light through the curtains fell on Mateo's face, giving it a pink glow, his freckles like ruddy stars. The lines around his eyes had multiplied in recent weeks and new splotches of gray peeked out from his curly hair. But his beauty still took my breath away. I put a hand on his knee. He turned toward me. "What?"

"You're so fucking beautiful."

"I know that look. Don't get any ideas. We must shower and get ready for dinner."

"Have you ever slept in a single bed with someone?" As soon as the words were out of my mouth, I regretted it. My brain automatically flipped through memories of sleeping close to another person in a small bed and landed on the night I spent with the abusive scoutmaster when I was thirteen in an even smaller bed on a train to the national Boy Scout Jamboree. If I was bitter about being gay, I could have blamed it on the scoutmaster, but I knew the signs were there before that incident, like the uneasiness in my gut the first time I saw the young doctor down the street. Still, the disturbing incident had left its mark and popped into my head more than I would have liked.

"When I was little, sometimes my brother and I slept in the same small bed," said Mateo. "He used to get scared at night. I bet you've slept with someone in every sized bed imaginable."

"What's that supposed to mean?" My Boy Scout memory left me in a foul mood. It wasn't the first time he had implied that I had been a slut a good part of my life, which had a certain truth to it.

"Are you angry? I was just kidding."

I pushed him back on the bed and climbed on top of him. "Take it back."

"Get off. What if someone walks in?"

"Are you worried?" I said, trying to control my laughter.

I laughed so hard I almost peed my pants because when I had gone to the bathroom before, I hadn't actually peed, but stood at the mirror and taken a few deep breaths. Okay, I had also looked in the medicine cabinet, a life-long habit just to see what there was to see. It had been many years since I'd popped any potentially entertaining meds into my pocket from a home I visited, and I certainly wasn't about to do it now, not in the home of Mateo's family.

Mateo wiggled and pushed me. "This is not funny!" Now, he was pissed off.

I got off him and stood up. "I have to pee."

"Didn't you just...?"

"I'm an old man. What can I say?"

An hour later we were sitting around a large table in what seemed a verbal equivalent of a soccer game: a constant back and forth, a din in the background from the spectators, the excitement of the announcers talking over each other, especially when one player got close to scoring a goal. Daisy and her father, Oscar, tended to be the loudest, though a husband of one of the daughters kept trying to compete. While Daisy passionately made the case for women's rights, her seven-year-old boy, Sebastian, stared at me with blank curiosity from across the table. It was much too noisy to try and engage him in conversation and a smile was useless in establishing any kind of rapport. He continued to stare.

Julia asked why family conversations always had to be so political. Undaunted, Daisy asked Mateo how it was possible that the United States allowed a person with fewer votes to win the presidency and why the U.S. hadn't elected a woman president. Others chimed in with questions about more idiosyncrasies of American politics. Mateo threw up his hands, reminding them he was just an immigrant. Everyone turned to me. If they were expecting me to defend the U.S. election system or anything about our government, they were coming to the wrong person. I shrugged. "*Estoy de acuerdo con Julia. Porque no hablamos de otras cosas, por ejemplo la Ciudad Perdida o la música de Colombia.*" My comment that I agreed with Julia and suggesting we talk about The Lost City or Colombian music was met with groans from Daisy and several others.

Mateo laughed at my idea. "Are you ready for a five-day hike through the jungle getting eaten by mosquitoes and dying from the heat to reach the Lost City?"

They all admitted they had never done it, but the pictures of the site did look amazing.

"Colombian music is a little more accessible," said Daisy in perfect English. "But most foreigners only know about Shakira. She's hardly Colombian anymore."

The conversation switched to questions about Mateo's work at the hospital. I watched in admiration as his eyebrows flexed, the water in his eyes ebbed and flowed, the corners of his mouth twitched as he talked about the life and death intensity of his job. What they didn't ask was how I fit into his life, how we met, and how long we had known each other. I glanced across the table again at the boy who continued to focus on me as I tried to focus on Mateo's words. What was going on in his head?

Sebastian had a pretty face, soft brown eyes, and a mop of curly hair such that he could easily have been taken for a girl. His skin was paler than most at the table. Mateo's family offered a mixed bag of skin tones, reflecting Colombia's history of intermarriage between Europeans, Afro-Colombians, and indigenous peoples. Daisy had married lighter; her two sisters darker. Mateo told me that when his mother married a man with darker skin, it had caused a scandal in her family, and he imagined it was why his father was obsessed with proving he could provide for his family.

The evening finished with "the tales of Tayrona," which, by their wild-eyed delight, was obviously an attempt to scare the shit out of the newbie as they told stories of knee-deep mud on the trails, spiders the size of one's hand, blood-thirsty mosquitoes, poisonous snakes, the relentless burning rays of the sun, and an undertow at the beaches that had carried away countless tourists.

I used his family's teasing to make Mateo climb into the single bed with me, claiming that I was going to have nightmares. He held me and stroked the top of my head until he thought I was asleep and then moved to the other bed.

# Chapter 33

Instead of the perils of Tayrona, I was immediately delighted by the absolute beauty of the park, the verdant mountains towering over white sand beaches sprouting palm trees and lined with giant gray boulders that looked like beached whales or, as Mateo believed as a child, petrified elephants. Along the worn paths between the shore and the mountains, the jungle gave up its mysteries of plants, birds, insects, and chattering capuchin monkeys leaping from tree to tree.

We had arrived early at the El Zaino entrance to the park to avoid crowds. It was a weekday but the beginning of the dry season when foreigners and Colombians flocked to the beaches. In the parking lot we strapped the backpacks filled with food and blankets and swimwear over our shoulders; Mateo carried Carmen in his pack.

I wore a floppy hat and cargo pants that could be zipped off at the knee to make shorts and a white polo shirt. The women had all decided on white dresses or white blouses with white gauzy pants, while the men wore white guayaberas. Daisy and her sisters had woven flowers into their thick hair. Mateo had gotten his guayabera on an afternoon shopping trip to the local artisan market after we spent the morning lounging around the family pool, Mateo still playing catch-up with Julia about his and Carmen's life in the United States.

Mateo came up beside me on the trail. “Did you put on sunscreen?” Sweet. He was thinking of me despite all the other things that must have been going on in his head.

“Yep. And lots of bug spray.”

A young woman passed us, headed back to the parking lot with a distressed look on her face, her white legs dotted with hundreds of red spots after probably having camped the night on the beach.

As it was still early, there were few other people on the trail that weaved through hushed jungle with sunlight splashing through the green foliage and birds calling out to herald our passing. The dirt path sometimes changed to wooden walkways around or over huge boulders where we would catch a glimpse of the bright blue water of the Caribbean with its treacherous frothy waves, waves my hosts proclaimed were poised to snatch an unwary tourist. After a twenty-minute walk we came out on a deserted beach where the surf pounded the sand and large birds hovered and screeched above the shoreline. We stopped for a rest, everyone dropping their backpacks and plopping down on the sand under the already intense sun. A red flag snapped in the wind, telling us no swimming was allowed.

“Why don’t we go sit under those palm trees?” I asked Daisy.

She laughed. “Those are coconut palms. Lovely to look at, but you really don’t want to have a coco fall on your *coco!*”

Mateo separated himself from the group and walked toward the shore, staring at the waves, lost in thought, his eyes focused on a distant memory.

“I have so many questions for you,” said Daisy.

I raised my eyebrows. “I’m sure you do,” I said with a wry smile.

“Is he okay?”

"Most of the time. The letters he found from his father hit him hard."

Daisy shook her head. "What did Carmen think of...you know...you and Mateo?"

"By the time I met her, she was already confused, and her mind would go in and out. Mateo tried to make her aware that he had met someone, but she never really got it or, at least, she acted like she didn't. We didn't push it in order not to upset her."

"I remember her as a strong woman who would do anything for her kids. After Sergio passed, she changed."

"That's what Mateo said."

Sebastian stood behind her, watching us with his curious brown eyes.

Daisy looked over her shoulder, then back at me. "Perhaps this is a conversation for another time," she said.

Mateo returned and stood over Daisy and me. "What are you two talking about?"

"Colombian music," she said with a grin.

"It's just another fifteen minutes. Should we go on?"

Our destination was a small cove with a protected beach that had been the family's favorite spot when Mateo was growing up. With the sun still low in the sky, the mountains provided us with a sliver of shade where we unpacked the food onto the blankets. Julia's oldest daughter, Lidia, had wrapped bunches of carnations, chrysanthemums, and roses in newspaper inside her pack, the stems cut short, and though they had suffered in the journey, they would still be usable. She worked for a company that exported Colombian flowers all over the world.

Mateo studied the flowers that were laid out on one of the blankets. "Carnations were her favorite," he mumbled. "She always said they represented love and innocence." He choked on the word innocence, an innocence he now seemed to question. The carnations were red, white, and pale pink ones with veins of rose running through them. The chrysanthemums were purple, yellow, and rust-colored; the roses yellow, white, and red. With my phone I photographed them, framing just the flowers, half in shade and half in sun, and felt the opening lines of a poem emerging.

We all removed our shoes and walked ankle-deep into the gentle waves that crept beyond us up the beach and erased our footprints. In a half-circle, holding flowers in our hands, we gazed out to sea in the direction where Carmen had fled with her son. Mateo opened the box and undid the twisty of the plastic bag. I offered to hold the box, allowing those that would be participating in the scattering to have their hands free.

They had decided to do things quickly without speeches to avoid drawing attention to the secret ceremony though the beach was empty, and it was unlikely anyone would spot what we were doing. Mateo dug his hand into the bag of ashes, his face wincing as he touched them, and came up with a handful. He tossed a cloud of ash on the water and threw a white carnation in the middle of it.

"I return you, dear mother, to a place where we were once happy."

All the adults followed suit, grabbing a handful, throwing a flower, and then dipping their hands in the water to clean off the ash. Even Daisy's son, Sebastian, stepped up and said he wanted to join in. He stuck his small hand deep into the bag and came up with a fistful, tossing it with a delicate sideways motion onto the water.

While everyone was focused on Sebastian, I glanced over to the right where a man in street clothes stood in the shadows next to a giant boulder. At first, I bristled, thinking we had been caught by the park authorities, but I noticed he was carrying three red carnations in his hand. His hair was close-cropped, and he had a stocky body. The features of his dark face melted into the shadows, but I knew immediately I was looking at Mateo in twenty-five years. It made me sad to think I probably wouldn't live to see it.

I shook the box and Mateo peered down into its depths. "I guess I should do the rest myself."

"No, wait," I said.

"Everyone's had a chance."

"There might be one more." I looked in the direction of the man by the rock, and all the eyes of the group followed mine.

Mateo shuddered and looked like he might collapse as he, too, knew immediately who it was. Julia hurried to his side in a move of support. I gave the box to Sebastian and told him to hold on tight as I positioned myself on Mateo's other side. Julia whispered that she hadn't said anything because she wasn't sure he'd come.

"*Qué hago?*" Mateo had no idea what to do.

He didn't wait for an answer but pushed himself out of the group and trudged toward his father, each step appearing like a child's first hesitant paces, the possibility of toppling over ever-present, but the impulse to go on a force out of his control.

Mateo and his father stood a couple of yards apart. We couldn't hear what words were spoken. Mateo senior offered one of the three red carnations he was holding; a gruff-looking man formerly or in some way still connected to the Medellin cartel, who may or may not have known his son was gay, held out a flower to his son. Mateo took it. We could see his body shaking from where we were, feel his heart ready to explode. Just as he was about to disintegrate into a thousand pieces on the sand, his father took him into his arms, both their bodies now shaking as if an earthquake was happening under their feet.

I tried to control my emotions but began sniffling. Julia put an arm around me. Sebastian looked up at me. "*No llore, tio.*" He called me uncle and told me not to cry.

After a lengthy hug, Mateo and his father separated and shook out their shoulders. They walked with heads high back to the group, in control, though red-eyed. Mateo took the box from Sebastian and offered it to his father. Mateo senior spread the rest of the ashes on the water and threw his two remaining flowers on top of the gray dust of Carmen bobbing and mixing with the froth of the waves while the little bits of bone fell below the surface. We stared at the two flowers, at first together like two hearts, and with the tide they began to separate, growing farther and farther apart.

Mateo pointed out that his father's black sneakers and the hem of his dress pants were soaked. The two Mateos laughed, and I saw the same laugh lines I had grown to love on the father's face, the same soulful eyes, the same splash of freckles though fewer of them.

As we all headed for the blankets and food awaiting us, I held back as Julia, Mateo, and his father chatted like it was a normal excursion to the beach, a moment from the past. Mateo turned around and looked for me, motioning for me to join them, but I waved him on.

"I want you to meet my father," he said. The simple words hit me like a storm, the idea that he would want me to be part of this newfound union. I waved him on again. Mateo stopped and came back to me.

"He wants to meet you."

"I doubt that."

"You know what he said to me when we hugged? He said he embraced all of what I am because I am his son and he never..." Mateo's emotions throttled his words, but he took a couple of breaths, "...he never stopped loving me."

Despite Mateo's confidence that his father would accept me too, I didn't feel much warmth as Mateo senior gave me a hard stare when we shook hands. He continued holding my hand in a tight grip and pumped it after the polite three seconds. And then he began to laugh, a gnarly version of Mateo's laugh, but not unpleasant. "You have nothing to fear from me," he said in English. "That you are here tells me everything I need to know."

A few minutes later, we were stretched out on the sand, gazing at the water like figures in a Seurat painting minus the parasols, waiting for the food to be dished out. Daisy and Julia prepared plates of arepas, shrimp ceviche, sun-dried beef called carne oreada, and deep-fried plantains stuffed with cheese called aborrajados. To drink, we had a choice of lulo juice or iced coffee. I took the juice made from lulo fruit I had tried that morning and found the citrusy flavor refreshing. Mateo senior removed a flask from his pocket and offered me a little aguardiente for my drink. Lidia's husband remarked with a chuckle how alcohol was not permitted in the park as he pulled beers out of his bag. He passed one to Mateo. Then everyone joked how gringos were searched carefully at the gate while Colombians were waved through. Julia complained that it was too early to be drinking.

After lunch, the kids were anxious to go in the water, and the adults wrapped towels around themselves as they changed into swimsuits to accompany their children into the water. Mateo's father turned to his son. "You ever learn to swim?"

"Hah!" Mateo scoffed. "You should know."

"You were so angry at me that day. You marched out of the water and sat down next to your mother, refusing to talk to me the rest of the afternoon." Mateo senior swiveled to me. "It was very rough water, not like now. Was not a good day for teach swimming."

"I almost drowned," said Mateo. "And you laughed at me."

"*Hijo*, I would never let you drown." Mateo's father laughed freely and seemed to relish teasing his son in what looked like a return to Mateo's childhood, as if the last twenty-five years hadn't happened. "Remember Playa Blanca, *hijo*? I think that's the place you really learned to swim."

"Oh, now you remember?"

"You should take Nathan there."

"We are spending a few days in Cartagena after we leave here."

"*Que Bueno!* I'm going there too. We will be there at the same time."

"And our house?" asked Mateo.

"I sold it many years ago. There was no reason to go back there." His voice fell with sadness.

Mateo stared at the sand between his knees. "It wasn't my choice."

"I know."

"I...I never got your letters...until I found them a couple weeks ago...after her death."

"I suppose that was a possibility, but I needed to write them, anyway."

"I think I'll go swimming," I said. I wanted to give Mateo and his dad time to be alone.

"Come, *hijo*. Walk with me." They stood up and walked down the beach.

I dove in the warm water where flowers still floated, rose to the surface, and stood contemplating everything that had happened in the last year. A few days before this trip, I had glanced at the calendar and was slammed with the fact that it was the one-year anniversary of Anthony's death. With all the focus on the trip and the delicate balance of this new relationship, it had slipped my mind, and I felt horrible for it. I should have reached out to Anthony's mother, but I hadn't.

As lovely as Mateo's family had been, everything about the visit had been intense, and I couldn't wait to have a few relaxing days alone with Mateo in Cartagena. But now we knew his father would be there as well. The aguardiente Mateo's father had poured in my drink, instead of relaxing me, had ramped up the feels.

Without warning, something attacked me from below the surface of the water. Multiple tentacles like an octopus wrapped around my legs and pulled me under. In the turbulent water agitated by hands and legs, I saw Sebastian with a look of triumph on his face and the other boys were laughing at me. I came up, coughing and snorting out the water I had swallowed. Daisy's husband saw what had happened and scolded the boys. He asked me if I was all right.

"They just took me by surprise."

"I'm sorry."

Daisy grabbed Sebastian's arm. "*Qué haces? Pida perdón a Nathan.*"

"It's okay," I said. "I'm fine."

I left the water and walked back to the blankets. "Is there any beer left?" I asked Lidia's husband. He handed me one that was no longer cold, but it tasted right, a beer on the beach in Colombia as the temperature steadily rose. I put on my hat and sunglasses and leaned my head back on my backpack, gazing at the Caribbean sky with its thick, muscular clouds.

# Chapter 34

I lay awake, not specifically waiting for Mateo to come home, but the emotional events of the day and my revved-up brain made it hard to drift into sleep. I was only a passenger on Mateo's emotional roller coaster day, but I wondered how things would play out in terms of our relationship. Mateo had gone out to dinner with his dad who had been cordial, even friendly with me despite what must have been going on inside his head, the notion that after all these years he had reconnected with his son only to find he was a homosexual involved with a man several years his senior. In this vulnerable time of Mateo's life, could the newfound relationship with his father make him question his choices? Could his father put doubts in his head about me? Even in situations where parents have been absent for many years, parents are parents. Their influence can be profound and mysterious.

In the six months since Mateo and I had met, there had been no time to get our footing with one crisis or another staring us in the face: the lingering trauma of Anthony's death, his mother's health, his accident, my financial woes and flight to Mexico, his mother's death, and the reunion with family, particularly his father. No down time had allowed us to ease into being with each other. And yet, Daisy had surprised me by privately telling me she thought we were good for each other. She had seen a hint of the love that I was sure seasoned the air around us.

I heard a noise outside the door, and it creaked open, allowing in light from the hall. His movements had the bungling nature of someone who had been drinking.

"Hi," I said.

"Sorry. I woke you."

"No. I was awake."

"Oh." I waited for him to come to my bed, greet me with a kiss, touch my head, something. He sat on the edge of his bed and sighed.

"How did it go?"

"I drank too much."

"You should take an aspirin. Do you have any?"

"I don't have a headache." He sounded annoyed.

"Sometimes it helps, so you don't have a hangover."

He struggled to take off his boots. "Fuck!"

"Do you need help getting undressed?"

He groaned. "Don't be silly. Just go to sleep."

"Did something happen?"

"No. Fine. Everything's fine. Go to sleep."

"But I just..."

"Nathan, chill," he said in a harsh voice.

I threw off the covers and started to get up.

"Nathan," he said, louder this time. "Stay in bed. Go to sleep."

I cowered back under the covers, but the more he told me to go to sleep, the less chance of that happening. He succeeded in removing both boots and tossed them over by his bag. He lay back without removing his clothes, and in a few minutes, he began to snore.

In a relationship, you reach a point where you can comfortably remove your loved one's clothes when they come home drunk. I had done it many times with both Vladimir and Anthony. I felt that Mateo and I weren't there yet, especially since he had scoffed at my offer to help him, and that depressed me, conjuring up the fears I'd had earlier in the evening.

I spent the next few hours being annoyed, tossing and turning. Each time I turned to look at Mateo, the streetlight outside the window hit me in the face and annoyed me. Mateo's position, now on his side facing away from me, annoyed me. The sour alcohol smell of his breath, riding on the humid air of the room, annoyed me. That he was fully clothed, and I didn't feel comfortable doing anything about it, annoyed me.

So much annoyance must have exhausted me to the point of falling asleep because the next thing I knew, someone was crawling in bed with me, a fully unclothed person, while a hint of a new day glowed outside the window. He wrapped me in his arms. "I'm so sorry."

"Why?" I croaked on the verge of tears of relief, of joy, of ecstasy.

"I think I was mean to you last night."

"You've had a lot on your plate."

"It nearly killed me to be sitting across from my father, feeling his excitement, his interest, his love, and knowing that it had been denied me all these years. And it was all my mother's fault. I hated being angry at her, the woman who had sacrificed everything to keep me safe. So, I had another drink. And another. And another. And when we said goodnight, I cried like I would never see him again and he held me in his arms. And I cried more because he could have been there for me over the years. I'm not a crying person, but lately I shed tears everywhere."

"I was afraid he said something that made you doubt us."

"Hate to burst your bubble, *querido*, but the dinner was not about you."

"I know. I'm an idiot."

"Don't ever let me be mean to you." He kissed my forehead and nuzzled closer. "Except..."

"Except what?"

"When you abandon me like that time you ran off to Mexico and I wasn't even healed from my accident."

"You were too. I waited."

"*Sinvergüenza.* That made it okay? That I was healed?"

I ran my hand from his neck down to his knees. "You don't have any clothes on."

"So?" He slipped his hand inside my underwear. He didn't necessarily do it to arouse me but to enter covered and restricted territory and lay claim to a ridge between my hip and my pelvis or a valley between my glutes. It wasn't a forgone conclusion where this was going in a small bed in his aunt's house with day breaking and the birds tweeting outside.

"I didn't abandon..." His kiss garbled the rest of my message.

His lips pulled back and he looked at me.

"My father said you were nice-looking."

"But..."

He kissed me again. "And a gentleman."

"I thought you didn't talk about me."

He wiggled my underwear down and crawled on top of me. "I didn't have a chance to tell him about your finer qualities. That's true."

"Will we see him again?"

"He's going to Cartagena today," he said, with his lips close to my ear. "We'll see him the day after." The simple communication and the "we" whispered in my ear sparked through my body. Where we were going was now obvious. I just had to remember not to shout out if things got too crazy.

***

Daisy insisted we spend the last night in Santa Marta at her house, even enticing us in a low voice that the sofa in the guest room folded down into a double bed. Julia looked disappointed but made us promise to have breakfast at her house. Then she would take us to the station to get on a bus to Cartagena.

The evening with Daisy and her family was more relaxed than at Julia's where, as kind as she and Oscar were, we were a novelty. Daisy invited a neighbor who was a professor of linguistics at the University of Magdalena in Santa Marta for dinner, and shockingly (not), he turned out to be gay. Perhaps a performative gesture to show that they were cool and had gay friends, but it was still a fun evening. Before dinner, Sebastian even corralled me into playing a video game with him at which I was terrible, giving him great pleasure to beat me.

The joy of being able to sleep in the same bed was considerably dampened by the back-numbing flimsy mattress allowing the springs to poke through. After a quick morning coffee, Daisy's husband dropped us off at Julia's on his way to work, one more kind gesture in a long line of treating us like royalty; we hadn't paid for a thing since we arrived, nor had it been necessary to arrange our own transportation.

Julia had made pandebono to accompany the large breakfast of fruit, arepas, scrambled eggs, and quesito. As we were finishing the meal, the doorbell rang, and Oscar went to answer it. He came back to the dining room and whispered something to Julia. She stood up with a concerned look and went to the door with Oscar. A few minutes later we heard, "Mateo. Nathan. Come."

A man in a dark suit and aviator sunglasses stood at the door, and beyond him in the driveway was a black Cadillac Escalade. "Señor Falla, I'm here to take you to Cartagena."

Mateo looked at his aunt with concern. It had been twenty-five years since the attempted kidnapping, but the memory was on both their faces.

The driver stood outside the door with his hands folded behind his back, stiff as a soldier. A text notification sounded from Mateo's phone. He read the message and then held the screen up to me. It was his dad telling us to enjoy the ride and he would see us soon.

We said an emotional goodbye to Julia and Oscar with promises to stay in touch and Julia said she might even consider getting on Facebook so it would be easier. She also told me to take care of Mateo, which made me smile.

The car had a cooler with sodas and beer, a basket of snacks, and the driver let us choose the music. We spent a good portion of the four-and-half-hour drive going in and out of naps since we had slept so poorly the night before.

We woke up as we entered the historic walled part of Cartagena, easing down a narrow one-way street with pastel-colored buildings on either side, and came upon a small plaza. He pulled in front of an entrance that said Hotel Santa Clara.

"This isn't the hotel we booked," I said to Mateo.

He had a discussion with the driver who assured him this is where he was told to take us and there was a reservation in our name. Once we had passed through the unassuming portal to the hotel, we entered a land of luxury that neither of us could afford.

"Let's see how much it is," said Mateo. "Maybe we could splurge for one night and then move to our regular hotel."

We stepped up to the front desk in shorts and T-shirts, but it felt like we should have been wearing linen suits and Panama hats, entering a colonial world of privilege and charm, having our valets handle the trunks.

The woman welcomed us with a smile, unfazed by our casual attire. "Yes, Mr. Falla and Mr. Landis. I have you in a deluxe room for four nights."

"Well...um...it might just be one night. Do you need a credit card?"

"Everything's taken care of, including any bar and restaurant tabs, room service, everything. Are you sure it's just one night?"

Mateo looked at me. "What do we do? Can we accept this?"

I returned the desk clerk's broad smile. "Does it have a view?"

"Oh, yes. The balcony looks out over the pool and the sea beyond that."

"We'll take it," I said.

The hotel room was the nicest either of us had stayed in, with a king-size bed and a bathroom you could have a party in. On the desktop was a welcome basket with fruit and a bottle of champagne. The card on the basket said, "*Disfruta, hijo.*"

Mateo held the card in a shaky hand. "I don't know what to say."

"Just shoot him a thank-you text."

"I don't want him to think he has to buy my love."

"He wanted to do something nice for you and he has the means."

"I still wonder what he does. It came up briefly in our conversation at the beach. He said he was a businessman now and left it at that."

"Did he bring it up, or did you?"

"I asked him why he didn't come to the States and try to find us if he had Mom's address. He said he wasn't allowed in the country due to his previous associations. Then he assured me he was a legit businessman."

***

After touring the old town, we sat in the hotel restaurant, waiting for Mateo's father to join us. He was a half hour late. We had another drink. And then it was an hour.

Mateo's frustration crinkled his forehead in a way that seemed deeper than the immediate situation of possibly being stood up by his newly found dad. "I can't tell you the number of times my mother and I sat at the dinner table, waiting for Dad to show up. He was always late and sometimes never appeared at all. It used to upset my mother, though she tried not to show it. We were surrounded by luxury and had people to cook and serve our food. But we had no father or husband to enjoy it with." He tried a half-smile, but it collapsed into a sigh. "We should go ahead and order."

Halfway through our dinner, he showed up, contrite and begging forgiveness. He had been in a meeting. His charm, engaging eyes, and warm handshakes made it difficult to be angry with him, and Mateo's irritation melted away at first sight of him. He asked me a lot of questions about my life, my travels, and my teaching. I appreciated that he showed an interest.

"Dad, stop interrogating Nathan and tell me about my half-brother and sister. How old are they?"

Mateo senior's eyes bore down on his son as Mateo's sometimes did on me. "Are you really curious or are you trying to calculate how long before I found a new wife?"

Mateo was momentarily stunned. "It was an innocent question."

"I wouldn't blame you for wanting to know. I waited five years for you and your mother to come back. It was painful. It became obvious I was waiting in vain." He took a pause with a dramatic sigh. "But that's history. Both your brother and sister are at university. They want to meet you."

"I wish I had more time. On the next trip we can go to Medellin."

"I like this, you say next trip. I hope it is so. There is much to see in this country."

Mateo picked up a spoon the waiter had set down in anticipation of the flan we were going to share. He twirled it in his fingers as I had seen him do in other times of nervousness. "I don't know when I'll have time off again."

"Maybe you think to move here someday."

Mateo dropped the spoon. "What are you saying? My life is there."

"Relax, *hijo.* I know your job is important to you. I'm happy for that. But you can do this job anywhere, no?"

"There are other things." It wasn't a great leap to believe he was referring to me.

Mateo senior's gaze fell on me. "You like to experience other countries, yes? You speak the language. This is a country of many famous writers."

I grinned at his cleverness. The enthusiasm I had expressed to him earlier of traveling and living abroad was now being used to cajole me. At least he wasn't trying to separate us. "I do want to see other parts of Colombia, but I had never thought of living here."

"Your flan," said his father as the server set the dessert in the middle of the table.

Mateo, obviously thankful for the interruption, picked up his spoon again and dipped into the custard. "We're going to take a boat out to the Islas del Rosario tomorrow. Probably have lunch at Playa Blanca."

"Ah, I remember beautiful days there."

"Me too." He pushed the flan toward his father, but he shook his head. Then he slid it across the white tablecloth toward me.

"You don't see so many amazing fish like before. Climate change, I suppose." He turned to me again. "He was timid about the water at first, but when he became confident, he didn't want to come out of the sea."

"I can imagine," I said, though water-Mateo was not someone I had gotten to know yet. In the Bay Area, we had plenty of water and beaches, but temperatures limited the chance to enjoy them. And even when the air temperature heated up, the ocean never did.

After dinner, Mateo's father wanted to take us for drinks to Café del Mar on top of the ramparts of the wall around the city. I begged off, saying I was tired. It seemed a good time to give Mateo more time alone with his father as he didn't know when he'd see him again. Mateo kissed me goodnight in the lobby in front of his father, and I went to the room with a smile on my face.

# Chapter 35

Mateo squirmed in his seat but remained silent the first half of our plane ride home. In the air above Mexico, he put a hand on my leg and said, "Yes."

"What?" I stopped the music and unplugged one ear. I was listening to the Red Hot Chili Peppers. "How long? How long?" echoed in my ear.

"Yes," he repeated.

"Yes, what?"

"What we talked about at the beach." After saying goodbye to Mateo senior, we had gone by boat to Playa Blanca, and I got acquainted with water-loving Mateo. We rented snorkel gear and swam among multicolored fish on the coral reef which begins just off the beach. We got out of the water and stretched out on the sugary sand. I sat up and hugged my knees, thumbing my thighs and arms to see if I was burning despite having used SPF 50, while Mateo lay face down, using his arm as a pillow, his body relaxed, and the sun turning his skin to an even more delicious golden brown. It probably wasn't an ideal time to broach a serious conversation, but when I had something in my head, it was hard to let it go.

"There's really no point in paying two rents," I said.

Mateo took so long to respond I thought he didn't hear me. He sucked back some drool and groaned at the interruption of his nap. "Are you saying we should move in together?"

"We could both save money."

He rolled over and put his arm over his eyes to block the sun. Sand had stuck to his sweaty chest. "So, it's an economical thing?"

"I just thought you might want to get out of your apartment because of...uh...the memories."

"And move in with you in the house of your memories?" He sat up and brushed sand from the hair of his chest.

"I know it's not ideal, but just until we figure things out."

"It's a cheaper, practical solution, you're saying." He snorted. "God, you're so romantic!"

"Thinking of it in a romantic way is too terrifying."

He gave me a sour look, and I dropped the subject, not bringing it up again for the rest of the time in Cartagena. We enjoyed walks around the city, tried a variety of restaurants, slept late in the giant king bed, and showered together. I tried to put a lid on my stewing brain, stop the nagging doubts, the notion that things were too good, so something bad was bound to happen. And Mateo spent a lot of time staring off into the space of his new reality, his reunion with his family, particularly his father. At times he would grin contentedly, and at others frown as if unsure what to do with this new truth. Cocktails and sex helped to distract us, but our different anxieties kept creeping back.

The flight attendant with the drink cart arrived at our side, delaying my response to his affirmative answer about moving in together. We ordered beers.

After the cart moved on, Mateo turned to me. "Fuck your practicality. I like the idea of crawling into bed with you every night after a long shift." The words caused me to both blush and tingle. I was seventeen all over again and Cindy invited me over to her house to study French.

"If it's too soon you could sleep in the spare bedroom."

"You're such a jerk. Even if I did, you'd be creeping over every night to slide in with me."

"Are we really ready to play house?"

"It's not playing. This trip has made me realize how important you are to me. I've got a family. I've got a dad. But it's you I want."

"If you could hear yourself right now. You sound like a soap opera."

"You can make fun of me all you want because I know you feel the same. You just don't have the guts to say it."

"I'm the one who proposed it."

"To save money."

"I'm afraid. I admit it."

"Millions of people love soap operas, by the way."

"Because it's an escape from their boring little lives. They're dying to feel something."

"I have no problem feeling something in case I haven't made myself clear. Something real, and I want to follow it to the natural conclusion. I've missed out on so much in my life. In the last few months, I've had to face that my life was small and limited because of my mom." The last few words barely made it out of his constricted throat. He took a breath. "There, I said it." It sounded strange that he described his life as small when he was in the business of life and death every day at work.

"You could also use that argument to say you wanted to go out and explore your options."

"You mean like, have hookup sex with lots of guys?"

"How do you know what car you want to drive unless you've test-driven the field? You might find you want a fancy new car with all the bells and whistles instead of this old jalopy."

"Why do you find it so difficult to believe I want you? Anyway, you're more like a classic car."

"Pink Cadillac? Little Red Corvette? Little G.T.O? Mercedes Benz?"

"Hmm. Not Little red Corvette. Maybe Pink Cadillac?"

"I'm mortified. All my life I wanted to be a Mercedes Benz. Oh, Lord won't you give me..." I sang.

"The Aretha song is much better. We're going riding on the freeway. Oh, no, we can't stop now..." He began a surprisingly good rendition of the song.

"This is an absurd conversation. Of course, I want you. You're annoyingly adorable. And you've got pipes." I set my cup on the tray table and took his hand between the seats. "I'm formally asking you to move in with me and be my mate." I guess my tone was still in the skeptical range.

"Could you be serious for once?"

"I am! I swear."

Mateo held up his cup of beer and we touched plastic to plastic. A little beer splashed onto my fingers and I licked it off. "It's a deal then," he said. "I'll give my landlord notice." His eyes searched mine for a hint that I was messing with him.

I lifted his hand to my mouth and let the tufts of knuckle hair tickle my lips, sparking a thrilling moment of happiness before my contrary brain jumped in. I continued to drag around a lot of relationship baggage. He carried the burden of recent family revelations, challenged by his long-held notions of who his parents were. Barriers stood in our way: differences in age, styles, life experiences. The turmoil of the 1960s and 1970s had molded my beliefs, feelings, and worldview before he was born into this world a continent away. I had loved, lived with, and lost a man, and had embarked on a second relationship before he, an innocent pre-teen, was uprooted from everything he knew and brought to the United States. He had never lived with another man, and yet was ready to dive in, ignorant of the trials that awaited us. To get past them we had banter and affection. We had sex and caring and laughter. We had family and a few friends who would support us. Was that enough?

A move to a neutral home that was ours could be in our future, but for now, my house would have to do. I squeezed his hand. "All right! We're going to live together. Gulp."

"Get used to it," he said. "Your best years are yet to come."

"I want to do something fun when we get back."

"Like?"

"I have something in mind. A surprise. I'm going to invite Cindy and Marcelo."

"I'm not big on surprises."

"Trust me."

***

Sunday found us having brunch with Cindy and Marcelo at Brown Sugar Kitchen on Mandela Parkway. Mateo had been badgering me since we got back from Colombia to tell him our surprise destination after the meal.

"I love surprises," said Marcelo as he pulled off a piece of fried chicken skin dripping with maple syrup and popped it in his mouth. We had all gotten the chicken and waffles. "Since we're in West Oakland, I'm wondering if we're going someplace nearby."

"I've never been in this neighborhood before," said Mateo.

"I have to admit," said Cindy. "When you said we were eating in West Oakland, I was a little taken aback."

"See?" said Marcelo. "It was a surprise, and it turned out great." He took a bite of waffle. "*Delicioso!*"

"Okay," I said. "A hint. The place is nearby, and it involves music and dancing."

"It's two in the afternoon," said Mateo in a grumpy voice, still peeved that I had kept him in the dark.

"A tea dance!" Cindy shouted. "Perfect for old people."

"Speak for yourself," said Marcelo. "Not that you're old, *minha vida.*"

"What kind of music?" asked Mateo.

"You'll see." I didn't want to tell him it was house music, knowing he would probably turn up his nose. "Anyway, it's about the scene, the people more than the music."

Mateo rested his chin in his palm. "I can't believe I'm with a party boy."

"An afternoon party boy, mind you. And I only do it once every six months to a year." My gut pinged, remembering the last time I was at the Sunday afternoon party with Anthony. It was about a month before he died. Maybe this wasn't such a good idea.

I questioned my choice again as we neared the entrance to the patio behind a large warehouse painted with murals. The heavy beat of house music reached us, and Mateo's face looked like I was dragging him to an execution. But Marcelo's head bobbed, and his body jerked like he couldn't wait to get on the dance floor while Cindy stared at me in awe that I could still surprise her after all these years. I slipped my arm into Mateo's and whispered, "Give it a chance? For me."

"A half hour."

"I feel overdressed," said Cindy. She wore a summer dress printed with colorful butterflies over a pair of tight jeans and ankle boots.

"That's the thing. Anything goes here in terms of dress, look, and behavior as long as it's chill." I pointed out a sign that said kids and dogs welcome. "Just in case you have a dog into heavy beats."

We paid the entrance and started weaving through the patio filled with a multi-ethnic crowd of all ages, sexual orientations, and personal styles. A bearded drag queen bumped into Mateo and then looked him up and down like he was the statue of David. I laughed and put an arm around him. "He's mine."

"Lucky you," he said, straightening his wig.

"Let's get drinks," said Marcelo.

"Please," said Mateo in a desperate voice. "I've never seen so many freaky people in one place."

I put a finger over his lips. "Be open."

*It'll be alright. He'll let go. He needs to let go. I need to let go.*

Being early in the afternoon, the DJ played a melodic yet danceable house mix. We got drinks and stood at the edge of the dance area where the concrete was painted in geometric circles and lines in primary colors. A Black woman in her fifties with long dreads shimmied with her Asian girlfriend in a tiger-print jumpsuit. A long-haired man without a shirt, despite it being a little cool, danced alone with twists and turns, thrusts and bends as if he were in his living room and didn't care who saw him. An elegantly dressed young couple might have just escaped a wedding reception and come to a place that was more fun.

Marcelo coaxed Cindy with rolling hand gestures closer to the thumping bass of the speakers, and they began to move. I was transported to prom night when Cindy was my date. We had boogied to Sly and the Family Stone's "Everyday People," laughing hysterically from having smoked a joint in the car before the dance. Combined with the diet pills I had taken and the high of Cindy agreeing to go to prom with me, I had sailed on silver clouds.

I took a joint out of my pocket and showed it to Mateo.

"Wanna get high?"

"Here?"

I sniffed the air. "Other people are doing it."

"It makes me horny, ya know. I might have to drag you to the men's room."

"One drink and he gets all sloppy. Who's the freak now?"

*Thank you, Jesus. He's relaxing.*

I waved Cindy and Marcelo over and we headed to a corner where we wouldn't be so obvious. Cindy leaned down and petted a golden retriever that was lazily stretched out in the shade, oblivious to the loud music. A little girl in a ballerina dress a few yards away stared at me just as I was about to take a hit. I lifted my other hand to try and hide it. Her mother smiled at me and shrugged. "Don't worry about it."

"She probably thinks it's a cigarette," said Marcelo. "Kids don't know."

"I have a feeling this one knows."

A minute later we were all on the dance floor and the DJ had abandoned the melodic mix for deep house, bringing in heavy basslines of jazz and funk. More people were dancing now, and there was a joy in the air that was contagious. It was the perfect combination of diversity, bliss, and freedom of movement.

People smiled at each other just to smile. Next to us three Spanish-speaking guys danced in a circle. They had shaved heads and tattooed necks. If I had run into them on the street at night, I would have been petrified. One of them grabbed his buddy by the neck and kissed the top of his head. He saw me staring and gave me a thumbs-up.

"Four on the floor," shouted Marcelo.

Cindy pointed at each of us and said, "One, two, three, four."

"No. I mean a four-on-the-floor beat. House. I'd say about 120 bpm. I used to do some DJing."

"Of course, he did," I said to Cindy.

Mateo put his hands on either side of my torso and pulled me close, landing a kiss on my lips.

"I will not go to the men's room with you!"

"Please."

I hugged him tightly and whispered in his ear. "I love you. Now, behave."

I peered over his shoulder at Cindy. Damn it. Her eyes were on us, getting misty. I wagged my finger at her, but it was too late. Emotions had reached the point of bubbling over, and my body began to shake. Everybody looked so beautiful in their various skin colors, tattoos, stylish sunglasses, and hats, and the music pulled the ropes of my emotions like a bell ringer in a church tower. I took a step back from Mateo and covered my face.

He lifted his hand and put it softly on my shoulder. "What is it, amor?"

Through my fingers, his face appeared distorted, worried. "I'm so happy. You still don't know me that well, but you will." I pointed at my face. "This is me happy. You make me happy."

"I make you happy? It's something I do?"

Cindy and Marcelo boogied toward us and we had a group hug, bobbing to the music.

"This is what heaven looks like," I said. "Forget the clouds and harps and white robes."

"Since the first day I met you," Cindy said over the loud music. "You've had your own take on things."

"Back then, with your hippie-dippy shit, you inspired me."

Cindy looked over the top of her yellow-framed sunglasses. "You were born weird. That's what attracted me to you."

Marcelo laced an arm around Mateo's waist and pulled him away from us. "Let's leave these lovebirds to it." He put his hands on Mateo's shoulders and danced close, looking into his eyes.

"Are you sure about this guy?" I said to Cindy.

She laughed. "That's what I love about him. He keeps everybody guessing. But in the end, he's devoted."

We continued to flail our arms and bob. "He's got that incredibly enticing Vladimir thing that unsettles me," I said.

"But he's not Vladimir. Not by a long shot. I trust him. Completely."

"I'm happy for you."

"And I for you."

"Who woulda thought?"

"I know."

"Okay. I want my boyfriend back." I went behind Mateo, slipped my arms around him, and for a minute, he was sandwiched between Marcelo and me. He laid his head back and his ear landed next to my mouth. "*Sinvergüenza,*" I whispered. And he shook with laughter. Marcelo broke away, took Cindy's hand, twirled her around, and kissed her.

We had the sun on our faces. A feeling of community. The proximity of loved ones. We had a shimmering sense of hope without reason. About us. About an uncertain world.

Mateo turned around to face me, as innocent as a child and at the same time as wanton as a fallen angel. We pressed our bodies together, so close I felt the buzz of his phone in his pocket. One after another. A series of text notifications. At first, he ignored it. But when the buzzes continued, curiosity got the better of him. The screen lit up his face, and then froze it. His lashes blinked rapidly as he scrolled through the messages and photos.

"Everything okay?"

He let out an unconvincing "Uh-huh" and drifted toward a bench. He plopped down on it, his face still pasted to the messages.

I followed and sat next to him. "What is it?"

He showed me a picture of a modern apartment building with mountains in the background. "I own a penthouse in Medellin. In this building."

"That's insane."

"My father. He says it's mine to do with what I want."

I threw my arm over his shoulders as he scrolled through the shots of the interior. Furnished and decorated. Architectural Digest-y. Tasteful but cold. He returned to the initial messages and read through them again. At the end of the photos, he closed his phone and put it in his pocket.

"I'm going to pretend that didn't just happen," he said.

We sat for a moment and stared at the thumping joy of the little universe around us. The crowd had started jumping up and down in sync. Far, far away in a tower in his native land, a home awaited Mateo. His father awaited him. A patter of panic ran through me.

"Should I get some drinks?" I said, my voice shaky. "You probably need one."

"Why?"

"Because of that." I nose-pointed at his pocket.

He looked at me with his mischievous smirk, a daunting sparkle in his eyes, his freckles dancing. "I have no idea what you're talking about."

"Right." I began to breathe again.

"Only one thing I'm sure about."

"What?"

"You."

I nodded and smiled and tapped my foot to a messy remix of a song that sounded familiar.

"Let's dance." I pulled Mateo to his feet, and we ran over to Cindy and Marcelo.

"It's 'Show Me Love,'" said Marcelo. "Crazibiza remix."

Mateo put his finger in the middle of my chest. "Right here."

My mind took off in a thousand directions of gratitude and doubt and tenderness and fear. On and on. The DJ ramped it up as if he could see inside my head and it was his job to silence my brain. I obeyed the music and let my body go. The four of us danced like there was no tomorrow. And maybe there wasn't. Now was good. I didn't know if we would end up in a condo in Medellin. I didn't know how long Mateo and I would be together, but hope now seemed my friend rather than an entity full of trickery. I didn't know if I would one day get a poem in The New Yorker or if another book of poetry was forthcoming. My life had been full of fits and starts, tragedies and moments of joy, successes and failures. Life and death.

*Come on, DJ. Get all of this out of my head. Let me just gaze on this beautiful man and hold him as long as I can.*

## Acknowledgements

I would like to thank the team at Spectrum Books for inviting me into the family and being supportive of and sympathetic to my vision in this book as well as the two previous ones with them.

Thanks to all the readers and reviewers of The Mayor of Oak Street who encouraged me to continue Nathan's story, though I'm not sure it counts as a sequel when the main story of this book takes place forty years after the end of that book. I trust you will be pleased where Nathan's journey has taken him.

I also want to thank my early readers. Bevan Vinton helped me with proofing an early draft. Other readers offered suggestions and gave me a lot of positive feedback. These include Mary Hardcastle, Onia Wellman, Ashley Spring, Erin Scholnick-Lee, Kelsea Reeves, Maciek, Bancy, Pat Henshaw, and Laury Egan.

I must also acknowledge Natasha, who has tirelessly worked to help with promotion of my two previous books and has come on board again to work on this one.

My fellow members of BAQWA (Bay Area Queer Writers Association) have offered support, encouragement and suggestions about writing and promotion. A community of writers makes this solitary profession a better place to be in this world.

It is important to acknowledge my ethnically and racially diverse group of friends and family, particularly my husband, who give me inspiration to write characters from all walks of life.

And lastly, I thank the people of San Leandro, California who have been supportive of my writing and helped me plan events like City Council member, Victor Aguilar, and the staff at The San Leandro Public Library. Though my last six books have been written since I moved to San Leandro, this is the first that has been set there.

## About the author

Vincent Traughber Meis is a fiction writer, a world traveler, and a former ESL community college teacher. When he's not traveling, he divides his time between writing and working in the garden. Most of the characters in his novels and short stories come from across the LGBTQ+ spectrum and are racially and ethnically diverse. He has published eight novels: *Eddie's Desert Rose, Tio Jorge, Down in Cuba, Deluge, Four Calling Burds* and *The Mayor of Oak Street, First Born Sons, and Colton's Terrible Wonderful Year. Tio Jorge, Down in Cuba,* and *Deluge* have all won Rainbow Awards. *The Mayor of Oak Street* and *First Born Sons* have won Reader Views Reviewer's Choice Awards. His short stories have appeared in several collections both in print and online, and have reached finalist status in several short story contests. A collection of short stories, *Far from Home,* was published in October 2021. He lives with his husband in San Leandro, California and Puerto Vallarta, Mexico.